A CRY FOR HELP

EVA RAE THOMAS MYSTERY - BOOK 21

WILLOW ROSE

Books by the Author

HARRY HUNTER MYSTERY SERIES

- All The Good Girls
- Run Girl Run
- No Other Way
- Never Walk Alone

MARY MILLS MYSTERY SERIES

- What Hurts the Most
- You Can Run
- You Can't Hide
- Careful Little Eyes

EVA RAE THOMAS MYSTERY SERIES

- So We Lie
- Don't Lie to me
- What you did
- Never Ever
- Say You Love me
- Let Me Go
- It's Not Over
- Not Dead yet
- To Die For
- Such A Good Girl
- Little Did She Know
- You Better Run
- Say It Isn't So
- Too Pretty To Die
- Till Death Do Us Part
- Rest In Peace
- Dark Little Secrets
- Not My Daughter
- The Girl In The Closet

- Liar Liar
- No More Lies
- A Cry For Help

EMMA FROST SERIES

- Itsy Bitsy Spider
- Miss Dolly had a Dolly
- Run, Run as Fast as You Can
- Cross Your Heart and Hope to Die
- Peek-a-Boo I See You
- Tweedledum and Tweedledee
- Easy as One, Two, Three
- There's No Place like Home
- Slenderman
- Where the Wild Roses Grow
- Waltzing Mathilda
- Drip Drop Dead
- Black Frost

JACK RYDER SERIES

- Hit the Road Jack
- Slip out the Back Jack
- The House that Jack Built
- Black Jack
- Girl Next Door
- Her Final Word
- Don't Tell

REBEKKA FRANCK SERIES

- One, Two...He is Coming for You
- Three, Four...Better Lock Your Door
- Five, Six...Grab your Crucifix
- Seven, Eight...Gonna Stay up Late
- Nine, Ten...Never Sleep Again
- Eleven, Twelve...Dig and Delve
- Thirteen, Fourteen...Little Boy Unseen
- Better Not Cry

- Ten Little Girls
- It Ends Here

MYSTERY/THRILLER/HORROR NOVELS

- Sorry Can't Save You
- In One Fell Swoop
- Umbrella Man
- Blackbird Fly
- To Hell in a Handbasket
- Edwina

HORROR SHORT-STORIES

- Mommy Dearest
- The Bird
- Better watch out
- Eenie, Meenie
- Rock-a-Bye Baby
- Nibble, Nibble, Crunch
- Humpty Dumpty
- Chain Letter

PARANORMAL SUSPENSE/ROMANCE NOVELS

- In Cold Blood
- The Surge
- Girl Divided

THE VAMPIRES OF SHADOW HILLS SERIES

- Flesh and Blood
- Blood and Fire
- Fire and Beauty
- Beauty and Beasts
- Beasts and Magic
- Magic and Witchcraft
- Witchcraft and War
- War and Order
- Order and Chaos
- Chaos and Courage

THE AFTERLIFE SERIES

- Beyond
- Serenity
- Endurance
- Courageous

THE WOLFBOY CHRONICLES

- A Gypsy Song
- I am WOLF

DAUGHTERS OF THE JAGUAR

- Savage
- Broken

Prologue

Central Florida

Tuesday Afternoon

Chapter 1

DIANE MERCER'S fingers hovered over her keyboard, a half-empty cup of coffee cooling at her elbow. Four hours into her shift, and the familiar weight of other people's emergencies pressed against her temples. She adjusted her headset, the cushioned ear pads worn thin from years of use, and took the next call with the practiced calm that had become as much a part of her as her prematurely gray hair.

"911, what's your emergency?" The voice that answered was high-pitched, fragile—a child's voice stretched thin over terror. Her heart beat faster. It was always harder when children called in. And this one was worse than any of the others. Four simple words that would haunt Diane for the rest of her life.

"My mom shot me."

The words landed like ice in Diane's stomach. Her fingers froze above the keyboard for precisely one second before muscle memory took over. She clicked the priority alert button, watched it flash red on her screen, and kept her voice steady.

"I'm here to help you."

She typed furiously as she spoke, already triangulating the call's origin point.

"Sweetie. You're doing great. Can you tell me your address?" Her voice remained level, betraying nothing of the dread coiling through her chest. On her second monitor, blue dots represented available patrol units. Two were less than three minutes from the caller's approximate location.

"I don't—" The child's voice cracked. "It's in the forest. We're in a cabin somewhere."

"Ocala Forest?"

"Y-yes, that's it. Please hurry."

Diane's training clicked into place like tumblers in a lock. She knew that area very well and knew exactly where the cabins were. She and her husband often hiked there, and their children loved swimming in the springs. Her supervisor, alerted by the priority signal, appeared behind her chair, a silent presence watching the information populate the screen.

"Are you somewhere safe right now? Away from the shooter, away from… your mother?" She signaled to her supervisor, pointing at the dispatch status. The woman nodded and stepped away to coordinate the emergency response.

"I'm in the bathroom." His breathing sounded wrong—shallow and liquid. "The door doesn't lock good."

Diane felt the frantic flutter of her heart against her ribs, a caged bird beating against her professional detachment. Her eyes locked on the screen where dispatch had confirmed two units *en route*, ETA two minutes. She noted how her own hand remained steady as she typed additional notes: JUVENILE GUNSHOT VICTIM, SHOOTER IN HOME, BATHROOM DOOR COMPROMISED.

"You're very brave, honey. Help is coming right now. Can you tell me where you're hurt?" Her voice took on the gentle cadence she reserved for the youngest callers—warm but clear, each word precisely enunciated.

A sound escaped him—half sob, half something worse. "My stomach. It's all wet."

Diane swallowed, her throat suddenly dry as sand. The call center around her continued its constant hum of activity, but it seemed to recede, as if she and this young child existed in a bubble of shared crisis.

"Listen to me. I need you to find something—a towel or shirt—and press it against where you're hurt. Can you do that for me?"

Rustling sounds came through the line. Something clattered to the floor.

"It hurts," he whispered.

"I know it does." Diane's free hand clenched into a fist, nails digging half-moons into her palm. "But you're doing so well. The police and an ambulance are almost there." On her screen, the blue dots moved with agonizing slowness through the digital streets. "Can you hear any sounds? Where is your mother now?"

The silence stretched for three eternal seconds. When the boy spoke again, his voice had dropped to a whisper. "She's coming. I can hear her."

Diane's heart rate spiked, sending a cold rush through her veins. "Try to stay very quiet. Help is almost there." She checked the dispatch timer: one minute, twenty seconds until arrival. Too long. "Is there anywhere you can hide in the bathroom?"

The boy's breathing had grown more labored, each inhale a struggle. "She's outside the door."

The words hit Diane like a physical blow.

"Stay with me. The police are almost—"

A new sound came through the line—a woman's voice, distant but clear enough. "Baby, open the door. Open the door, sweetie."

Diane's skin prickled with goosebumps. "Don't open the door. The police will be there in less than a minute." Her voice remained steady, but sweat beaded along her hairline, a cold trickle running down her spine.

Scraping sounds—the bathroom door being forced open. The boy's breath came faster.

"She's coming in," he whispered.

"You need to hide. Now." Diane abandoned protocol, the urgency breaking through her professional veneer.

She heard movement, a whimper of pain. The sound of the door slamming against the wall.

"Oh, baby." The woman's voice was closer now, saturated with an emotion Diane couldn't name—something between grief and rage. "Why did you call them? Why would you do that?"

Diane pressed her headset tighter against her ear, as if she could physically reach through the connection to shield the boy. "Units arriving now," her screen informed her, but too late, too late.

The gunshot came without warning—a deafening crack that sent Diane's headset tumbling from her hands. It dangled from its cord, swinging like a hanged man as she stared at it in shock. The line went dead, leaving nothing but the hiss of an empty connection.

For one suspended moment, Diane remained perfectly still, her body frozen while her mind processed the unthinkable. Then reality crashed back—the fluorescent lights suddenly too harsh, the murmur of the call center too loud. Her hands trembled violently as she reached for her headset, fumbling it back into place with clumsy fingers.

"Hello?" Her voice cracked. "Are you there?"

Nothing.

Cold sweat broke across her forehead. The screen before her blurred as her eyes widened, focusing on everything and nothing. Her stomach heaved once, threatening rebellion. Someone was speaking—her supervisor, hand on her shoulder, asking questions Diane couldn't process.

"I lost him," she said, her voice unnaturally flat. "The mother… There was another shot."

The supervisor was saying something about the responding officers, about protocol, about taking a break, but Diane barely heard her. All she could hear was the young boy's voice—"My mom shot me"—and the final gunshot that had severed their connection.

She reached for her coffee, knocking it over with trembling fingers. The brown liquid spread across her desk, soaking into her notepad. She stared at the expanding stain, watching it blur the words like tears.

In her twenty-three years as a 911 operator, Diane Mercer had heard gunshots before. She had listened to the last breaths of strangers, had guided callers through the worst moments of their lives. But as she sat in her ergonomic chair, with coffee dripping onto her sensible shoes and her headset buzzing with a new incoming call, she knew with terrible certainty that this boy's voice would join the few that still visited her in the dark hours before dawn.

Part I

Tampa, Florida

Chapter 1

I STOOD by the central fountain at Tampa Mall, the cascading water failing to drown out the pounding in my chest. My fingers brushed against the cold metal of the handgun in my pocket—a last resort I never thought I'd use this way. Around me, shoppers drifted between stores, consumed by their normal lives: teenagers posing for selfies, mothers corralling excited children, elderly couples walking arm-in-arm. None of them noticed me—a slightly overweight, middle-aged woman with red hair streaked with silver. Invisible. That was about to change. I'd spent twenty years hunting criminals; now I needed to become one.

The weight of the decision pressed down on me like a physical force. Ten days on the run had taught me that playing defense would only end one way—with me in handcuffs or a body bag. Rule Six of the Profiler's Code echoed in my mind: The hunter can become the hunted. I needed to flip the script and create a controlled chaos that would serve my purpose.

I scanned the mall's upper level methodically, not randomly. There—the security camera blind spot near the food court entrance. And there—the service corridor leading to the back parking lot.

A young security guard strolled past, radio crackling at his hip, not even glancing my way. Two Tampa PD officers stood by the north entrance, chatting with the mall's head of security. They were here because of the increased patrol presence throughout the city, hunting for me. The irony wasn't lost on me.

My hand closed around the grip of my weapon. I'd never fired a gun in a public place outside of duty.

I took a deep breath and pulled the gun out in one smooth motion, raised it, and squeezed the trigger three times in rapid succession.

BANG! BANG! BANG!

The shots echoed off the high ceiling, amplified by the mall's acoustics. For one frozen moment, nothing happened—as if everyone's brains needed time to process the impossible event unfolding in their safe, ordinary space.

Then the screaming started.

A wave of panic rippled outward from me like a stone dropped in water. People dove behind planters, scrambled under tables, and pulled children to the ground. A teenage boy knocked over a rack of sunglasses as he bolted for the exit. A security guard reached for his radio with shaking hands, ducking behind a kiosk.

"Active shooter! Active shooter!" someone shouted, and the panic redoubled.

I remained standing, the gun still in hand. Not moving. Not threatening. Just waiting. The crowd parted around me like water flowing around a rock, creating an empty circle of space with me at its center. The two police officers at the entrance drew their weapons and began pushing through the fleeing crowd, but the human current worked against them.

A middle-aged woman stumbled in her haste to escape, shopping bags spilling from her hands. As she struggled to her feet, her eyes locked with mine. I saw the moment of recognition wash across her face—the widening eyes, the slight gasp. She pointed a trembling finger at me.

"That's her!" she screamed, her voice piercing through the chaos. "That's that rogue FBI profiler from the news!"

Just as I'd expected. My face had been plastered across every news channel. The media had told the story of the dangerous former agent gone rogue, a woman with inside knowledge using it to commit the perfect crime.

I kept my expression neutral, though inside, my stomach churned. For twenty years, I'd been the one people ran toward for safety, not away from in terror.

Mall security guards converged from multiple directions, trying to coordinate through their crackling radios. The younger ones looked terrified, while the older guards moved with more purpose, creating a loose perimeter. None of them had firearms—mall policy—but they were trying to contain the situation until police arrived in force.

I calculated the timing in my head. From the moment the first shot was fired to full police response: approximately four minutes. I'd already used nearly two. The initial responders would be whoever was closest—the two officers already inside—followed by patrol units, then SWAT. They would secure the perimeter first, then begin clearing the building.

My plan relied on this predictable response. Law enforcement would follow protocol, and protocol was something I knew intimately.

I lowered my gun slowly, making sure everyone saw the deliberate motion. Several phones were pointed at me—recording, livestreaming. Perfect. The more digital footprints, the better. I needed the world to see.

The first police officer had finally pushed through the crowd, gun drawn, positioned behind a concrete planter thirty feet away. "Drop the weapon!" he shouted, his voice steady despite the chaos. "Do it now!"

I made eye contact with him and slowly placed the gun on the floor, sliding it away from me with my foot. Not surrendering—just changing tactics.

"Eva Rae Thomas!" he called out, recognition dawning on his face. "Get on the ground! Hands where I can see them!"

Instead of complying, I checked my watch. Three minutes eighteen seconds. Right on schedule. The service corridors would be my exit route, but I needed the timing to be exact. Too early, and I'd be caught. Too late, and the opportunity would vanish.

The second officer flanked from the left, moving cautiously between abandoned shopping bags and overturned chairs. Mall security had formed a loose ring around the first officer and me, keeping frightened stragglers back.

I raised my hands slowly to shoulder height—not surrender, just buying seconds. My eyes locked on the fire alarm on the wall near the food court entrance. The commotion had emptied most of the mall, but the alarm would trigger the sprinkler system, adding another layer of confusion.

As the officers inched closer, I tensed my muscles, ready to move. This was my one chance to access what I needed, and I wouldn't get another. If I failed now, I'd never clear my name.

"Now, on your knees!" the officer shouted, just fifteen feet away.

I took one last deep breath.

Four minutes.

Time to move.

Chapter 2

I BOLTED toward the food court, moving against the tide of fleeing shoppers. My body operated on pure instinct now, weaving between obstacles with practiced efficiency.

"Stop her!" someone shouted, but the command was swallowed by the chaos. The mall's fire alarm began to wail—whether triggered by security or some panicked shopper, I couldn't tell. Perfect timing. The sprinklers would activate soon. People collided with me as they rushed for the exits, shoulders bumping, hands grabbing briefly before letting go. No one wanted to be a hero today. No one except the security guards and police officers, now in pursuit behind me.

An abandoned food tray crashed to the floor as I dodged around a corner. The service corridor entrance waited ahead—a gray door marked "Staff Only," partially hidden behind a decorative palm. A young employee in a green polo shirt stood frozen before it, his eyes wide with indecision as the chaos unfolded around him.

"FBI!" I lied without breaking stride. "I need access now!"

The familiar authority in my voice worked—a reflex from my twenty years with the Bureau. The young man stumbled backward, his shoulder hitting the door as he moved aside. I pushed past him, shouldering through the door before he could question why an FBI agent would be running from mall security.

The service corridor hit me with its stark contrast to the mall's polished public face. Fluorescent tubes buzzed overhead, every third one flickering with a sickly pulse that cast moving shadows against cinderblock walls. The concrete floor was stained with decades of spills and tracked-in dirt. Exposed pipes and electrical conduits ran along the ceiling like industrial veins and arteries.

I paused, orienting myself. The heavy door swung shut behind me, muffling the alarm and screams. For a moment, the relative quiet was jarring—just the distant wail of sirens and the hum of the building's mechanical systems. The corridor stretched in both directions, intersecting with others to form a hidden maze behind the mall's gleaming façade.

I needed to go east. From memory, I recalled the mall's layout from the public safety briefing I'd attended two years ago as part of an anti-terrorism task force. The irony wasn't lost on me—using knowledge gained as law enforcement to evade that same system.

I turned right, moving at a controlled jog. Running would attract attention; walking would waste precious seconds. My footsteps echoed despite my efforts to step lightly. I passed storage rooms with padlocked doors, a break room with empty vending machines, and a wall of electrical panels labeled with store names and numbers.

A door opened ahead of me. I pressed myself against the wall, hand instinctively reaching for a weapon that wasn't there anymore—I'd left it on the mall floor as planned.

A janitor backed into the hallway, pulling a yellow mop bucket. He turned and froze, the mop clattering to the ground as his eyes locked on me. Middle-aged, Hispanic, his name badge reading "Miguel." Recognition flashed across his face—my photo had been on every news station for the last couple of days.

His mouth opened to shout. I closed the distance between us in three quick steps, pressing my finger to my lips in a universal gesture for silence. His eyes widened further, darting between my face and the corridor behind me.

"Please," I whispered, my voice barely audible. "I didn't do what they're saying."

He hesitated, and I saw the calculation behind his eyes—the risk assessment. I could see him wondering if I would hurt him, if I was armed, if helping me would cost him his job, or worse.

"Five minutes," I said. "Just give me five minutes before you tell anyone you saw me."

The distant door I'd entered through burst open, voices echoing down the corridor. The janitor's eyes flicked toward the sound, then back to me. He gave an almost imperceptible nod and pointed toward a narrow hallway branching to the left.

"That way," he whispered in a heavy accent. "Through kitchen storage."

I touched his shoulder briefly in thanks and slipped away, guilt mingling with gratitude. I'd just made him complicit in aiding a fugitive. Another innocent person potentially damaged by this nightmare that had become my life.

The narrow hallway led to a large storage area filled with pallets of supplies for the food court restaurants. I navigated between towers of napkins, plastic cutlery, and industrial-sized food containers. Beyond them, a heavy metal door with a push bar promised escape.

I paused, my hand on the bar, calculating. Four minutes and thirty-seven seconds since the first shot. Police response would be in full force now. The parking lot would be swarming with officers, who would be establishing a perimeter. SWAT would arrive within minutes if they weren't already on scene. Helicopters would follow shortly after.

My options were shrinking by the second.

I'd spent my career tracking killers who tried to stay one step ahead of law enforcement. Now I was living their experience, understanding their desperation in ways I never could have imagined.

Through my mind ran calculations of escape routes, police response times, and the stark reality that I had no choice but to keep moving.

The wail of police sirens grew louder, their Doppler effect indicating multiple units converging from different directions. I pressed my ear against the metal door, listening for movement outside—nothing distinct—just the general commotion of an evacuation.

With a deep breath, I pushed the emergency exit bar.

An alarm immediately shrieked—a local door alarm separate from the mall's main system. I stepped out into blinding afternoon sunlight, momentarily disoriented by the transition from the dimly lit corridor.

To my left, the flashing lights of police cruisers created a blue-and-red strobe effect against the buildings. To my right, the service road curved behind a dumpster enclosure before disappearing around the corner. No officers visible in that direction—yet.

I made my choice and ran, the distant thunder of helicopter rotors beginning to build overhead. The hunt was on, and I was both predator and prey.

Chapter 3

ONE WEEK EARLIER

Chapter 4

THE PARADISE BAY Motel was anything but paradise. Its faded blue sign flickered in the gathering dusk, half the neon letters dead, the remaining ones casting a sickly glow across the crumbling stucco facade. I leaned my head against the passenger window of our stolen sedan, fatigue pressing down on me like a physical weight. Three days on the run had left me hollow-eyed and desperate, my body aching from too many hours crammed in car seats and makeshift hiding places. Matt's hand found mine in the darkness, his fingers giving a gentle squeeze—a silent reminder that I wasn't alone in this nightmare. At least not yet.

"You ready?" he asked, his voice low and rough with exhaustion.

I nodded, though every fiber of my being wanted to stay hidden in the anonymous safety of the car. "Let's get this over with."

The motel office smelled of stale cigarettes and lemon-scented cleaner that failed to mask decades of human transience. A bell above the door announced our arrival with a cheerful ding that felt obscene against our grim purpose. Behind the counter, an elderly man looked up from a dog-eared paperback, his eyes narrowing as they landed on my face.

My pulse quickened. I'd pulled my hair back under a baseball cap and traded my usual clothes for a shapeless sweatshirt, but my face had been plastered across every news channel in Florida for days. Recognition was a luxury I could no longer afford.

The old man's gaze lingered, making my skin crawl with the uncomfortable sensation of being cataloged, memorized. His eyes—surprisingly sharp in his weathered face—moved from my hair to my eyes, down to my mouth, then back up again.

"Need a room," Matt said, stepping slightly in front of me, his bulk creating a partial shield between me and the owner's probing stare.

The man's attention shifted reluctantly to Matt. "How many nights?"

"Just one," Matt replied, placing several worn bills on the counter. Cash only—one of our new rules for survival. No credit cards, no paper trails, nothing that could be traced or tracked.

The owner's gnarled fingers sorted through the bills with practiced efficiency.

I held my breath, watching the man's face for any hint of suspicion. After what felt like an eternity, he reached beneath the counter and produced a key attached to a plastic diamond-shaped fob with the number 17 faded almost to illegibility.

His fingers closed around the key for a moment too long before extending it toward Matt. "Last one at the end," he said, his voice like sandpaper on wood. "Check out's at eleven. No exceptions."

Matt nodded his thanks, reaching for the key.

"You folks in town for business or pleasure?" the owner asked, his eyes sliding back to my face with uncomfortable intensity.

"Just passing through," Matt replied, his tone casual but firm, signaling an end to the conversation.

The owner nodded slowly, his hawk-like gaze following us as we turned away. "Enjoy your stay," he called after us, the words carrying an undercurrent that raised the hair on the back of my neck.

We walked down the open-air hallway, our footsteps echoing against peeling paint and concrete. The air smelled of mildew and ocean salt, the nearby bay asserting its presence.

"He recognized you," Matt murmured, his voice barely audible above the distant sound of traffic from the highway.

I kept my eyes forward, counting room numbers. "Maybe. Maybe not."

"We'll be gone by morning either way."

Room 17 greeted us with a blast of stale air when Matt pushed open the door. I stepped inside, my eyes adjusting to the dimness. A double bed dominated the space, its faded floral spread sagging in the middle like a hammock. Wood-paneled walls gave the room a claustrophobic feel, and the carpet beneath our feet was worn thin along a path from the door to the bathroom.

Matt locked the door behind us, using both the standard lock and the flimsy chain. Without a word, he began his security sweep—a routine we'd established over the past three days. He moved methodically through the small space, checking the phone for taps, examining air vents for cameras, and unscrewing lamp bases to look for bugs. I watched him probe behind the framed landscape print on the wall—a generic watercolor of a sunset that had probably hung there since the Reagan administration.

While Matt worked, I drew the curtains tight against the darkening evening and switched on the ancient television set, keeping the volume low. The screen flickered to life with local news, and my stomach dropped as my own face stared back at me from behind the broadcaster's shoulder. My official FBI headshot—professional, composed, a lifetime away from the desperate woman I'd become.

"The manhunt continues for former FBI profiler Eva Rae Thomas, now considered armed and extremely dangerous," the anchor intoned gravely. "Thomas is wanted in connection with the homicide of 55-year-old Richard Collins earlier this week. Police warn the public not to approach Thomas if spotted, but to contact authorities immediately."

My fingers dug into the edge of the mattress, the springs creaking beneath my white-knuckled grip. Seeing myself and hearing myself getting portrayed like this was unbearable. But it was my reality right now.

Matt finished his sweep and sat beside me on the bed, the

ancient mattress sagging under our combined weight. "No bugs. No cameras. We're clean."

I nodded, but the temporary security offered little comfort. The walls of this trap were closing in around us.

"We can't keep running," I said, my voice hollow in the shabby room. "They'll find us eventually."

Matt's hand covered mine, warm and solid. "Then we stop running and start fighting back."

I turned to him and studied the determination in his blue eyes. After twenty years in the FBI, I'd learned to read faces like most people read street signs. Matt wasn't offering blind optimism or false hope. He had a plan.

Through the thin walls, I could hear a television playing in the next room, the muffled voices of guests in the parking lot, and the distant hum of traffic on the highway. The mundane soundtrack of normal lives continued while mine imploded spectacularly.

"How?" I asked.

Outside, car headlights swept across our curtained window, momentarily illuminating the room with harsh light before plunging us back into shadow. In that brief flash, I caught sight of our reflections in the bathroom mirror—two exhausted, hunted people, backed into a corner with nowhere left to run.

But still fighting.

Chapter 5

"I'VE BEEN THINKING about reaching out to Juan Ramirez," Matt said, his weight shifting on the creaking mattress. I turned from the television, my body tensing involuntarily at the name I knew so well. Juan Ramirez—former crime scene technician with Tampa PD, now working as a private investigator, specializing in helping people disappear. A brilliant mind with questionable ethics and an extensive network of contacts that spanned both sides of the law. The last person I wanted involved in our situation—and possibly the only person who could help us.

"No." The word came out sharper than I'd intended. "We can't trust anyone right now, especially not someone with connections to local law enforcement."

Matt's expression remained steady. "We need resources, Eva. Someone who understands forensics well enough to spot the inconsistencies in the evidence against you."

I pushed myself off the bed and began pacing the small room, five steps in one direction before being forced to turn. The worn carpet beneath my feet had been walked thin by countless others before me—fugitives, lovers, travelers, all passing through, leaving nothing behind but indentations in a mattress and cigarette burns on the nightstand.

"Juan isn't law enforcement anymore," Matt continued. "He left the department three years ago after that evidence contamination scandal. Remember? The one where they tried to pin the whole thing on him despite systemic problems in the lab."

I did remember. Juan had been the scapegoat in a mess that went all the way up to the commissioner's office. He'd fought back, threatened to expose everything he knew, and eventually walked away with his reputation damaged but his freedom intact. It had been ugly, political, and deeply unfair.

"That's exactly my point," I said, stopping to face Matt. "He has every reason to hate the system. But he also has every reason to curry favor with it now if it helps his PI business. We'd be placing our lives in his hands."

Through the paper-thin walls came the sound of a couple arguing in the next room—a woman's voice rising in frustration, a man's lower tones trying to placate her. On the other side, a television blared a game show, the host's manufactured enthusiasm a jarring counterpoint to our desperate planning. Each sound made me flinch, my nerves raw with the constant vigilance of prey.

"He owes me," Matt said simply, his voice dropping lower. "From before."

I paused my pacing.

"What kind of debt?" I asked.

Outside, a car door slammed in the parking lot. I moved instinctively to the window, pulling back the edge of the curtain just enough to peer out. An elderly couple shuffled toward the motel office, nothing suspicious about them except perhaps their willingness to stay in such a dismal establishment.

"The kind we need right now."

I let the curtain fall back into place but remained standing by the window, my back pressed against the wall. "So, you trust him because you helped him once?"

"I trust him because he risked his career to expose a lie. That's what

I helped him with. I don't want to go into details, but he did it when there was nothing in it for him." Matt's eyes held mine. "He could have walked away and not fought back. Most people would have. He didn't."

Another door slammed somewhere down the hall. Footsteps passed our room, heavy and purposeful. I found myself holding my breath until they faded away. Part of me knew my hypervigilance bordered on paranoia, but I'd learned that paranoia was often just good sense wearing an unflattering name.

"We can't trust anyone right now," I repeated, but with less conviction.

"We can't do this alone," Matt countered softly. "You know that, Eva Rae. Whoever framed you has resources, access, and a plan that's been in motion for longer than we've been aware of it. We need someone who can move in circles we can't access anymore."

He was right. The precision of the frame against me suggested someone with intimate knowledge of forensic procedure and evidence collection. Someone who understood how to construct a case that would withstand scrutiny. Someone who knew me well enough to anticipate my movements and reactions.

Someone who might leave traces that only an expert like Juan Ramirez could detect.

Matt's phone buzzed with an incoming text. He glanced at the screen, then turned it so I could see.

Tomorrow. 9 a.m. Old fishing pier at Henderson Beach. Come alone.

"So, you did more than just think about reaching out to him," I say. "You knew I'd cave."

"He'll help us," Matt said, tucking the phone away.

I rubbed my temples, feeling the dull throb of a tension headache building behind my eyes.

"Fine. But we change locations immediately afterward, regardless of how the meeting goes." I dropped my hand and met his gaze directly. "And I'm coming with you. If he's setting us up, we face it together."

Matt didn't argue, just nodded once in acknowledgment. The room's single overhead bulb cast harsh shadows across his face, deepening the lines of exhaustion around his eyes, highlighting the stubborn set of his jaw. Three days on the run had aged us both, stripped away pretense and comfort, leaving only the bare essentials of who we were.

"We should try to get some sleep," he said, though we both knew rest would be elusive. "Tomorrow could change everything."

Or end everything, I thought, but didn't say.

Through the wall, the arguing couple had gone quiet. The game show had ended, replaced by the dramatic score of a crime procedural. The irony wasn't lost on me—fictional detectives solving crimes in neat forty-minute packages while real-life law enforcement hunted an innocent woman across Tampa Bay.

The single bulb flickered overhead, threatening to plunge us into darkness at any moment—a fitting metaphor for our circumstances—as we clung to a faltering light while shadows gathered around us.

"We're down to our last few hundred dollars," I said, mentally calculating our dwindling resources. "Three more prepaid phones. One change of clothes each." I met Matt's eyes. "If Juan can't or won't help us, what's plan B?"

Matt's expression was solemn in the harsh light. "There is no plan B, Eva. Not yet."

The truth hung between us, heavy and undeniable. We were running out of time, money, and options. Tomorrow's meeting with Juan might be our last chance.

Chapter 6

I WAITED until Matt stepped into the shower before retrieving the burner phone from the bottom of my duffel bag. My fingers trembled slightly as I unwrapped it from the T-shirt I'd used to cushion it—one of only three phones we had left, each to be used once and then discarded. Three calls, three chances to hear my family's voices before we'd need to find another untraceable way to communicate.

Three days felt like a lifetime when you were running for your life, but it must have seemed even longer for the people waiting for news, for any sign that you were still alive.

I dialed my mother's number, the familiar sequence burned into my muscle memory despite the unfamiliar phone in my hand. Each ring felt like an eternity, my heart accelerating with each second of silence. What if they'd been questioned? What if their phones were being monitored? What if—

"Hello?" A young voice answered, bright and slightly breathless.

Something in my chest cracked open. "Angel," I whispered, my daughter's name emerging like a prayer.

"Mom?" The word exploded with joy and relief. "Mom! Is that really you?"

"Hey, sweetie," I said, my voice softening instantly. Tears gathered in my eyes, hot and insistent. I hadn't cried during the entire nightmare of the past three days—not when I'd seen my face plastered across news channels labeled as armed and dangerous, not even when I'd realized someone had constructed an elaborate frame designed to destroy my life. But the sound of my daughter's voice undid me completely.

"I miss you so much," Angel continued, words tumbling out in a rush. "When are you coming home? Grandma made lasagna yesterday, but it wasn't as good as yours, and I got an A on my vocabulary test and—"

"Angel," I interrupted gently, "is Christine there?"

"Yeah, she's right here with the baby. Hold on."

I heard shuffling and muffled voices, someone saying, "Give me that," with gentle insistence. Then my older daughter's voice came through the line, controlled but tinged with worry.

"Mom? Where are you? Are you okay?"

I closed my eyes, picturing Christine's face—so much like my own at her age, but with a steadiness I'd never possessed. Being a single mom at only eighteen had given her a gravity I hadn't acquired until decades later, if ever.

"I'm okay," I reassured her, the lie coming easily for her sake. "How's it going with the baby? How's my little Ellie?"

A brief hesitation, then she followed my lead into safer conversational territory. "She slept through the night for the first time," Christine said, her voice warming. "And she's so much fun now. She's starting to recognize faces, I think. She definitely knows when Grandma's holding her versus me."

I smiled despite everything, imagining my granddaughter's tiny face. Another piece of my heart that I couldn't be with right now. "That's wonderful," I managed, though the words felt hollow against the weight of my absence.

Christine's voice dropped lower, more serious. "How are you doing, Mom? I saw your face on the news again. What's happening? I've been so worried and tried to get ahold of you. But your phone goes directly to voicemail."

"I had to get rid of it," I explained, picturing the phone I'd destroyed and abandoned in pieces across three different dumpsters in the Tampa Bay Area. "It wasn't safe."

"Mom." Her voice tightened with fear poorly disguised as frustration. "They're saying you killed a man. They showed your picture and everything. What's happening?"

I pressed my fingers against the bridge of my nose, fighting for composure. How could I explain that someone had constructed an elaborate frame against me? That every piece of evidence pointing to my guilt had been meticulously fabricated? That I was running not because I was guilty, but because I knew I couldn't trust the system to uncover the truth?

"I didn't do what they're saying," I said finally, each word deliberate and clear. "I'm working to fix things and come home soon. I promise." My voice cracked on the last word. "I miss you so much."

"Are you still with Matt?" she asked, ever practical, ever concerned for my welfare even when I should be protecting hers.

"Yes."

"Good." A single word carrying layers of meaning—relief that I wasn't alone, approval of the person watching my back, acknowledgment that at least one thing in this nightmare made sense.

In the background, I heard my mother's voice calling something I couldn't make out, then Christine responding away from the phone. When she returned, urgency had entered her tone. "Mom, there are two men who keep driving by the house. Police, I think, but they never stop. They just… watch."

My stomach tightened. Of course, they would be monitoring my family. It was standard procedure for fugitive cases. I would have ordered the same surveillance myself when I was with the Bureau.

"Don't approach them," I instructed, slipping back into FBI mode. "Don't give them any reason to do more than observe. I'll contact you again when I can, but it might not be for a few days."

"Mom—"

"I love you," I said quickly. "Tell Alex, Elijah, Angel, and Grandma I love them too. And kiss that baby for me. And don't tell Olivia what's going on if she calls from college. It will only distract her, and she has midterms coming up. I don't want her to worry, okay?"

"She already knows, Mom," Christine said with a deep sigh. "You think she doesn't watch TV?"

"I hoped she wouldn't. Okay, then tell her I'm okay, and everything will be fine."

"I don't think she'll buy that, but I'll try."

"Gotta go."

I ended the call before my voice could betray me further, before I could make promises I wasn't certain I could keep. For several minutes, I remained seated on the edge of the bed, head bowed, the silent phone clutched in my hand like some talisman that could transport me back to my normal life.

The shower had stopped running, but Matt hadn't emerged. Giving me privacy, I realized, even in this cramped space where privacy was a luxury we could no longer afford.

The door hinges creaked as Matt pushed it open wider. He stood in the doorway, hair damp against his neck, saying nothing as he placed a hand on my shoulder. The simple weight of human connection nearly undid me again. I covered his hand with mine and squeezed once before straightening my spine.

"They're watching the house," I said, focusing on facts rather than feelings. "But everyone's safe for now."

Matt nodded, understanding everything I wasn't saying. We'd both been law enforcement long enough to know the playbook. Watch the family. Monitor communications. Wait for the fugitive to make contact. It was what I would have done.

Through the small bathroom window, a movement caught my eye. The elderly motel owner walked past our room, his gait slow but purposeful, his head turned toward our curtained window. Something about the deliberate nature of his path raised my internal alarms.

"That's the third time he's walked by in the last hour," Matt said, following my gaze.

I rose from the bed's edge, slipping the phone into my pocket. Later, I'd disassemble it and dispose of the pieces separately, as we'd done with the others. For now, I needed to focus on the immediate threat.

"We need to be ready to move quickly if we have to," I said, wiping away the last traces of tears with the back of my hand. The vulnerability I'd allowed myself during the call vanished, replaced by the hypervigilance that had kept us alive these past three days.

I moved into the main room and began methodically repacking our few belongings. Matt mirrored my movements with practiced efficiency, our partnership requiring few words. We both knew we had to be ready, in case we needed to leave fast.

Outside, the motel owner passed by again, slower this time, his shadow briefly visible through the gap in the curtains.

"He made a call after we checked in," Matt said quietly, zipping his bag closed. "I couldn't hear what he said, but he kept looking out the window toward us, while he talked."

I nodded, processing this new information. "Could be nothing. Could be calling the cops. Either way, we must be ready."

The emotional warmth from hearing my family's voices still lingered somewhere deep in my chest, but I tucked it away, a luxury I couldn't afford right now. Later, when this was over—if this were ever over—I would allow myself to feel the full weight of what I stood to lose.

We had hours before our meeting with Juan Ramirez, hours we'd planned to use for much-needed rest. But rest, like privacy and safety, had become another casualty of this nightmare.

Chapter 7

THEN:

The afternoon sun slanted through the windows of Granger's restaurant, casting long rectangles of light across the polished floors. Ann Porter moved between tables with the fluid precision of someone who had walked these paths a thousand times before. She balanced three plates along her left arm, her right hand steadying them with practiced ease, her attention divided between the weight of porcelain and the mental catalogue of who had ordered what. Table seven needed ketchup. The couple by the window would want their check soon. The man in the corner booth had already eaten half his fries but hadn't touched his sandwich. Ann noted it all and filed it away, a constant stream of small observations that kept her shift running smoothly.

"Here you are," she said, setting down plates before a family of four. "Chicken strips for you, burger medium-rare, Caesar salad, and the fish special." Her smile appeared and disappeared efficiently—present long enough to be polite, brief enough to move on.

The restaurant hummed around her with its familiar symphony

—knives scraping plates, ice clinking in glasses, the sizzle and hiss from the kitchen, bursts of laughter from the bar. Ann navigated through it all, her body on autopilot while her mind categorized and prioritized each task. Check on table two. Refill waters at nine. Drop off the check at five.

Tom Granger appeared from the back office, his eyes scanning the dining room with the quick assessment of a man who'd spent twenty-five years in the business. He nodded at Ann as she passed, a silent acknowledgment that things were running as they should.

"Need more ranch dressing at table twelve," she murmured as she passed him, and he gave a curt nod, already moving toward the kitchen to relay the message.

Ann swept past the wait station, grabbing a fresh ketchup bottle and napkins in one fluid motion. Her steps faltered slightly when the front door opened, admitting a rush of cooler air and a figure whose presence seemed to fill more space than his physical body should allow.

The policeman stood in the entrance, the afternoon light catching on his badge. He was in full uniform—dark blue that looked almost black until the light hit it just right, utility belt heavy with equipment, the unmistakable bulge of a holstered gun at his hip. Ann wasn't the only one who noticed; a brief hush rippled through the nearest tables, that momentary collective intake of breath that accompanied authority entering a room.

The hostess approached him with a menu, but he shook his head, gesturing toward Ann's section with a confidence that suggested he'd been here before, though Ann couldn't recall seeing him. Her fingers tightened around the ketchup bottle as the hostess led him to table eight—one of her four-tops, now occupied by just him, his broad shoulders making the space seem smaller.

Ann took her time delivering the ketchup to table seven, her mind racing ahead to the interaction that awaited her. She checked her reflection in the polished surface of the coffee machine—hair still tucked neatly behind one ear, lipstick faded but presentable. She wasn't sure why she checked.

"Good afternoon," she said, approaching his table with a professional smile fixed in place. "Welcome to Granger's."

"Officer Marcus Hale," he said, though she hadn't asked. His eyes—a deep brown that caught the light in fragments—met hers directly. "I've heard good things about this place."

Ann nodded, aware of a subtle shift in her breathing pattern. Shallower now. Faster. "First time visiting us?"

"First time in uniform," he said with a slight smile that creased the corners of his eyes. "Usually I'm off-duty when I make it here."

That explained why she didn't recognize him. Ann pulled out her notepad and uncapped her pen. Her palm felt damp against the plastic. "Can I get you started with something to drink?"

"Just water for now." He didn't look at the menu. "What do you recommend?"

The question was standard, but something in his tone made it feel more personal. Ann found herself unusually conscious of her posture, the way she held her pen, the sensation of being watched with an intensity that exceeded the normal server-customer dynamic.

"The smash burger is good," she said, her voice steadier than she felt. "Chef Cho makes them with a blend of three meats. Or the special today is blackened salmon with roasted vegetables."

Marcus nodded slowly, his gaze never leaving her face. "I'll trust your judgment. The burger, medium."

Ann wrote it down, though the order was simple enough to remember. Her handwriting looked different somehow—tighter, more careful strokes. She was aware of his gun again, the holster's leather worn with use, its weight pulling slightly at his belt. The authority it represented. The danger.

"I'll get that in for you," she said, turning to leave.

"Ann," he called after her, and she froze, not remembering having told him her name. Her gaze flicked to her name tag—of course. "Could I get some coffee while I wait?"

She nodded, not trusting her voice for a moment. "Cream and sugar?"

"Black is fine."

In the kitchen, the familiar chaos welcomed her—Chef Cho barking orders at the line cooks, steam rising from pots, the rhythmic chop of knives against cutting boards. Ann punched in the order, her fingers tapping the screen with unusual force.

"You okay?" Miriam asked, sidling up next to her with a tray of dirty dishes. "You look like you've seen a ghost."

"I'm fine," Ann said, pouring coffee with a hand that wasn't quite steady. "Just… there's a cop at table eight."

Miriam glanced through the kitchen window. "Oh, he's cute though."

Ann didn't respond, but heat crept up her neck as she arranged the coffee cup on a saucer. When she returned to the dining room, she could feel Marcus watching her, tracking her movements as she delivered the coffee. His eyes seemed to follow her as she checked on her other tables, took orders, and delivered food. Every time she glanced in his direction, he was looking at her with that same steady, evaluating gaze.

The weight of his attention made her hyperaware of her body —the swing of her hips as she walked, the movement of her hands as she jotted down orders, the way she tucked her hair behind her ear when she was concentrating. Actions that had been automatic for years suddenly felt deliberate, performed.

When his food arrived, Ann set the plate before him with care, conscious of the proximity of their hands, the smell of his cologne —subtle but present, something woodsy and clean that contrasted with the cooking odors that typically surrounded her.

"Anything else I can get you?" she asked, stepping back slightly, needing the distance.

"This looks great," he said, then added with unexpected directness, "How long have you worked here, Ann?"

The question startled her—personal in a way customers rarely were. "About three years," she answered, unsure why she felt compelled to be honest rather than deflecting.

He nodded as if confirming something. "You know everyone's patterns. I've been watching you work. Very efficient."

The observation felt invasive yet flattering. Ann's chest tightened with a confusion of emotions—pride, discomfort, and something else she couldn't name. "Enjoy your meal," she said, retreating to check on her other tables.

Throughout his meal, she remained conscious of his presence, like a persistent itch between her shoulder blades. When she brought his check, he handed her a credit card without looking at the total.

"Everything was excellent," he said, his voice lower than before. "Exactly what I needed today."

Ann processed his payment and returned with the receipt. He added a tip that was nearly half the cost of the meal itself, signed with a confident flourish.

"I'll be seeing you again," he said as he stood. It wasn't phrased as a question.

Ann watched him leave, the strange flutter in her stomach persisting long after the door closed behind him. She picked up his empty plate and noticed he'd eaten every bite, leaving it nearly clean. Something about the thoroughness unsettled her. As she cleared the table, she found herself picturing his face, replaying their interactions, and wondering exactly when he would return.

Chapter 8

THREE DAYS EARLIER, I'd been driving down Morrison Avenue with the windows cracked, letting in the warm Tampa air that carried hints of exhaust and flowering jasmine. The late afternoon sun glinted off my rearview mirror, momentarily blinding me just before the flash of red and blue lights appeared behind me. I checked my speed—five over the limit, nothing that usually warranted a stop—and pulled to the curb with the practiced calm of someone who'd spent two decades on the other side of law enforcement. Just a routine traffic stop. The last normal moment before my entire life imploded.

I watched in my side mirror as the officer approached, noting his unhurried gait and the casual way his hand rested near his holster—relaxed, not anticipating trouble—a routine stop for him, too. The heat rising from the asphalt created wavering distortions around his figure as he drew closer. I rolled down my window, the electric motor whirring in protest.

"License and registration, ma'am." His voice carried the flat affect of someone who'd repeated the same phrase thousands of times. Young guy, maybe early thirties, with a neatly trimmed mustache and the beginning of sweat stains darkening his uniform collar.

"Officer." I nodded, reaching slowly for my purse. Twenty years with the FBI had taught me how to interact with law enforcement—deliberate movements, respectful tone, nothing that could be misinterpreted as a threat. "May I ask why I was pulled over?"

"Taillight's out." He leaned slightly to glance at the back of my car. "Driver's side."

I frowned. I'd checked all my lights before we left a week earlier. It was actually Matt's old car. We had decided to take this instead of my minivan so my daughter Christine could use that back home for her and the baby.

I kept my confusion to myself as I handed over my license and the registration I'd retrieved from the glove compartment. His eyes flickered with recognition as he read my name.

"FBI?" he asked, looking at me with new interest.

"Twenty years," I confirmed. "Though I'm more of a consultant these days."

"You're the one who wrote that book on the profiler's code," he said.

"That would be me. That's actually why I'm in town. I live over in Cocoa Beach, but was invited to a book signing event here in Tampa this week. My boyfriend and I are leaving town today. Going home to the children."

He nodded, that subtle shift in posture that comes when one law enforcement officer recognizes another. His shoulders relaxed a fraction. "I'll just run this and have you on your way, Agent Thomas."

I watched him walk back to his patrol car, my fingers drumming lightly on the steering wheel. Matt was at the mall waiting for me to pick him up. He had been buying presents to take home to the kids, as we usually did when going places. They had been staying with my mom while we were gone. I guess we kind of felt guilty for being away. I was a grandmother now, and it was hard to be away from that little munchkin. Ellie was the most adorable little thing in the world, and everyone loved her. Even my youngest, Angel, Matt's and my mutual child, who, up until now, had been the adorable one in the family. She hadn't seemed to mind leaving her position to Ellie.

Through my open window came the steady hum of passing traffic, the distant wail of an ambulance, the chirping of birds in the trees lining the boulevard. Ordinary sounds on an ordinary day.

The officer returned faster than I expected, his expression now carefully neutral—the professional mask I recognized from my own days of delivering bad news. Something had changed. My fingers stilled on the steering wheel.

"Ma'am, I'm going to need you to step out of the vehicle."

I felt the first flutter of unease in my stomach. "Is there a problem, Officer?"

"Please step out of the vehicle." His hand had moved closer to his weapon, and his stance widened slightly—preparing for trouble.

I complied, moving slowly, my mind racing through possibilities. Outstanding warrant? Some database error? "What seems to be the issue?" I asked as my feet hit the pavement. The heat rose through the thin soles of my shoes.

He didn't answer immediately; instead, he gestured toward the rear of my car. "Ma'am, is there any particular reason why your trunk might smell the way it does?"

The question hit me like a physical blow. "I don't understand."

"When I walked past your vehicle, I detected a strong odor consistent with decomposition." His words were careful and precise—the language of a report being mentally drafted. "Do you mind if I take a look in your trunk?"

Cold dread pooled in my stomach. "Officer, I assure you—"

"Ma'am, I need you to open the trunk." His hand now rested directly on his holster.

I swallowed hard, my throat suddenly dry. "I don't know what you're talking about. There shouldn't be any smell." But even as I spoke, I became aware of it—faint but unmistakable in the heat. That sweet, sickly odor that every experienced investigator knows.

The smell of death.

With trembling fingers, I pressed the trunk release button on my key fob. The lock disengaged with a soft click that seemed to echo in the space between us.

The officer stepped forward and lifted the trunk lid.

His reaction told me everything before I could see inside. His body went rigid, his hand immediately drawing his weapon as he stumbled back a step. "Jesus Christ," he breathed, the professional veneer cracking to reveal naked shock.

I moved to look, even as everything in me screamed not to. The world narrowed to the contents of my trunk—a man's body, curled in a fetal position, blood had soaked through the light-colored shirt, darkening to rust around what appeared to be a gunshot wound. His face was turned away, but I could see dark hair and pale skin with the gray undertone of death. I didn't recognize him. I had never seen this man before in my life.

My training kicked in automatically—assessing time of death (12-24 hours based on early decomposition), wound pattern (gunshot wound to the back of the head, and another in the back at close proximity, personal), body positioning (placed post-mortem)—even as my mind reeled in horrified disbelief.

"Don't move," the officer ordered, his weapon now trained on me. “Hand over your service weapon.”

I reached down, took my gun out of the holster, and handed it to him. His free hand reached for his radio. "Dispatch, I need backup at West Morrison Avenue. Code three. I have a 187 and a suspect in custody." His voice shook slightly on the last word.

Time seemed to stretch and compress simultaneously. I could hear my own breathing, too fast, too shallow. Sweat trickled down my spine. A car passed, the driver slowing to rubberneck before speeding away. The sun beat down mercilessly from a cloudless sky.

"Officer," I managed, my voice sounding strange to my own ears, "I don't know who that is. I didn't put him there. Someone must have—"

"Hands where I can see them," he cut me off, his earlier recognition of me as a colleague completely erased. Now I was just a killer caught with her victim.

I raised my hands slowly, mind racing. If I submitted to arrest now, I would be at the mercy of whoever had planted this body in my car. Someone with enough knowledge and access to frame me for murder. Someone who wanted me imprisoned or worse.

Rule Seven of The Profiler's Code echoed in my head: Truth before badge. The ultimate loyalty is to finding the truth, even when it conflicts with official positions.

The officer had positioned himself between me and the driver's door. His radio crackled with dispatch confirmation. Backup was on the way. Minutes, perhaps seconds, before my chance evaporated.

"Turn around and place your hands on the vehicle," he instructed, shifting slightly to retrieve his handcuffs.

In that moment of movement, I made my decision. Twenty years of respecting the law, of following procedure, of building cases meticulously within the system—all abandoned in a heartbeat of survival instinct.

I lunged forward, driving my shoulder into his midsection. He wasn't expecting resistance from a fellow law enforcement officer. His back hit the pavement hard, the impact knocking the wind from his lungs in a surprised whoosh. His weapon clattered away.

"I'm sorry," I gasped, though he likely couldn't hear me through his own desperate attempts to breathe. "I didn't do this. I have to find out who did."

I scrambled back into my car, hands shaking so violently I could barely get the key into the ignition. The engine roared to life. In my rearview mirror, I could see the officer struggling to his feet, shouting into his radio, his face contorted with anger and disbelief.

I floored the accelerator, tires screaming against asphalt as I pulled away. The red and blue lights receded in my mirror, but I knew they would soon multiply. Every patrol car in Tampa would be looking for me within minutes.

As Morrison Avenue stretched before me, the reality of what I'd just done crashed over me in waves of nausea and terror. I had assaulted an officer. I had fled a murder scene. I had left behind physical evidence connecting me to a homicide.

I had become exactly what the Profiler's Code warned against—a suspect running from justice.

Chapter 9

THE MEMORY DISSOLVED as I snapped back to the present, my fingernails digging half-moons into my palms. The Paradise Bay Motel room materialized around me in all its depressing glory—water stains spreading across the ceiling like disease, thin curtains that let the neon sign outside pulse through in sickly red intervals, and the ever-present smell of industrial cleaner failing to mask decades of cigarettes and desperation. I resumed pacing the five steps the narrow room allowed, wearing an invisible trench between the bathroom door and the foot of the sagging bed, where Matt sat, watching me with concern etched in the lines around his eyes. On the day of the escape, I grabbed our bags from the back seat, then left the car in an alley behind the mall before running to Matt, who was waiting for me at the entrance to Macy's. After explaining to him what had happened, he had abandoned all the gifts for the kids and stopped a passing car using his badge. He then asked the driver for his vehicle for police matters, and as the driver got out, we took his car and drove off.

"Richard Collins," I said, the name still unfamiliar on my tongue despite having repeated it dozens of times since learning the victim's identity. "Fifty-five years old. Accountant at Meridian Financial.

Divorced, no children. No criminal record. Not even a parking ticket." I ran my fingers through my unwashed hair, wincing as they caught in tangles. "I've never met him, never heard of him, never worked a case connected to him. There is absolutely no reason why his body should have been in my trunk."

Matt shifted on the bed, the ancient springs protesting beneath his weight. His prosthetic leg was propped against the nightstand, and he massaged his residual limb absentmindedly—a habit when he was deep in thought. The day's stubble darkened his jaw, making the scar above his right eyebrow stand out in stark relief.

"Rule Four," he said quietly.

I stopped pacing, my shoulders tensing at the reference. The Profiler's Code had been my professional bible for years. Now it seemed to be mocking me.

"The innocent run differently," I recited mechanically. "Those falsely accused behave distinctively from the guilty; they seek to prove innocence rather than merely escape consequences." A bitter laugh escaped me. "And here I am, running. Making myself look guilty with every mile I put between myself and that crime scene."

Matt's gaze was steady and analytical without judgment. "You made a split-second decision based on your instincts. Those same instincts have solved dozens of cases that stumped everyone else. I trust them."

A cockroach scuttled across the baseboard and disappeared behind the ancient television stand. The ice machine down the hall groaned and clattered, the sound carrying through paper-thin walls. Somewhere nearby, a couple was arguing in hushed, intense tones—the words indistinct but the emotion unmistakable.

"My instincts are telling me this is methodical," I said, resuming my pacing. "Someone chose Collins specifically. Someone put him in my trunk knowing I'd be pulled over." I stopped, a new thought forming. "That taillight—I checked all the lights last week. Someone tampered with our car to ensure I'd be stopped."

"That's a lot of variables to control," Matt observed, leaning forward.

I sank onto the edge of the bed beside Matt, suddenly

exhausted. Three days of running, three days of barely sleeping, the constant hypervigilance wearing me down to raw nerves and bone-deep fatigue.

The TV was still on, but muted. The news wheel returned to my story. The headline scrolled beneath: "Manhunt Intensifies for Former FBI Profiler Eva Rae Thomas." I turned on the volume just to hear the reporter then detailing my "violent escape" from the traffic stop, the "premeditated murder" of Richard Collins. Every word twisted reality into a darkly distorted version of events. Beneath it, another headline announced the reward for information leading to my capture had doubled.

"They're making me sound like a dangerous criminal," I whispered, my stomach turning. "Like I've completely lost control."

Matt took the remote from my trembling hands, then muted the TV again. "Which means whoever is framing you knows what they're doing."

"But why?" I pressed my palms against my eyes, trying to think through the exhaustion. "Why me? Why Collins? There has to be a connection I'm not seeing."

"We need more information on Collins," Matt said, his detective's mind already plotting investigation angles. "Bank records, phone records, recent contacts. Something that connects him to whoever is setting you up."

I nodded, my thoughts aligning with his. "We need resources we don't have—access to databases and contacts who can run searches without triggering alerts." I sighed, letting my hands drop to my lap. "We need help. We need allies."

"That's why we're meeting Juan tomorrow," he said. "He can help us get all the info on Collins."

"We need more than one," I said. "In case Juan can't be trusted. I don't have a good feeling about him. He's shady."

The neon sign outside flashed, painting the room briefly in crimson before plunging it back into shadow. The rhythmic pulse reminded me of emergency lights, of the moment my life had shattered three days ago.

"Sarah Winters," I said suddenly, sitting straighter.

Matt's eyebrows rose slightly. "The bookstore owner? How would she help us?"

"I don't know, but she's the one who invited me here and arranged the event. She's a big fan of mine. Maybe she'll believe me when I say I'm innocent? I can't think of anyone else who would."

Matt considered this, his expression cautious. "Reaching out to anyone right now is risky. You don't know who you can trust."

"I don't need to trust her with everything. Just enough to get information about Collins." I reached for my jacket—a nondescript hoodie borrowed from Matt that hung loose on my frame. "She gave me her personal number. Said I could come by the store any time if I wanted to browse after hours."

Matt watched me, his eyes narrowing slightly as he measured the risk against our dwindling options. "And you think she won't immediately call the police when a fugitive shows up at her door?"

I hesitated, remembering Sarah's warm smile, her enthusiastic questions about my profiling work, her obvious admiration. "She's fascinated by criminal psychology. She was talking about how the system fails people, how false convictions happen. If anyone might listen before judging, it's her."

Matt reached for his prosthetic, strapping it on with practiced movements. "Then we go together. If she seems suspicious, we leave immediately."

I nodded, already mentally mapping the least conspicuous route to downtown Tampa. As I gathered my purse and burner phone, I caught my reflection in the bathroom mirror—a stranger staring back at me with haunted eyes and desperate determination. The woman in the mirror looked guilty, looked hunted.

Looked exactly like the fugitive they were claiming I was.

Chapter 10

BOOKMARK HAVEN STOOD dark and silent on the corner of the street, its windows reflecting the lamps in dull yellow squares against the night. Matt and I watched from across the street, sheltered in the shadow of a closed café, studying the bookstore for any sign of surveillance. The "CLOSED" sign hung in the front door, but a soft light glowed from the back office window. Sarah was working late, just as I'd hoped. I pulled the hood of my borrowed jacket lower over my face, painfully aware that my distinctive red hair made me far too recognizable despite my attempts at disguise.

"Police cruiser passed twice in the five minutes we've been watching," Matt murmured, his voice low. "Could be routine patrol, or they could be monitoring potential contacts."

I nodded, tension coiling between my shoulder blades. "We'll use the back entrance. Quick and quiet."

We crossed the street separately—Matt first, then me, thirty seconds later—moving casually as if we belonged there, as if we weren't fugitives in a city-wide manhunt. The alley behind the bookstore was narrow, lined with dumpsters from neighboring businesses, filling the humid air with the sweet-sour smell of food waste. A single security light cast long shadows.

"This is a risk," Matt whispered as I grabbed the handle to see if she had left the door unlocked. "We're bringing her into this without warning. Putting her in danger."

The handle turned with a soft click. "We're out of options," I replied, though guilt twisted in my stomach. He was right—we were potentially making Sarah an accessory, whether she wanted that role or not.

The door opened into a small storage area stacked with cardboard boxes labeled "New Releases" and "Special Orders." The familiar scent of paper and binding glue enveloped us—a sharp contrast to the alley's stench. I closed the door silently behind us, my eyes adjusting to the dimmer light filtering in from the main shop.

We moved carefully through the storage room into Bookmark Haven. The bookstore spread before us like a literary sanctuary—floor-to-ceiling shelves creating intimate corridors between sections, comfortable reading nooks tucked into corners with plush armchairs worn smooth by years of readers, and small lamps casting pools of golden light that seemed to make the books' spines glow with promise. A coffee counter stood silent along one wall, its espresso machine gleaming dully in the low light. The air carried notes of cinnamon and old paper, of leather bindings and the faint citrus of furniture polish.

In another life—a normal life, the life I'd had just three days ago—this place would have been a haven indeed. Now it was just another calculated risk.

A soft thud came from the office at the back of the store, followed by the scrape of a chair on hardwood. Matt shifted beside me, his body angling slightly to shield mine, despite knowing I was perfectly capable of defending myself—an old habit born of affection rather than doubt in my abilities.

The office door opened, spilling brighter light across the floorboards. Sarah Winters emerged, a stack of papers in her hands, her head bent over them in concentration. She took three steps before freezing, her awareness of our presence hitting her like a physical blow. The papers scattered as her hands flew up in startled defense.

"Who's—" she began, then her eyes widened with recognition. "Eva Rae?"

"I'm sorry to frighten you," I said quickly, keeping my voice low and my hands visible. "We needed somewhere safe to talk."

Sarah's gaze darted between Matt and me, then to the door behind us, then back again. Her hand moved to her throat in that unconscious self-protective gesture humans make when threatened. I watched emotions chase across her face—shock, fear, confusion, and then something that looked like determination.

"I've seen your face all over the news," she said, bending to gather the fallen papers with trembling fingers. "They're saying you killed someone. That you're dangerous."

"I didn't kill anyone," I said, staying where I was to avoid frightening her further. "I'm being framed, Sarah. Someone planted a body in my car and broke my taillight to make sure I'd be caught with it."

Sarah straightened, papers clutched against her chest like armor. She wore the same kind of casual, comfortable clothes I remembered—a loose sweater over jeans, practical flats, her brown hair pulled back in a simple ponytail. Nothing about her appearance suggested anything but the bookish, friendly woman I'd met during my signing.

"Come into my office," she said after a moment, glancing toward the front of the store as if expecting police to burst through at any moment. "You shouldn't be standing out here where someone might see you through the windows."

We followed her into the cramped office—a space made smaller by overflowing bookshelves and stacks of publisher catalogs. A desk dominated the center, its surface buried under paperwork, coffee mugs, and a laptop displaying a spreadsheet. Sarah closed the door behind us, then leaned against it, still clutching her papers.

"I need to understand what's happening," she said, her voice steadier now.

I sank into one of the visitor chairs, suddenly aware of how exhausted I was. "The man—Richard Collins—was planted in my trunk. I never met him before seeing his body."

"He was at the book signing, though," Sarah said.

"He was? I don't remember him," I said.

"Well, you signed thousands of books and read to an entire room filled with hundreds of people, so why would you remember one face?" Sarah's eyes widened slightly as she continued. "He worked at Meridian Financial as an accountant, but loved mysteries and anything related to policework."

I leaned forward. "You knew him?"

Sarah set the papers on her desk with deliberate care. "He was a regular customer. Came in every Thursday for the new mystery releases. Always bought two—one thriller, one classic detective story." Her voice softened. "I can't believe he's dead. He was such a lovely man."

Matt and I exchanged glances. Our first real connection to the victim, our first potential thread to pull. The bookstore.

"Sarah," I said carefully, "I need to know everything about him. Who he spoke to, what he was like, and if he ever mentioned any troubles. Anything that might help me understand why someone would kill him and use him to frame me."

Sarah pushed a strand of hair behind her ear, her fingers noticeably unsteady. "I don't know much about his personal life. He was quiet and polite. Mentioned work sometimes, complaining about audits and deadlines. I guess you could say we flirted a little. Maybe that's why he kept coming in." She hesitated, glancing at her phone on the desk. "But he did seem... nervous these past few weeks—looking over his shoulder a lot. I asked if he was okay, and he said something about discovering numbers that didn't add up."

My pulse quickened. "Numbers that didn't add up? Like financial discrepancies?"

"I think so." Sarah wrapped her arms around herself. "I can't believe he's gone, though. It makes me so sad."

I reached for her hand, and she let me grab it. Our eyes met, and I could tell she wasn't afraid of me. "I... we... need your help. Can we trust you?"

Her lips became narrow, her eyes scrutinizing both of us. Then she nodded. "Okay. I want to believe you. How can I help?"

Relief washed through me—a potential ally, and our first lead, all in one conversation.

Chapter 11

THEN:

Ann's alarm blared for the third time, finally piercing through her dreams of watchful brown eyes and a smile that transformed severity into warmth. She blinked, momentarily disoriented, before the realization crashed over her—today she might see Marcus again. The thought sent her lurching upright, sleep forgotten as anticipation flooded her system, her heart already racing though her feet hadn't even touched the floor.

The digital clock's red numbers accused her of indulgence: 9:17 a.m. She wasn't due at Granger's until eleven, but Ann had planned to arrive early, to ensure everything in her section would be perfect when—if—Marcus appeared. She swung her legs over the side of the bed, her toes curling against the cool hardwood as images from yesterday replayed in her mind—his steady gaze tracking her movements, the way his presence had filled her awareness even when she wasn't looking directly at him, the deliberate way he'd promised to return.

Ann stood before her closet, suddenly critical of options she'd never questioned before. The standard black pants and white button-down that comprised Granger's unofficial uniform seemed insufficient now. She pulled out three nearly identical pairs of black pants, laying them across her unmade bed, scrutinizing each for subtle differences. The first was slightly faded at the knees. The second had a loose thread at the hem. The third—her newest pair, worn only a handful of times—hugged her hips more closely than the others. She selected these, holding them against herself as she studied her reflection in the full-length mirror attached to her closet door.

"This is ridiculous," she whispered to herself, the same words she'd spoken to her reflection in the rearview mirror while driving home the night before. But she didn't put the pants back. Instead, she spent another fifteen minutes selecting a white shirt—choosing one that was slightly more fitted than her usual preference—and her most comfortable black flats.

In the bathroom, Ann leaned close to the mirror, examining her face with unusual scrutiny. She opened her makeup bag—typically only used for special occasions—and began applying foundation with careful strokes. Her hand trembled slightly as she lined her eyes, a thin smudge of brown rather than her usual bare lids. Mascara next, two coats, then a tinted lip balm that enhanced her natural color without looking obvious. Professional enough for work but more polished than her everyday appearance.

Her hair, typically pulled back in a simple ponytail, received similar attention. She spent precious minutes with a round brush and blow dryer, coaxing it into soft waves that framed her face. When she finally stepped back to assess the full effect, the woman in the mirror looked like a more vivid version of herself—still Ann, but Ann with the contrast turned up, the details sharpened.

The clock read 10:27 when she finally grabbed her purse and keys. She was cutting it close now, especially with the morning traffic. Tom expected servers fifteen minutes before their shift to review the daily specials and prep their sections. Being late wasn't an option, not when she needed everything to go perfectly today.

Ann's car started with its familiar rattle. As she pulled out of her apartment complex, she found herself humming happily.

Traffic moved sluggishly, every red light seeming to last an eternity. Ann drummed her fingers against the steering wheel, checking her watch, calculating minutes. She was cutting it too close. Ten minutes to get across town. She'd need to be lucky with the lights.

When the traffic signal ahead turned yellow, Ann made a split-second decision. She pressed harder on the accelerator, her car surging forward through the intersection just as the light shifted to red. A flash of guilt mixed with triumph as she cleared it—technically legal, but pushing the boundaries of safety.

The brief satisfaction evaporated as red and blue lights flared in her rearview mirror. Ann's stomach dropped, her mouth suddenly dry. She eased her car toward the curb, heart hammering against her ribs as the patrol car pulled in behind her. This couldn't be happening, not today of all days, when she was already running late and needed everything to be perfect for when Marcus arrived at the restaurant.

Through her side mirror, she watched a uniformed figure emerge from the patrol car. The morning sun caught on something metallic—a badge pinned to a broad chest. Ann's breath stopped in her throat as recognition dawned. Even at this distance, the officer's posture and build were unmistakable.

Marcus.

Ann's hands gripped the steering wheel, her palms suddenly slick with sweat. She watched his methodical approach in the mirror, each step bringing him closer, his face becoming clearer. The same intense eyes that had tracked her movements across the restaurant yesterday now focused solely on her vehicle. His expression was neutral, professional—the face of a police officer performing a routine traffic stop, not the man who had watched her with such interest, who had promised to return to see her.

She fumbled with the window control, her finger slipping off the button twice before the glass finally lowered. The morning air rushed in, carrying with it the subtle scent of his cologne—that same woodsy clean smell she'd noticed yesterday when he'd sat at her table.

"License and registration, please," Marcus said, his voice revealing no recognition, no special acknowledgment.

Ann swallowed hard, her throat clicking audibly in the silence. "Officer Hale," she managed, hating how breathy her voice sounded. "I—I didn't realize it was you."

His expression shifted then, a slight softening around the eyes as he leaned down to get a better look at her face. The sunlight caught on his badge, sending fractured light across the interior of her car.

"I recognize you from Tom Granger's restaurant, don't I?" he said, his tone warming a fraction, though his posture remained professional. "Ann, right?"

She nodded, her chest tight with a mixture of relief and anxiety. "Yes. I-I'm sorry about the light. I'm running late for my shift."

"I still need to see your license and registration," he reminded her, the authority in his voice unmistakable despite the hint of familiarity.

"Of course," Ann said, turning to reach for her purse on the passenger seat. Her hand shook visibly as she rummaged for her wallet, papers spilling out in her haste. She extracted her license, then opened the glove compartment for her registration and insurance card. The small cards slipped through her trembling fingers not once but twice, falling to the floor mat before she finally secured them and handed everything over.

Marcus took the documents, his eyes scanning them briefly before returning to her face. Ann couldn't help but notice the way his uniform stretched across his shoulders, how the fabric looked freshly pressed, the neat line of buttons drawing her eye down the center of his chest. His utility belt held the equipment of his profession—gun, handcuffs, radio—each item a reminder of his authority, his power.

"You seem nervous," he observed, his voice lower now.

"I hate being late," Ann said, which was true, though it wasn't the primary reason her heart was pounding so hard she could feel it in her fingertips. "Tom—my boss—he's strict about punctuality."

Marcus nodded, his eyes lingering on her face. Ann became acutely aware of her makeup, the extra care she'd taken with her appearance this morning. Had he noticed? Could he tell it was for him?

"You changed your hair," he said, confirming that he had indeed noticed. The comment wasn't professional, wasn't related to her traffic violation, but Ann felt a surge of pleasure at his observation.

"Just… trying something different," she said, her fingers automatically reaching up to tuck a strand behind her ear, a gesture he'd seen her make repeatedly during her shift yesterday.

Marcus's gaze followed the movement, a slight smile playing at the corners of his mouth before his expression returned to professional neutrality. "Let me run these," he said, holding up her documents. "Sit tight."

As he walked back to his patrol car, Ann exhaled shakily, suddenly aware she'd been holding her breath. She watched him in her side mirror—the crisp lines of his uniform, the confident way he moved. This couldn't be a coincidence—being pulled over by Marcus of all people, on the very morning after he'd promised to see her again. The universe didn't work that way.

Unless he had been looking for her.

The thought sent a fresh wave of adrenaline through her system, a mixture of fear and something dangerously close to excitement.

Ann watched Marcus through her side mirror as he stood by his patrol car, her documents in hand. He appeared to be taking longer than necessary, studying her information with unusual thoroughness before finally making his way back to her window. His steps were measured, unhurried, as if he had all the time in the world despite her evident rush to get to work. The sunlight caught in his short dark hair as he approached, and Ann found herself holding her breath again, her fingers resuming their nervous dance against the steering wheel.

"Well, Ann Porter," he said, leaning down to her window. Her name in his mouth sounded different somehow—more significant. "Everything checks out. You've got a clean record."

She nodded, not trusting her voice immediately. "So… am I getting a ticket?" The question came out smaller than she intended, almost hopeful in its uncertainty.

Marcus studied her face for a moment, his expression unreadable. "I think we can let this one slide with a warning." He held out her documents. "But yellow lights mean slow down, not speed up. You know that."

Ann reached for the papers, her fingertips brushing against his as she took them. The contact wasn't accidental—his fingers lingered against hers a fraction too long, the pressure slight but deliberate. Her skin tingled where they touched, the sensation traveling up her arm like an electric current.

"Thank you," she managed, hyper-aware of the blush spreading across her cheeks. "I really appreciate it."

Their eyes met, and in that moment, something passed between them—a current of recognition, of mutual awareness that transcended their brief encounters. His professional mask slipped just enough to reveal a hint of the man who had watched her with such interest in the restaurant.

"Be more careful next time," he said, his voice dropping slightly. "I'd hate to see anything happen to you."

The words were standard enough for a traffic stop, but the way he said them—with a soft intensity, a hint of a smile playing at the corners of his mouth—transformed them into something more intimate, more personal. Ann felt her chest tighten, her breath shallow.

"I will," she promised, meaning it.

Marcus straightened, taking a step back from her car. "Have a good day, Ann. Drive safely." The professional tone had returned, but his eyes held hers a moment longer than necessary before he turned away.

Ann watched in her rearview mirror as he walked back to his patrol car. Halfway there, he paused, looking back at her vehicle as if considering something. What was he thinking? Had he planned to find her this morning? The questions buzzed in her mind like trapped insects as she watched him finally continue to his car.

Only when his patrol car pulled away did Ann release the breath she'd been holding. She pulled back into traffic, her mind racing faster than her car.

The coincidence seemed too perfect to be random. How likely was it that of all the officers who could have pulled her over, it would be Marcus Hale? Ann had never believed much in fate, but this—this felt like something aligned by forces beyond her understanding. Or perhaps more deliberately arranged by human intention.

Had he followed her home last night? The patrol car she'd glimpsed outside her apartment complex as it passed by—had that been him? The thought should have alarmed her, but instead it sent a thrill of excitement through her. He was interested enough to seek her out, to learn where she lived, to engineer another meeting before their planned encounter at the restaurant.

By the time Ann pulled into the employee parking lot at Granger's, her emotions had cycled through confusion, excitement, anxiety, and back again. She checked her appearance in the rearview mirror, reapplied her lip balm, and tucked her hair behind her ear—the gesture she now recognized as something she did when nervous, something he had noticed.

The kitchen's heat hit her as she pushed through the back entrance, the familiar sounds and smells grounding her after the surreal morning encounter. She hurried to the break room to stow her purse, nearly colliding with Miriam, who was emerging with her order pad in hand.

"There you are!" Miriam's eyes widened as she took in Ann's appearance. "Whoa. What happened to you? You look… different."

Ann touched her hair self-consciously. "Just felt like making an effort today."

Miriam's eyes narrowed with interest. "This wouldn't have anything to do with Officer Dreamy from yesterday, would it?"

"Don't be ridiculous," Ann said, the denial automatic even as heat rose to her cheeks.

"Mmhmm." Miriam's knowing smile made Ann look away. "Well, Tom was asking for you. You're cutting it close."

Ann nodded, checking her watch—11:13. She was late. "I got pulled over," she said, the truth escaping before she could consider whether sharing was wise.

Miriam's eyebrows shot up. "Ticket?"

"Just a warning."

"Lucky you." Miriam studied her face. "You okay? You seem… I don't know. Wired."

"I'm fine," Ann said, moving past her friend to clock in. "Just a weird morning."

The restaurant was always quiet in the lull before the lunch rush, giving Ann time to prep her section. She arranged salt and pepper shakers with unusual precision, aligning them perfectly at the center of each table. Her mind kept drifting back to the traffic stop—Marcus's fingers against hers, the way his eyes had held hers, his parting words. "I'd hate to see anything happen to you." As if he were concerned about her well-being. As if he cared about her.

Tom emerged from his office, clipboard in hand, eyeing Ann with mild suspicion. "You were cutting it close today, Porter."

"Sorry. Traffic issue." She didn't elaborate, and he didn't ask.

"Chef's special today is pan-seared trout with lemon caper sauce." He studied her face. "You feeling alright? You look flushed."

Ann nodded quickly. "I'm fine. Just rushed in."

The first customers arrived shortly after eleven-thirty, and Ann fell into her familiar routine—greeting, seating, taking orders, delivering food. But beneath her professional exterior, a countdown had begun. Each time she passed the wall clock, her eyes flicked to it, calculating the minutes until 1:15, the time Marcus had come in the day before.

By 12:30, the restaurant was half-full, the lunch crowd trickling in steadily. Ann found herself looking toward the door each time it opened, a small jolt of anticipation followed by disappointment when the customer who entered wasn't Marcus. She'd forgotten to bring her table seven's extra napkins, brought unsweetened tea to a customer who had specifically requested sweet, and nearly collided with Chef Cho as she backed through the kitchen door without looking.

"Eyes forward, Porter," Chef Cho snapped, though her expression held more curiosity than anger as she took in Ann's distracted state.

"Sorry, Chef," Ann murmured, heat rising to her face.

At 12:45, Ann found herself in the restroom, checking her appearance in the mirror. She reapplied her lip balm for the third time that day, smoothed her hair, and pinched her cheeks for color. The woman staring back at her had bright eyes and flushed cheeks—a woman waiting for something, or someone.

By 1:00, Ann's section had filled with the peak lunch crowd, but she handled her tables with mechanical efficiency, one part of her mind always aware of the clock, of the door. When Jonah Myers arrived at 1:05 and took his usual table in her section, she greeted him with a distracted smile, her eyes darting to the entrance over his shoulder.

"Everything okay, Ann?" Jonah asked, his brow furrowed with concern. "You seem a little off today."

"I'm fine," she said, the words automatic now. "Just busy. Coffee?"

As she poured his usual cup, her hand trembled slightly, sloshing a few drops onto the saucer. 1:10. Just five more minutes until Marcus's time. Would he be punctual? Would he request her section again? The anticipation was almost unbearable, a physical sensation like electricity beneath her skin.

At precisely 1:15, the front door opened. Ann's head snapped up, her heart leaping into her throat. A couple entered—an elderly man and woman, definitely not Marcus. Disappointment crashed through her with surprising force. She turned away, busying herself with refilling water glasses, trying to tamp down her irrational reaction.

The minutes ticked by—1:20, 1:25, 1:30. Each time the door opened, Ann's pulse spiked, only to plummet when the entering customer wasn't Marcus. By 1:45, a gnawing anxiety had taken root in her chest. He'd promised to return. Had this morning's encounter changed his plans? Had she somehow disappointed him?

At 1:52, the door opened once more, and Ann didn't allow herself to look up immediately, having learned from her repeated disappointments. It was only when Miriam passed by, whispering, "Officer Dreamy just walked in," that Ann's head jerked up, her eyes finding Marcus's tall figure standing in the entrance, scanning the restaurant until his gaze landed on her.

Their eyes locked across the room, and the smile that spread across his face sent a surge of relief and pleasure through Ann's body so intense she had to grip the edge of a table to steady herself.

He had kept his promise after all.

Later that same night, the glow from Ann's laptop cast blue shadows across her face as she sat cross-legged on her couch, the room otherwise dark except for a small lamp in the corner. She'd changed into sweatpants and an old T-shirt while washing her work clothes so they would be ready for tomorrow. Her fingers hovered over the keyboard for a moment before she typed: "Officer Marcus Hale, police department." The search felt simultaneously thrilling and forbidden, as if she were crossing some invisible line between curiosity and intrusion.

The search results populated her screen, and Ann leaned forward, scanning the links. The first was the official police department website. She clicked, navigating through the site until she found the "Our Officers" section. There he was, third row down: "Officer Marcus Hale, Patrol Division." The photograph was formal, clearly taken for professional purposes—Marcus in his dress uniform, cap tucked under one arm, expression serious and composed. So different from the slight smile he'd given her at the restaurant, the intensity in his eyes when he'd pulled her over this morning.

Ann studied the image, noting details she hadn't had time to observe in person. The strong line of his jaw, the subtle cleft in his chin, the precise way his uniform fit across his shoulders. Even in this formal photograph, there was something magnetic about him—an authority that transcended the uniform.

The biographical information beside his photo was sparse: five years with the department, community policing specialist, recipient of the department's Service Excellence award two years ago—nothing personal—no mention of family, hobbies, or life outside the force.

Or a wife.

Ann clicked back and continued scrolling through the search results. A link to a local newspaper article caught her eye: "Local Officers Support Children's Hospital Fundraiser." She clicked, finding a group photograph of several uniformed officers at what appeared to be a charity run. Marcus stood in the back row, his height making him visible despite his position. Unlike his official photograph, this one caught him mid-laugh, his face transformed by genuine amusement. Ann found herself smiling in response, as if his joy had reached across time and the digital divide to touch her.

The article mentioned him only in passing—"Officers Marcus Hale and Dennis Brower organized the department's team"—but it offered another glimpse into his life. He cared about sick children. He organized charity events. He had a real smile that transformed his face.

Next, Ann turned to social media. Facebook yielded nothing under his name—either he didn't have an account or, more likely, his privacy settings kept his profile hidden from searches. Instagram was similarly fruitless. She found a LinkedIn page that confirmed his position with the police department but offered no personal details or connections.

His digital footprint was minimal and controlled. In an age where most people's lives were sprawled across multiple platforms, Marcus Hale maintained an unusual degree of privacy. Ann wasn't sure whether to find this intriguing or concerning.

She tried another search: "Marcus Hale police department traffic stops." Nothing relevant appeared. "Marcus Hale restaurant regular." Again, nothing. She tried various combinations, seeking some thread that might connect him to her beyond their chance encounters, but the internet remained silent on the matter.

Ann closed her laptop and leaned back against the couch, her mind circling back to this morning's traffic stop. The coincidence felt too perfect—of all the officers who could have pulled her over, it had been him. Of all the moments she could have run a yellow light, it had happened when he was nearby.

Unless it hadn't been a coincidence at all.

The thought that had excited her earlier now took on a different shade in the darkness of her apartment. Had he been following her? Waiting for her to make a minor traffic violation so he could engineer another meeting before their scheduled encounter at the restaurant?

Ann rose from the couch, moving to her window. She pulled back the curtain slightly, peering down at the parking lot below. The street lamps cast pools of yellow light across the asphalt, illuminating the familiar row of residents' vehicles. No patrol car sat among them. No figure waited in the shadows.

Yet the unease remained, a slight pressure in her chest that wasn't entirely unpleasant. Being the object of someone's attention—especially someone like Marcus, with his authority and intensity—was both flattering and frightening. A shiver ran down her spine that had nothing to do with the temperature of her apartment.

Ann let the curtain fall back into place but found herself returning to the window twice more in the next hour, checking for a vehicle that wasn't there. Each time, relief and disappointment mingled in equal measure.

As she prepared for bed, brushing her teeth in front of the bathroom mirror, Ann studied her reflection. She looked the same as always—perhaps a bit more color in her cheeks, a brightness in her eyes that hadn't been there before Marcus walked into the restaurant. But beneath this surface animation, something else stirred—a wariness, a vigilance that felt new.

She rinsed her mouth and turned off the bathroom light. Before climbing into bed, she checked the front door's deadbolt, then the lock on her balcony door—both secure. As she settled under the covers, she wondered if Marcus was thinking about her too.

Chapter 12

THE WAIL of police sirens jolted me from a fitful sleep the next morning in the motel room. My eyes snapped open in the darkness, body tensing before my mind had fully registered the sound. Beside me, Matt was already moving, years of detective work having conditioned him to wake instantly at the first hint of danger.

"How many?" I whispered, my voice rough with sleep, but my mind suddenly, painfully clear.

Matt didn't answer immediately. He crossed to the window in three quick strides, his prosthetic leg making a barely audible sound against the thin carpet. He edged the curtain aside—faded yellow fabric that might once have been white—and peered through the gap.

"Three patrol cars," he confirmed, voice tight. "Lights flashing. No sirens now. They're trying not to spook us."

The digital clock on the nightstand glowed 4:17 a.m. in angry red numerals. We'd been back here from Sarah's store for less than five hours. Someone had ratted us out—the motel clerk, perhaps, recognizing my face from the news and making a call after we'd checked in. The "how" didn't matter now. Only the escape.

"Back window?" I asked, already moving, already calculating.

"Only option." Matt reached for his jeans draped over a chair.

I slid off the bed, pulling on my sneakers without bothering with socks. We'd slept in our clothes—another adaptation to life on the run. My fingers trembled slightly as I reached for the backpack we kept packed with essentials: what little cash we had left, the last two burner phones. Matt grabbed the duffel bag with the few clothes we had brought for this trip, which was supposed to last only a week.

The motel room told the story of our desperate circumstances in pathetic detail—rumpled sheets on a sagging mattress, takeout containers from the all-night diner down the street, newspaper clippings about the manhunt spread across the small table where we'd searched for any information that might help us understand who was framing me and why. The articles painted me as unstable, dangerous—a rogue agent spiraling into violence. The narrative was being controlled with frightening precision.

Matt moved to the bathroom and tested the small window above the shower. I pressed my ear to the door, listening. Footsteps outside now, heavy and purposeful. Radio chatter, too muffled to make out words but carrying the unmistakable cadence of police communications. They were moving carefully and methodically, securing exits and establishing a perimeter. They were following the protocol I knew by heart.

"It's stuck," Matt muttered from the bathroom. "Frame's swollen from humidity."

I joined him, assessing the window. Barely eighteen inches square, set high in the wall. Beyond it, darkness and the promise of temporary freedom. I handed Matt his pocket knife.

"Cover your hand," I whispered.

He nodded, wrapping his jacket sleeve around his fist as he worked the knife between window and frame, gently prying. The wood groaned in protest. A splinter broke free, then another. Sweat beaded on Matt's forehead despite the room's chill.

The footsteps outside were closer now. Low voices conferring just beyond our door. I counted at least three officers, maybe four. My pulse hammered in my throat, but my mind remained analytical, detached—cataloging escape routes, calculating odds, processing information through the lens of my training.

The window gave way with a soft crack. Matt pushed it open, grimacing at the noise. The early morning air rushed in, carrying the scent of rain-soaked asphalt and distant garbage.

"You first," Matt insisted. "I'll cover."

No time to argue. The window was chest-height for me. I grabbed the sill and pulled myself up, Matt's hands supporting my legs. The opening was tight—painfully so. My shoulders scraped against the frame as I wriggled through. A jagged edge caught my jacket, tearing the fabric and scoring a line across my ribs that burned like fire.

I suppressed a gasp, focusing instead on the drop to the ground outside. Not far. I twisted my body, bracing for impact. The landing sent a jolt through my knees, but I rolled with it, coming up in a crouch against the building's back wall.

Through the window, I could hear a sharp knock at our room door. Then another, harder.

"Police! Open up!"

Matt was already halfway through the window, his larger frame struggling against the narrow opening. His prosthetic leg complicated the maneuver, catching awkwardly on the sill. I reached up to help guide him through, my hands gripping his forearms. He dropped beside me with less grace than he'd have liked, stumbling slightly before righting himself.

The door to our room splintered inward with a crash that carried clearly through the thin walls. Shouts followed—officers discovering an empty room, immediately moving to check the bathroom. We had seconds, nothing more.

"Move," Matt urged, already pulling me toward the darkness beyond the parking lot's dim lights.

Chapter 13

WE RAN through the back alley behind the motel, our footsteps splashing through puddles left by the early morning rain. The night air stuck to my skin, humid and heavy with the smell of rotting food from overflowing dumpsters. Chain-link fences lined one side of the alley, separating the motel's property from an abandoned lot overgrown with weeds. My lungs burned, but I knew how to push my body through discomfort. Matt kept pace beside me despite his prosthetic leg, his breath coming in controlled measures. Neither of us spoke. We didn't need to.

The distant shouts from the motel faded as we put more distance between ourselves and our pursuers. Fifty yards ahead, the alley opened onto what looked like a service road.

"We need transportation," I said, scanning our surroundings with the methodical attention I'd once given crime scenes.

To our right, beyond another chain-link fence, was what appeared to be a small parking lot adjacent to a closed repair shop. Three vehicles sat in the dimly lit space: a minivan, a sedan up on blocks, and an older-model pickup truck parked nearest to us. The truck's faded red paint was peeling along the hood, and rust had claimed the bottom edge of the driver's door, but it was our best option.

"That truck," Matt said, already assessing the fence separating us from it. "Looks like an '86 or '87 Ford. Simple ignition system. I can get it started."

I didn't question his knowledge of hot-wiring vehicles. Before he'd become a detective, when we were both teenagers figuring ourselves out, Matt had worked auto theft for a few years. He knew cars from both sides of the law.

"Now," I whispered.

We moved in tandem, staying low and using the shadows and abandoned debris for cover. The chain-link fence was only six feet high, but climbing it would make us visible. Instead, Matt led us to where the fence met the building wall, where years of neglect had created a gap just wide enough to squeeze through if we turned sideways.

I went first, the metal edge of the fence scraping against my back as I edged through. Matt followed, his larger frame requiring more effort. I scanned the parking lot for cameras or witnesses, seeing neither. The area was deserted, the repair shop's windows dark. Even the streetlamp at the corner flickered intermittently, creating more shadows than light.

We approached the truck from behind, staying out of sight of both the alley and the main road. Matt paused at the driver's side, examining the window and lock.

"Keep watch," he murmured, wrapping his jacket around his elbow.

The sound of Matt's elbow hitting the window was muffled but still seemed too loud in the quiet night. Glass cracked, then collapsed inward in a shower of fragments. He reached through carefully, unlocking the door before climbing in. I remained outside, watching.

From the motel came new sounds—radios squawking commands, flashlight beams probing the darkness. They'd figured out which way we'd gone and were organizing a search. Minutes, maybe seconds, before they'd check this lot.

Inside the truck, Matt had pulled down the steering column cover and was working on the wires. His face was a mask of concentration, fingers moving with precision despite the pressure. I'd seen this expression before—when he was working difficult cases, when he was focusing through pain on his worst days with his prosthetic. It was the face of someone who refused to fail.

"Almost there," he said, not looking up.

The back door of the motel crashed open. Flashlight beams cut through the darkness of the alley. Dogs barking now—they'd brought K-9 units.

"Matt," I urged, my voice tight.

"I know." His hands moved faster, twisting wires together beneath the dashboard.

The engine coughed once, twice—then fell silent. Matt swore under his breath, adjusting something I couldn't see. A flashlight beam swept along the fence line, coming closer to the gap we'd used.

The truck's engine suddenly roared to life, the sound impossibly loud in the tense silence. I yanked open the passenger door and threw myself inside as Matt shifted into reverse. Through the cracked side mirror, I saw the flashlight beams converge on our position, followed by shouts of discovery.

Matt backed the truck out of its space with controlled urgency, then shifted into drive. The tires squealed against the pavement as we accelerated toward the exit on the opposite side of the lot.

"They'll call it in," I said, watching the rearview mirror as officers spilled into the parking lot behind us. "Every patrol car in the area will be looking for this truck."

Matt nodded grimly, hands tight on the steering wheel. "Then we'd better make sure they don't find it."

As we pulled onto the street, I glanced back one last time. The officers were returning to their vehicles, already beginning the pursuit.

Part II

Chapter 14

THE TRUCK LURCHED FORWARD as Matt pushed it beyond its aging engine's comfort zone. I twisted in my seat, looking back at the motel through the cracked side mirror. Police flashlights bounced like fireflies in the darkness as officers scattered to their vehicles to begin the pursuit. But it wasn't the police that caught my attention. Standing under a streetlamp at the edge of the property was a figure I recognized immediately—broad shoulders, military stance, and the distinctive glint of a silver ring on his right hand.

Victor Reeves.

The man who collected newspaper clippings of violent crimes, like some people collected stamps. The man whose restraining orders I'd studied during my last major FBI investigation before everything fell apart. What was he doing here?

"We've got company besides the police," I said, my voice tighter than I intended. "Victor Reeves is back there watching."

Matt's hands gripped the steering wheel harder, knuckles whitening. "The security contractor? The one with the temper?"

"And the collection of crime scene photos. Yes." The image of Reeves standing motionless under the harsh glow of the streetlamp burned in my mind. He hadn't been trying to hide. If anything, he'd positioned himself to be seen.

The silver snake ring on his finger had caught the light as he'd watched us flee—the same ring that had left distinctive bruising patterns on three different women who'd filed restraining orders against him. During the investigation years ago, I'd noted his meticulous collection of newspaper clippings detailing violent crimes, stored in labeled binders in his apartment. "Research," he'd called it. Among law enforcement, he was nicknamed "The Collector" for his disturbing hobby.

Matt drove with controlled aggression, taking sharp turns down unlit back roads, cutting through an abandoned parking lot, doubling back along a service road behind a row of warehouses. The truck's suspension protested each maneuver, metal groaning beneath us. My fingers gripped the cracked vinyl of the dashboard as we bounced through a pothole deep enough to lift us from our seats momentarily.

"Trying to break any pattern," Matt explained unnecessarily. "If anyone's following, they'll expect us to head straight out of town."

I nodded, dividing my attention between the side mirror and the road ahead. No headlights appeared behind us. No police sirens wailed in the distance. The quiet felt almost more threatening than pursuit.

The truck's headlights carved a narrow path through absolute darkness as Matt turned onto what appeared to be a logging road, trees pressing close on either side. My body tensed with each curve, anticipating the flash of lights or the sudden appearance of a roadblock. Twenty years of chasing suspects had taught me all the standard containment protocols. Now those same protocols were being used against me.

Rule Three of The Profiler's Code echoed in my mind: Maintain emotional distance. A profiler who becomes emotionally invested loses objectivity and risks missing crucial details. I'd taught that rule to trainees and had lived by it during countless investigations. How could I maintain emotional distance when I was the subject of the manhunt? When every instinct for self-preservation screamed against the detachment my training demanded?

I forced myself to breathe deeply, to analyze rather than react. Victor Reeves had appeared too conveniently. His presence suggested either incredible luck or deliberate planning. Given everything else that had happened—the planted body, the taillight sabotage—luck seemed increasingly unlikely.

"Reeves fits the profile," I said, thinking aloud. "He has a history of violence, a fascination with crime scenes, and a grudge against me personally for the investigation and for putting him away."

My analytical mind continued dissecting possibilities even as my body betrayed me with physical responses to fear—elevated heart rate, cold sweat beading along my hairline, the slight tremor in my hands that I tried to hide by clenching them into fists. I'd interviewed countless killers, had stared into the eyes of people who'd committed unspeakable acts, all without losing my professional composure. But this was different. This time, I wasn't just the profiler. I was the prey.

Matt reached over, his right hand briefly squeezing mine before returning to the wheel. The simple gesture of connection grounded me, pulling me back from the edge of my spiraling thoughts. His face remained focused on the road ahead, but that momentary touch conveyed everything words couldn't—we were in this together, we would find a way through, we had each other when we had nothing else.

The truck climbed a gentle rise, its engine straining against the incline. At the crest, Matt killed the headlights, and we continued in darkness, guided only by ambient moonlight filtering through the trees. Below us, the twinkling lights of Tampa are now a place of danger. Somewhere in that sprawl of light and shadow were answers—and people determined to stop us from finding them.

As we descended the far side of the rise, disappearing into the protective darkness of the forest, I thought about Victor Reeves standing under that streetlamp, his silver ring catching the light. Had he been there as a participant in the frame against me, or as a messenger? Either way, his presence confirmed what I'd already suspected—someone was watching our every move, anticipating our decisions, using my own profiling techniques against me.

Chapter 15

THEN:

Ann's fingers tapped a rhythmic pattern against the laminated order pad as she watched the wall clock tick its way toward 1:15. The minute hand seemed to move with deliberate slowness, as if aware of her scrutiny. Three days now. Three consecutive days, Marcus Hale had appeared at exactly 1:15, requested her section, ordered black coffee with one sugar, and watched her every move until precisely 2:00, when he would leave, leaving behind a too-generous tip and the weight of his attention that lingered long after he was gone.

The lunch rush swirled around her—families with fussy children, businesspeople with laptops open beside their plates, the regular crowd of office workers from the building across the street. Ann moved between tables with practiced efficiency, but her eyes kept returning to the clock, to the front door, to the empty four-top in the corner of her section.

1:13. She refilled water glasses at table twelve, her hands steady despite the flutter in her chest.

1:14. She delivered a club sandwich and fries to the man in the blue tie, smiling automatically at his thanks.

1:15. The door opened.

Marcus stood in the entrance, uniform crisp, posture military-straight. His eyes found hers immediately, as if drawn by some magnetic force. Ann felt a jolt of excitement.

The hostess approached him, menu in hand. Ann watched their exchange from across the room, saw the hostess glance at her section, saw the slight shake of her head as she consulted her seating chart. A ten-minute wait for Ann's section. Other sections had immediate availability.

Marcus said something, his expression pleasant but firm. The hostess looked toward Ann again, then nodded reluctantly. He would wait for Ann's section just as he had yesterday. And the day before.

"Your cop's back," Miriam appeared at Ann's elbow, voice low and teasing. "Right on time. Man's punctual, I'll give him that."

Ann's smile felt stiff on her face. "He's not my cop."

"Tell that to the way he looks at you." Miriam nudged her playfully as they both retreated to the service station. "Like you're the only menu item he's interested in."

The metaphor made Ann's skin prickle uncomfortably. "Don't you think it's weird? He comes in at exactly 1:15 every single day and only wants my section."

Miriam shrugged, reaching past Ann for a stack of napkins. "I think it's flattering. Guy's obviously into you."

"But the timing. Always 1:15. Never 1:14, never 1:16." Ann's fingers had resumed their tapping against the order pad. "And that first day, then pulling me over the next morning, then back here again…."

"Some guys are creatures of habit. And the traffic stop was just a coincidence." Miriam glanced over at Marcus, who had taken a seat in the waiting area, his eyes never leaving Ann. "Besides, he tips well, right? And he's not grabby or creepy like some customers. I think you should count yourself lucky."

"I guess so."

But there was something about the constancy of his gaze that felt more invasive than a wandering hand ever could. Ann nodded distractedly, moving to clear a recently vacated table in her section. The sooner she cleaned it, the sooner Marcus would be seated.

As she wiped down the table, she felt his eyes on her back—a tangible weight between her shoulder blades. She'd once found his attention thrilling. Now, as it continued day after day, minute after precise minute, something about it felt less like admiration and more like… surveillance.

The hostess approached with Marcus in tow. "Table for one," she announced, setting down a menu with more force than necessary. Ann suspected the hostess didn't appreciate being overridden about the seating arrangement.

"Officer Hale," Ann said, the name sticking slightly in her throat. "Nice to see you again."

"Ann." He smiled, transforming his features from severe to almost charming. Almost. "How are you today?"

"Fine, thank you." The script was the same each day. "Coffee, black with one sugar?"

"You remember." His smile deepened, as if pleased by this evidence of her attention. "Yes, please."

As Ann turned toward the coffee station, a commotion erupted from table twenty. A red-faced man in an expensive suit was gesturing angrily at his plate, his voice carrying across the restaurant.

"This is raw! Completely raw in the middle! Are you trying to poison me?"

Ann detoured smoothly, approaching the table with her professional smile firmly in place. "I'm so sorry about that, sir. Let me take this back to the kitchen immediately."

"Sorry doesn't cut it!" The man's voice rose further, attracting stares from nearby diners. "I'm on a tight schedule. I don't have time for incompetence."

"Of course, sir. I'll have Chef rush a new order for you." Ann maintained her calm tone despite the man's increasing volume. "And we'll certainly remove this from your bill."

"You're damn right you will!" He pushed the plate toward her, causing some of the sauce to slosh onto the tablecloth.

Ann was acutely aware of Marcus watching this exchange, his gaze a physical pressure on her skin. She handled the plate carefully, apologized once more, and retreated to the kitchen, feeling Marcus's eyes tracking her all the way to the swinging door.

In the kitchen's relative safety, she exhaled shakily.

"Problems?" Chef Cho asked, eyeing the returned plate.

"Table twenty says it's raw." Ann set down the offending steak, which looked perfectly medium-rare to her experienced eye.

Chef Cho prodded it with a knife, face impassive. "Customer's always right," she said flatly, though her expression suggested the opposite. "I'll make another, well-done this time."

When Ann returned to the dining room, Marcus's coffee was her priority. As she set the cup before him, she noticed anew how he had positioned himself—back to the wall, facing both her section and the front entrance. It was a positioning she'd seen him take each visit, a detail she'd mentally filed away alongside his consistent arrival time and coffee order.

"Thank you," he said, his eyes never leaving her face. "Everything okay with that table?"

"Just a cooking preference issue." Ann's smile felt stretched across her face. "Can I get you anything else?"

"Just the coffee for now." The same answer as always. He never ordered food; that was only the first time. Now, he just nursed the single coffee for exactly 45 minutes.

As Ann dealt with the angry customer—delivering his well-done steak with profuse apologies, offering free dessert, enduring his continued muttering—she felt Marcus's eyes following her every movement. When she served other tables, when she chatted with Miriam, when she refilled salt shakers at the service station. Always watching, always tracking.

By the time 2:00 arrived and Marcus rose to leave, Ann's shoulders had knotted into tight coils of tension. He paid his check—$2.50 for the coffee, $10 tip—and gave her that same smile that had once made her heart race but now made her pulse quicken for entirely different reasons.

"See you tomorrow, Ann," he said. Not a question, but a statement of fact.

Ann's shoulders ached as she punched out for the day, the tension that had accumulated during her shift settling into a knot in her stomach. Six hours of serving, smiling, and feeling Marcus's eyes on her had left her physically drained and mentally frayed. The employee lounge suddenly felt too small, the walls pressing in, and she hurried to gather her purse and jacket, eager for the relative safety of her car, her apartment, her locked door.

"See you tomorrow!" Miriam called from the break room table where she was counting her tips.

Ann managed a tight smile. "Yeah, see you."

"You sure you're okay?" Miriam's brow furrowed with concern. "You've been jumpy all day."

"Just tired," Ann lied, the words feeling hollow even to her own ears. She pushed through the back door before Miriam could press further.

The employee parking lot was half-empty now, the afternoon shift having replaced the lunch crew. Ann's car waited in its usual spot, unremarkable among the other vehicles. She walked quickly, keys clutched in her right hand with the longest key protruding between her fingers.

Each step on the asphalt seemed to echo too loudly. Ann glanced over her shoulder twice before reaching her car, though the parking lot contained nothing more threatening than a stray paper bag tumbling in the breeze. She unlocked her car, slid inside, and immediately pressed the lock button, the solid thunk of the mechanisms engaging providing momentary comfort.

For several seconds, she sat motionless, hands gripping the steering wheel, staring at nothing. Marcus's face appeared in her mind—his watchful eyes, his precise movements, his smile. Three days of the same routine. The traffic stop that couldn't have been a coincidence.

Ann started her car, the engine's familiar rattle grounding her slightly. She was being ridiculous. Plenty of people had routines. Plenty of cops regularly patronized the same restaurants. It didn't mean anything.

She backed out of her parking space and headed for the exit, following her usual route home—left onto Maple, right at the second light onto Westfield Avenue. The flow of afternoon traffic enveloped her car, anonymity providing a sense of security that began to ease the tightness in her chest.

At the first stoplight, Ann glanced in her rearview mirror—a habitual check that became anything but routine when she spotted the white and blue patrol car two vehicles behind her. Her hands clenched involuntarily on the steering wheel, knuckles blanching white against the black vinyl.

"It's not him," she whispered to herself. "It can't be him." But she couldn't see the driver clearly through the windshield glare, couldn't confirm or deny her suspicion.

The light changed. Ann accelerated, perhaps a touch too quickly, earning an irritated horn blast from the car beside her. She eased off the gas, forcing herself to drive normally. Her eyes flicked to the rearview mirror again. The patrol car remained two vehicles back.

At the next intersection, one of the cars between Ann and the patrol car turned right. Now, only one vehicle separated them. Ann's breathing grew shallow, her chest tight with each inhaled breath. She turned left onto Henderson Street—still her regular route home, nothing unusual, nothing that would suggest she was aware of being followed.

The car between them turned into a strip mall parking lot.

Now the patrol car was directly behind her.

Ann's fingers tightened further on the steering wheel, her knuckles now bloodless. She could feel her pulse in her temples, a rapid drumming that seemed to match the frantic pace of her thoughts. Was it Marcus? Was he following her? Or was this an ordinary patrol, a coincidence that her paranoia was transforming into something sinister?

Three consecutive intersections, and the patrol car remained behind her. Not tailgating, not flashing lights, just… present. Persistent. Following the same route she took every day from work to home.

The route Marcus would know if he'd been watching her.

Ann made a decision that felt like it belonged to someone else—someone braver or more foolish than she considered herself to be. At the next intersection, instead of continuing straight toward her apartment complex, she turned right, toward the grocery store she occasionally visited but hadn't planned to stop at today.

Her heart hammered against her ribs as she watched the rearview mirror, waiting to see if the patrol car would make the same unexpected turn.

It didn't.

The police cruiser continued straight ahead, growing smaller in her mirror until it disappeared from view altogether. Ann pulled into the grocery store parking lot, steering into a space near the back, and killed the engine. For several long moments, she simply sat there, hands trembling slightly as she released her death grip on the steering wheel.

"You're overreacting," she told her reflection in the rearview mirror. "It's a patrol car. They patrol. That's literally their job."

But the rational explanation did nothing to slow her racing heart or ease the tightness in her chest. Ann forced herself to take several deep breaths—in through the nose, out through the mouth. Gradually, her pulse slowed, though her hands continued to tremble.

After five minutes, she started the car again and pulled back onto the road, resuming her route home. Every few seconds, her eyes darted to the rearview mirror, checking for white and blue vehicles. Each mirror check became more frantic than the last—side mirror, rearview, other side mirror, rearview again—a compulsive pattern that left little attention for the actual road ahead.

A siren wailed in the distance, the sound faint but unmistakable. Ann jolted so violently that her car swerved, crossing briefly into the opposite lane before she corrected with a jerky motion of the wheel. A horn blared as an oncoming car passed, its driver gesturing angrily through the windshield.

"Sorry," she whispered, though no one could hear her. "I'm sorry."

The siren grew fainter, headed in another direction, responding to some emergency that had nothing to do with her. Ann forced herself to focus on driving, on maintaining a steady speed, on signaling properly for turns—all the mundane details of operating a vehicle that had never required conscious thought before.

By the time she turned into her apartment complex, her shirt was damp with sweat despite the car's air conditioning. She scanned the parking area before pulling into her assigned space, checking for patrol cars, for unmarked vehicles that might contain watching eyes, for anything out of the ordinary.

Nothing seemed amiss, yet Ann couldn't shake the feeling of exposure as she walked from her car to her building, keys clutched in her defensive grip once more. She found herself looking over her shoulder every few steps, scanning rooftops and parked cars for any sign of surveillance.

The rational part of her mind understood she was spiraling, seeing threats where none existed. But another part—the part that had cataloged Marcus's precise arrivals, his consistent seating position, his unwavering gaze—whispered that patterns never lied, and coincidences accumulated past the point of random chance became something else entirely.

Something deliberate. Something targeted.

Something dangerous.

Ann burst into her apartment, slammed the door behind her, and immediately engaged all three locks—the standard doorknob lock, the deadbolt, and the chain. The metallic clicks and scrapes sounded unnaturally loud in the silence, but each secured mechanism eased her breathing incrementally. Only when the final lock was in place did she allow her shoulders to drop slightly, though the knot of tension remained firmly lodged between her shoulder blades. She moved to the windows next, drawing the blinds with quick, jerky movements, shutting out the fading afternoon light and any eyes that might be watching from below.

The living room seemed different somehow—the familiar furniture transformed into shadowy shapes in the dimness she'd created. Ann flicked on a lamp, its warm glow dispelling some of the gloom but not the unease that had followed her home like a stray dog.

She moved to her desk with purpose, pulling open the second drawer. Beneath a stack of bills and old greeting cards lay a small collection of unused notebooks—birthday gifts from well-meaning relatives who didn't know she rarely wrote anything by hand anymore. She selected one with a plain black cover, its pages crisp and empty, waiting to be filled.

At the kitchen table, Ann opened the notebook to its first blank page. She uncapped a blue pen, then reconsidered and reached for a black one instead. More official. More factual. She wrote the date at the top of the page, then underlined it twice.

"Marcus Hale," she wrote in careful block letters, then underlined his name three times. The act of writing his name made him more tangible somehow, transformed him from a nameless anxiety into something she could analyze, categorize, and understand.

Ann created her first section: "Physical Description." She wrote methodically, recalling details with the precision that came from hours of observation. Height (approximately 6'2"). Build (athletic, broad shoulders, narrow waist). Hair (dark brown, short, military cut). Eyes (brown, watchful). Distinctive features (small scar right below right eye, calluses on right hand knuckles, slight asymmetry to smile).

She started a new section: "Behavioral Patterns." Here she noted his consistent arrival time (1:15 p.m., precise to the minute, never early, never late). His seating preference (always facing the door, back to the wall). His order (black coffee, one sugar added by himself, never by her). Duration of stay (45 minutes exactly). Tip amount (always disproportionate to order size).

The act of documentation calmed her, transformed her fear into something analytical, something she could control. Ann created additional categories: "Conversation Topics" (minimal, professional, personal questions about her schedule and history at the restaurant). "Observed Interactions with Others" (minimal, polite but distant with other staff, no engagement with other customers).

Her pen moved faster now, filling the pages with observations she hadn't even realized she'd made. The way his eyes tracked her movements across the restaurant. How he positioned himself to maintain sight lines to both her and the exits. The careful way he handled his coffee cup, leaving minimal fingerprints on the ceramic.

Ann flipped to a fresh page and drew a simple timeline. She marked their first meeting with a star, then the traffic stop the following morning, then each subsequent restaurant visit. The pattern, laid out visually, seemed undeniable. She uncapped a red pen and connected the traffic stop to their first meeting with a crimson line, then drew another from the traffic stop to his first 1:15 arrival.

No coincidences. Only patterns.

On another page, she sketched a rough map of her route home, marking the spot where she'd noticed the patrol car today with a red X. She couldn't prove it was Marcus in that vehicle, but couldn’t say it wasn’t him either.

Ann sat back, surveying her work—six pages filled with observations, theories, and connections. Seen individually, each incident could be explained away. The traffic stop—coincidence. The regular restaurant visits—a creature of habit. The consistent seating position—a cop's professional paranoia.

But together, they formed something unmistakable. Something deliberate.

Something terrifying.

Ann wrote one final note at the bottom of the last page: "Not paranoia if they're really watching you."

Chapter 16

THE WAREHOUSE LOOMED BEFORE US, a hulking shadow against the pre-dawn sky. I assessed it with the methodical eye I'd developed—rusted corrugated metal exterior, broken windows along the upper level, chain-link fence with a gap large enough to slip through unnoticed. Not ideal, but better than the truck we'd been forced to abandon two miles back when the engine finally gave out. Matt's hand brushed against mine, a silent question. I nodded once. This would be our sanctuary for now, however temporary.

"Stay close to the wall," I whispered, leading the way through the fence gap, careful not to catch my clothing on the jagged metal edges. The lock on the side entrance had long since rusted away, leaving only an empty hole where it once secured the door. Another small mercy in a week that had offered few.

Inside, the smell hit me first—damp concrete, motor oil, the musty scent of abandonment. My eyes adjusted to the gloom, cataloging details automatically—vast open space, at least ten thousand square feet. The ceiling is thirty feet high, with broken skylights allowing thin shafts of early-morning light to penetrate the darkness. Rusted shelving units stood like industrial sentinels along the walls, some toppled, others still defiantly upright. The concrete floor was stained with dark patches—oil spills, water damage, perhaps worse. Not a place anyone would choose to be, which made it perfect for us.

"How long do you think this place has been empty?" Matt asked, his voice low despite the isolation.

"Based on the dust patterns and vegetation growth through the floor cracks, I'd say at least five years." I moved further inside, keeping my back to the wall, instinctively avoiding the light beams from the broken skylights. "The local economy tanked in this district around 2018. Everything shut down when the shipping routes changed. I read that somewhere."

Matt nodded, his detective's mind following the same analytical path mine had. We'd spent the drive looking for a place exactly like this—forgotten, isolated, but with multiple exit points. The industrial district had been our best bet, and the gamble had paid off.

"I'll secure the perimeter," he said, already moving toward the far side of the warehouse. "Check for any signs of recent visitors. I bet this is a popular place for the homeless."

I watched him go, his silhouette distorted by shadows, the slight limp from his prosthetic barely perceptible to anyone who didn't know to look for it.

My priority was mapping escape routes. I moved methodically through the warehouse, noting each potential exit. Main entrance at the front, the side door we'd used, two loading dock doors on the east wall, and what appeared to be a collapsed section of roof in the northwest corner that could serve as an emergency exit if necessary. High windows that could be reached by climbing the shelving units. A rusted fire escape on the western exterior wall, visible through one of the broken windows.

I circled back to where we'd entered and set my backpack down against the wall, wincing as my muscles protested—days on the run had taken their toll. My body ached for rest, but my mind refused to quiet. I pulled out the burner phone—our last one—and powered it on, aware that even this small digital footprint was a risk. But we needed information more than we needed perfect security right now.

Matt returned as I connected to a public network through the VPN we'd set up. "All clear," he said, settling beside me. "No fresh footprints in the dust except ours. No signs anyone's been here in months."

I nodded, already focused on the search results loading on the small screen. "I need to find out more about Richard Collins. There has to be a reason his body was in my trunk specifically."

"I'll make a supply run," Matt said after a moment of watching me work. "We need water, food, and first aid supplies. That cut on your side needs proper cleaning."

I'd almost forgotten the injury from our escape through the motel bathroom window. The adrenaline had masked the pain, but now that Matt mentioned it, I could feel the sting along my ribs where the jagged edge had caught me.

"Be careful," I said, meeting his eyes. "One hour. If you're not back—"

"I'll be back," he interrupted, his tone leaving no room for doubt. He leaned in, his lips brushing my forehead—a gesture so normal, so incongruous with our current situation that it almost broke my composure. Then he was gone, slipping out the side entrance as quietly as he'd entered.

Alone in the vast space, I returned to the phone, running searches on Richard Collins while keeping my ears attuned to every sound in the warehouse. Water dripped somewhere to my left, a steady plinking against metal that marked time like an arrhythmic clock. Rats scurried in the dark corners, their tiny claws scratching against concrete. The distant hum of traffic filtered through the broken skylights, reminding me of the world continuing outside our temporary refuge.

After twenty minutes of searching through public records, I found something—a court filing from six months ago. Richard Collins had requested a restraining order against someone. The details were sealed, but the timing caught my attention.

I dug deeper. The restraining order had been granted, but the subject's name remained hidden behind legal barriers I couldn't breach with a burner phone and limited time.

The warehouse seemed to grow more cavernous around me as I contemplated the implications. Collins hadn't been a random victim. He'd been chosen specifically, placed in my trunk specifically, to create a narrative of my guilt. But why? What had he known or seen that made him both valuable and dangerous to someone?

I closed my eyes, not to sleep but to think, to let my trained mind make connections my conscious thoughts might miss. The dripping water. The scratching rats. The whisper of wind through broken windows. Each sound was registered and categorized, background noise to the greater puzzle I was trying to solve.

Someone had gone to elaborate lengths to destroy my life—someone with resources, knowledge, and a specific grudge. The answer was out there in the growing daylight, while I sat in shadows, a fugitive from the very system I'd served for twenty years.

When Matt returned, I would share what I'd found. Together, we would build a case, piece by scattered piece. Not just for my freedom, but for justice—the principle I'd devoted my life to and refused to abandon now, even when it had abandoned me.

Chapter 17

MATT'S RETURN announced itself by the subtle change in air pressure as the side door opened and closed. When his familiar silhouette appeared in the dim light, I exhaled slowly. He carried our black backpack, bulging with supplies. His sneakers squeaked against the concrete as he crossed the space between us, each footfall a scream in the warehouse's cavernous silence.

"Anyone follow you?" I asked, the question automatic after days of constant vigilance.

Matt shook his head, setting the backpack down carefully. He glanced at the phone on the floor beside me. "Find anything?"

"Collins filed a restraining order six months ago. Details are sealed, but it's something that could be interesting." I slid the phone into my pocket and stood, wincing as the movement pulled at the cut along my ribs.

Matt noticed, his eyes narrowing with concern. "Let's take care of that first." He unzipped the backpack, revealing a surprisingly comprehensive collection of supplies—bottled water, energy bars, and a first aid kit.

He gestured toward my side. "Let me see."

I lifted the edge of my shirt, revealing the angry red line that curved along my ribs. Not deep enough to need stitches, but the edges were inflamed, and dirt from the motel window was embedded in the wound.

Matt cleaned it with gentle efficiency, his touch clinical yet intimate in a way that spoke to our years together. As he applied antibiotic ointment and a clean bandage, I studied his face—the lines of exhaustion around his eyes, the stubble darkening his jaw, the absolute focus he gave to the task at hand. Even now, hunted and desperate, he remained solid and dependable—my anchor in a storm that threatened to drown us both.

"Thanks," I said simply when he finished, pulling my shirt back down.

He then reached into his bag for his laptop and dragged an overturned wooden crate to serve as a makeshift desk. He positioned another crate beside it as a seat, then opened the laptop. The screen's blue glow illuminated his face from below as he typed in passwords and connected to a network through multiple VPN layers.

"I'm downloading recent Tampa Bay newspaper archives," he explained. "I'm focusing on unsolved homicides from the past year. I thought there might be a connection to what's happening now."

I moved my crate closer, shoulder pressed against his as we hunched over the screen. The contact grounded me, a physical reminder that despite everything, I wasn't facing this alone. Matt opened the first article—a three-month-old report about a corporate lawyer found strangled in his downtown office. Nothing about the case resonated with our current situation.

We moved through the files methodically, examining crime scene photos when available, analyzing police statements, and reading between the lines of carefully worded press releases. My trained eye picked up details the reporters had missed—blood spatter patterns that contradicted official theories, body positioning that suggested staging rather than natural falling, wound patterns that told stories about the killers' emotional states during the attacks.

The fifth file stopped me cold. A man in his fifties was found beaten in his home six weeks ago. The official report cited robbery as the motive, but the crime scene photos showed something different. The violence had been excessive, frenzied. Yet the unconscious body had been carefully arranged afterward, hands folded across the chest, face cleaned of blood. The man had survived, but barely. He claimed he didn't see his attacker, that he didn't remember anything from the attack.

"That's Reeves," I said, tapping the screen. "Victor Reeves' signature."

Matt zoomed in on a particular photo showing the victim's bedroom. "Excessive violence followed by carefully arranging the beaten-up victim. You're right." His fingers moved across the keyboard, opening another file. "And there's something else you should see."

The new document was a prison release record dated four months ago. Victor Reeves was released on parole after serving three years of a five-year sentence for aggravated assault—current address listed in Tampa.

"He's been out for months," I murmured, the timeline arranging itself in my mind.

"The Collector," Matt said, using the nickname Reeves had earned. "You think he's still keeping his newspaper clippings of crime scenes?"

"Definitely, and nursing a grudge." I leaned back, memories surfacing from the case that had put Reeves away. "I was the one who built the profile that led to his arrest. He threatened me during the trial, said I'd regret the day I crossed his path." I shook my head, fragments connecting.

The warehouse had grown darker as we worked, the shafts of light from the broken skylights fading as evening approached. Now only the laptop's glow illuminated our faces, casting harsh shadows that emphasized the exhaustion etched into our features. The vast space around us seemed to grow larger in the darkness, our small pool of light a fragile barrier against the encroaching night.

"You said you saw him at the motel?" Matt asked, his voice lower as if the darkness demanded quiet.

"Yes. Standing under a streetlamp, watching us escape." The

image remained vivid in my mind—Reeves' broad shoulders, military stance, and that distinctive silver ring catching the light. "He wanted me to see him. It was deliberate."

"A message," Matt agreed, closing one file and opening another. "But what's he trying to tell you?"

I stared at the screen, at the crime scene photos of victims whose deaths mirrored the excessive violence of Reeves' signature style. "That he's coming for me. That he wants me to know it." I rubbed my eyes, fighting fatigue.

Matt's fingers stilled on the keyboard. The laptop's battery indicator blinked a warning—twenty percent remaining. Another resource with limited time.

"Let's focus on what we know for certain," he said, opening yet another file. "Reeves is out. He's in Tampa. He has a history with you. And he was watching us escape." His eyes met mine, the blue glow from the screen reflecting in them like cold fire.

I nodded, leaning closer to the screen as Matt pulled up more files. The darkness pressed against our backs as we worked, two fugitives hunched over digital breadcrumbs, searching for the path that would lead us back to truth—and freedom.

Complete darkness had claimed the warehouse by the time Matt closed the laptop, the battery finally surrendering after hours of use. I lit the small emergency candle from our supplies, its flame casting our shadows in giant, distorted versions against the walls. The sudden absence of the screen's glow left an afterimage on my retinas—crime scene photos, prison records, and newspaper headlines, all bleeding together in a grotesque collage. I rubbed my eyes, fighting the fatigue that threatened to cloud my judgment when I needed it most. That was when Matt cleared his throat in the particular way he did before delivering news he knew I wouldn't like.

"I've arranged another meeting with Juan Ramirez," he said, his voice steady but cautious. "Since we couldn't make it today. Tomorrow morning, seven a.m."

I looked at him. "Are we sure that's safe?"

"It's our only option right now. We have to at least try."

Chapter 18

THEN:

The evening shift at Granger's felt alien to Ann, the familiar restaurant transformed by the dimmer lighting and the different clientele that occupied the tables. She had traded shifts with Miriam, partly to avoid the 1:15 ritual that had become the center of her days, partly to see if breaking her pattern would break his. Her fingers trembled slightly as she folded napkins at the service station, the white paper squares refusing to form clean triangles under her unsteady hands. Beside her, Lena hummed tunelessly, her movements quick and practiced, dark hair escaping from her messy bun as she worked.

"You're folding those like they personally offended you," Lena remarked, nudging Ann's shoulder with her own. "That's your fifth crooked one in a row."

Ann set down the misshapen napkin, flexing her fingers. "Sorry. My mind's elsewhere."

"Clearly." Lena's gaze was piercing, assessing. "You've been jumpy all night. Almost dropped that tray of drinks when the kitchen door swung open too fast."

The overhead lights caught in Lena's silver hoop earrings as she turned, creating brief flashes that drew Ann's eyes. Beyond Lena's shoulder, the entrance to the restaurant remained firmly closed, no one entering or leaving. Still, Ann couldn't help checking it every few minutes, as if Marcus might materialize despite the hour, despite her schedule change.

"Lena," Ann began, her voice lower than necessary in the half-empty restaurant, "have you ever felt like someone was… watching you? Following you?"

Lena's hands stilled on the napkin she was folding. "Like a creepy customer? We get those sometimes. That businessman who always sits in your section and touches your arm when he orders?"

"No, not like that." Ann shook her head, resuming her folding with renewed determination, though her fingers still betrayed her with their trembling. "Like someone… someone with power. Someone who could know your schedule, your routes, where you live."

"You're being cryptic as hell, girl." Lena set down her napkin and turned fully toward Ann, eyebrows raised in question.

Ann glanced around, ensuring no customers were within earshot. Tom was in his office. Chef Cho was focused on the abbreviated evening menu. The nearest occupied table was a good fifteen feet away, its occupants engrossed in their own conversation.

"That police officer," Ann whispered, the words feeling dangerous even as they left her mouth. "Marcus Hale. The one who's been coming in for lunch."

"Officer Dreamy?" Lena's expression brightened. "Miriam mentioned him. Said he always sits in your section, tips like a dream."

"He comes in at exactly 1:15. Not 1:14, not 1:16. Exactly 1:15." Ann's hands had stopped pretending to fold, the napkin clutched tightly between her fingers. "Every single day. And he just watches me. For exactly forty-five minutes."

Lena's smile faltered slightly. "Maybe he's on a strict schedule? Cops have routines, right?"

"The day after he first came in, he pulled me over on my way to work." Ann's voice had dropped even lower, forcing Lena to lean in to hear her. "Of all the police officers in this city, it was him. He knew my name before I showed him my license."

"Your name tag—"

"No. The way he said it—it was like he'd been waiting for me. Testing me." Ann's eyes darted involuntarily to the entrance again. "And I've been seeing patrol cars. Following routes similar to mine. Parked near places I go."

Lena waved a dismissive hand. "This is a small city, Ann. There are police cars everywhere."

"No, you don't understand." Desperation edged into Ann's voice now. "I've been keeping track. Writing it all down. The patterns, they're too specific to be a coincidence."

"Writing it down?" Lena's tone sharpened with sudden interest. "Like a log?"

Ann nodded, folding another napkin with mechanical precision. "Dates, times, locations. Where he sits, what he orders, how long he stays." She hesitated. "Yesterday I made a turn I never make—just to see. And the patrol car that had been behind me went straight instead. But then when I got home…."

"What happened when you got home?" All traces of dismissal had vanished from Lena's voice.

"There was a different patrol car parked two blocks from my apartment." Ann's hands had begun to tremble again, more violently now. "As if he knew I was testing him, so he switched vehicles."

Lena's expression shifted, her earlier amusement draining away like water down a sink. She reached out, gripping Ann's wrist with surprising strength, her silver bangles clinking softly with the movement.

"My cousin Elisa," Lena began, her tone heavy with significance, "dated a cop in Baltimore three years ago. Just a couple of dates, nothing serious. But when she tried to end it, he started showing up everywhere—her work, her gym, the coffee shop she liked." Lena's grip tightened. "He said it was his patrol route. Said it was coincidence. It wasn't. He was totally stalking her."

Ann felt a chill spread through her chest despite the heat seeping into the service area from the kitchen. "What happened?"

"She found out he was using police resources to track her movements. Running her plates to see where she'd been. Getting her phone records." Lena's eyes had hardened. "He knew things he shouldn't have known. When she threatened to report him, suddenly, there were traffic tickets. Parking violations. A neighbor called in a noise complaint that never happened."

Ann's mouth had gone dry. "Did she report him?"

"Eventually. But it took months, and half the department closed ranks around him at first." Lena released Ann's wrist but kept her voice low. "Some men with badges think they're entitled to whatever—or whoever—they want. The badge just gives them tools most stalkers don't have."

The word hung in the air between them. Stalker. Ann had been circling around it in her mind for days, unwilling to give it substance by saying it aloud. But hearing it in this context, from someone else, made it suddenly, terribly real.

"He's so polite," Ann said, her voice small and uncertain. "Always smiles, always leaves a good tip. Never says anything inappropriate."

"The well-behaved ones are the scariest," Lena countered. "They're the ones who know exactly how far they can push before crossing a line anyone else would notice."

The front door opened, admitting a couple seeking dinner. Ann flinched visibly, her eyes darting to the entrance before she could stop herself. The automatic reaction didn't escape Lena's notice.

"You're scared of him," Lena observed, not a question but a statement.

Ann nodded, unable to deny what was clearly written in her body's instinctive response. "I feel like I'm going crazy. Like maybe I'm seeing patterns that aren't there."

"You're not crazy," Lena said firmly. "And from what you're

telling me, those patterns are real." She glanced toward the kitchen, then back at Ann. "Have you told anyone else?"

"No. I mean, Miriam knows he comes in regularly, but she thinks it's... cute. That he has a crush or something." Ann forced herself to resume folding napkins, needing the small task to ground her. "I sound paranoid when I say it out loud."

"You don't sound paranoid to me," Lena said, her voice hard with conviction. "You sound like someone whose instincts are trying to protect her."

Ann swallowed hard, relief at being believed mingling with the terror of having her fears confirmed by someone else. "What do I do?"

"We'll figure this out," Lena promised, squeezing Ann's arm. "For now, just try to act normal. We'll talk more after close."

Ann pushed through the swinging door into the kitchen, the relative sanctuary of stainless steel and steam enveloping her like a cocoon. She leaned against the wall briefly, eyes closed, trying to steady her breathing. The conversation with Lena had left her feeling exposed, as if her private fears had been written across her face in ink, visible to everyone but herself. When she opened her eyes, she found Chef Cho watching her from the prep station, hands never pausing in their rhythmic dicing of red peppers, the knife's blade catching the overhead lights in quick, controlled flashes.

"You look like someone just walked over your grave," Chef Cho observed, her tone matter-of-fact rather than sympathetic. She swept the diced peppers aside with the flat of her knife and reached for an onion, peeling it with efficient movements.

"I'm fine," Ann said automatically, the denial worn smooth from repetition throughout the evening.

Chef Cho snorted, the sound sharp and dismissive. "And I'm Julia Child." She began slicing the onion into perfect, translucent half-moons, each cut precise and measured. "Table seven's order will be up in two minutes. You might want to fix your face before you deliver it."

Ann moved to the sink, splashing cold water on her wrists the way her mother had taught her to do when anxiety threatened to overwhelm her. The kitchen's familiar sounds surrounded her—the sizzle of the grill, the rhythmic chopping of Chef Cho's knife, the low hum of the industrial dishwasher. Normally, these sounds grounded her, but tonight they seemed distant, as if she were hearing them through water.

"It's that police officer," Ann said suddenly, the words escaping before she could reconsider. "Marcus Hale."

Chef Cho's knife paused mid-slice, hovering above the cutting board for a beat before resuming its work. "The one who sits in your section. Punctual as a German train."

Ann nodded, surprised that Chef Cho had noticed from her position in the kitchen. "Yes."

"What about him?" Chef Cho's tone remained neutral, but something in her posture had shifted, a subtle tensing that Ann might not have noticed if she hadn't worked with the woman for three years.

"He's…" Ann hesitated, still struggling to give voice to her suspicions despite the conversation with Lena. "I think he might be following me. Outside the restaurant, I mean."

The knife stilled entirely this time. Chef Cho set it down deliberately, the blade parallel to the edge of the cutting board, and wiped her hands on her apron. For the first time that evening—perhaps for the first time ever—she gave Ann her complete attention.

"Tell me," she said simply.

Ann found herself recounting the story again—the traffic stop, the precise timing of his visits, the patrol cars that seemed to shadow her movements. As she spoke, Chef Cho's expression remained impassive, but her eyes grew harder, more focused, like polished stones.

Chef Cho was silent for a long moment, her gaze seemingly fixed on the half-prepared vegetables before her. When she finally spoke, her voice carried an edge Ann had never heard before.

"Lena is right. Trust your instincts," she said. "Especially around men in positions of authority."

Ann blinked, surprised by the personal tone from the typically reserved chef. "I thought maybe I was being paranoid."

"That's what they want you to think." Chef Cho picked up her knife again but didn't immediately resume chopping. Instead, she turned it slightly, examining the blade as if seeing something reflected there. "My ex-husband was a police sergeant in San Francisco. Nineteen years ago now."

Ann remained silent, sensing that interrupting would cause Chef Cho to retreat into her professional shell.

"When I filed for divorce, he didn't take it well." Chef Cho's voice remained even, matter-of-fact, as if discussing a recipe rather than a personal trauma. "Suddenly, patrol cars were driving past the restaurant where I worked. Officers I'd never met would come in, sit at the bar, and watch me while they nursed a single drink."

The knife moved again, resuming its rhythmic work on the onions. Chop. Chop. Chop. The sound punctuated her words like a metronome.

"When I confronted him, he always had an excuse. He was 'just checking on me' or 'happened to be in the neighborhood.'" Chef Cho's mouth tightened. "Then he started showing up at my apartment. At the grocery store. At my sister's house, when I visited her."

Ann leaned against the counter, her legs suddenly feeling too weak to support her weight. Each detail of Chef Cho's story aligned with her own experience, each parallel reinforcing the cold fear that had taken root in her chest.

"How did it end?" she asked, dreading the answer yet needing to hear it.

"I documented everything. Dates, times, places, witnesses." Chef Cho's knife continued its steady rhythm, the blade glinting under the harsh kitchen lights. "I went to his superior officer with my evidence. Then to that officer's superior when nothing happened. Then to the police commissioner. Then to a lawyer."

Ann's breathing had become shallow again, her chest tight. "Did it work?"

"Eventually." Chef Cho swept the chopped onions into a waiting pan, the sizzle and aroma filling the immediate area. "But patterns don't lie, Ann. When someone shows you who they are through consistent behavior, believe them the first time."

The kitchen's sounds seemed to grow louder around them—the scrape of spatulas, the clatter of plates, the hiss of steam. The ordinary cacophony of restaurant work continued while Ann's world tilted on its axis, reality reshaping itself around the confirmation that her fears were justified.

"I thought I was losing my mind," Ann admitted, her voice small against the kitchen's backdrop. "Seeing connections that weren't there."

"You're not losing your mind." Chef Cho's gaze was steady, unwavering. "You're paying attention. There's a difference."

She turned back to the grill, flipping a piece of fish with practiced ease. The conversation seemed to be over, Chef Cho retreated into her professional persona. But then she reached for a plate, arranged the fish on a bed of vegetables with artistic precision, and slid it toward Ann.

"Table seven," she said, nodding toward the swinging door. Then, her voice dropping slightly, she added, "And Ann? Document everything. Dates, times, places. It matters."

Ann picked up the plate, her hand steadier now despite the fear coursing through her. As she pushed through the swinging door back into the dining room, her eyes automatically scanned for threats—checking the entrance, the windows, the shadows between tables. The weight of Marcus's invisible surveillance pressed down on her, but alongside it grew something new—a seed of determination, small but stubborn.

She had already been writing things down, but from now on, she would document everything. She would build her case. She would trust her instincts.

And she would not become another victim whose warnings went unheeded until it was too late.

Chapter 19

THE UNDERGROUND PARKING garage swallowed us in its concrete maw, the air heavy with the scent of motor oil and damp cement. Matt and I descended the ramp in silence, our footsteps echoing despite our efforts to move quietly. My eyes adjusted to the dimness, automatically mapping the space—flickering fluorescents creating alternating pools of harsh light and impenetrable shadow, concrete pillars offering cover at regular intervals, and most importantly, the three visible exit points. I counted six parked cars, all empty, their shapes hulking and still in the half-light. The garage felt both exposed and confining, a paradox that set my nerves on edge.

"Seven minutes early," Matt murmured beside me, checking his watch.

I nodded. Being with the FBI had ingrained certain habits—arrive before anyone else, secure the location, identify threats, establish control. Even as a fugitive, those instincts remained intact.

We positioned ourselves behind a concrete pillar near the east wall, selecting a spot that offered clear sightlines to all entrances while providing immediate cover if needed. The pillar was stained with decades of automotive fluids, dark streaks mapping a history of neglect. I noticed Matt's subtle shift in posture as he distributed his weight evenly, compensating for his prosthetic leg without conscious thought.

"If this goes sideways—' I began. "If he shows up here with police…."

"Northwest stairwell, eight seconds to cover," he replied, completing my thought.

A water pipe dripped somewhere in the distance, the steady plink-plink marking time like a metronome. Each drop echoed off the concrete, creating an acoustic map of the space that my trained ear used to confirm we were still alone.

At precisely 7:00 a.m., headlights swept across the entrance ramp, cutting through the murk like searchlights. The distinctive purr of a well-maintained vintage engine announced Juan Ramirez's arrival before his car came into view. The Cadillac—1960s model, immaculately restored—glided into the garage with the stately presence of an ocean liner. Its polished black surface reflected the lights in distorted patterns as it circled once before parking twenty yards from our position.

The engine died, leaving only the settling sounds of cooling metal. I watched Juan through the windshield, noting how he sat motionless for seventeen seconds—counting, perhaps, or gathering thoughts. His silhouette remained perfectly still, betraying none of the nervous energy most people would display in such circumstances.

When he finally emerged, it was with the deliberate grace of someone who'd choreographed his own movements. His shoes—Italian leather, expensive but practical—made almost no sound on the concrete. He wore a charcoal suit that would have looked appropriate in any courthouse or high-end restaurant, the perfect camouflage for moving between worlds. Nothing about his appearance suggested a man meeting fugitives in a deserted parking garage at dawn.

Juan reached into his pocket, and I tensed. He withdrew only a pocket watch, checking it with methodical precision before returning it to his vest. The gesture seemed performative, almost theatrical, as if he were establishing a character rather than checking the time.

"You can come out now," he called, his voice neither raised nor particularly directed. He spoke as if addressing the garage itself, confident we would hear. "I came alone, as promised."

Matt and I exchanged glances. I gave a slight nod, and we stepped from behind the pillar in tandem, maintaining the defensive formation we'd silently agreed upon. Juan's eyes—sharp and assessing—tracked our movements without surprise. His gaze lingered on Matt's face for a moment before settling on mine.

"Eva Rae Thomas," he said, my name sounding like a case number in his mouth. "You look remarkably composed for someone the entire state is hunting."

"Cut the commentary, Ramirez," I replied, keeping my voice level despite the irritation flaring beneath my skin. "Matt says you can help us. I need to know if that's true before we waste any more time."

A smile flickered across his face—there and gone so quickly I might have imagined it. "Direct as ever." He gestured toward his car. "I brought information. Shall we discuss it here in the open, or would you prefer the privacy of my vehicle?"

"Here is fine," I said immediately, unwilling to surrender any tactical advantage by confining ourselves in his car. "What do you know about Richard Collins?"

Juan's eyebrows rose fractionally. "Not even a 'thank you for coming' or 'how have you been since the department threw you under the bus'?" He checked his watch again, the action deliberate, almost taunting. "Interesting. Why would you begin with Collins specifically, rather than asking about the frame-up more broadly?"

My jaw tightened. This was exactly what Matt had warned me about—Juan's tendency to answer questions with questions, to probe for reactions rather than provide information freely. I could feel my patience fraying at the edges, threads of control threatening to unravel.

"I don't have time for games," I said. "Collins was placed in my trunk for a reason. I need to know why."

"Everyone has time for games, Agent Thomas," Juan replied, emphasizing my former title. "That's what this is, isn't it? Someone's elaborately constructed game, with you as the unwitting player." He took three measured steps forward, stopping at what he clearly calculated was the edge of my comfort zone. "The question isn't why Collins was in your trunk—it's why you specifically were chosen as the frame."

Matt shifted beside me, his posture subtly protective though he remained silent. I could feel his analytical gaze moving between Juan and me, assessing, calculating.

"We know I was chosen deliberately," I said, struggling to keep the edge from my voice. "What I need are facts, not philosophical observations about my situation."

"Facts." Juan let the word hang in the air between us. "Like the fact that Collins' death wasn't random? Or the fact that someone with intimate knowledge of forensic procedure used a murder weapon so similar to yours, it's hard to explain away?" His eyes—dark and unnervingly perceptive—never left my face. "Or perhaps the fact that Victor Reeves has been following you since his release?"

My breath caught. We'd discovered Reeves' potential involvement on our own, but Juan's casual mention of it suggested he knew far more than he should. My mind raced, trying to determine how he'd acquired this information and what else he might know.

"How long have you been watching me?" I demanded, taking an involuntary step forward.

"Long enough to know you're running out of time and options," Juan replied, unperturbed by my advance. "The question is, Agent Thomas, are you ready to hear what I've found, or would you prefer to continue this verbal sparring until the next shift of security guards arrives in approximately forty-three minutes?"

The overhead light flickered, casting Juan's face in momentary shadow before illuminating it again. In that split second, I made my decision—not based on trust, which I couldn't afford, but on necessity, which I couldn't ignore.

"Show me," I said simply, forcing my shoulders to relax even as every instinct screamed for caution.

Juan nodded once, a gesture that acknowledged the reluctant truce between us. "Then let's not waste any more time. Let me show you."

Chapter 20

JUAN MOVED to his car with deliberate steps, opened the passenger door, and retrieved a sleek laptop. His movements were precise and economical, as if choreographed to convey professionalism. He placed the computer on the Cadillac's hood, the metal still warm from the engine's heat. When he opened it, the screen cast an eerie blue glow across our faces, transforming the dim garage into something otherworldly. I watched his fingers tap across the keyboard with practiced efficiency, noting how he positioned the screen so both Matt and I could see it clearly while maintaining control of the device. Trust only extends so far in our world.

"These are internal police reports," Juan said, opening a folder labeled with an alphanumeric code I recognized as Tampa PD's filing system. "Not the sanitized versions released to the press."

I leaned closer, my eyes scanning the document that appeared on screen. Autopsy report for Richard Collins, complete with crime scene photos I hadn't seen before. The clinical language of death contrasted with the violent reality captured in the images. Photos from what appeared to be his living room floor, blood patterns suggesting he'd been standing when first shot, then fallen and been shot again.

"Page four," Juan directed, his manicured finger tapping the screen. "Cause of death and ballistics."

Matt shifted beside me, moving into a better position to see while maintaining his vigilance of our surroundings. I felt the slight pressure of his arm against mine—a small, anchoring touch in the midst of chaos.

I scrolled to page four, my eyes immediately locking onto the highlighted section. "Victim sustained two gunshot wounds, consistent with .38 caliber rounds, likely fired from a Smith & Wesson Model 642."

My blood went cold. The Smith & Wesson 642 was a common enough weapon, but it was also my weapon of choice throughout my FBI career. The gun I'd carried for years, the one I'd trained with until it felt like an extension of my hand.

"That's my gun," I said, the words barely audible above the drip of water somewhere in the distance. "Not just the same model—that specific description matches my service weapon exactly."

Juan's expression remained neutral, but his eyes tracked my reaction with scientific interest. "I thought it might," he said. "So, the killer used an identical weapon. That suggests they know you intimately. Not just your movements or your schedule, but your preferences, your history."

The implication hung in the air between us, heavy with menace. Someone who knew me well enough to choose the exact weapon model I preferred. Someone who understood that this detail would add another layer of circumstantial evidence against me, another thread in the tapestry of my supposed guilt.

"There's more," Juan continued, scrolling to another document. "The bullets recovered from Collins' body had rifling marks consistent with a newer weapon—manufactured within the last two years. But according to your service records, you've had your .38 for over a decade."

Matt spoke for the first time since Juan had opened the laptop. "So, whoever did this knew enough to match the caliber and model but didn't account for the age difference in the ballistics."

"A small mistake," Juan agreed, "but potentially significant. It's the kind of detail that might eventually create reasonable doubt—if your case ever made it to trial."

"If," I repeated, the word bitter on my tongue. "If I'm not killed before then."

"Collins was killed by the first gunshot, a shot to the back of the head. Execution style." His finger tapped rhythmically against the hood of his car as he spoke. "No defensive wounds, no signs of struggle. No signs of forced entry."

I processed this information, turning it over in my mind like a puzzle piece seeking its fit. "He knew his killer."

"Or at least didn't perceive them as a threat until it was too late," Juan corrected. "You don't turn your back on someone you're afraid of."

"Or maybe they snuck up on him from behind."

"Sure."

Matt had moved slightly behind Juan while he spoke, his detective's eyes studying the man's every micro-expression and body language. I caught Matt's gaze briefly—a subtle nod indicating that, so far, he detected no deception. Juan was telling us what he believed to be true, though that didn't necessarily make it accurate.

I thought about Victor Reeves—his brute-force approach, his lack of subtlety, his preference for direct confrontation rather than manipulation. "But this murder doesn't have Reeves' signature. It doesn't look like his work."

Juan's lips curved in what might have been approval. "Maybe he's changing things up? He knows you know his methods, so perhaps he changed to hide that it was him? If the main goal was to frame you, he would be smart enough not to leave a trace that could lead to him."

I stared at the autopsy photos still displayed on the screen, the clinical documentation of violence that had set this nightmare in motion. Someone had selected Richard Collins specifically, had executed him with a weapon chosen to implicate me, had planted his body in my trunk, and ensured I would be discovered with it. Someone who knew me well enough to anticipate my reactions, to predict how I would respond when cornered.

Someone who was still watching, still maneuvering pieces on a board I couldn't fully see.

"There's something connecting Collins to me," I said, certainty hardening in my voice. "Something beyond the frame-up. He wasn't chosen at random."

Juan nodded slowly. "That's what I believe as well. The question is—what was that connection, and why did it make him a target?"

Matt shifted his weight, drawing my attention. His expression remained neutral, but I recognized the slight narrowing of his eyes—he was processing something, seeing a pattern I hadn't yet grasped.

"We need to dig deeper into Collins' life," I said, my mind already mapping the investigation that needed to happen. "Financial records, phone logs, social media—anything that might reveal who he was in contact with in the weeks before his death."

"Already working on it," Juan replied, closing the laptop. The blue glow disappeared, plunging our faces back into the garage's dim lighting. "But there's something else you should keep in mind."

I waited, tension coiling between my shoulder blades.

"Whoever is behind this," Juan said, his voice dropping lower, "I don't think they're finished. They could be constructing a narrative of escalation—making you appear more desperate, more dangerous with each passing day."

The implication was clear: more bodies would follow. More deaths would be laid at my feet and more lives destroyed in the effort to destroy mine.

Chapter 21

I CLOSED my eyes for a moment, processing the implications of what Juan had just shared. When I opened them again, the garage seemed colder somehow, the dripping water in the distance marking time with metronomic persistence. Juan had delivered facts with clinical precision, each one another piece in the puzzle of my framing. But I sensed he was holding something back—a final revelation he was reluctant to share. His fingers tapped against the closed laptop, a subtle tell that betrayed his internal debate.

"We should move," Matt said, his voice low as he checked his watch. "We've been stationary too long."

Juan nodded, sliding the laptop into a sleek leather case. "I'll continue investigating Collins' background. Financial records sometimes reveal connections that personal histories obscure." He secured the case with practiced efficiency, his movements betraying no wasted energy.

"How do we contact you?" I asked, already calculating our next moves, the safe houses we might use, the identities we might temporarily assume. "Without anyone being able to find out that you're helping us?"

"You don't," Juan replied, straightening his immaculate suit jacket. "I'll find you when I have something concrete."

I didn't like that arrangement—it placed too much control in his hands, left us waiting rather than acting. But I recognized the logic behind it. Every communication was a risk, every contact point a potential trap. Juan was relying on his resources within the force and couldn't risk losing them.

Juan turned toward his car, then paused, his hand resting on the door handle. The hesitation was slight but noticeable—a disruption in his otherwise fluid movements. Something in his posture shifted, a subtle squaring of the shoulders that suggested he'd made a decision.

"There's something else you should know," he said, not turning to face us. "I was at the police station yesterday, following up on a different case."

The change in his voice—a slight flattening of tone—triggered my internal alarms. Whatever came next wouldn't be good news.

"I saw your friend there," he continued. "The bookstore owner. Sarah Winters."

The name hit me like a physical blow. Sarah, who had spoken with such conviction about helping me clear my name. Sarah, whose eyes had darted nervously to her phone more than once during our conversation.

"What was she doing there?" I kept my voice neutral despite the sudden thundering of my pulse.

Juan finally turned, his expression carefully composed. "Giving a statement. About your 'erratic behavior' when you came to her store at night and asked her for help. About how Collins was a huge fan of yours and was at the bookstore for the signing." His eyes met mine, watching for my reaction. "I have a source there who gave me the details."

My face had hardened into a mask, but beneath it, my mind raced through every interaction with Sarah, searching for signs I'd missed: The too-convenient offer of help, the nervous glances at her phone, the way she'd directed our conversation toward specific topics while avoiding others.

Did she believe I was guilty? Was that why she went to the police? Was she reporting back to them about me?

Why?

Maybe she was just covering herself, making sure she wouldn't be in trouble for helping me. Maybe she was just pretending to believe me, because she was afraid I might harm her? I guess I couldn't blame her, but it still hurt.

"Did she see you?" Matt asked, practical as always.

Juan shook his head. "I made sure she didn't."

The betrayal settled in my stomach like ice. I'd trusted Sarah—not completely, not blindly, but enough to accept her help when we were desperate. Enough to reveal our presence to her when staying hidden was our only advantage.

"She's an informant," I said, the words barely audible.

Matt's hand came to rest on my shoulder, a warm weight that anchored me as my mind spun through implications. "We have to be more careful who we trust."

The garage suddenly felt exposed and vulnerable. If Sarah had betrayed us, she might have shared information about our whereabouts, maybe that's how they found us at the motel the next morning. Of course it was. That only made sense. The walls seemed to close in, the shadows harboring new threats.

"We should go," I said, moving toward our exit route—the northwest stairwell we'd identified upon arrival. "This location is not safe."

Matt fell into step beside me, his movements as fluid and controlled as my own. We'd developed a rhythm in our days on the run, a synchronized dance of survival that required no verbal coordination.

Chapter 22

THEN:

Ann's hands trembled as she tied her apron strings, fumbling twice before the bow took shape behind her back. She'd arrived fifteen minutes early for her shift, scanning the parking lot before darting inside Granger's through the back entrance. No patrol cars today—at least none she could see. Her neck prickled with the phantom sensation of being watched anyway. This feeling had become her constant companion since Marcus Hale first walked into the restaurant and fixed those observant eyes on her.

The break room was mercifully empty except for Miriam, who sat at the small table folding napkins into perfect triangles, her dark hair pulled back in a neat ponytail. She looked up as Ann entered, her brows immediately knitting together.

"Jesus, Ann. You look like you haven't slept in days."

Ann touched the shadows she knew must be visible beneath her eyes. "Is it that obvious?"

"Like a neon sign." Miriam pushed a stack of napkins toward her. "Here, make yourself useful while you tell me what's going on."

Ann sank into the chair opposite Miriam, taking a napkin with unsteady fingers. The white cloth felt cool and crisp, a small anchor to reality as her thoughts threatened to spiral. The rhythmic motion of folding—corner to corner, smoothing the crease, folding again—gradually steadied her hands, though her heart continued its rapid drumming against her ribs.

"It's Marcus," she said finally, her voice barely above a whisper, though they were alone. "Officer Hale. I think… I think he's stalking me."

The word hung in the air between them, ugly and stark. Ann had avoided saying it aloud until now, as if naming the fear would make it more real, more dangerous.

Miriam's fingers stilled mid-fold. "What makes you think that?"

Ann recounted everything—the traffic stop the morning after their first meeting, his daily arrivals at precisely 1:15, the patrol cars that seemed to shadow her movements, the feeling of being watched in her own apartment. With each detail, her voice grew steadier, more certain, even as her hands resumed their trembling.

"And last night," Ann continued, leaning closer, "A neighbor told me she's seen patrol car number 37 parked outside my apartment complex several evenings this week. Just watching."

"Really?" Miriam frowned.

"Yeah, this neighbor—Rosa Alvarez—is always watching everything. She keeps track of unusual activity in the neighborhood. Has for years." Ann swallowed hard, her throat suddenly dry. "And Chef Cho—she believes me too. She said her ex-husband was a cop who did the same thing to her after they separated."

Miriam set down her napkin, reaching across to squeeze Ann's wrist. "Why didn't you tell me sooner? This is serious, Ann."

"I thought I was being paranoid." Ann looked down at her half-folded napkin, now crumpled from her grip. "Everyone keeps saying how charming he is, how he must just have a crush on me."

"Men," Miriam muttered, rolling her eyes. "Look, you shouldn't have to deal with him today. Let's switch sections."

Ann's head snapped up. "You'd do that?"

"Of course I would. He always comes at 1:15, right? You take my section by the kitchen, and I'll handle his table when he comes in." Miriam stood, smoothing her apron. "Let's check the chart and make it official."

They moved to the staff rotation chart posted near the time clock, Miriam running her finger down the laminated surface to find their assignments. Ann peered over her shoulder, hope flickering for the first time in days.

After changing the assignments, Miriam clapped her on the shoulder. "Section four is as far from your usual tables as possible. Even if he comes in, he won't be anywhere near you."

Relief washed through Ann, loosening the knot between her shoulders. Section four was the smallest, tucked away in the corner farthest from the entrance. If Marcus took his usual table, he'd have to crane his neck to see her. For the first time in days, she felt like she could breathe.

The lunch shift began smoothly. Ann settled into a rhythm with her new tables—an elderly couple who ordered the soup of the day, a mother with two well-behaved children, a businessman engrossed in his laptop. The familiar routine of taking orders, delivering food, and refilling drinks soothed her frayed nerves. By 1:00, she had almost convinced herself that today would be different.

At precisely 1:15, the front door opened.

Ann's head jerked up, her body reacting before her mind could catch up. Marcus Hale stood in the entrance, uniform pristine as always, eyes scanning the restaurant with the practiced assessment of a predator seeking prey. Their gazes locked across the room, and the small bubble of security Ann had built around herself burst instantly.

The hostess approached him with a menu, but he shook his head, gesturing toward Ann's corner. Ann watched in growing horror as the hostess looked confused, checking her seating chart, then leading Marcus across the restaurant—not to his usual table in section two, but directly to an empty four-top in Ann's new section.

"How did he know?" Ann whispered, her pulse pounding in her ears. “He must have specifically asked for my section.”

Marcus took his seat, his eyes never leaving Ann as she stood frozen by the service station, notepad clutched so tightly her knuckles whitened. Miriam appeared beside her, face taut with concern.

"Did you tell anyone we were switching sections?" Ann asked, her voice barely audible.

"No one. I swear." Miriam squeezed her arm. "Maybe it's just a coincidence."

But they both knew it wasn't. Somehow, Marcus had known exactly where to find Ann, despite a last-minute schedule change that even she hadn't been aware of until minutes before her shift.

Ann forced her legs to move, approaching his table with the mechanical steps of a wind-up toy. The notepad trembled visibly in her grip as she stopped before him, summoning a brittle smile that felt like it might shatter her face.

"Officer Hale," she said, the words sticking in her dry throat. "Your usual coffee?"

"Black, one sugar," he confirmed, his eyes never wavering from her face. That steady gaze—once merely intense, now terrifying in its focus—tracked her every microexpression. "How are you today, Ann? You seem tense."

"Just busy," she lied, the words automatic.

His smile didn't reach his eyes. "I noticed your car as I drove in. Looks like you need your tires rotated soon."

Ann's breath caught, a cold weight settling in her stomach.

"I'll take care of it," she managed, the words coming from far away, as if someone else were speaking through her mouth. "Just the coffee today?"

"That's all I need." His smile widened slightly, showing the edges of his teeth. "For now."

Ann nodded mechanically, turning away with wooden movements. Her mind raced with terrible questions. None of them did she have answers for.

Behind her, she felt the weight of his eyes, steady and unrelenting, tracking her retreat across the restaurant floor.

Ann placed the coffee cup before Marcus with deliberate care, disguising how badly her hand wanted to shake. She kept her body angled slightly away from him, as if the additional inches of distance might somehow protect her. The sensation of his gaze followed her as she moved to her other tables, a tangible weight pressing between her shoulders. She found herself taking circuitous routes across the restaurant floor to avoid passing directly in front of him, though she knew his eyes tracked her regardless of where she went.

The lunch rush intensified around her—clinking silverware, overlapping conversations, the rhythmic swing of the kitchen door as other servers moved between dining room and kitchen. Ann clung to these ordinary sounds, using them to anchor herself in normality.

When Daniel Reed walked in at 1:30, Ann felt a surge of relief at the sight of his familiar face. The attorney was a steady presence at Granger's, arriving daily with his leather-bound notebook and thoughtful manner. Unlike Jonah Myers with his excessive familiarity, Daniel maintained a polite professional distance that Ann had always appreciated. Today, his predictable presence felt like a lifeline.

"Your usual table is free," she told him, leading him to a small two-top along the wall, blessedly distant from where Marcus sat nursing his coffee.

Daniel settled in with a nod of thanks, unfolding his napkin with precise movements. "Just an iced tea today, Ann. I have a court appearance at three."

"Coming right up." Ann's shoulders relaxed slightly as she stepped away from Marcus's line of sight to prepare Daniel's drink. These small moments of invisibility felt precious, like catching her breath while treading water.

When she returned with the tea, Daniel was scanning a newspaper, his brow furrowed as he read a headline about a local trial.

"Following the Westbrook case?" Ann asked, setting down his drink. Small talk with regular customers was routine, safe—a script she could follow without thinking.

Daniel looked up, his expression thoughtful. "Hard to avoid it. It's all anyone at the courthouse is discussing. The evidence seems fairly straightforward."

"That's what the paper's been suggesting," Ann agreed, glancing at the headline. She didn't mention that she'd barely had time to follow the news lately, her mind too occupied with her own concerns.

"Most of my colleagues think—"

"That's not what you said the other day, though." Marcus's voice cut through their conversation like a knife, though he remained seated at his own table several feet away. "You mentioned you thought the defendant was being framed."

Ann's head snapped toward Marcus, her body going cold despite the restaurant's warmth. He was watching her with that same steady gaze, coffee cup held midway to his lips, as if his interjection into a private conversation was perfectly natural.

"I—what?" Ann managed, her voice sounding strange to her own ears.

"The Westbrook case," Marcus continued, setting down his cup. "You said Tuesday that you thought someone was setting Westbrook up. That the evidence seemed too perfect." His smile was pleasant, conversational. "You have a good eye for inconsistencies."

The blood drained from Ann's face so rapidly she felt light-headed. She had never discussed the Westbrook case with anyone at the restaurant and never shared an opinion about it, certainly not with Marcus. She'd barely registered the headlines, too consumed with her own situation to follow local news.

Daniel looked between them, confusion evident in his furrowed brow. "I didn't realize you followed legal cases so closely, Ann."

"I don't," she said, the words emerging too quickly, too forcefully. "I never—I haven't been following the case at all."

Marcus's expression didn't change, but something in his eyes hardened. "Must be thinking of someone else, then," he said smoothly. "Memory plays tricks sometimes."

Ann's fingers lost their grip on her order pad. It fell to the floor with a soft slap against the hardwood, pages splaying open. She bent to retrieve it, grateful for the moment to hide her face as her mind raced. Was Marcus deliberately lying to make her seem forgetful? Or worse—had he somehow been listening to private conversations she'd had elsewhere?

When she straightened, Marcus was watching her with that unnervingly steady gaze. "Are you feeling all right, Ann? You seem pale."

The concern in his voice sounded genuine, which made it all the more disturbing. Ann forced her lips into what she hoped resembled a smile. "Fine. Just busy." She turned to Daniel, desperate to escape. "I'll check back in a few minutes."

She retreated to the kitchen, pushing through the swinging door with more force than necessary. Inside, she pressed her back against the wall, closing her eyes as she fought to steady her breathing. Chef Cho glanced at her from the grill but said nothing, her gaze knowing and sympathetic.

Ann stayed in the kitchen longer than necessary, using the excuse of waiting for an order to avoid returning to the dining room. When she finally emerged, Marcus was gone, his table empty except for his coffee cup and a twenty-dollar bill tucked beneath it. Relief flooded through her so powerfully that her knees nearly buckled.

She finished her shift in a daze, moving between tables with mechanical efficiency while her mind circled endlessly around Marcus's strange outbursts. The Westbrook case. Her tires needing rotating. Her new section assignment. None of these were coincidences. None could be explained away.

As her last table cleared, Ann found herself standing outside Tom's office, hand raised to knock before she'd consciously decided to seek him out. Her knuckles rapped against the wood before she could reconsider.

"Come in," Tom's gruff voice called.

She pushed open the door to find him behind his cluttered desk, surrounded by the sports memorabilia that covered every wall—signed baseball bats, framed jerseys, team pennants from games attended decades ago. Tom looked up from his paperwork, reading glasses perched low on his nose.

"Porter. What's up?"

Ann closed the door behind her, fingers twisting in her apron. "I need to talk to you about a customer."

Tom leaned back in his chair, the springs creaking in protest. "The elderly couple at table nine? I already comped their dessert after that mix-up with their order."

"No, it's—" Ann took a deep breath, steadying herself. "It's about Officer Hale. The police officer who comes in at 1:15 every day."

"Marcus? Good tipper, from what I hear." Tom removed his glasses, setting them on a stack of invoices. "Problem with his order?"

"No, it's more personal than that." Ann's words tumbled out in a rush. "He's been following me. He knows things about me he shouldn't know. Today, he mentioned that my tires need to be rotated. And he tried to make Daniel Reed think I'd discussed the Westbrook case with him, but I never did. And somehow, he knew I'd been moved to section four, even though that change wasn't posted anywhere."

She paused, breathless, hands shaking visibly now. Tom's expression had shifted from mild interest to something closer to concern, though not the kind she'd hoped for.

"Porter," he said, folding his arms across his chest, "sounds to me like you're reading too much into things."

"I'm not," Ann insisted. "Chef Cho believes me. And my neighbor—she's seen his patrol car watching our apartment building."

Tom sighed, rubbing a hand across his stubbled jaw. "People see conspiracy theories everywhere." He leaned forward. "Look, Ann, the guy's obviously sweet on you. Police officers notice details—it's literally their job. He probably saw your tires needed rotation when passing your car, maybe for your safety? The section thing was just a coincidence."

"It wasn't a coincidence," Ann said, her voice rising slightly. "None of this is a coincidence."

"Then he probably just asked to be seated in your section because he likes you."

"I don't think—"

"Hey, most women would be flattered by this kind of attention from a good-looking officer of the law." Tom's tone had taken on a paternal quality that made Ann's skin crawl. "If you're not interested, just let him down easy. But don't go making accusations about a respected member of the police force based on what might just be him showing interest awkwardly."

Ann stared at him, the full weight of her isolation crashing down on her. Tom didn't believe her. He wouldn't help her. His dismissive wave as he reached for his glasses again made it clear the conversation was over.

"That'll be all, Porter. I've got inventory to finish."

She left his office with wooden steps, shoulders slumped in defeat. The door closed behind her with a soft click that felt somehow final, like a cell door being locked. Tom's words echoed in her mind: "Most women would be flattered." The implication stung: that her fear was an overreaction, that she should be grateful for Marcus's attention rather than terrified by it.

No one who could actually help her would believe her. Ann was on her own.

The employee door creaked open as Ann stepped outside for her break, the mid-afternoon sun temporarily blinding her after hours under the restaurant's artificial lighting. She hugged her arms against her chest despite the mild spring temperature, a chill that had nothing to do with the weather seeping into her bones. The alley behind Granger's was empty except for stacked produce crates and the large dumpster whose perpetual sour smell mingled with cooking aromas from the kitchen vent. Ann leaned against the brick wall, closing her eyes briefly as she drew a deep breath of outside air

—her first moment alone since Marcus's unsettling comments about the Westbrook case.

When she opened her eyes, her gaze automatically swept the alley, then the street beyond—a habit she'd developed lately, this constant vigilance that exhausted her yet felt necessary for survival. She had almost convinced herself that she was being paranoid when she spotted it: a white and blue patrol car parked across the street, partially obscured by a FedEx delivery truck. From this angle, she could just make out the number on its door: 37. The same car her neighbor Rosa had seen watching her apartment.

Ann's pulse quickened as she pushed away from the wall, moving closer to the alley entrance for a better view. The car's windows were tinted, making it impossible to see who sat behind the wheel, but she knew with bone-deep certainty that it was Marcus. The small dent on the rear bumper confirmed it was his vehicle.

With trembling fingers, Ann pulled out her phone and snapped several photos, making sure the patrol car's number and the dent were clearly visible. She checked the time: 2:30 p.m.

"Documentation," Ann whispered to herself, adding a note to the photos with the date, time, and location. Chef Cho's words echoed in her mind: Dates, times, places. It matters.

The employee door opened again, and Miriam stepped out, unwrapping a piece of gum.

"God, it's stuffy in there," she said, stretching her arms overhead. "Chef's making that spicy soup again, and the whole place smells like—" She broke off, noticing Ann's rigid posture. "What's wrong?"

Ann pointed across the street. "That patrol car. It's his."

Miriam squinted in the direction Ann indicated. "The one behind the delivery truck? How do you know it's his?"

"The dent on the back bumper. And it's car 37—the same one my neighbor's seen watching my apartment." Ann held up her phone, showing Miriam the photos she'd taken.

Miriam's expression shifted from skeptical to concerned as she studied the photos. "You're sure?"

As they watched, the patrol car's engine started, its lights remaining off as it pulled smoothly away from the curb. It circled the delivery truck and disappeared down the street without haste, as if it hadn't been caught in the act of surveillance.

"That's… weird," Miriam admitted, her earlier dismissiveness fading. "Did he see us watching him?"

Ann's stomach clenched. "I don't know. Maybe." She checked the photos on her phone again, making sure they were clear. "This isn't a coincidence, Miriam. None of it is."

The remainder of her shift passed in a blur of tension, Ann's attention split between her tables and the windows that looked out onto the street. Every passing car, every shadow movement outside made her flinch. By closing time, her shoulders ached from being held rigid for hours, and a persistent headache throbbed behind her eyes.

As the final customers trickled out and the evening staff began their closing routines, Ann wiped down tables with uneven, distracted movements. Her cloth moved in erratic patterns rather than her usual efficient circles, her eyes darting to the windows every few seconds. When a car drove past with headlights on high beam, she dropped her spray bottle, the plastic clattering loudly on the wooden floor.

Tom emerged from the office at the noise, his keys jangling at his belt. He paused, watching as Ann retrieved the bottle with visibly shaking hands.

"Everything alright?" he asked, concern finally showing in his expression.

Ann straightened, clutching the spray bottle like a talisman. "Fine," she said automatically, the lie so practiced it came without thought.

Tom's eyebrows drew together as he studied her pale face. "You don't look fine. You've been jumping at shadows all night. Lena said you nearly screamed when that busboy dropped a tray."

Ann's throat tightened. She hadn't screamed, but it had been close—the sudden crash bringing her heart into her throat, her body instinctively bracing for danger.

"I saw his patrol car today," she said finally, her voice barely above a whisper. "During my break. Parked across the street, watching the restaurant."

Tom sighed, scrubbing a hand over his face. "Porter—"

"I took photos," she interrupted, reaching for her phone. "Car number 37. The same one my neighbor Rosa's seen outside my apartment. It has a dent on the rear bumper—it's definitely his car. He was watching me, Tom.'

Tom glanced at the photos without really examining them. "Look, I know you're convinced there's something sinister going on, but—"

"There is something going on. I'm telling you Tom."

"Ann." Tom's use of her first name rather than her surname caught her attention. "Have you considered that maybe you're seeing connections that aren't there?"

"No." Ann shook her head firmly. "These aren't coincidences. They can't be."

Tom's expression softened into something like pity. "Why don't you take tomorrow off? Get some rest. Things will seem clearer with a good night's sleep."

The dismissal in his tone was unmistakable. Though his concern seemed genuine, he still didn't believe her—not really. Ann nodded mechanically, too exhausted to argue further. She finished cleaning her tables in silence, then gathered her belongings from the break room, hyperaware of Tom watching her with that same pitying expression.

Chapter 23

I KEPT my shoulder blades pressed against the wall, the position giving me an unobstructed view of both library exits. The fluorescent lights buzzed overhead in an irregular pattern that matched my frayed nerves. Seventeen people occupied the computer lab—two elderly men researching genealogy, a college student with headphones nodding to music as she typed, a woman with three restless children, and eleven others whose behaviors I'd categorized from least to most concerning. My eyes never stopped moving, cataloging new arrivals, tracking the bored security guard by the main entrance, watching for any face that lingered too long on Matt as his fingers flew across the keyboard in the corner terminal.

I shifted my weight slightly, easing the pressure on my injured side. The cut from our motel escape had mostly healed, but the tender flesh still protested when I stood too long in one position. The library's air conditioning raised goosebumps on my arms, a stark contrast to the humid Tampa heat outside. I adjusted my baseball cap lower, feeling exposed.

Matt's posture betrayed nothing of our desperate circumstances—shoulders relaxed, expression neutral as he navigated through digital barriers with practiced efficiency. Only I could see the tension in his jaw, the slight narrowing of his eyes as he concentrated. His body blocked most of the screen from casual observers, a precaution we'd discussed before entering. If anyone asked, we were researching local history for a family project. Our story wouldn't hold up to intense scrutiny, but it didn't need to. We only needed enough time to find what we came for and disappear again.

A teenage boy entered the computer lab, hood pulled low over his face. I tracked his movements, noting the nervous energy in his gait, the way his eyes darted around the room. Just a kid skipping school, not a threat. Still, I maintained my vigilance as he settled at a terminal across the room.

"Eva Rae," Matt's voice reached me as the barest whisper, audible only because I was attuned to it after years together. His right hand made a subtle gesture we'd established earlier—two fingers tapping against his thigh. He'd found something.

I casually moved to stand behind him, positioning myself so I could see the screen while maintaining sight lines to both exits and the security guard, who had now turned his attention to an elderly woman asking for help finding a book. My fingers brushed Matt's shoulder, a touch that might appear affectionate to observers but served as acknowledgment of his signal.

"Collins' email," Matt murmured, his voice barely audible. "I've bypassed the security questions. He wasn't particularly creative with his passwords."

The screen displayed Richard Collins' Gmail account, the inbox populated with the mundane correspondence of everyday life—work emails, shopping receipts, newsletters. Matt had already sorted them by sender, highlighting a recurring address that stood out from the corporate domains and services: TrueLove4Ever@mailsecure.com.

"Twenty-three messages in the last month alone," Matt said, clicking on the oldest one.

The email opened, revealing a message that seemed innocuous at first glance:

. . .

Saw you at Parkside Café today. You looked so handsome in that blue shirt. I loved how you stirred your coffee three times before drinking it—always so precise. Maybe next time I'll find the courage to say hello instead of watching from across the room.

"Check the next one," I whispered, unease crawling up my spine at the intimate details observed without Collins' knowledge.

Matt clicked through to a message sent three days later:

You didn't come to the café today. I waited for two hours. Did something happen? Are you sick? I drove by your office but couldn't see you through the windows. Hope you're taking care of yourself. Remember that chicken soup you mentioned liking when you were talking to the barista last week? I could bring some by...

The progression continued through the emails, each revealing a deeper descent into delusion and obsession:

Why aren't you responding to my messages? I know you read them—I can see the read receipts. Are you playing hard to get? That's okay. I understand the game. I've always known we're meant to be together.

Saw you having lunch with that woman from your office today. She touched your arm twice and laughed at everything you said. She's not right for you. She can't understand you like I do. We have a connection that's special.

Three days and no response to my last seven messages. I'm worried about you. Or maybe you're deliberately ignoring me? After everything I've done? After how patient I've been? I deserve better than this silence.

. . .

The final message sent chills through me despite the library's warmth:

If I can't have you, no one will. You've forced my hand, Richard. I've been so patient, so understanding. I've given you every chance to recognize what we have. This is your last warning. Choose wisely.

This message had been sent two days before Collins' body appeared in my trunk.

"This is classic erotomaniac stalking progression," I whispered, my profiler's training automatically analyzing the pattern. "The delusional belief in a non-existent relationship, the perceived slights, the escalation from adoration to entitlement to threats." I pointed to specific phrases, my finger hovering over the screen without touching it. "See how they move from observation to interaction to possession? The language becomes increasingly proprietary—'after everything I've done,' 'you've forced my hand.'"

Matt nodded, continuing to navigate through Collins's inbox. "Collins never replied to any of these. Not once. But he saved them all in a separate folder labeled 'Evidence.'" He clicked into the folder, revealing dozens more messages, meticulously preserved.

"He knew he was being stalked," I said, my mind racing through the implications. "He was documenting it, probably planning to go to the police. We know he got a restraining order on someone. This must be that same person." I glanced toward the security guard, who had returned to his post by the entrance after helping the woman get to the librarian. "Can you access his sent mail? See if he reached out to anyone about this?"

Matt nodded, fingers dancing across the keyboard as he navigated to Collins's sent items. I maintained my vigilance, cataloging each person who entered or left the computer lab and assessing their body language for potential threats. The teenage boy had settled into what appeared to be an online game. The woman with children was now helping her youngest use a drawing program. Nothing triggered my internal alarms, but I remained alert.

"Look at this," Matt said, opening a message Collins had sent to himself as a draft. "It's a list of incidents—dates, times, and observations."

The document detailed multiple encounters with someone Collins believed was following him—a figure glimpsed outside his apartment, a car that frequently appeared in his office parking lot, and flowers delivered with no sender information. The final entry, dated three days before his body was found in my trunk, read simply: *Called Sarah to discuss concerns. Meeting tomorrow night.*

Sarah. Again, her name appeared, another thread connecting her to Collins. My jaw tightened as I processed this new information, the betrayal burning fresh. She did tell me that she and Collins flirted and knew each other from her store. But it sounds like they were more than that. Like they were actually friends? Or maybe lovers?

"Keep searching," I instructed Matt, my eyes scanning the room once more. "We need to know exactly what connection Sarah had to Collins, and why she never mentioned knowing him this well."

Matt nodded, already diving deeper into Collins' digital footprint as I resumed my position by the wall, more determined than ever to unravel the web closing around us.

The sharp squeak of rubber-soled shoes against linoleum cut through the library's hushed atmosphere. My head lifted fractionally at the sound, tracking its source without appearing to look directly. A middle-aged woman with steel-gray hair cut in a precise bob approached from the reference desk, glasses hanging from a beaded chain around her neck. Her cardigan—navy blue with pearl buttons—and sensible shoes marked her as staff rather than security, but the purposeful line of her mouth concerned me more than any uniform. She was heading straight for our terminal, her eyes narrowing with the particular focus of someone who has spotted something out of place.

I shifted my weight imperceptibly, preparing to move. The woman's gait was unhurried but determined, each footstep a soft squeak against the polished floor. My assessment was immediate and automatic—late fifties, no obvious physical training, likely unarmed except perhaps for pepper spray on her keychain, but her hand was already drifting toward the phone clipped to her belt. Far more dangerous than her physical presence was what a single call from her could summon.

I tapped Matt's shoulder twice—our prearranged signal for approaching threat. His response was immediate, though nothing in his posture betrayed alarm. Without breaking rhythm in his typing, he minimized Collins' files and inserted a flash drive into the USB port.

"Starting transfer," he murmured, his voice barely audible as his fingers initiated the copying process. A progress bar appeared on screen—15% complete and crawling forward with excruciating slowness.

The librarian was thirty feet away now, her path taking her between computer stations, gaze focused on our corner. She'd removed the glasses from around her neck and perched them on her nose, squinting slightly as she looked in our direction. The recognition hadn't happened yet, but it was coming—I could see the process beginning as her brow furrowed, mental connections forming.

"Library security protocols," I whispered to Matt. "She'll check ID first before making accusations. Standard procedure gives us approximately forty-five seconds from initial contact."

Matt nodded almost imperceptibly, his eyes fixed on the progress bar: 27%.

I moved from my position against the wall, deliberately placing myself between the approaching librarian and Matt's screen. The transfer needed another minute at least—time we might not have once recognition sparked. I adjusted my baseball cap lower, though I knew the gesture was likely futile. My face had been plastered across every news outlet in Florida for days; the cap was camouflage at a distance but wouldn't withstand scrutiny.

The librarian stopped three feet away, close enough that I could smell her light floral perfume and see the Tampa Public Library name badge pinned to her cardigan: HEAD LIBRARIAN in block letters beneath the library logo.

"Excuse me," she said, her voice carrying the practiced quiet of someone who had spent decades in hushed spaces. "I need to see some identification, please." Her eyes moved between Matt and me, settling more intently on my face with each passing second.

I shifted my stance, angling my body to block her view of the screen where the progress bar had reached 42%. Every microsecond mattered now.

"Identification?" I repeated, injecting confusion and slight indignation into my tone while keeping my voice low. "We're just doing some research for a family project."

Her eyes narrowed slightly, head tilting as she studied my face more carefully. "I believe all patrons were informed upon entry that ID is required for computer use." Her gaze drifted toward the screen, but I subtly shifted again, maintaining the visual barrier.

"My husband has his license," I said, nodding toward Matt without taking my eyes off her. I could see the moment recognition began to crystallize—the slight widening of her eyes, the parting of her lips, the small step backward she took unconsciously. She knew who I was now.

"You're—" she began, her hand moving decisively toward the phone at her belt.

I didn't let her finish. "We'll be going now," I said calmly, keeping my voice steady despite the adrenaline flooding my system. "No need to call anyone."

Matt's subtle head tilt told me the transfer had completed. He ejected the flash drive and pocketed it in one smooth motion, then closed the browser and cleared the history with three precise keystrokes. We had seconds at most before the librarian recovered from her shock.

"You're that FBI agent," she said, voice rising slightly above appropriate library volume. "The one who—"

"Ma'am, please step aside," I interrupted, my tone firm but not threatening. The last thing we needed was to create a scene that would draw immediate attention.

Her hand had reached the phone now, fingers curling around it as she took another step back. "I need to call security," she announced, louder now.

Matt stood, gathering our minimal belongings with calm efficiency. We moved in tandem, stepping away from the terminal in perfect synchronization born from days on the run together. The librarian's voice rose behind us—"Stop right there!"—but we were already moving through the stacks, our pace deliberate rather than panicked.

"Don't run," I murmured to Matt as we navigated between shelves of reference materials. "Running draws attention. Walk with purpose."

He nodded, matching my stride as we wound through the library's labyrinthine arrangement of bookcases. Behind us, I could hear the librarian on her phone, her urgent whispers carrying in the quiet space. Other patrons had begun to look up from their books and computers, curiosity drawing their attention to the commotion.

We reached the non-fiction section, where I'd noted a side exit during our arrival. Standard library security protocol would focus on covering the main entrances first, leaving secondary exits vulnerable for precious extra seconds. The door—marked EMERGENCY EXIT ONLY—would trigger an alarm when opened, but by then we'd be moving through the adjacent courtyard.

"Security's coming from the main entrance," Matt observed quietly, nodding toward the front of the library where two uniformed guards had appeared, scanning the space with practiced efficiency.

"Ten seconds," I responded, maintaining our measured pace through the American History section. We reached the emergency door just as one of the guards spotted us, his hand moving to the radio at his shoulder as he pointed in our direction.

Matt pushed the door open, and the alarm immediately blared through the previously hushed library. Bright afternoon sunlight momentarily blinded me as we stepped into the courtyard, but I'd memorized the layout when we arrived—fifteen steps to the wrought iron fence with the broken section, then across Palmetto Street to the alley where we'd left our latest "borrowed" vehicle.

We moved with controlled urgency, not the panicked flight of the guilty but the strategic withdrawal of trained operatives. Behind us, voices shouted orders as the security team organized pursuit. Too late. We slipped through the gap in the fence and crossed the street, blending into a group of college students waiting at the crosswalk.

Matt's hand found mine, his fingers warm as they closed around my cold ones.

"She recognized me immediately," I said as we reached the alley, our pace never faltering despite the sounds of pursuit fading behind us. "Our window for moving freely in public is closing fast."

As we pulled away from the curb, I glanced back at the library once more. The security guards had reached the fence but stopped there, speaking into their radios. They hadn't seen which vehicle we'd entered. Another small victory in a war that seemed increasingly desperate.

Chapter 24

THEN:

The minute hand on the wall clock crept toward the three, each incremental movement drawing Ann's eyes like a magnet. 1:15 approached—the time that had become the center of her days, the hour that divided her life into before and after. Her fingers trembled slightly as she delivered a club sandwich to table seven, her shoulders rigid despite her attempts to appear relaxed. Three consecutive days she'd switched shifts, worked evenings, called in sick—anything to break the pattern, to avoid being where Marcus expected her to be. But Tom had insisted she return to her regular lunch shift today, his patience with her "paranoia" visibly wearing thin.

"You can't keep rearranging your life over this," he'd told her that morning, arms crossed over his chest. "Either file a formal complaint or move on."

As if it were that simple. As if a complaint against an officer would be taken seriously without overwhelming evidence. Ann's documentation had grown to pages of notes, photographs, and timestamps—but would it be enough? The question twisted in her mind like a knife as she refilled water glasses, her eyes darting to the clock again. 1:12.

The lunch crowd hummed around her—clinking silverware, murmured conversations, the occasional burst of laughter from the corner booth where three women in business attire shared a bottle of wine. Normal sounds, everyday life continuing, while Ann's world had narrowed to watching and waiting, to the constant awareness of potentially being watched herself.

She made her way to the kitchen, pulse quickening as she pushed through the swinging door. From here, she could see the wall clock and the front entrance simultaneously. 1:13. Her chest tightened, restricting her breathing to shallow sips of air that couldn't quite satisfy her lungs.

Chef Cho glanced up from plating a salmon dish, her eyes narrowing as she took in Ann's rigid posture. "It's almost time," she said quietly, the words not a question but a recognition.

Ann nodded, unable to form words as her throat constricted. She collected her waiting order—Cobb salad, dressing on the side—and returned to the dining room, the plate's weight requiring conscious effort to keep steady. 1:14.

The front door opened, and Ann nearly dropped the salad. An elderly couple entered, the man helping his wife remove her light jacket. Not Marcus. Ann's shoulders dropped slightly, her breathing resuming a more natural rhythm as she delivered the salad to table four.

1:15 arrived and passed. No Marcus.

By 1:20, Ann felt the tightly coiled tension in her back begin to unwind, vertebra by vertebra. Her movements between tables became more fluid, less mechanical. She even managed a genuine smile when the businesswomen complimented the wine selection.

"He's not coming," she whispered to herself as she arranged clean silverware at the service station. "He broke the pattern."

But the relief was short-lived, dissolving like sugar in hot liquid as a new thought crystallized: What if his absence was deliberate? What if the break in the pattern was itself part of the pattern?

Ann's head jerked up, eyes scanning the dining room with

renewed intensity. The large windows facing the street suddenly seemed like vulnerable points rather than sources of natural light. Her gaze swept across the parking lot visible through the front windows, searching for patrol car 37, for any vehicle that might contain watching eyes.

"Table nine needs more napkins," Miriam said as she passed, frowning when Ann didn't immediately respond. "Ann? You still with us?"

"Sorry," Ann murmured, grabbing a stack of napkins without looking away from the windows. "I'll take care of it."

She approached table nine with a brittle smile, depositing the napkins while positioning herself to keep the entrance in her peripheral vision. The door remained closed. No new customers entered. No patrol car appeared in the parking lot. Still, the absence felt calculated rather than coincidental, as if Marcus had deliberately created this uncertainty to heighten her anxiety.

On her next trip to the kitchen, Ann detoured slightly, passing by the side window overlooking the alley and the adjacent street. Nothing. No sign of him. She collected a cheeseburger for table twelve, then lingered near the hostess stand, peering through the tinted glass door as if Marcus might materialize from the rippling heat rising off the asphalt.

"You're going to burn a hole in that door with your eyes," Lena said, appearing beside her with a stack of menus. "I could feel you staring from across the room."

Ann startled, nearly losing her grip on the order pad. "I'm just—checking."

"For your police officer?" Lena studied Ann's face, her usual easy smile replaced by genuine concern. "It's almost 1:45. He's not coming today."

"That's what worries me," Ann said, keeping her voice low as she turned toward the service station, Lena following close behind.

The service station offered a brief illusion of privacy—a corner of the restaurant where servers could regroup, refill water pitchers, and collect clean silverware. Ann's fingers trembled as she arranged forks, knives, and spoons into neat bundles, her eyes still flicking to the windows, the door, and the street beyond.

"Are you okay? You seem jumpier than usual," Lena asked, reaching for a stack of napkins and folding one absently. "I thought you'd be relieved he didn't show."

"I was. At first." Ann's voice dropped to a whisper, though no customers were within earshot. "But what if this is calculated? What if he's watching from somewhere else? What if this is part of his game?"

The silverware in Ann's hands clinked audibly as her tremor worsened. Lena's expression shifted from concern to something more serious, her earlier dismissive attitude fading.

"Maybe he just had the day off," she suggested, though her tone lacked conviction. "Or got assigned to a different patrol area."

"No," Ann shook her head firmly. "He's too consistent. Too deliberate. Breaking his pattern means something." She set down the silverware, afraid she'd drop it. "He's not gone. He's just… changing tactics."

Lena was quiet for a moment, watching as Ann's eyes darted to the windows again, scanning for threats that remained invisible but no less real to her. When Lena spoke again, her voice had lost its casual edge.

"Have you considered that maybe—" she began, then paused, reconsidering her words. "I mean, is there a chance you might be overthinking this? Just a little?"

Ann met her gaze directly, a spark of desperate intensity in her eyes. "That's what he wants everyone to think. That's why he's so careful—never saying anything inappropriate, always maintaining plausible deniability." Her fingers curled into tight fists at her sides. "But the patterns are real, Lena. And now the pattern has changed, which means…."

She trailed off, unable to articulate the nameless dread that curled in her stomach. The implications hung in the air between them—if Marcus had changed his approach, it meant he was adapting, evolving, and perhaps escalating.

Lena's doubtful expression softened, concern replacing skepticism. "Okay," she said quietly, reaching out to touch Ann's arm. "I hear you. What can I do to help?"

The simple question—the first time anyone had offered practical assistance rather than doubt or dismissal—nearly undid Ann's fragile composure. She blinked rapidly, fighting back the burn of potential tears.

"Just… watch with me," she whispered. "Tell me if you see him. Or his car. Or anything unusual."

Lena nodded. "I can do that."

Ann turned back to the dining room, forcing her body through the motions of her job while her mind remained hyperalert, scanning, searching for the threat she knew was there—unseen but present, like radiation or carbon monoxide. Deadly things didn't need to be visible to destroy.

And Marcus Hale's absence felt more dangerous than his presence had ever been.

Ann's fingers moved methodically through her end-of-shift routine, each motion precise and deliberate. Apron folded into her locker. Tips counted and sorted. Phone checked for messages, then slipped into her back pocket within easy reach. She pulled her car keys from her purse, arranging them between her fingers in the defensive position she'd adopted years ago—the longest key protruding between her middle and index fingers like a small, jagged weapon. The employee exit loomed before her, its small square window revealing a slice of the darkening parking lot. She took a deep breath, squaring her shoulders as if preparing for battle rather than simply leaving work.

"Want me to walk you out?" Lena asked, appearing in the break room doorway, her own purse already slung over her shoulder.

Ann hesitated, torn between wanting the safety of numbers and not wanting to put Lena at risk. "No, I'm fine," she said finally.

Lena frowned but nodded. "Text me when you get home, okay?"

Ann pushed through the employee door and into the cool evening air, her eyes immediately scanning the parking lot. She catalogued each vehicle, comparing them to the mental inventory she'd compiled when arriving that morning. A blue sedan that hadn't been there earlier. A motorcycle was parked near the dumpster. Neither matched the vehicles she'd associated with Marcus, but that didn't mean safety. She waited, counting to thirty, watching for movement, for a silhouette behind a windshield, for anything out of place.

Nothing. Just the ordinary sounds of a restaurant parking lot at dusk—distant kitchen fans, the occasional car passing on the main road, the hum of the streetlights as they flickered to life.

Ann approached her car with measured steps, circling it once before unlocking the door. She checked the back seat before sliding behind the wheel, then immediately locked all the doors with a decisive press of the button. The familiar click of the mechanisms engaging provided momentary comfort, like the sound of a castle drawbridge being raised.

Her routine continued inside the vehicle. Check mirrors. Adjust seat position slightly, then readjust to the original position. Verify all windows are closed. Place the phone in the holder with emergency contacts pre-loaded. Only when these protective rituals were complete did she start the engine.

The drive home had become an exercise in precision. Ann maintained exactly the speed limit, her eyes flicking regularly to the speedometer to ensure she never crept above or below the posted numbers. Too fast might attract attention; too slow might suggest awareness of being followed. Either could give him an excuse to pull her over. Again.

"Complete stop at stop signs," she whispered to herself as she approached an intersection. "Signal one hundred feet before turning. Stay in lane. Both hands on the wheel."

Her knuckles whitened as she gripped the steering wheel at precisely ten and two, her back rigid against the seat. The familiar route home now felt like navigating a minefield—each intersection a potential trap, each traffic signal an opportunity for Marcus to materialize behind her with those flashing lights that had become a recurring feature in her nightmares.

As she turned onto Westfield Avenue, Ann's chest tightened. The police station lay three blocks ahead on the right—a brick building with blue-trimmed windows that she'd once found reassuring. Now it represented danger, a headquarters from which her personal nightmare was dispatched and supported by an institution that would likely close ranks around one of their own if she reported him.

Her breathing quickened as she approached, eyes darting between the road ahead and the station's parking lot. Patrol cars lined up in neat rows, their roof lights dormant but ready. Was car 37 among them? She couldn't tell from this distance, couldn't risk slowing down to check.

Ann passed the station, exhaling shakily as it receded in her rearview mirror. She'd made it past the most dangerous stretch. Just four more miles to her apartment, where she would double-lock her door, place a chair beneath the knob, and spend another night jumping at every sound from the parking lot below.

The flash of lights in her rearview mirror shattered her momentary relief.

Red and blue strobes pulsed through her car interior, painting her hands in alternating colors as they clutched the steering wheel. For a terrible moment, she considered accelerating—fleeing from the inevitable confrontation—but rationality prevailed. Running would only make things worse. It would give him justification for escalation.

Ann guided her car to the curb with trembling hands, her breathing so shallow and quick that dark spots danced at the edges of her vision. The patrol car stopped behind her, its headlights blinding in her mirrors. She watched the driver's door open, the familiar silhouette emerging, and her worst fears were confirmed.

Marcus approached with unhurried confidence, his hand resting casually on his utility belt near his holstered weapon—not a threat, but a reminder of his authority. His flashlight beam swept briefly across her face before lowering slightly, the harsh light still illuminating her white-knuckled grip on the steering wheel.

"Good evening, Ms. Porter," he said, his tone professionally pleasant, as if they were meeting by chance rather than through his deliberate pursuit. "License and registration, please."

Ann turned slowly to face him, fighting to keep her voice steady. "What did I do wrong, Officer Hale?"

His expression remained neutral, though something in his eyes—a flash of something she couldn't name—suggested he'd expected her question. "You rolled through the stop sign at Westfield and Elm. Didn't come to a complete stop."

The accusation hit her like a physical blow. She had stopped completely and had counted one-Mississippi, two-Mississippi in her head while her tires were motionless against the asphalt. She had been meticulous about every single traffic law precisely to avoid giving him any legitimate reason to stop her.

"No, I didn't," she said, the words emerging with unexpected strength despite her racing heart. "I came to a complete stop. I was counting in my head."

Marcus's expression didn't change, but his posture shifted slightly—a subtle straightening of his spine, a minute narrowing of his eyes. He withdrew his notepad from his breast pocket, flipping it open with practiced ease.

"I observed the violation clearly, Ms. Porter," he said, his voice carrying the calm authority of someone whose word would be believed over hers in any official proceeding. "License and registration, please."

The request hung in the air between them—not a question but a command, backed by the weight of his badge, his gun, the flashing lights that bathed them both in alternating scarlet and sapphire. Ann stared into his impassive face, searching for some crack in his professional veneer, some acknowledgment that they both knew what was really happening.

She found none. Just the patient expectation of compliance, of submission to his authority, whether legitimate or manufactured for this very purpose.

Slowly, her hands still trembling, Ann reached for her purse to retrieve her driver's license, the sense of being trapped intensifying with every passing second.

Ann's fingers fumbled with the clasp of her purse, the simple action made difficult by her trembling hands. She extracted her driver's license and reached toward the glove compartment for the registration, acutely aware of Marcus watching every movement through her window. His presence felt physical, like a weight pressing against her skin, even though he hadn't touched her. When she turned to hand him the documents, she found him leaning slightly closer than necessary, his upper body angled into the window space she'd rolled down. The invasion—small but deliberate—sent a cold ripple through her chest.

"Thank you," he said, taking the documents with practiced efficiency. His flashlight beam swept across them, illuminating her photograph, her address—information he already knew intimately, given his surveillance. The light cast harsh shadows across his face, transforming his professional expression into something more ominous.

He didn't step back after taking her license and registration. Instead, he leaned further into her window space, his body blocking her view of the side mirror, eliminating her peripheral escape route. The subtle scent of his cologne—that same woodsy clean smell she remembered from his visits to the restaurant—invaded her car's interior, marking his territory in yet another way.

"You seem nervous tonight, Ms. Porter," Marcus observed, his tone carrying a note of concern that might have sounded genuine to anyone else. "Everything all right?"

Ann pressed her back against the driver's seat, creating what little distance she could in the confined space. Her heart hammered against her ribs with such force she wondered if he could see her blouse moving with each beat.

"I'm fine," she managed, the lie automatic and unconvincing. "Just tired after my shift."

"Long day at Granger's?" His casual reference to her workplace, while not surprising, felt like another intentional reminder: I know where you work. I know your routines.

"Yes."

"I missed lunch today," he continued conversationally, as if they were having a casual chat rather than a traffic stop. "Had a training session that couldn't be rescheduled."

The explanation for his absence—offered without being requested—confirmed what Ann had feared. He wanted her to know that his break in pattern had been deliberate, not a reprieve. That he remained in control of their interactions, determining when and where they would occur.

"Any plans for the evening?" Marcus asked, shifting slightly to examine her car's interior with his flashlight. The beam swept across the passenger seat, the dashboard, the back seat—checking for what? Other passengers? Evidence of some kind?

"Just going home," Ann said, her voice higher than normal despite her efforts to control it.

"Taking a different route home tonight?" he asked, the casual question landing like a punch to her stomach.

Ann froze, her breath catching painfully in her throat.

"What do you mean?" she asked, fighting to keep her voice steady, to mask the terror blooming in her chest.

Marcus didn't look up from his examination of her documents. "Just noticed you heading down Cedar Lane. It's not the fastest route to your address that I see here on your license." His eyes flicked to her face then, watching for her reaction. "Scenic route?"

Ann's hands clenched in her lap, nails digging half-moons into her palms. The pain helped ground her, prevented her from visibly falling apart as the confirmation of her fears crashed over her. He had been following her and had tracked her deliberate attempts to evade surveillance.

"How would you know what route I take home?" The question emerged stronger than she'd expected, direct and challenging despite her fear.

Marcus's expression didn't change, but something shifted in his eyes—a flicker of acknowledgment that she'd called out the game they were playing. He didn't answer directly.

"I noticed you went all the way to Pinecrest before doubling back. That's quite a detour. Almost like you were checking to see if someone was following you." His tone remained conversational, but the underlying message was clear: I see you. I know what you're doing. You can't escape me.

"I wasn't—" Ann began, but the protest died on her lips. Denying the obvious would only make her appear irrational, paranoid—exactly how he wanted her to seem if she ever reported him.

"You should be careful in that neighborhood. We've had reports of suspicious activity in the area."

The warning—delivered with apparent concern—contained its own implicit threat. Ann swallowed hard, her mouth dry as desert sand.

"Thank you for your concern," she managed, each word feeling like glass in her throat.

Marcus nodded, his gaze holding hers a moment too long before he finally straightened, pulling back slightly from her window. He held out her license and registration along with a yellow slip of paper.

"Just a written warning this time," he said, his tone suggesting magnanimity rather than the manipulation Ann knew it to be. "Everyone makes mistakes. Just be more careful at that intersection in the future."

Ann took the documents with fingers that had gone numb. The warning citation felt like a prop in an elaborate performance—a physical reminder of his power to create official records, to establish a paper trail that would make her look like a problematic driver rather than his target.

"Drive safely, Ms. Porter," Marcus said, stepping back from her car with a slight nod. "I'll be seeing you around."

Not a question. Not a casual farewell. A statement of fact. A promise.

Ann's hands shook so violently that she could barely shift the car into drive. She pulled away from the curb with careful precision, hyperaware of Marcus watching her departure. In her rearview mirror, his figure remained motionless by the side of the road, growing smaller but no less threatening as she increased the distance between them.

Part III

Chapter 25

THE FLASH DRIVE felt like a loaded weapon in my pocket as Matt guided our newly "borrowed" sedan through the winding streets of Oakridge Estates. Sarah Winters lived in a neighborhood of manicured lawns and flowering crepe myrtles, where mailboxes matched front doors, and children's bicycles lay trustingly unattended in driveways. The suburban perfection made my skin crawl.

"Number thirty-four," Matt murmured, slowing as we approached a cheerful yellow two-story colonial with white shutters and a wrap-around porch. The house looked like it belonged in a real estate magazine—hanging baskets of ferns flanking the entrance, stepping stones leading through a perfectly edged lawn, and not a weed in sight.

"Remember," I said, my voice low, "we're here for information, not confrontation. We play along until we understand exactly what her role is in this."

Matt nodded, his fingers tightening almost imperceptibly on the steering wheel. "Just two friends seeking refuge with someone they trust." His voice carried the weight of irony.

As we pulled into the driveway, I spotted a small figure crouched in the front yard—a boy of about nine, dark-haired and slender, pushing toy cars through the grass with sound effects that carried through the open car windows. Tommy Winters. I'd never met Sarah's son at my book signing at her store, but I knew she had one. She had told me she adopted him two years ago. His parents had died in a car accident, leaving him in the foster system.

The front door opened before we even stepped from the car. Sarah stood framed in the doorway, one hand raised in greeting, the other balancing a plate of what appeared to be freshly baked cookies. Her casual attire—jeans and a light-blue button-down shirt with the sleeves rolled up—projected a sense of relaxed domesticity. Her smile stretched wide across her face, revealing perfectly straight teeth.

"Eva! Matt! Thank goodness you're okay!" Her voice carried the precise notes of concern and relief that someone would expect. Too precise. Too practiced. She rushed down the steps toward us as we exited the car, the plate of cookies balanced carefully in her hand. The scent of vanilla and brown sugar wafted toward us.

"I've been so worried." She enveloped me in a hug, her free arm squeezing me with what felt like genuine emotion. I forced myself to return the embrace, my body stiff despite my best efforts to appear natural. Over Sarah's shoulder, I watched Tommy look up briefly from his cars before returning to his play, apparently accustomed to his mother's visitors.

"We didn't know where else to go," I said, the lie coming easily as I stepped back from her embrace. "Things have escalated, and we needed somewhere safe."

"Of course, of course," Sarah replied, her voice dropping to a confidential tone. "You can stay as long as you need to." She turned toward her son. "Tommy, say hello to Ms. Thomas and Mr. Miller."

The boy stood, dutifully wiping grass from his knees. "Hello," he said with the automatic politeness of a well-trained child. His eyes assessed us with quiet intelligence before he returned to his cars, apparently dismissing us as uninteresting adult concerns.

Sarah ushered us inside, her hand pressing lightly against my back in a gesture that seemed both comforting and controlling. The interior of her home continued the theme of magazine-perfect domesticity—gleaming hardwood floors, coordinated furniture that managed to look both stylish and lived-in, family photos arranged in matching frames along the staircase wall.

"Let's get you both some coffee," Sarah said, leading us toward the kitchen. "You must be exhausted." Her movements were graceful and efficient as she navigated her space, the plate of cookies never tilting despite her animated gestures.

The kitchen gleamed with stainless steel appliances and white marble countertops. Copper pots hung in precise gradations above a professional-grade range. Everything was immaculate—no dirty dishes in the sink, no mail scattered on countertops, no magnets cluttering the refrigerator. The perfection felt deliberate, staged rather than lived-in.

"Cream and sugar?" Sarah asked, already reaching for matching ceramic mugs from a cabinet. "Or do you still take it black with just a touch of cinnamon, Eva?" She smiled over her shoulder, her eyes crinkling at the corners. "I remember from your book signing."

"That's right," I replied, filing away this demonstration of her attention to detail. "Good memory."

"I pay attention to people I admire," she said, her back turned as she prepared the coffee. While she worked, I noticed her phone on the counter, screen facing down. As she set out cream and sugar for Matt, her fingers brushed against the device, turning it slightly to check for notifications. The gesture was subtle, almost unconscious, but repeated twice more as she poured coffee and arranged cookies on a serving plate.

"This is quite a home you have," Matt commented, his tone conversational as he accepted his mug. His eyes, I noticed, were methodically scanning the kitchen, taking in exits, sightlines, potential weapons or threats—the same assessment I was conducting.

"Tommy and I love it here," Sarah replied, bringing her own coffee to the table and gesturing for us to sit. "When I adopted Tommy, I moved us here. I wanted somewhere that felt..." she paused, selecting her word with care, "...secure."

A small sound from outside—a car door closing down the street—caused her to stiffen momentarily, her gaze darting toward the window before returning to us with a forced smile. Her reaction seemed disproportionate, a hairline crack in her composed facade.

"So," she said, pushing the plate of cookies toward us, "tell me everything. The news is saying awful things about you, Eva. I've been sick with worry."

I took a cookie I had no intention of eating, buying time to formulate my response. "It's been a nightmare," I admitted, allowing genuine emotion to color my voice. "Someone planted Collins' body in my trunk, and now they're systematically destroying my reputation and credibility."

"Oh, Eva." Sarah reached across the table to squeeze my hand, her skin cool against mine. "Who would do such a thing?"

"That's what we're trying to figure out," Matt interjected, his tone measured. "Eva Rae has made enemies over the years, working for the Bureau. But this feels personal."

Sarah nodded sympathetically, releasing my hand to tuck a strand of hair behind her ear. "Let's move to the living room," she suggested. "It's more comfortable for talking."

The living room continued the theme of calculated comfort—plush sofas arranged for conversation, books artfully displayed on built-in shelves, family photos capturing Sarah and Tommy in moments of orchestrated happiness. No husband or partner appeared in any of the frames I could see.

"I was telling Matt about Richard Collins," I said once we were seated, launching the conversational probe we'd planned in the car. "We're trying to understand why he was targeted, who might have wanted him dead."

Sarah's expression remained sympathetic and attentive. "Such a horrible crime," she murmured.

"The strange thing is," I continued, watching her face carefully, "we discovered he was investigating financial irregularities at his firm. He seemed to be building a case against someone."

"That sounds dangerous," Sarah replied, her fingers curling more tightly around her mug. "I knew Richard pretty well. Like I told you, he was a regular at my bookstore."

“But you knew him as more than that, am I right?” I asked. “What was the nature of your relationship?”

Before Sarah could respond, the front door banged open, and Tommy raced in, his cheeks flushed with exertion. "Mom, I'm hungry," he announced, stopping short when he noticed we were still in conversation.

"Tommy, what have I told you about interrupting?" Sarah's voice remained pleasant, but something shifted in her eyes—a sudden intensity that seemed disproportionate to the minor social transgression. She stared at her son with a focus that made the hairs on the back of my neck stand on end.

"Sorry," Tommy mumbled, backing away slightly under his mother's gaze.

"It's fine, sweetheart," Sarah said, her expression softening as quickly as it had hardened. "Get an apple from the fruit bowl. We'll have dinner soon."

I watched the interaction with practiced observation, noting how Tommy's shoulders relaxed only after he'd left the room, how Sarah's eyes tracked him with an ownership that went beyond maternal concern.

Sarah turned back to us, her smile firmly in place once more. "Now, where were we? Oh, yes, Richard. Such a terrible shame what happened to him. He had such a keen mind for patterns and inconsistencies."

I leaned forward slightly, maintaining eye contact. "Sarah, how well did you know Richard Collins?"

Her smile never faltered. "Well enough to know he deserved better than what happened to him," she replied, her voice smooth as glass. "Don't you agree?"

The question hung between us, charged with unspoken meaning as we regarded each other across the coffee table. Sarah's expression remained open and friendly—but her eyes were calculating, measuring my response with an intensity that belied her casual posture.

“Do stay for dinner, please. It would make me so happy.”

I nodded. We could use a home-cooked meal right about now,

and what was cooking in the kitchen smelled divine. I watched her as she got up with a smile.

"I'll need to stir the sauce. Please excuse me."

She was the perfect hostess in her perfect home, serving cookies with one hand while possibly reporting my whereabouts to the police with the other. I took a sip of coffee, buying time as I considered my next move in this dangerous game of chess we were playing.

Chapter 26

STEAM ROSE from a pot on the stove as Sarah stirred what smelled like homemade marinara sauce. "I hope you both like pasta," she called over her shoulder, her movements fluid and practiced as she reached for dried herbs from a rack arranged in alphabetical order. "Tommy's favorite is spaghetti with my special sauce."

I stood in the kitchen doorway, watching her perform domestic normality with the precision of an actress who had rehearsed her role for years. Everything about her house felt deliberate—not just clean and organized, but curated, as if each object had been selected and placed to tell a specific story about the woman who lived here.

"Can I help with anything?" I offered, more to establish my movements through the house than from any genuine desire to assist.

"No, no," Sarah replied, waving a wooden spoon dismissively. "You're my guests. Besides, cooking relaxes me." She glanced at the kitchen clock—a vintage piece that looked authentically retro rather than reproduced. "Dinner will be ready in about thirty minutes. Please, make yourselves at home."

The invitation was exactly what I needed. "Mind if I use your restroom?"

"Of course not. Down the hall, second door on the left." She turned back to her cooking, humming softly—a lullaby I vaguely recognized but couldn't name.

I moved through the dining room with its table already set for four—cloth napkins folded into perfect triangles, water glasses filled to identical levels, a small vase of fresh-cut flowers as a centerpiece. Matt caught my eye from the living room, where he'd been examining family photos with deliberate casualness. A subtle nod passed between us—the mutual understanding of seasoned partners who could communicate volumes with the smallest gestures.

The hallway was lined with more framed photographs—Tommy's school portraits in chronological order, Sarah receiving a community service award, the two of them at various tourist destinations. I noticed the absence of spontaneous shots—those imperfect, candid moments that most family collections include. Every image appeared staged, composed for maximum effect.

As I approached the bathroom, a partially open door on the right caught my attention. Light spilled from the gap, illuminating a slice of cream-colored carpet. I glanced back toward the kitchen—Sarah was still occupied, the sound of chopping and the radio she'd turned on providing auditory cover. Making a split-second decision, I altered my path and slipped toward the office door.

The room was small but meticulously organized—a glass-topped desk with a closed laptop, color-coded file folders in a wall-mounted organizer, and a stylish ergonomic chair pushed neatly into place. What stopped me cold was the corkboard that dominated the wall opposite the desk. It was covered with newspaper clippings, printouts, and handwritten notes—all about me from the last couple of days.

My breath caught as I moved closer.

"Finding something interesting?"

Sarah's voice behind me sent ice through my veins. I turned slowly, my face composed despite the alarm bells ringing in my head. She stood in the doorway, wooden spoon still in hand, her expression pleasant though her eyes were sharper than before.

"I was looking for the bathroom," I said, gesturing toward the corkboard. "What is all this, Sarah?"

She laughed—a light, tinkling sound that didn't reach her eyes. "Oh, that must look strange! I've just been trying to keep up with what was going on." She stepped into the room, casually placing herself between me and the door. "I haven't been able to sleep since it happened. I've been concerned about you and how I could help. I feel slightly guilty for this happening to you. I'm the one who invited you here, and now you're in this total mess of a situation. It's not fair."

Sarah smiled, her head tilting slightly to the right. "The bathroom is the next door down. Dinner is almost done."

I slipped past her, feeling her eyes tracking my movement down the hall. In the bathroom, I locked the door and leaned against it, processing what I'd discovered. Sarah had been keeping track of me and what the media wrote about me. Why? Because she felt guilty? Because she wanted to help?

Something about it didn't feel right.

By the time I rejoined everyone for dinner, Sarah had transformed into the perfect hostess again, serving homemade pasta with a flourish. "Tommy, smaller bites please," she instructed as her son twirled spaghetti onto his fork. Matt sat across from me, his expression carefully neutral, though I could read the tension in the set of his shoulders.

"This is delicious," I commented, the food turning to ash in my mouth as I forced myself to maintain our charade. Sarah had deflected when I asked her about the nature of her relationship with Collins, so it was time to try another approach.

"You mentioned knowing Richard Collins from your bookstore. What did he usually look for?"

"Oh, yes," Sarah replied, refilling Matt's water glass without being asked. "He loved mystery novels—the more complex the better. Said they helped him think outside the box in his work."

"His work as an accountant?" Matt asked, taking a careful sip of water.

"Mmhmm." Sarah nodded, her attention momentarily diverted to Tommy's messy eating. "He mentioned auditing was like detective work—finding inconsistencies in the narrative."

I seized the opening to keep her talking. "Did he ever mention what he was working on specifically? Any cases that troubled him?"

Sarah's eyes flicked to mine, then away—a tell so subtle most would miss it. "He kept the details confidential, of course. Professional ethics and all that." She turned toward Matt. "Would you like more pasta, Matt? You've barely touched your plate."

"Actually," Matt said, folding his napkin beside his plate, "would you mind if I washed my hands again? Got a bit of sauce on them."

"Of course." Sarah smiled. "Bathroom's—"

"Down the hall, second door on the left," Matt finished for her. "I remember."

As he left, I engaged Sarah in conversation about her bookstore, asking detailed questions that required her full attention. "How did you get into selling books? Have you always loved literature?"

Sarah launched into what sounded like a rehearsed narrative about her lifelong passion for reading, her voice animated as she described opening Bookmark Haven five years ago. I nodded at appropriate intervals, my peripheral vision tracking the hallway where Matt had disappeared.

Instead of heading to the bathroom, Matt slipped silently into the living room. I kept Sarah talking, watching as she checked her phone again beneath the table—the third time since we'd sat down to eat. Her story about the bookstore's grand opening droned on as I divided my attention between her words and the mental clock tracking Matt's absence.

In the living room, Matt moved directly to the side table he'd noted earlier—the only piece of furniture with a locked drawer. Using the small set of picks we both carried, he worked the simple lock open in seconds. Inside, nestled in a felt-lined compartment, lay five identical burner phones. He removed one, checked its call history, and found multiple outgoing calls to the same number, as recently as that morning. He photographed the number with his own burner phone, then carefully replaced everything exactly as he'd found it.

As he closed the drawer, a shadow fell across the room. "Finding everything okay?"

Matt looked up to see Sarah standing in the doorway, holding a pitcher of iced tea. Her smile remained in place, but her eyes had hardened to chips of blue ice.

"Just admiring your book collection," Matt responded smoothly, gesturing to the shelves behind the table. "You have a first edition Agatha Christie. My grandmother collected her works."

Sarah's posture relaxed fractionally, though her eyes remained watchful. "The Queen of Mystery," she said, stepping into the room. "No one's ever solved crimes quite like her characters." She placed the pitcher on a coaster, her movements precise. "I've made up the guest room for you both. I insist you stay the night. It's far too dangerous for you to be driving around after dark."

The offer hung between them, framed as hospitality but carrying the weight of a command. I heard it all from the kitchen.

When I joined them moments later, Sarah turned to me with renewed enthusiasm. "Eva, I was just telling Matt that you simply must stay tonight. I've prepared the guest room already."

"That's very kind," I began, "but we don't want to impose—"

"Nonsense!" Sarah interrupted, her voice rising slightly. "I won't hear of you leaving. It's settled." Her smile stretched wider. "Let me show you the room. I put out fresh towels and turned down the sheets. The bathroom has new toothbrushes still in their packages and travel-sized toiletries—all the amenities of a luxury hotel but with the comfort of a friend's home."

She led us upstairs, chattering about thread counts and hypoallergenic pillows, her enthusiasm becoming increasingly disconcerting. The guest room itself was impeccable—a king-sized bed with plump pillows arranged in descending order of size, bedside lamps with matching shades, and even wrapped chocolates on the pillows. It was a haven for someone like us who had been living in sleazy motels and who had slept on the concrete floor of an empty warehouse just the night before.

"Everything you might need should be here," Sarah said, opening the attached bathroom door to reveal an array of products arranged by size on the counter. "But if you think of anything else, anything at all, my room is just across the hall."

As she finally left us alone, closing the door with a soft click, Matt and I exchanged glances laden with unspoken concern. Sarah's meticulous hospitality had taken on an increasingly oppressive quality—less the generosity of a friend and more the calculated control of a jailer ensuring her prisoners remained exactly where she wanted them.

Chapter 27

THE GUEST ROOM felt both luxurious and suffocating, with its high thread-count sheets and abundance of pillows that Sarah had pointed out with such peculiar pride. Matt sat on the edge of the bed, removing his prosthetic with practiced movements. Neither of us spoke until we heard Sarah's footsteps retreat down the hall, followed by Tommy's bedroom door closing and the muffled sounds of a bedtime routine in progress.

"She has burner phones," Matt finally murmured, his voice barely audible above the soft hum of the central air conditioning. "What do you think she uses them for?"

I removed my earrings and placed them on the nightstand with deliberate care. The small gold hoops—a gift from my daughter Christine years ago—were one of the few personal items I'd managed to keep with me through our desperate flight. "Five identical phones, you said?"

"All the same model, prepaid. The one I checked had outgoing calls to the same number." Matt massaged his residual limb, easing the discomfort from a day spent on the move.

"The office wall—it had newspaper clippings of me, all from the past few days. She said she has been following the news because she was worried and wanted to help, but something about it rubbed me the wrong way. Why would she hang up newspaper clippings?"

The weight of what I'd seen in that home office pressed against my chest.

"I've started to wonder if her interest in me coming here is more than just doing a speaking engagement and book signing," I continued, keeping my voice low enough that it wouldn't carry through the walls. "Me coming here, doing the speaking engagement. It feels planned."

Matt's hand found mine in the semi-darkness, his fingers warm against my perpetually cold ones. "The question is why. What does she want from you specifically?"

I stood, moving restlessly to the window overlooking the backyard. Security lights illuminated a perfectly maintained lawn, a child's swing set, and a stone patio with arranged seating. Like everything in Sarah's life, the yard was meticulously organized, unnaturally perfect. "The stalking emails we found in Collins' account showed classic progression—observation, perceived intimacy, entitlement, then rage when the fantasy relationship wasn't reciprocated."

"And when Collins rejected the stalker…" Matt began.

"If it was Sarah, she eliminated him and found a way to make me pay simultaneously." I turned from the window, arms crossed over my chest. "But there's something else bothering me. Her behavior toward Tommy seems off—possessive beyond normal maternal concern."

Matt nodded slowly. "I noticed that too. The way she watches him and corrects him for minor infractions. That intensity when he interrupted our conversation."

"Like he's an extension of her rather than his own person," I added, remembering the look that had passed between mother and son—Tommy's subtle flinch, Sarah's controlling gaze. "Children raised by narcissists often develop that hyperawareness of parental moods. They learn to read subtle cues for self-preservation."

"You think the boy might be in danger?" Matt's expression darkened with concern. Despite the risks we faced, his instinct to protect an innocent child remained undiminished.

I sighed, returning to sit beside him. "I don't know. But if Sarah is unstable enough to commit murder and frame me for it, she's unpredictable. That unpredictability makes her dangerous to everyone around her, including Tommy."

Matt ran his hand through his hair—a gesture I recognized from our years together, his way of processing disturbing possibilities. "We need to be out of here by dawn. Whatever Sarah's involvement, this house isn't safe."

"Agreed." I reached for my bag at the foot of the bed. "We take shifts sleeping. Four hours each."

We continued planning in whispers—exit strategies, rendezvous points if we got separated, what information we still needed to gather before leaving. Eventually, Matt stretched out on the far side of the king bed, his breathing gradually deepening as exhaustion claimed him despite the danger. I remained sitting upright against the headboard, listening to the house settle around us.

The central air shut off, leaving a sudden silence that amplified smaller sounds—the refrigerator's hum downstairs, the occasional creak of expanding and contracting wood, the soft tick of a clock somewhere down the hall. Through the window, I watched clouds slide across the moon, casting shifting shadows across the too-perfect lawn.

An hour passed, then another. Matt slept soundly beside me, his face relaxed in a way it never was during waking hours. I envied his ability to shut down when necessary, to grab rest in the spaces between crises. My own mind continued to race, assembling and reassembling the puzzle pieces of our situation.

A soft sound drew my attention—a voice, muffled but distinct, coming through the wall that separated our room from what I presumed was Sarah's bedroom. I tensed, straining to hear. She was speaking, her tone animated, though I couldn't make out specific words. No second voice responded. A phone call, perhaps?

I eased off the bed, careful not to disturb Matt, and moved silently to the wall, pressing my ear against the painted surface.

Sarah's voice became clearer—still hushed, but distinct enough that I could catch fragments:

"...don't suspect anything... perfect timing having them here..."

I held my breath, straining to hear more. Sarah's voice dropped lower for a moment, then rose again with what sounded like excitement:

"...everything's going according to plan... The evidence is all in place..."

My blood ran cold. I glanced back at Matt, debating whether to wake him, but decided to gather more information first. I leaned closer to the wall, pressing my ear harder against the surface.

"...he'll be mine soon enough... Once she's completely discredited..."

The pronouns sent a fresh wave of alarm through me. She. Me. He? Who was she referring to? Matt? Someone else?

"...I've waited long enough... Tommy needs a proper father figure..."

I jerked back from the wall as if it had burned me, the implications of Sarah's words crystallizing into a horrifying possibility. I moved quickly to the bed, shaking Matt's shoulder gently but urgently.

His eyes opened immediately. One look at my face, and he was fully alert, sitting up without a sound.

"What is it?" he whispered, reaching automatically for his prosthetic.

"Sarah's on the phone in her room, at least I think she is; she could be talking to herself," I murmured, my lips close to his ear. "She's talking about us not suspecting anything, about evidence being in place. And something about Tommy needing a 'proper father figure.'"

Matt's expression hardened as he processed this information. "You think I'm the target? Beyond framing you?"

"It fits the pattern of erotomanic obsession," I whispered, the profile forming in my mind with sickening clarity. "She eliminates perceived rivals and obstacles to create space for her fantasy relationship. Collins rejected her advances. I'm an independent woman in your life who could be seen as competition."

Through the wall, Sarah's voice continued, though her words were now indistinct—the one-sided conversation carried on, punctuated by soft laughter that raised goosebumps along my arms.

Matt and I exchanged alarmed glances in the darkness, the full dimension of our danger becoming clear. We weren't just staying in the home of someone who had betrayed us or who was feeding information to whoever framed me.

We were sleeping under the roof of the killer herself, a woman who had already murdered once and seemed to be orchestrating our destruction with methodical precision. And the most disturbing realization of all—she had invited us into her web deliberately, bringing the prey right to the predator's lair.

"We need to get out now," I breathed, reaching for my bag.

Matt nodded grimly, already moving with silent efficiency. "And we need to find a way to protect Tommy, too."

As we gathered our few belongings in the darkness, Sarah's voice continued its one-sided conversation beyond the wall, her pleased, confident tone more chilling than any threat could have been.

Chapter 28

THEN:

Ann's fingers fumbled with her apron strings as she hurried through the employee entrance of Granger's, her eyes darting to each shadowed corner of the hallway before she fully committed to stepping inside. She'd parked her car directly beneath a light pole today, had checked the back seat twice before getting in, and had taken three different routes on her drive to ensure no one followed her. The precautions exhausted her, but the alternative—letting down her guard even for a moment—was unthinkable after what she'd witnessed outside her apartment window at 2:00 a.m.

"Ann?" Tom's voice made her jump as he emerged from his office. "Jesus, you look like hell."

She forced her lips into what she hoped resembled a smile. "Just didn't sleep well."

Tom frowned, taking in the dark half-moons beneath her eyes, the pallor of her skin. "You know, if you need another day off—"

"I'm fine," she cut him off, the words automatic by now. "Really."

He didn't look convinced but nodded anyway, retreating into his office as Ann continued toward the break room. Her gaze swept across the restaurant through the kitchen pass-through—scanning tables, doorways, and windows. No sign of Marcus. Not yet.

She spotted Miriam by the service station, arranging silverware into rolled napkins with quick, efficient movements. Relief flooded through her—a friendly face, someone who'd at least begun to believe her. Ann approached swiftly, glancing over her shoulder before touching Miriam's elbow.

"I need to show you something," she whispered, her voice strained even to her own ears. "Break room. Now."

Miriam's eyebrows rose, but she followed without question, abandoning her task. Ann led the way, checking the employee hallway once more before pulling Miriam into the empty break room and shutting the door with more force than she'd intended.

"What's going on?" Miriam asked, concern replacing her usual easy smile. "You look terrible."

Ann's hands trembled as she fumbled with her phone, nearly dropping it in her haste to unlock the screen. "Last night," she began, her voice catching. "Two in the morning. He was there, Miriam. Outside my apartment."

"Marcus?" Miriam stepped closer, her voice dropping instinctively.

Ann nodded, pulling up her photo gallery with fingers that wouldn't quite obey her commands. "I couldn't sleep. I've barely slept in days. I was checking the windows—I do that now, every hour or so—and there he was."

She turned the phone toward Miriam, displaying the first image—a patrol car parked at night, partially obscured by a hedge but clearly visible in the harsh glow of her phone's night mode. The timestamp in the corner read 2:07 a.m.

"This is from last night?" Miriam took the phone, studying the image with narrowed eyes.

"Swipe right. I took several." Ann's voice quivered. "He was there for over an hour. Just sitting. Watching."

Miriam swiped through the photos, each showing the patrol car from slightly different angles. The final image was the clearest. The number 37 was clearly visible on its door.

"That's definitely his car," Miriam said, her tone shifting from curious to concerned. "The one with the dent in the rear bumper?"

Ann nodded vigorously. "And it gets worse. After the traffic stop the other day—"

"He pulled you over again?" Miriam's head snapped up, her fingers tightening around Ann's phone.

"On my way home. Said I rolled through a stop sign on Westfield and Elm." Ann's voice rose slightly before she caught herself, glancing at the closed door. "I didn't, Miriam. I swear to God I didn't. I've been so careful—counting in my head at every stop sign, watching my speed exactly. I knew he'd use any excuse to pull me over."

"What happened?"

Ann hugged her arms around herself, as if the physical pressure might keep her from falling apart. "He kept me there for twenty minutes, just asking questions. Where was I going? Was I heading straight home? What route was I taking home?" She swallowed hard. "He said he'd noticed I took Cedar Lane the night before—that's the detour I made when I was checking if someone was following me."

"How did he know that?" Miriam whispered.

"Because he was the one following me." Ann's voice cracked. "He wanted me to know he was watching."

Miriam took a step back, her expression shifting as the full implications sank in. She zoomed in on one of the photos, focusing on the license plate and the distinctive dent in the bumper. "This is the same patrol car you've seen before? You're absolutely sure?"

"Positive." Ann rubbed her hands over her face, smearing the concealer she'd carefully applied to hide the evidence of her sleepless night. "Number 37. The same one I've seen him arrive here in, the same one my neighbor saw. The same one he used to pull me over."

"And he didn't give you a ticket? Just a warning?"

Ann nodded. "He doesn't want official records. He wants me scared." Her voice dropped to a whisper. "It's working."

Miriam handed back the phone; her earlier skepticism had completely evaporated. "You need to tell Tom about this," she said firmly, squeezing Ann's arm. "This is beyond uncomfortable customer territory now."

"I tried." Ann scrolled through the photos again, as if confirming to herself that the evidence was real, that she wasn't imagining the escalating nightmare. "He thinks I'm overreacting. That I should be flattered by the attention."

"Show him these photos," Miriam insisted. "The timestamp, the car number—it's all right there. This isn't some police officer with a crush. This is stalking, Ann."

The word hung in the air between them, stark and undeniable. Ann had been circling it for weeks, afraid to give voice to her fears, but now it stood plainly before them. Stalking. By a man with a badge, a gun, and the institutional power to make any complaint disappear.

"What if telling Tom makes it worse?" Ann whispered. "What if Marcus finds out I'm documenting this? What if—"

The break room door swung open, and both women jumped. Lena stood in the doorway, her eyebrows rising at their obvious tension.

"Sorry to interrupt whatever's going on, but Ann, you've got customers at table four," she said, her gaze moving between them with open curiosity.

Ann nodded, hastily shoving her phone into her apron pocket. "I'll be right there."

Lena hesitated, clearly sensing the charged atmosphere. "Everything okay?"

"Fine," Ann said automatically, the lie worn smooth from repetition. "Just showing Miriam some photos."

As Lena retreated, Miriam grabbed Ann's wrist, holding her back. "This isn't going away on its own," she said softly. "And I'm worried about what happens next if you don't get help."

Ann nodded, acknowledging the truth in Miriam's words even as fear knotted in her stomach. "I'll talk to Tom after the lunch rush," she promised, though her voice lacked conviction. "I need to get to my tables."

She straightened her shoulders and smoothed her apron, summoning the professional mask she'd perfected over years of service work. But as she pushed through the door into the dining room, her eyes automatically swept the entrance, the windows, the parking lot beyond—scanning for a white and blue patrol car, for the man whose surveillance had transformed her life into an unending nightmare.

Ann balanced the water pitcher with both hands as she refilled glasses for the elderly couple seated by the window. The afternoon sun streamed through the glass, warming her back as she bent over the table, smiling mechanically at the woman's comment about the *wonderful weather we're having*. She'd managed to maintain a veneer of normalcy for the first half of her shift, though each jingle of the bell above the entrance door sent a jolt of electricity up her spine, her body constantly braced for the moment she dreaded. When it finally came—the distinctive sound of the door swinging open with more force than necessary—she didn't need to turn to know. Something in the sudden stillness of the restaurant, the shift in air pressure, told her exactly who had entered.

Ann's hands froze mid-pour, water hovering just above the rim of the glass. Through the window's reflection, she caught a glimpse of crisp blue uniforms—not one but two. Marcus had brought backup.

"Is everything alright, dear?" the elderly woman asked, noticing Ann's sudden rigidity.

Ann's grip on the pitcher slipped, water sloshing dangerously close to the edge. She steadied it with a jerky movement, spilling a few drops onto the tablecloth.

"I'm so sorry," she managed, the words barely audible as her throat constricted. "I'll bring some extra napkins."

She turned, keeping her gaze fixed on the floor, but peripheral vision betrayed her—Marcus stood at the hostess stand with another officer. Officer Ramirez, she saw on her name tag. Marcus's head was already turning, scanning the restaurant with deliberate thoroughness until his eyes locked onto her position by the window. The slight curve of his lips wasn't quite a smile, but a recognition, an acknowledgment of prey spotted.

The pitcher threatened to slip from Ann's suddenly numb fingers. She clutched it against her chest, pivoted sharply, and walked with measured steps toward the kitchen. Not running. Running would attract attention, would confirm her fear. But every instinct screamed at her to flee, to escape those eyes that tracked her movement across the dining room floor.

Ann pushed through the swinging kitchen doors with her shoulder, the familiar sounds of the kitchen—the sizzle of the grill, the clatter of plates, Chef Cho's precise instructions to the line cook—enveloping her like a protective cocoon. She set the water pitcher down with trembling hands, breathing in short, shallow gasps that couldn't quite satisfy her lungs.

"Porter? You look like you've seen a ghost." Chef Cho glanced up from the grill, her knife pausing mid-slice through a red pepper.

"He's here," Ann whispered, the words catching in her dry throat. "Marcus. With another officer."

Chef Cho's expression shifted, understanding immediately. She set down her knife with deliberate care. "In your section?"

"They'll request it." Ann moved toward the chef, desperation evident in her rigid posture. "I can't go out there. Please—can someone cover my tables? Just until they leave?"

Chef Cho wiped her hands on her apron, her eyes narrowing as she moved to the pass-through window, peering discreetly into the dining room. Ann watched her take in the situation—the two officers now being led by the hostess toward a table in Ann's section, Marcus's rigid posture and searching gaze.

"Jake," Chef Cho called to the junior line cook. "Take over the grill."

The young man nodded, sliding into position as Chef Cho

stepped away. She turned to Ann, her expression resolute. "Stay in the kitchen. I'll tell Miriam to cover your tables." She hesitated, then added, "Use the pass-through window. Watch what happens."

Ann nodded gratefully, positioning herself where she could observe the dining room without being easily spotted from the tables. She kept her body angled away from the direct line of sight, only her eyes and part of her face visible through the narrow opening.

In the dining room, Marcus and Ramirez were being seated at table twelve, directly in her section as she'd predicted. The hostess placed menus before them, her smile professional but tight. Ann watched as Marcus's gaze swept the restaurant again, lingering on the kitchen doors, his expression darkening when minutes passed without Ann's reappearance.

He leaned toward Ramirez, saying something Ann couldn't hear from her position. The other officer nodded, her expression neutral, hands folded on the table in front of her. Unlike Marcus, Ramirez seemed relaxed, as if this were simply a normal lunch break rather than part of whatever game Marcus was playing.

Ann's heart pounded against her ribs as she watched Miriam approach their table, notepad in hand. Miriam's posture was stiff, her professional smile not reaching her eyes as she took their drink orders. When Marcus spoke to her, gesturing toward the kitchen, Miriam's shoulders tensed visibly.

"He's asking about you," Chef Cho murmured, standing close enough to observe without drawing attention to Ann's position. "Miriam's handling it well."

As if on cue, Tom emerged from his office, his eyes immediately finding the officers' table. Ann watched as Miriam gestured subtly toward him, then retreated to the service station. Tom approached Marcus and Ramirez, his broad shoulders squared, hands clasped behind his back—the stance he took when dealing with difficult customers.

The conversation that unfolded was visible only through body language from Ann's limited vantage point. Tom stood stiffly, nodding occasionally at whatever Marcus was saying. Marcus leaned forward in his chair, one hand on the table, fingers splayed—a position of dominance, of claiming space. Officer Ramirez remained mostly silent, her eyes drifting around the restaurant, occasionally settling on the kitchen doors where Ann hid.

"What are they saying?" Ann whispered to Chef Cho, who had moved closer to the window.

"Can't hear from here," Chef Cho replied, her expression grim. "But your officer doesn't look happy."

Ann flinched at the possessive—"your officer"—but couldn't deny the accuracy of Chef Cho's observation. Marcus's posture had grown increasingly rigid, his gestures more clipped as the conversation with Tom continued. Tom's stance remained firm, though Ann noted the slight shifting of his weight from foot to foot—a tell she recognized from when customers complained about the food.

After what felt like an eternity but was likely only a few minutes, Tom nodded once more and turned toward the kitchen. Ann backed away from the window, her heart hammering so loudly she was certain everyone could hear it. Chef Cho squeezed her shoulder briefly before returning to the grill, leaving Ann standing alone, arms wrapped around herself as if holding her body together by force.

The kitchen door swung open, and Tom entered, his expression troubled. His eyes found Ann immediately, noting her position away from the pass-through, her defensive posture.

"Ann," he said, his voice uncharacteristically gentle. "Can I speak with you?"

"What did he want?" The question burst from her before she could stop herself.

Tom glanced over his shoulder at the closed kitchen door. "He asked where you were. Said he was concerned when he didn't see you on the floor." He paused, his brow furrowing. "He mentioned something about checking on your welfare after your traffic incident the other day."

Ann's chest tightened, the air suddenly insufficient in the warm kitchen. "Did you tell him I'm here?"

"I said you weren't feeling well and were taking a short break,"

Tom replied, studying her face with new intensity. "Ann, he seemed to know an awful lot about your schedule. Asked if you were still planning to close tonight, whether you usually parked in the back lot or the side entrance."

A small sound escaped Ann's throat—not quite a sob, not quite a gasp, but something between the two. "Did he leave?" she managed.

Tom shook his head. "They ordered lunch. He said he'd wait to make sure you're okay before he leaves." He hesitated, then added, "He seems pretty determined to see you."

Ann pressed her back against the cool metal of the prep station, the edge digging into her spine—an anchor point of physical discomfort to distract from the spiraling terror in her mind. Marcus wasn't going to leave. He would wait, watching the kitchen doors, trapping her in the back of the restaurant like a cornered animal.

And he'd brought another officer with him this time—a witness, perhaps. Someone who would see only a concerned colleague checking on a citizen after a traffic incident, not the calculated pursuit that had become Ann's waking nightmare.

Ann pressed herself into the corner of the empty staff room, the hard plastic chair digging uncomfortably into her back as she hunched over her phone. The small space felt like her only sanctuary in the restaurant since Marcus and Officer Ramirez had finally left twenty minutes ago, after lingering over their meal for nearly two hours. She'd remained in the kitchen the entire time, helping Chef Cho prep vegetables, wiping down already clean counters, anything to justify her continued absence from the dining room. Now, during her delayed break, her trembling fingers typed words into her phone's search bar that made her stomach clench: "police officer stalking."

The search results populated her screen instantly—a cascade of links that seemed to pulse with foreboding. "When Your Stalker Wears a Badge." "Police Powers: The Perfect Cover for Predatory

Behavior." "Few Consequences When Cops Stalk, Harass, Threaten Women." Ann's throat tightened as she clicked the first link, scrolling through a detailed article about a Florida woman whose complaints against a police officer were repeatedly dismissed until he broke into her home.

She clicked back and selected another article. This one profiled three separate cases of women stalked by officers who had pulled them over for minor traffic violations—the initial point of contact that had spiraled into months of surveillance, intimidation, and fear. Ann's hands began to shake more violently as she recognized the pattern: traffic stops for infractions that hadn't occurred. Patrol cars driving by homes at odd hours. Officers "coincidentally" appearing at workplaces.

The third article detailed how officers could access driver's license databases, vehicle registrations, and even criminal history systems to gather personal information about their targets. One woman had moved three times, each time finding her stalker had her new address within days. Another had her friends and family members pulled over repeatedly when the officer couldn't locate her directly.

"Jesus," Ann whispered, the word escaping on a shaky exhale as she scrolled further.

The most disturbing section detailed the lack of accountability: police departments investigating their own; officers placed on paid leave, then reinstated. Complaints dismissed for "insufficient evidence." Victims labeled as unstable, attention-seeking, or mentally ill when they persisted in reporting the harassment.

Ann took screenshots of the most relevant sections, creating a new folder on her phone labeled "Research." She added them alongside her growing collection of photos.

The staff room door swung open, and Ann startled violently, nearly dropping her phone. Miriam stood in the doorway, concern etched across her features.

"You okay? Tom's looking for you," she said quietly.

Ann nodded, locking her phone screen with trembling fingers. "Did he say what he wants?"

"Just that he needs to speak with you before you clock out." Miriam hesitated. "They're gone, Ann. Both of them left about twenty minutes ago."

"I know." Ann stood, smoothing her apron with hands that wouldn't quite steady. "I saw them leave from the kitchen window."

As Ann made her way back to the dining room, the knot in her stomach tightened with each step. Tom stood by the host stand, his brow furrowed as he checked reservations on the computer. He glanced up as she approached, his expression shifting to something between concern and frustration.

"There you are," he said, guiding her to a quiet corner near the entrance, his voice low but firm. "We need to talk about what happened earlier."

Ann hugged her arms across her chest, creating a physical barrier between them. "I couldn't face him, Tom. I just couldn't."

"Marcus specifically asked where you were," Tom said, watching her reaction carefully. "He said he was worried about you after pulling you over. Something about you seeming unusually distressed during the stop."

A bitter laugh escaped Ann's throat before she could stop it. "Of course, I was distressed. He's been following me for weeks. Watching my apartment. Driving past my building at two in the morning." Her voice rose slightly before she caught herself, glancing around to ensure no customers were within earshot.

"Ann—"

"I have proof," she interrupted, fumbling with her phone. She pulled up the photos from the previous night, the timestamp clearly visible in the corner. "This is his patrol car outside my apartment at two a.m. Look at the car number—37. The same one that's been following me. The same one my neighbor saw."

Tom took the phone, squinting at the small screen. "It's a patrol car, Ann. They patrol. That's literally their job."

"At two in the morning? Parked in the same spot for over an hour, watching my building?" Ann swiped to the next photo, then the next. "And what about the traffic stop two days ago? I didn't roll through that stop sign, Tom. I was counting in my head, making sure I came to a complete stop specifically so he wouldn't have an excuse to pull me over."

Tom handed back the phone, his expression softening into something that looked uncomfortably like pity. "Ann, are you sure you're not reading too much into this? He seems like a devoted regular to me."

Ann's voice cracked. "Who showed up at my apartment complex at two in the morning?"

"Listen," Tom placed a hand on her shoulder that was clearly meant to be comforting, but felt like a weight pinning her in place. "I've known Marcus for years. He's a good officer with a solid reputation. If he pulled you over, I'm sure he had a reason."

"That's exactly the problem," Ann whispered, the fight suddenly draining from her body. "Everyone thinks he's just a good cop doing his job. No one can see what's happening."

Tom sighed, running a hand through his thinning hair. "Look, finish your shift, go home, and get some rest. Things will seem clearer after a good night's sleep."

Ann nodded mechanically, recognizing the dismissal in his tone. The assumption that she was overreacting, imagining connections that weren't there, creating problems where none existed.

As her shift wound down, Ann moved through her closing duties with mechanical efficiency, her mind racing with the information she'd discovered during her research. Every few minutes, her eyes darted to the windows, scanning the parking lot for white and blue patrol cars.

Just as she finished, movement outside the front window caught her eye. A patrol car cruised slowly past the restaurant, its headlights illuminating the darkening parking lot with sweeping beams. Though she couldn't make out the driver's face or the car number from this distance, Ann's body responded with immediate, visceral recognition—her heart rate doubling, her palms growing damp with cold sweat, and her lungs constricting until breathing became a conscious effort.

She ducked behind the host stand, pressing her back against the wooden structure as if it could shield her from those searching lights. With trembling fingers, she pulled out her phone and called Lena.

"Hey, what's up?" Lena's voice came through, casual and warm.

"Are you still at the restaurant?" Ann whispered, her eyes fixed on the windows where the patrol car's taillights were still visible at the edge of the lot.

"Just left ten minutes ago. I'm almost home. Why?"

"I need a ride," Ann said, the words tumbling out in a desperate rush. "Please. I can't walk to my car alone. He's out there—the patrol car just drove by. I think he's waiting for me to leave."

"Oh, my God, Ann." Lena's tone shifted immediately from casual to concerned. "I'll turn around. Don't leave the building. Stay where there are other people."

"Thank you," Ann whispered, relief momentarily overwhelming her fear. "I'll wait by the kitchen entrance."

As she ended the call, Ann pressed her forehead against the cool wood of the host stand, trying to steady her breathing. She just needed to stay safe for ten more minutes. Then Lena would arrive and would ensure she wasn't alone in the darkened parking lot where Marcus might be waiting.

The patrol car circled back, moving more slowly this time as it passed the restaurant's front entrance. Ann shrank further behind the host stand, making herself as small as possible. Through the window, she could just make out the car number illuminated briefly by the streetlight: 37.

Her documentation folder would gain another entry tonight. Another timestamp. Another sighting. More evidence that would likely be dismissed as a coincidence, as paranoia, as a woman over-reacting to a man's attention.

But Ann knew better. And as she huddled behind the host stand, waiting for Lena's rescue, Ann faced the terrifying reality that her evidence might never be enough until something happened that couldn't be ignored—something she might not survive to document.

Chapter 29

THE BOATHOUSE CREAKED AROUND US, timbers groaning with each gentle rock of the water beneath. We'd fled Sarah's perfect suburban prison before dawn, slipping out through the kitchen door while she and Tommy slept. Now, six hours later, the stench of mildew and fish guts permeated our new sanctuary—an abandoned structure jutting over the murky waters of Copper Bay, far enough from the main channels that casual boaters wouldn't notice us.

Matt was reading the news on his burner phone. His prosthetic leg was propped beside him, giving his residual limb a break after our rushed escape and subsequent hours of searching for a safe location.

Our temporary home was little more than a forgotten fisherman's shelter—rotting floorboards, a partially collapsed roof patched with blue tarp, and the skeletal remains of rod holders mounted to walls that listed dangerously toward the water. We'd pushed moldering crates and broken equipment against one wall to create a small living space, our few belongings arranged with the careful precision of people accustomed to quick departures. Matt played a video.

"Turn it up," I whispered, leaning forward on the overturned bait bucket that served as my seat. The news anchor's mouth moved silently for a moment before Matt found the volume control.

"—breaking news tonight in what police are now calling a pattern of violent murders across Tampa Bay." The anchor's voice emerged from the phone's speaker, his professionally concerned expression giving way to a field reporter standing in front of crime scene tape, red and blue lights pulsing in the background. "We go live to Melissa Chen at the scene downtown."

The reporter's face filled the screen, her expression appropriately somber as wind whipped her hair. "Thank you, Jack. I'm standing just outside the police perimeter where the body of a woman in her forties was discovered less than three hours ago in what authorities are describing as a methodical, execution-style murder with disturbing similarities to the killing of Richard Collins last week."

My breath caught as the screen changed to show the cordoned-off area. Even with the camera keeping a respectful distance, I could make out the chalk outline on the pavement. A sheet-covered form lay at the center of the activity, partially visible as crime scene technicians worked methodically around it.

"Jesus," Matt breathed, his hand reaching instinctively for mine. "This happened right downtown."

The reporter continued, her voice taking on the hushed tone reserved for particularly gruesome details. "Sources close to the investigation tell us that, like Richard Collins, the victim was shot twice in the back with a .38 caliber weapon. However, what makes this case particularly disturbing is that a note was found pinned to the victim's clothing."

The screen showed a blurred image of what appeared to be a piece of paper that was hard to read. But I could make out what looked like my name at the top.

"While police have not released the contents of the note, our sources confirm it was a letter from former FBI agent Eva Rae Thomas, the prime suspect in both murders."

My face appeared on screen—my official FBI photograph from years ago, looking confident and professional in my Bureau jacket.

The image dissolved into a more recent shot from my book jacket, then a grainy surveillance photo that must have been taken in the past week. The collection of images created a visual progression, transforming me from a respected law enforcement officer to a fugitive.

"This is—" I began, but the words died in my throat as the broadcast continued.

"Police are now openly referring to these killings as the work of a serial offender," the reporter said, her expression grave. "Tampa PD has upgraded their advisory, warning that Thomas should be considered armed and extremely dangerous."

Matt cursed under his breath, his fingers tightening around mine as the anchor reappeared, looking directly into the camera. "If you're just joining us, we have breaking news on what police are now calling the 'Profiler Murders.' A second victim has been found, and authorities believe former FBI profiler Eva Rae Thomas is responsible for both killings."

The screen split to show my photograph alongside the crime scene. The juxtaposition made my stomach turn—my face and the shrouded body, linked forever in viewers' minds. The banner across the bottom read: "MANHUNT INTENSIFIES: FORMER FBI PROFILER SUSPECTED IN SERIAL KILLINGS."

"I'm being framed for another murder," I whispered, my voice sounding distant to my own ears. The analytical part of my brain—the part trained through decades of FBI work—continued functioning despite the horror washing over me. "She's escalating, creating a pattern that fits the profile of a serial killer."

Matt's phone rang. He checked the display before answering. "I recognize the number. It's Juan," he acknowledged, his voice low as he put the call on speaker.

"Are you watching the news?" Juan Ramirez's voice crackled through the small speaker, tension evident even through the poor connection.

"We are," Matt confirmed, his eyes never leaving my face.

"It's worse than what they're reporting," Juan said. "The victim was shot twice from behind, just like Collins, but this time there was obvious staging of the body. And the note—" he paused, the silence heavy with implication.

"They're calling you a serial killer now," Juan continued, his voice tense. "Every cop in three counties is looking for you. The FBI has been officially called in. I've never seen a manhunt of this magnitude."

"Well, technically, you have to have killed three people to be called that, but who's counting?" I said.

I opened my own phone and went through the news channels. Each showed variations of the same coverage—my face splashed across the screen with warnings about my dangerous nature, experts speculating about my "psychological break," talking heads discussing my FBI career as if searching for signs of instability that had been there all along.

"They've created a task force," Juan added. "The director held a press conference an hour ago. Your former colleagues are leading the manhunt, Eva Rae."

I closed my eyes briefly, imagining the faces of agents I'd trained, worked alongside, and trusted with my life—now hunting me like an animal. When I opened them again, the television showed split-screen coverage: the crime scene on one side, and on the other, a photograph of me with my daughter at her high school graduation three years ago. The image had been cropped to isolate me, my smile now recontextualized as something sinister.

The water lapped gently against the pilings beneath us, the boathouse shifting with each wave. Like my former life, it was a structure on the verge of collapse, held together by nothing more than stubborn determination and increasingly fragile connections to solid ground.

Chapter 30

MATT ENDED the call with Juan, the phone's screen going dark in his hand like a snuffed candle. I stared at my own face on the news—a face now synonymous with murder in the minds of millions. Outside, the wind picked up, sending ripples across the bay water and causing our fragile shelter to protest with creaks and groans. Matt pushed himself to his feet, reattaching his prosthetic with quick, practiced movements before pacing the narrow confines of our hideout, his footsteps heavy on the weathered planks.

"We need to get as far away from Tampa as possible," he said, his voice tight with controlled urgency. "North Carolina, maybe even further. Somewhere they won't be looking." He gestured toward the door. "Juan has contacts who can get us new identities. We disappear, regroup, figure out our next move from somewhere safe."

I remained seated, watching him move back and forth across the uneven floorboards. Five steps one way, turn, five steps back—a caged tiger measuring the limits of his confinement. The news anchor continued speaking, but I reached over and silenced him with a press of the button. The sudden quiet amplified the sounds of our refuge—water slapping against the pilings, wind whistling through gaps in the walls, the distant call of a night bird somewhere along the shore.

"We can't leave," I said finally, my voice calm despite the storm of emotions beneath the surface. "Not yet."

Matt stopped pacing, turning to face me with disbelief etched across his features. "Did you miss the part where every law enforcement officer in Florida is hunting for you? Where they've just upgraded you from suspect to serial killer?" He ran his hand through his hair— his tell when frustration threatened to overwhelm him.

"Rule One of The Profiler's Code," I replied, meeting his gaze steadily. "Trust the evidence, not the narrative." I leaned forward, resting my elbows on my knees. "The narrative says I'm killing people execution-style and leaving notes. The evidence—if we could access it—would tell a different story."

"Eva—" he began, but I continued, my voice gathering strength as I spoke.

"Sarah Winters is behind this," I said, certainty hardening my tone. "She killed Collins. She killed this woman. She's systematically framing me, and if we run now, she wins. I'll never clear my name."

Matt's shoulders sagged slightly, his expression shifting from frustration to concern. "I know you think it's Sarah. And after what we saw in her house last night, I believe she's involved. But staying here is suicide."

I stood. "Think about it, Matt. Sarah knew Collins." I tapped the printed emails. "Someone was stalking him—someone whose writing exhibits classic erotomanic fixation patterns. Then he ends up dead the night after meeting with Sarah."

"Didn't he get a restraining order against the stalker? Why would he meet with Sarah if she was the stalker?" he asked. "If he had a restraining order against her?"

"Maybe he got a restraining order against the wrong person?" I said. "Maybe because Sarah was using burner phones, he thought it was someone else? Maybe he thought he could trust Sarah, but he couldn't."

"And since he refused her advances, she murdered him. Yeah, that makes sense," Matt said.

"In the mind of a very sick individual, it would."

The boathouse creaked around us as I walked to the opposite wall, where we'd taped up photographs and notes—our own investigation board, pieced together from scraps of evidence we'd managed to gather.

"Remember when we first went on the run? When I'd just been accused of Collins' murder?" I turned to face Matt, watching realization dawn on his face. "Sarah said she wanted to help clear my name."

Matt nodded slowly. "She seemed so genuine."

"Too genuine. Too prepared." I traced my finger along a timeline we'd created. "She had burner phones in her drawer. A wall covered with information about me. She knew my coffee preferences." I turned to face him fully. "She wasn't helping us, Matt. She was tracking us."

"Even if you're right—"

"I am right," I interrupted, certainty burning through me like a flame. "She orchestrated this entire frame. She's been planning it for quite some time, probably."

"Fine," Matt conceded, stepping closer. "Let's say she's behind everything. That's even more reason to get distance. We can gather evidence remotely, work through Juan, build our case from somewhere she can't reach us."

"No," I shook my head firmly. "We need proximity. We need to catch her making a mistake."

Outside, rain began to fall, light drops becoming a steady patter against the weathered roof. A tarp covering part of the ceiling billowed slightly with each gust of wind, water collecting in its center before spilling onto the floor in the corner. The storm was picking up, mirroring the tension in our small space.

"This is your life we're talking about," Matt said, his voice rising slightly. "Your freedom. Your future. Our children's future. We can't gamble that on the hope that a meticulous killer who's planned this for years will suddenly make a convenient mistake."

"She will," I countered, moving to stand directly in front of him. "Her obsession with details makes her vulnerable. She's not just framing me; she's playing a game with me."

The wind howled suddenly, sending a spray of water through a gap in the wall. Matt flinched as droplets hit his face, but I continued, my voice low and intense.

"Sarah sees this as some twisted courtship. Collins rejected her, and she eliminated him. Now she's eliminating what she sees as obstacles between you and her. She wants me discredited, imprisoned, or dead so she can create space for her fantasy life with you."

Matt's expression darkened. "The comment about Tommy needing a father figure."

"Exactly." I nodded. "This isn't just about framing me. It's about claiming you. In her mind, she's creating a vacancy in your life that she can fill." I reached out, my fingers brushing his arm. "If we run, she'll follow. And she'll keep killing to maintain the narrative she's creating."

The boathouse gave another protesting groan as the thunderstorm intensified outside. Water had begun to seep through cracks in the floorboards, forming small puddles. Matt looked down at my hand on his arm, then back to my face.

"So, what's your plan?" he asked, his resistance softening slightly. "We can't exactly walk into police headquarters with theories about Sarah's obsession."

"We need concrete evidence that links her to the murders," I said, stepping back toward our makeshift investigation board. "Proof she was stalking Collins. What's her connection to the second victim? Anything that disrupts the narrative she's—"

The distinct sound of footsteps on the wooden dock outside cut through my words—heavy, deliberate steps approaching the boathouse door. We both froze. Matt extinguished the lamp with one quick movement, plunging us into darkness.

The footsteps stopped directly outside our door. A pause, pregnant with threat. Then, the unmistakable sound of the rusted latch being tested from the outside.

Chapter 31

THEN:

Ann paused outside Granger's front entrance, her fingertips still burning with the memory of the small electronic device she'd discovered beneath her car the night before. A tracking device. This was how he knew where she was at all times.

She hadn't driven to work today—couldn't bear to sit in the vehicle that had been violated, transformed from transportation into surveillance. Instead, she'd asked Miriam to pick her up, had spent the fifteen-minute ride obsessively checking the rearview mirror for patrol car 37. The restaurant's familiar façade should have offered comfort, the routine of her job a respite from the growing nightmare of Marcus Hale's surveillance. Instead, she found herself scanning the parking lot for the patrol car with the telltale dent in its bumper, before forcing herself to push through the door.

The restaurant's interior enveloped her in familiar scents—fresh coffee, bacon from the breakfast rush, Chef Cho's signature soup simmering for the lunch crowd. Ann inhaled deeply, momentarily steadied by the ordinary. Her fingers moved automatically to tie her apron strings as she stepped past the hostess stand, nodding mechanically at the morning hostess who was gathering menus for the shift change.

Then she saw them.

Her body registered their presence before her conscious mind processed it—muscles seizing, lungs forgetting their rhythm, blood draining from her face with such speed that dark spots danced at the edges of her vision. Marcus Hale and Officer Ramirez sat at table eight, directly in the center of her assigned section. They'd positioned themselves with perfect tactical advantage: Marcus facing the main entrance, Ramirez with a clear view of both the kitchen doors and the employee entrance. Marcus's coffee cup was already half empty, suggesting they'd arrived well before her shift began and had deliberately established their presence in her territory.

Ann's order pad slipped from suddenly nerveless fingers, clattering against the hardwood floor. The sound drew Marcus's attention, his head turning with the fluid precision of a predator sensing movement. Their eyes locked across the restaurant, and the small, knowing smile that curved his lips sent ice spreading through her veins. He nodded once, a gesture that might have appeared friendly to anyone else but carried unmistakable meaning to Ann: I'm watching you. I'll always be watching you.

She broke eye contact with physical effort, stooping to retrieve her pad with trembling hands. Keeping her head down, she scanned the restaurant for Lena, desperate for an ally in the suddenly hostile space. The morning shift servers were gathering their things, preparing to clock out as the lunch crew filtered in. Ann spotted Lena near the service station, loading sugar packets into small ceramic containers, her dark hair escaping its practical bun as she worked.

Ann crossed to her with quick, jerky steps, her back crawling with the weight of Marcus's gaze tracking her movement.

"Lena," she whispered, her voice cracking. She gripped Lena's forearm with fingers that dug too deeply and would leave marks. "Please switch sections with me. I can't—I just can't serve him today."

Lena looked up, startled by the intensity of Ann's grip. "What? Who—" Her gaze followed Ann's quick, fearful glance toward table eight, understanding blooming in her expression as she registered Marcus and Ramirez. "Oh. Him."

"Please," Ann repeated, her voice barely audible now, desperation evident in every syllable. "Section four is empty right now. You can have all my tips from the other tables. I just—I can't go over there. Not after I found a tracker under my car."

Lena studied Ann's face, taking in her pallor, the slight tremor visible in her jaw, the way her eyes kept darting nervously toward Marcus's table before skittering away, like a wounded animal afraid to look directly at a predator.

"A tracking device?" Lena said slowly, keeping her voice low. "You think he—"

"I know he did," Ann interrupted, the words tumbling out in a desperate rush. "Who else would it be? He's a cop. He has access to that kind of equipment. And now he's here, with another officer as witness, trying to make it look like a casual lunch, but it's not, Lena. It's not."

Lena hesitated, glancing toward the officers' table. Ramirez was laughing at something Marcus had said, her expression relaxed and natural. Marcus's posture appeared casual, one arm draped over the back of his chair, but his eyes remained fixed on Ann's back with an intensity that belied his seemingly relaxed demeanor.

"Okay," Lena said finally, squeezing Ann's arm. "I'll take section two. You take four."

Relief washed through Ann with such force that her knees nearly buckled. "Thank you," she breathed, gratitude making her voice tremble. "Thank you."

Throughout her shift, Ann maintained a careful orbit around the restaurant floor, always positioning herself with at least one wall at her back, always keeping Marcus in her peripheral vision while pretending to focus on her tables. She moved with deliberate efficiency between the coffee station and her section, taking the long route that kept her farthest from table eight. Her shoulders remained hunched forward, an unconscious protective posture, her spine rigid with the effort of appearing normal while her instincts screamed danger.

Lena approached Marcus's table with professional detachment, notepad in hand, maintaining the polite but impersonal manner she used with difficult customers. From across the restaurant, Ann watched as Marcus's expression shifted from surprise to something harder, more calculating, as he registered the change in servers. He said something to Lena, his head tilting slightly in Ann's direction, and Lena responded with a tight smile and a shrug that Ann recognized as deliberately casual.

As the lunch rush intensified around her, Ann found herself tracking Marcus's movements with hyperaware precision. She noted how his eyes followed her path between tables, his head turning with measured restraint that wouldn't be obvious to anyone not watching for it. Whenever she emerged from the kitchen or approached the service station, his conversation with Ramirez would pause momentarily, both heads turning slightly in her direction before resuming their discussion.

At one point, while refilling water glasses for an elderly couple in her section, Ann glanced up to find Marcus and Ramirez with their heads bent close together, Marcus speaking in low tones that didn't carry across the restaurant. When Tom approached their table to check on their meal, their conversation stopped abruptly. Marcus leaned back in his chair with an easy smile that transformed his face into something almost charming. The moment Tom moved away, Marcus's expression returned to its previous intensity, eyes seeking Ann across the room as if drawn by magnetic force.

A cold weight settled in Ann's stomach as she realized the restaurant—once her sanctuary, the place where her routine had provided structure and safety—had been invaded. Marcus had colonized her workspace just as he'd colonized her sense of security, her freedom of movement, her peace of mind. Even here, surrounded by coworkers and customers, with Lena acting as a buffer, she wasn't safe from his watching eyes.

The realization pressed down on her chest like a physical weight, making each breath an effort as she moved between tables with mechanical efficiency, her mind racing with terrifying questions: What would he do next? How far would he go? And would anyone believe her before it was too late?

Ann's hands shook as she lined up salt shakers on the service counter, her motions mechanical while her attention remained fixed on table eight. Officer Ramirez stood, leaning slightly toward Marcus to murmur something Ann couldn't hear before gesturing toward the restroom hallway. Marcus nodded, his posture shifting subtly as his colleague walked away, leaving him momentarily alone. Without Ramirez's presence as a social buffer, something in his demeanor changed—a predator no longer needing to maintain the appearance of casualness. He straightened in his chair, his gaze sweeping the restaurant with new intensity before he reached into his pocket and pulled out his phone.

Ann's fingers froze on a half-filled shaker as Marcus lifted the device, not to his ear as if making a call, but out in front of him. He angled it first toward the main entrance, then in a slow, methodical sweep across the dining room. His movements had a practiced precision, the deliberate documentation of someone building a visual record rather than a customer taking casual photos of their meal.

The salt granules scattered across the counter as Ann's grip faltered. She watched, breath caught in her throat, as Marcus turned slightly in his chair, directing his phone toward the kitchen doors, capturing their location, the staff who moved through them. He paused, adjusted his position, then aimed the camera toward the employee entrance, the side exit leading to the parking lot, and the narrow hallway housing the restrooms.

He was mapping the restaurant, documenting its layout and points of egress and entry, and creating a tactical assessment of her workplace.

When he swiveled again, pointing his phone toward the service station where Ann stood, she ducked instinctively, her body responding before her conscious mind processed the threat. Salt crystals crunched under her palms as she pressed herself against the counter, momentarily hidden from his direct line of sight. The realization of what she'd just witnessed crashed over her like ice water—Marcus wasn't just watching her. He was documenting her environment, preparing for something more.

Ann's chest tightened, each breath becoming a conscious effort as the implications unfurled in her mind. A police officer photographing a restaurant wouldn't raise suspicions. If questioned, he could claim official business, a security assessment, or any number of plausible explanations that would satisfy casual observers. But Ann knew better. Those photos weren't for any police file; they were for his personal documentation of her movements, her routines, her escape routes.

She abandoned the salt shakers, wiping her trembling hands on her apron as she scanned the restaurant with growing desperation. Lena was in the kitchen. Chef Cho was focused on the lunch rush. Tom was nowhere to be seen. Her eyes settled on Daniel Reed, seated at his usual spot at the counter, legal papers spread before him as he ate his solitary lunch.

Daniel had been coming to Granger's for years and was respected in the community as an attorney with connections throughout the local justice system. If anyone might understand the legal implications of what she'd just witnessed, might have the authority to be taken seriously, it would be him.

Ann approached his spot at the counter, her steps quickening as she saw Marcus lower his phone, checking the images he'd captured. Daniel glanced up at her approach, his usual polite smile fading as he registered the tension in her face.

"Everything alright, Ann?" he asked, setting down his fork. "You look a bit pale."

"Daniel," she whispered, leaning close to avoid being overheard, acutely aware of Marcus's presence across the restaurant. "That police officer over there—I think he's stalking me."

Daniel's eyebrows rose slightly, his gaze shifting toward table eight, where Marcus now appeared absorbed in his phone.

"The one who comes in for coffee during his lunch break most days?" he asked, his tone careful, neutral.

"Yes." Ann's voice caught, the word emerging as barely more than a breath. "He's been following me for weeks now. Driving past my apartment at night. Pulling me over for traffic violations that didn't happen." Her words tumbled out in a desperate rush. "And now—just now—he was taking pictures of the restaurant. All the exits. The staff areas. Where I work."

Daniel studied her face for a long moment, his expression shifting from concern to something that looked uncomfortably like condescension.

"That's Officer Hale, isn't it?" he said finally, his voice lowering to match her whispered tone, though the gravity she'd hoped for was missing. "Marcus Hale?"

Ann nodded, hope flaring briefly that Daniel recognized the name and might know something about him that could help her case.

"Sounds like you've got yourself an admirer, Ann," Daniel said, his lips curving into a dismissive smile that extinguished her hope like fingers pinching out a candle flame. "Most women would be flattered by attention from a man in uniform."

The familiar refrain—the same dismissive response Tom had given her, that so many others had offered when she'd tried to explain her fears—hit Ann like a physical blow. Her mouth opened to protest, to explain the difference between admiration and obsession, between attention and surveillance, but the words died in her throat as she registered the look in Daniel's eyes. He wasn't taking her seriously. Wouldn't take her seriously.

"It's not—" she began, desperate to make him understand.

"He's just doing his job, Ann," Daniel interrupted, his tone gentle but patronizing, as if explaining something simple to a child. "Police officers maintain awareness of their environments. It's their training." He gestured vaguely toward where Marcus sat. "He's probably just security-conscious. Checking exits, entry points. It becomes a habit for them."

Ann's hands clenched at her sides, nails digging half-moons into her palms. Another person who couldn't—or wouldn't—see what was happening right in front of them. Another potential ally lost to the plausible deniability that Marcus so carefully maintained.

"But—" she tried again, only to be cut off by a sharp tapping sound from the corner of the restaurant.

Mrs. Mendez sat at her usual table, teaspoon clicking deliberately against her coffee cup as she stared directly at Ann. The elderly woman's eyes were keen and knowing, her mouth set in a firm line as she gestured imperiously for service.

"Your regular in the corner seems to need something," Daniel said, clearly relieved by the interruption. He turned back to his legal papers, effectively dismissing Ann and her concerns in one practiced movement. "Maybe bring me the check when you have a moment?"

Ann stood frozen for a second longer, the weight of Daniel's dismissal settling heavily across her shoulders. Even here, surrounded by people, she was alone with her fear. Isolated by the very plausibility of Marcus's behavior, by the respectability his uniform provided, by the natural inclination of others to believe there must be a rational explanation for what she was experiencing.

The tapping grew more insistent. Ann turned away from Daniel, blinking rapidly to dispel the burn of frustrated tears that threatened to form. As she moved toward the corner table, she felt Marcus's gaze tracking her, knew without looking that he'd observed her conversation with Daniel, and was likely assessing whether this interaction posed a threat to his surveillance.

Her isolation had never felt more complete, more terrifying.

Chapter 32

THE FOOTSTEPS STOPPED. Three heartbeats of silence followed, heavy and expectant. Matt and I exchanged a glance in the near-darkness, years of partnership allowing us to communicate without words. We both knew who might have found us—Sarah, the police, or someone else entirely. None of those possibilities promised anything but danger.

The latch rattled again, more insistently this time. Matt moved silently to position himself behind the door, his back against the wall, while I crouched behind an overturned fishing crate, ignoring the protest from my still-tender wound.

A gust of wind howled around the boathouse, the sound nearly masking the metallic snap of the lock giving way. Nearly, but not quite. The door flew open with a splintering crack that echoed across the water.

Moonlight spilled through the doorway, silhouetting a massive figure that filled the frame. I recognized him instantly—Victor Reeves, "The Collector." The man who'd watched us escape from the motel days ago, the volatile ex-security contractor with the silver ring that left distinctive marks on his victims.

My heart hammered against my ribs as I assessed the tactical situation with cold precision. Victor blocked our only obvious exit. His size and known combat experience made physical confrontation a last resort. The boathouse windows were too small for a quick escape, and the water beneath offered minimal cover for a retreat. In the dim light, I could make out the bulk of his shoulders, the military stance, the slight forward lean that suggested readiness to lunge.

Matt shifted his weight imperceptibly, angling his body to create a barrier between Victor and me despite the obvious disadvantage he faced. The slight sound drew Victor's attention, his head turning toward Matt's position. I seized that split-second of distraction, rising from behind the crate, standing behind him with a metal pipe pushed against his spine, a make-believe gun.

"Don't move," I commanded, my voice steady despite the adrenaline coursing through my system.

Victor froze, his features becoming clearer as my eyes adjusted. His breathing was controlled, but rapid, nostrils flaring slightly with each exhale. His hands—capable of inflicting the devastating damage I'd seen in crime scene photos—hung at his sides.

Then, to my astonishment, he slowly raised them in a gesture of surrender.

"I'm not here to hurt you," he said, his voice a gravelly rumble that seemed to vibrate through the floorboards beneath my feet. "I'm here to warn you. She's coming for you next."

The statement hung in the air between us, unexpected enough to momentarily disrupt my focus. Matt had emerged from his position, moving to stand slightly. I felt rather than saw his protective stance, his body angled to absorb any potential attack.

"Who's coming?" Matt demanded, though I suspected we both knew the answer.

"Sarah Winters," Victor replied, his hands still raised, palms forward.

"Why should we believe you?" I kept my fake weapon trained on him, unwavering. "Your own history with violence doesn't exactly inspire trust."

"I'm not asking you to trust me, Agent Thomas. I'm warning

you." His silver ring caught the light again as he slowly lowered his hands to waist level. "Sarah Winters is not who you think she is."

"We know exactly who she is," Matt said, his voice taut with suspicion. "What we don't know is why you're really here."

Another gust of wind buffeted the boathouse, sending ripples across the water beneath us. The moonlight filtering through the broken windows cast long, distorted shadows across the warped wooden floor, giving Victor's substantial form an even more menacing appearance. Yet something in his demeanor had shifted—a subtle change in posture that suggested vulnerability rather than threat.

"I've been watching you," he admitted, confirming what I'd already known. "But not for the reasons you think."

"Enlighten us," I said, ignoring the growing ache in my arm as I maintained my aim. "Quickly."

"Could you lower your weapon, please?" he said.

I lowered the pipe and put it in the pocket of my jacket. "No funny business."

Matt tensed beside me, ready to intercept any sudden movement. Water dripped steadily from a leak in the roof, marking time in the tense silence.

"Sarah hired me months ago," Victor explained, his voice dropping lower. "Said she needed security, protection from a stalker. But that wasn't the whole truth." He looked directly at me. "She wanted me to watch someone for her. Richard Collins."

The name of the murdered accountant sent a chill through me that had nothing to do with the damp night air.

"And now she's hired me again," Victor continued, urgency threading through his words. "To find you. To finish what she started."

I narrowed my eyes, searching for the lie in his statement. But what I saw instead was fear—genuine fear in the eyes of a man whose file described him as pathologically incapable of remorse or empathy.

"She killed that second woman," Victor said. "She told me about how she shot her in the back of the head. She placed the body downtown at night in a parking lot where it would be easy to find. She left your name on the body in a letter confirming your guilt and remorse, having you ask to be stopped, that you know you're out of control. And she's not finished."

The boathouse creaked around us, timbers protesting against the strengthening wind. I was weighing his words against everything we'd discovered about Sarah Winters—her obsessive wall of news clippings about me, her secret connection to Collins, her carefully constructed façade of normality hiding something deeply disturbed beneath.

"How do we know you're not working with her?" Matt challenged, still positioned protectively between us.

Victor's scarred face hardened. "You can't," he answered simply. "But I'm here, aren't I?"

The wind howled louder, rattling the loose boards of our shelter. In that moment, I had to make a choice—trust the violent man with a history of threats against me, or dismiss his warning and potentially miss crucial information about the woman who was systematically destroying my life.

Chapter 33

"IF I WANTED to hurt you, I wouldn't have announced myself. I would have come in with my weapon pulled."

In my experience, trust had to be earned, especially from a man whose file contained three years for assault, several restraining orders, and a history of explosive violence. But something in Victor's eyes—a haunted quality I recognized from interviewing witnesses who'd seen things they wished they hadn't—made me curious enough to listen, if not to lower my guard.

"Keep talking," I instructed, "but stay where you are."

Victor nodded once, accepting my terms. "Sarah Winters contacted me when I got out four months ago. Said she needed security work—discreet surveillance, no questions asked." His fingers brushed against his silver ring, turning it absently as he spoke. "She claimed Collins was obsessed with her, that he was following her, texting her, leaving notes at her bookstore. I thought it would be easy money."

Matt shifted beside me, his prosthetic leg making a barely audible adjustment on the warped floorboards. "And you believed her?"

"She paid well," Victor replied with a shrug that conveyed both defensiveness and shame. "And she had evidence—photographs of him that she said were taken outside of her home, copies of emails he'd supposedly sent. It looked legitimate enough."

I studied Victor's body language as he spoke. The slight downward cast of his eyes when mentioning the evidence suggested embarrassment—not at lying now, but at having been fooled then.

"What kind of surveillance did she want?" I asked, keeping my voice neutral despite the growing knot of tension in my stomach.

"Standard stuff at first. Where he went, who he met with. She said she needed documentation for a restraining order." Victor's face hardened. "Then things got weird. She wanted me to plant things in his apartment—receipts, movie tickets, even women's underwear."

My mind immediately connected this to the emails we'd found in Collins' account—the ones from an apparent stalker claiming to know intimate details about his life, his habits. "She was creating evidence that he was the stalker," I murmured, more to myself than to the men in the room.

Victor nodded. "It escalated fast. She started asking me to take photos of him sleeping." His expression turned grim. "That's when I knew something wasn't right."

Matt and I exchanged glances, both recognizing the pattern. Sarah had been manufacturing evidence against Collins the same way she was now framing me—meticulously, obsessively, leaving a trail of breadcrumbs for investigators to follow toward her preferred conclusion.

"Did you do it?" Matt's question carried an edge of judgment.

Victor's jaw tightened. "Some of it. Not the photos while he was sleeping—even I have standards." He shifted his weight, his massive frame casting a longer shadow across the floor as the moon moved behind a cloud. "By then, I was getting uncomfortable with the whole arrangement. I told her I was done."

"How did she react?" I asked, recognizing the critical moment in the narrative.

"She doubled my fee." Victor's laugh held no humor. "Said she just needed a few more weeks of surveillance. Then she started asking questions about you."

The revelation sent a chill through me despite the fact that I'd half-expected it. "What kind of questions?"

"At first, just professional stuff. Your investigation methods and cases you'd worked on. Said she was researching for a true crime book." Victor's expression darkened. "Then she wanted details about your personal life: where you lived, your relationship with Miller here."

"When did you realize what she was really doing?"

"The night Collins died." Victor's voice dropped lower, his eyes taking on that haunted quality again. "She called me, hysterical, saying Collins had attacked her. Asked me to come to her house right away." He rubbed his scarred jaw, the memory clearly disturbing him. "When I got there, she was perfectly calm. She had a drink waiting for me. Collins was already dead in her garage. She told me she had gone to his house for dinner, then shot him in the back and took him with her back home."

Matt stepped forward, his disbelief evident. "And you what—helped her dispose of the body? Did you put it in Eva Rae's trunk?"

"No." Victor's denial came sharp and immediate. "I walked out. Told her I wasn't getting involved in murder."

"Why are you telling us this now?" I demanded, needing to understand his motivation before I could trust anything he said.

"Because she's gone completely off the rails." Victor's voice took on an urgency that seemed genuine. "She's convinced herself that once you're gone, she and Miller can create some kind of perfect family with her kid. I think her obsession with you, Eva Rae, has made her believe she is you, and she wants to take over your life."

I remembered Sarah's words through the guest room wall: "Tommy needs a proper father figure." The memory made my skin crawl.

"I need specifics," I pressed, sensing there was more Victor wasn't telling us. "Anything that could help us prove she's behind the killings. Did you see evidence? Hear her confess? Were there witnesses?"

Victor's expression changed subtly, a flicker of something crossing his face. "I think she has a—"

The sharp crack of gunfire cut through his words. Glass exploded inward as a bullet shattered one of the few intact windows. Victor ducked instinctively, his military training evident in the fluid movement.

"Get down!" Matt shouted, already moving toward me as a second shot splintered the wooden wall just inches from my head.

I dropped to the floor, rolling behind the cover of the overturned crate as more bullets peppered the boathouse. The sound of splintering wood and breaking glass filled the small space as our fragile sanctuary came under attack.

Victor had flattened himself against the wall beside the door, his expression grim but unsurprised. He caught my eye across the room, his face illuminated by muzzle flashes from outside.

"It's her," he growled, the confirmation unnecessary as another volley of bullets tore through the boathouse walls.

The attack confirmed his warnings more effectively than any words could have. Sarah Winters had found us, and she had come to finish what she'd started.

Chapter 34

ANOTHER SPRAY of bullets tore through the boathouse wall, sending splinters flying across the room like deadly confetti. I pressed myself lower behind the crate, feeling the wound in my side scream in protest. Across the small space, Matt had taken cover behind an ancient outboard motor, his eyes meeting mine in a silent question: What now? We were rapidly running out of options. The tactical part of my brain calculated our survival odds as increasingly dismal with each passing second.

"Stay down!" Victor barked, his voice cutting through the chaos of splintering wood and shattering glass. He crouched by the doorway, surprisingly agile for a man his size, peering cautiously around the frame before jerking back as another shot punched through the spot where his head had been moments before.

Victor suddenly moved, not toward us but deeper into the boathouse, gesturing urgently with one hand. "There's a hatch under that tarp!" he shouted over the gunfire. "Back corner!"

I stared at him in momentary confusion, my FBI training screaming that this was a trap—that Victor was herding us into a corner where we'd be easier targets. Yet his actions contradicted everything in his psychological profile. The Victor Reeves in our files wouldn't risk himself to help federal agents; he'd be more likely to use us as human shields.

"Why are you helping us?" I demanded, even as another volley of bullets forced me to duck lower.

"Stop being so stubborn, for crying out loud. I'm trying to help you here. Because she used me!" Victor's face contorted with a rage I recognized wasn't directed at us. "Is that what you want to hear? She made me part of her sick game. Now, move!" He punctuated his command by firing back through the shattered window, providing cover fire with a handgun.

Matt caught my eye, silently communicating that we had few options. Staying meant certain capture or death. The water beneath the boathouse offered our only realistic chance, even if Victor's motives remained unclear. He grabbed our backpack with supplies, then signaled to me that it was time.

"Go," I mouthed to Matt, gesturing toward the back corner where a moldy blue tarp lay crumpled against the wall. He nodded once and began moving in a combat crawl, staying as low as possible while bullets continued to tear through the fragile wooden structure around us.

I followed, wincing as my injured side scraped against the rough floorboards. Each movement sent fresh pain radiating across my ribcage, but the alternative—remaining exposed to increasingly accurate gunfire—provided powerful motivation to ignore the discomfort.

We reached the tarp as Victor continued providing sporadic cover fire, his massive frame still positioned between us and the main assault. Matt yanked away the heavy canvas, revealing a square wooden hatch set into the floor. Decades of salt water and humidity had swollen the wood, making it stick in its frame.

"Pull harder!" Victor shouted, ejecting an empty magazine and slamming a fresh one into his weapon with practiced efficiency. "There's a drop to the water, about six feet!"

Matt braced himself against an old equipment rack and pulled with both hands. The hatch resisted, then surrendered with a groan of protesting wood. Cold, damp air rushed up from the opening, carrying the briny smell of the bay. Below, black water lapped against the pilings, invisible in the darkness beneath the structure.

Victor cursed, shifting position to fire back, when a bullet caught him high in the shoulder. The impact spun him halfway around, his face registering shock more than pain.

"Victor!" The shout escaped me before I could consider it, an instinctive response to seeing someone wounded, regardless of their past.

Blood spread across his shirt with alarming speed, but he waved off my concern with his good arm. "Go! Now!" he commanded, pressing his opposite hand against the wound. Despite the injury, he maintained his position, his body effectively shielding our escape route.

I hesitated, my gaze locked on Victor. The man who'd threatened me during his trial years ago was now bleeding to protect our escape. "Why?" I asked again, needing to understand even as bullets continued to shred our surroundings.

Victor's scarred face twisted into what might have been a smile in other circumstances. "Maybe I want redemption," he said, then fired another shot through the window. "Or maybe I just hate being manipulated more than I hate federal agents. What does it matter? Now, go!"

Matt's hand found mine, tugging me toward the hatch. "We need to move," he insisted, his eyes conveying what his words didn't —that staying would waste Victor's sacrifice.

I nodded, and moved toward the hatch. A final glance at Victor showed him reloading again, his movements slightly slower as blood loss began taking its toll. Our eyes met briefly, and I saw something I never expected to find in "The Collector"—a grim acceptance of consequences.

Another bullet splintered the wood near his head, showering him with debris. "Get underwater as soon as you hit. Swim under the dock to the east."

The tactical advice cemented my decision. I slipped through the hatch, hanging momentarily from the edge before letting go. The fall was brief, the shock of cold water intense as it closed over my head. My clothes immediately became waterlogged, dragging me deeper before I kicked back toward the surface.

I broke through just in time to see Matt drop through the hatch above, his body silhouetted briefly against the fractured ceiling of the boathouse before he plunged into the dark water beside me. Above us, the gunfire continued, punctuated by Victor's increasingly sporadic return fire.

The water was frigid, stealing my breath and sending sharp pains through my injured side. Matt surfaced beside me with barely a splash, his eyes immediately finding mine. No words were necessary—we both understood the gravity of what had just happened. Victor Reeves, the man I'd helped put away years ago, had just risked his life to save ours.

As we began to swim silently toward the eastern side of the dock as instructed, the boathouse behind us erupted in a new frenzy of gunfire. I couldn't tell whether Victor was still returning fire. Either way, his intervention had bought us precious minutes—and possibly revealed the key to unraveling Sarah's frame once and for all.

If we survived long enough.

Chapter 35

MATT'S HAND found my arm underwater, squeezing gently to get my attention before pointing toward the eastern shore where a cluster of seagrapes offered potential cover. I nodded, understanding his plan without words—we would stay submerged as much as possible, surfacing only for quick, silent breaths as we made our way to concealment.

We pushed off from the pier's shadow, using gentle, muffled strokes that barely disturbed the water's surface. The cold bit deeper with each passing second, numbing my fingers and sending shivers through my core. My wounded side throbbed in protest against the exertion, but I channeled the pain into focus, using it to keep my mind sharp despite the hypothermia gradually setting in.

Fifteen feet from the pier, I paused to tread water, taking another carefully controlled breath as I scanned our surroundings. The boathouse was now silhouetted against the night sky, its damaged structure creaking in the wind. No movement was visible through the shattered windows. No flashes of gunfire. No sign of Victor. The stillness felt calculated rather than coincidental—the quiet before another storm.

That's when I saw her.

A figure had appeared at the edge of the dock, illuminated by the same moonlight that had earlier revealed Victor in the doorway. Sarah Winters stood motionless, staring out across the water, her posture relaxed despite the violence she had just orchestrated. She wore dark clothing—practical for a night operation—with her hair pulled back in a neat ponytail. Even from a distance, I could see that she held a gun at her side with the comfortable familiarity of someone who knew how to use it.

What struck me most, however, was her expression. The Sarah I knew—or thought I knew—had always maintained a certain softness in her features, a helpful warmth in her eyes. That mask had fallen away completely. In its place was something predatory, almost hungry. Her lips curved in a smile that contained no warmth, only satisfaction. Her eyes scanned the water's surface with the calculated patience of a hunter tracking wounded prey.

I'd interviewed dozens of killers during my FBI career, had stared into the eyes of people who had committed unimaginable acts. I recognized what I was seeing now—the unguarded moment when a predator believes they're unobserved, when the performance drops away, and the true nature emerges. Sarah's transformation was so complete that she might have been a different person entirely from the warm bookstore owner who had served us cookies in her perfect suburban kitchen.

Matt tugged at my sleeve, urging me to keep moving. I followed his lead, pushing through the water with increasingly numb limbs. Each stroke sent fresh pain radiating from my injured side, but I focused on survival rather than suffering.

Sarah moved along the dock, her movements unhurried, confident. She held something in her other hand—a flashlight, which she now switched on, sweeping its beam across the water's surface in methodical passes. The light reflected off the gentle waves, creating deceptive patterns that would make it difficult to distinguish swimmers from natural movement. Her technique suggested training or research—one more detail that didn't align with the persona of a simple bookstore owner.

"She's hunting," I thought, the professional part of my brain continuing to analyze even as my body fought the cold water. Not searching in panic or anger, but hunting with precision and patience. This wasn't impulsive violence but calculated elimination of obstacles. In her mind, I was simply a problem to solve on her path to the life she believed she deserved.

Chapter 36

THEN:

The lunch rush hit Granger's like high tide—a surge of humanity filling every table, their collective voices creating a wall of sound that Ann used to find comforting. She moved between tables with practiced efficiency, her smile fixed in place. Each time the door opened, her shoulders tightened imperceptibly, her body braced for the moment she knew would eventually come.

Marcus Hale stood in the doorway, the afternoon sunlight casting him in silhouette for a moment before he stepped fully inside. Ann's hand froze mid-pour, water hovering dangerously close to overflowing the customer's glass as she watched Marcus scan the restaurant with deliberate thoroughness. Not searching, she realized—he already knew exactly where she was. The survey was performative, establishing his presence, letting her know he was aware of everyone and everything in the space.

The hostess approached with a practiced smile, menus in hand. Ann couldn't hear their exchange over the dining room chatter, but she saw the moment Marcus gestured in her direction, saw the hostess's expression shift to uncertainty as she consulted her seating chart.

"Everything okay?" The customer's question jolted Ann back to awareness.

"Yes, sorry." She completed the pour with a jerky motion, then stepped away from the table, moving toward the kitchen with swift, urgent steps. She needed a moment, just one moment to breathe before—

"Ann." Tom's voice caught her near the service station, his hand settling briefly on her arm. His expression was troubled, brow furrowed with lines that hadn't been there months ago. "Officer Hale is asking specifically for your section."

The words landed like stones in her stomach. "Please," she whispered, her voice nearly inaudible beneath the restaurant noise. "Don't make me serve him."

Tom's eyes darted toward the entrance where Marcus still stood, his posture military-straight, waiting with the patient stillness of a predator who knows his prey has limited escape routes. "I offered Miriam, but he was… insistent."

"Tom—" Ann began, desperation edging into her voice.

"Just take his order and bring his food," Tom said, his tone suggesting this was the most reasonable compromise available. "Professional, quick, and done. I'll keep an eye out."

The small assurance did nothing to ease the cold dread spreading through Ann's body. Tom might watch, might even intervene if something obvious occurred, but he still didn't truly understand. Didn't believe the depth of danger she sensed every time Marcus entered her orbit.

Tom raised his hand, gesturing toward the hostess with a small nod that signaled consent to Marcus's request. Ann watched, paralyzed, as the hostess led Marcus to a small table directly in the center of her section. This position allowed him unobstructed views of the entire restaurant, the kitchen doors, and the staff entrance.

Her order pad felt suddenly heavy, the small plastic pen slipping against her damp palm as she forced herself to approach his table. Each step required conscious effort, her body fighting the instinct to flee, to hide, to escape the watching eyes that tracked her movement across the floor.

"Good afternoon, Officer Hale," she managed, the professional greeting emerging as flat and lifeless despite her attempt at normalcy. Her hand shook visibly as she held the pen poised above the pad, the tremor so pronounced that the pad nearly slipped from her grasp.

"Ann." He spoke her name with a familiarity that made her skin crawl, though his tone was perfectly pleasant, even warm. "Thank you for coming over. I was afraid you might avoid me."

The direct acknowledgment of her fear—packaged as concern—sent a cold ripple down her spine. She said nothing, waiting with rigid posture for his order, unwilling to engage in the pretense of casual conversation.

Marcus studied her face with that same measured intensity she'd come to dread, his head tilting slightly as he observed her discomfort. "You seem afraid of me, Ann," he said, his voice lowered just enough to keep their conversation private despite the surrounding noise.

The statement—so accurate and yet so manipulative in its presentation—broke something in Ann's carefully maintained façade. "I think you've been following me," she said quietly, the words escaping before she could stop them, driven by days of accumulated fear and the violation she'd discovered underneath her car.

Marcus's eyebrows rose, his expression shifting to what appeared to be genuine surprise. If Ann hadn't seen the device with her own eyes, hadn't documented pattern after pattern of his surveillance, she might have doubted herself in the face of his convincing reaction.

"Following you?" He leaned back slightly, palms open on the table in a gesture of innocent confusion. "Ann, I'm not following you. Why would you think that?"

The denial—so smooth, so practiced—hit her like a physical blow. "The tracking device in my car," she said, her voice barely above a whisper. "The patrol car outside my apartment. The way you always know where I'll be."

"Tracking device?" He shook his head, concern creasing his brow. "Ann, I have no idea what you're talking about. I come here because the coffee is good and the service—your service—is excellent." His eyes held hers, unwavering. "As for patrol cars, we cover the entire town. It's not unusual for us to be in various neighborhoods."

Every word was plausible, reasonable—and utterly false. Ann gripped her pen tighter, her knuckles whitening with the effort of not screaming the truth at him.

Marcus leaned forward, lowering his voice further. "Listen, you seem genuinely distressed. Why don't we talk about this somewhere private? After your shift, perhaps? I can help you figure out what's going on."

The suggestion sent ice through her veins—the thought of being alone with him, away from witnesses, from the relative safety of the public space. "No," Ann said, taking a deliberate step back, putting distance between them. "I don't feel safe being alone with you." Her voice wavered despite her effort to keep it steady.

Something flickered in Marcus's eyes—a brief, dark expression quickly masked by renewed concern. "Ann, I'm a police officer. If you're experiencing problems, I'm literally the person who's supposed to help."

Before Ann could respond, before she had to find words to counter his practiced manipulation, a loud splash and clatter erupted beside them. She turned to find Lena standing there, an empty water pitcher in her hands, a spreading puddle at her feet.

"Oh, my God, I'm so sorry!" Lena exclaimed, her voice carrying across the restaurant as she made a show of dabbing ineffectually at the spill with her apron. "Ann, can you help me with this? I'll need towels from the back."

The manufactured emergency was transparent—at least to Ann—but it created the distraction she desperately needed. "I have to help," she told Marcus, already backing away from his table. "I'll send Miriam to take your order."

She didn't wait for his response, turning quickly to follow Lena toward the kitchen, feeling Marcus's eyes on her back with each retreating step, the weight of his gaze like a physical touch she couldn't escape.

The kitchen door swung shut behind Ann, muting the dining room's clamor and replacing it with the precise, ordered sounds of the kitchen. The familiar environment that had once felt like a sanctuary now seemed insufficient protection against the threat waiting just beyond the door. Ann's composure, held together by the thinnest threads during her confrontation with Marcus, unraveled completely. Her shoulders slumped as she pressed herself against the stainless steel prep table, its cold solidity the only thing keeping her upright as her body began to tremble uncontrollably.

The first sob escaped without warning, a ragged sound that tore from her throat and seemed to surprise even her. She pressed her palm against her mouth, trying to contain the breakdown, but it was like trying to hold back a flood with her fingers. Tears spilled down her cheeks, hot and unstoppable, as weeks of accumulated fear and tension sought release.

Chef Cho's knife stilled mid-chop. She set it down with deliberate care, wiping her hands on her apron before crossing to Ann's side. Her approach was neither hesitant nor overly emotional—just the steady movement of someone who understood crisis. She placed a firm hand on Ann's shoulder, the pressure grounding rather than constraining.

"Breathe," Chef Cho instructed, her voice low and steady. "In through nose, out through mouth."

The kitchen door opened again as Lena slipped inside, immediately positioning herself with her back against it, arms crossed—a sentinel ensuring their privacy. Her eyes met Chef Cho's over Ann's hunched form, silent understanding passing between them.

"He—he acted like I was crazy," Ann managed between shuddering breaths, her voice breaking on the words. She wiped roughly at her tears with the back of her hand, smearing mascara across her cheek. "Looked me right in the eye and denied everything. The device in my car, the patrol car outside my apartment—all of it."

"Gaslighting," Chef Cho said, the word sharp and precise as her knife work. "Making you question your reality."

"He's good at it," Ann continued, her words tumbling out faster now, as if she needed to expel them before they poisoned her. "So convincing that for a second—just a second—I almost doubted myself. Maybe I imagined the device. Maybe the patrol car was a coincidence." Her fingers curled into fists at her sides. "But I didn't. I have photos. Documentation. It's real, and he knows it's real, and he's still sitting out there pretending to be concerned about my 'distress.'"

Chef Cho's expression hardened as she listened, the lines around her mouth deepening. Her hand remained steady on Ann's shoulder, a quiet anchor in the storm of emotion.

"He suggested we meet somewhere private," Ann added, fresh fear flashing across her face. "To 'talk about what's going on.' Can you imagine?" A bitter laugh escaped her, sounding more like a sob. "He wants me alone, away from witnesses."

"You need to file a formal complaint," Chef Cho said, her direct manner cutting through Ann's spiraling thoughts. "The police department has internal affairs. Document everything, take it above his head."

Ann shook her head vigorously, fear replacing the momentary anger. "They're all cops. They'll protect him, not me." Her voice dropped to a whisper. "You know what happens to women who report police officers? Best case, they don't believe me. Worst case…." She trailed off, the unspoken possibilities hanging in the air between them.

"Ann's right," Lena said from her position by the door. "My cousin dated a cop in Baltimore. When she tried to report him for harassment, suddenly she was getting pulled over three times a week. Parking tickets. Noise complaints. They closed ranks around him."

Chef Cho's jaw tightened, but she didn't argue. "Then what is your plan?"

The question landed heavily in the kitchen's steam-laden air. Ann stared at the tiled floor, her tears slowing as the immediate emotional wave receded, leaving behind the cold clarity of her impossible situation.

"I don't know," she admitted. "I've documented everything. I've varied my routes. But he keeps finding me. Keeps watching. And now he's trying to isolate me, to make everyone think I'm paranoid." Her voice strengthened slightly with determination despite the fear. "I know what he's doing. I just don't know how to stop it."

Jake, the line cook, looked up from the grill, his expression uncomfortable but concerned. "My brother's a security consultant. Maybe he could check your apartment, your phone? Make sure there aren't more devices?"

"And I can stay with you," Lena offered immediately. "At a hotel or wherever. You shouldn't be alone right now."

The kitchen door swung open again, and everyone tensed. Tom stepped in, his gaze immediately finding Ann's tear-streaked face. His expression softened with concern, though the wariness in his eyes suggested he still wasn't fully convinced of the danger she faced.

"He's gone," Tom said simply. "Paid his bill in full and left."

A visible wave of relief washed over Ann's body, her shoulders dropping as the immediate threat retreated. But the respite was temporary, and she knew it. Marcus's departure only meant he'd shifted to a form of surveillance she couldn't see—perhaps waiting in his car across the street or driving past the restaurant at calculated intervals.

"Thank you," she said to Tom, straightening her posture with effort, attempting to reassemble her professional demeanor. "I can finish my shift."

"Ann—" Tom began, then seemed to reconsider whatever he'd been about to say. "Take a few minutes if you need them. Your tables are covered."

After Tom left, Chef Cho squeezed Ann's shoulder once more before returning to her station. "Strong doesn't mean facing danger alone," she said over her shoulder, her knife resuming its steady rhythm. "Remember that."

Ann nodded, taking several deep breaths as she smoothed her apron and wiped the remaining tears from her face. She couldn't hide in the kitchen forever. Her customers were waiting, and she needed this job, needed the normalcy it represented even as that normalcy crumbled around her.

For the remainder of her shift, Ann moved through the restaurant with brittle efficiency. Each time the door opened, her head snapped up, her body tensing in anticipation of Marcus's return. Though he didn't reappear, his earlier presence lingered like a noxious cloud, poisoning the air she breathed, transforming the familiar restaurant into hostile territory where danger could return at any moment.

Ann stood outside her apartment door, keys clutched so tightly between her knuckles that they left indentations in her palm. Lena had suggested that she go home with her and stay the night, but Ann had told her she would be okay. Now, staring at the door that stood ever-so-slightly ajar—perhaps a quarter-inch gap between door and frame where there should have been none—she regretted that decision with sickening clarity. She distinctly remembered locking it before leaving this morning.

Her body responded before her mind fully processed the implications, taking three quick steps back until her shoulders pressed against the opposite wall of the hallway. Her breathing quickened, short, shallow gasps that didn't seem enough for her lungs as her eyes remained fixed on that slender gap, that impossible space that shouldn't exist. Someone had been inside—was perhaps still inside.

Ann's hand trembled as she reached for her phone, her thumb hovering over the emergency call button before she hesitated. Who would come if she called 911? The same department where Marcus worked. The same colleagues who saw nothing wrong with his behavior, who might even be helping him. The realization that she couldn't trust the very people meant to protect her sent a wave of nausea through her stomach.

Instead, she called Lena.

"I'm at my apartment," she whispered when Lena answered, her voice barely audible even to herself. "The door's open. Someone's been inside."

"Don't go in," Lena replied immediately, all casual warmth vanishing from her tone. "I'm leaving now. Twenty minutes, tops."

"Hurry," Ann whispered, ending the call but remaining pressed against the wall, unable to tear her gaze from the door that represented yet another boundary Marcus had violated.

The twenty minutes stretched into an eternity of held breath and racing thoughts. Twice, Ann heard footsteps in the stairwell and pressed herself into the alcove near the fire extinguisher, heart pounding until the steps passed by her floor. When Lena finally appeared, slightly breathless from taking the stairs two at a time, Ann nearly collapsed with relief.

"It's still open," she said, gesturing toward the door. "Just like that. I haven't touched it."

Lena's expression hardened as she took in the scene, her usual easy smile nowhere in evidence. "Could be maintenance," she suggested, though her tone lacked conviction. "Or the building manager?"

Ann shook her head. "They always let me know, either by a call or text. And they'd close the door behind them."

They exchanged a look of shared understanding before Lena reached into her oversized purse and withdrew a small canister of pepper spray. "Stay behind me," she instructed, approaching the door with more confidence than Ann could have mustered alone.

Lena pushed the door open with her foot, pepper spray raised at eye level as they peered into the apartment's interior. The familiar space—Ann's small living room with its worn but comfortable furniture, the kitchen visible through the breakfast bar—appeared undisturbed. No drawers pulled open, no furniture overturned, no obvious signs of ransacking or theft.

"Hello?" Lena called, her voice strong despite the tension evident in her posture. "Anyone here?"

Only silence answered. They moved cautiously into the apartment, Lena leading the way as they checked each room methodically—the bathroom with its shower curtain still arranged exactly as Ann remembered, the bedroom with its unmade bed precisely as she'd left it this morning. Even the closet doors stood partially open at the same angle Ann recalled from her hurried departure.

"Nothing's missing," Ann said, confusion mingling with the fear that still coiled in her stomach. "The TV's still here. My laptop." She gestured toward the coffee table where her computer sat, seemingly untouched.

"Maybe it was just the wind?" Lena suggested, though they both knew the idea was absurd. Third-floor apartments didn't have their locked doors blown open by errant breezes.

"No," Ann shook her head, certainty hardening her voice. "He was here. This is a message." She wrapped her arms around herself, fingers digging into her own biceps. "He's showing me he can get in whenever he wants. That there's nowhere I can hide."

The violation felt more intimate than if he had ransacked the place. This subtle intrusion—leaving everything exactly as it was except for the unlocked door—demonstrated a chilling level of control. He hadn't needed to destroy her possessions to destroy her sense of safety.

"We need to document this," Lena said, already pulling out her phone. She photographed the door from multiple angles, capturing the lock mechanism and the slight scratch marks on the frame.

Ann joined her, moving through the apartment with her own phone, taking photos of each room. Not because anything was disturbed, but because the very lack of disturbance was itself evidence of the psychological game Marcus was playing.

"I brought you something," Lena said when they'd finished the documentation. She reached into her bag and pulled out a small security camera, its sleek black design suggesting a recent purchase. "It's not much, but it connects to your phone. Motion detection, night vision."

Ann took the device with trembling hands, gratitude momentarily overwhelming her fear. "Thank you," she whispered.

They positioned the camera on a bookshelf facing the apartment door, angled to capture anyone who entered. The small setup process—downloading the app, connecting the device to Ann's phone, testing its functionality—provided a welcome distraction from the knowledge that her private space had been invaded.

"I can stay," Lena offered as evening approached, her concerned gaze taking in Ann's pale face and the shadows beneath her eyes. "The couch looks comfortable enough."

Ann considered the offer, temptation warring with guilt. "You've done so much already," she said finally. "And you have the early shift tomorrow."

After several more assurances, additional checks of the lock, and a promise to call if anything—anything at all—seemed wrong, Lena finally left. The sound of the door closing behind her friend echoed through the apartment with finality, leaving Ann alone with her thoughts and the unsettling knowledge that Marcus had stood in this same space, touched her possessions, and invaded her sanctuary.

She moved to the kitchen table, pulling out her laptop and setting it carefully before her. The camera's small red light blinked reassuringly from its position on the bookshelf, but Ann knew it wasn't enough. If something happened to her—if Marcus's surveillance escalated to something worse—a security camera might capture the event but wouldn't explain the history, the pattern, the slow psychological torture that had preceded it.

And it would be too late.

Ann opened her laptop and activated the camera, adjusting her position until she sat centered in the frame. She took a deep breath, steadying herself before she began to speak.

"My name is Ann Porter," she said, her voice growing firmer with each word. "I'm recording this on April 21st as documentation of the ongoing stalking and harassment I've experienced from Police Officer Marcus Hale of the City Police Department."

She spoke for nearly an hour, recounting every incident chronologically—the daily restaurant visits that had evolved into traffic stops, the patrol car sightings near her apartment, the tracking device found in her vehicle, and now, the violation of her home. Her voice grew steadier as she spoke, the act of recitation transforming her fear into something more focused, more determined.

When she finished, Ann uploaded the video to her cloud storage account, naming the file "Insurance," then sent the access link to both Lena and Chef Cho. If something happened to her, the truth would survive. The documentation would remain, even if she did not.

She curled up on her bed fully clothed, phone clutched in her hand, security app open and active on the screen. Sleep would likely prove elusive, but for the first time in weeks, Ann felt something besides fear. A small spark of defiance had ignited within her—a determination that Marcus Hale would not silence her, would not erase her story, would not win his game of psychological warfare without a fight.

Part IV

Chapter 37

THE CHURCH'S basement smelled of industrial cleaner and cheap coffee, undercut by the unmistakable scent of unwashed bodies and damp clothing. I hunched deeper into the oversized coat we'd found in a donation bin three blocks back, keeping my head low as Matt and I shuffled through the entrance. My wet clothes clung to me beneath the coat, the chill from our swim in the bay having settled into my bones hours ago. Every muscle in my body screamed for rest, but rest meant vulnerability, and vulnerability meant death—or worse, capture by Sarah Winters.

"Keep moving," I murmured to Matt, noting how he favored his right side. The jagged piece of dock that had caught him during our underwater escape had torn a four-inch gash along his ribs. Not deep enough to require stitches, but enough to leave a trail of blood that had soaked through his shirt before we'd managed to press a scavenged T-shirt against it. "Corner spot. Better sightlines."

Matt nodded, his newly unshaven face making him look appropriately disheveled for our cover. He'd smeared dirt across his cheeks before we'd entered, completing the transformation from former detective to homeless veteran. I'd done the same, using mud from the bay's edge to streak my hair and face, concealing the features that had been splashed across every news outlet in Florida.

The shelter volunteers barely glanced at us as we made our way through the crowded room. That was the beauty of places like this—the social contract of averting eyes, of not asking questions. People came here to escape notice, making it the perfect cover for two fugitives with nowhere else to turn.

We found a spot against the back wall, positioned between a storage closet and a support column that offered partial concealment while maintaining clear views of both exits. I helped Matt lower himself to the floor, his face tightening with pain he refused to vocalize.

"Let me see it," I said, keeping my voice low as I helped him remove the filthy jacket he'd been wearing. The makeshift bandage we'd applied was soaked through, the blood having slowed but not stopped completely.

"It's fine," Matt insisted, though his pallor suggested otherwise. "Just needs cleaning."

I glanced around, assessing our position and the room's occupants before focusing on his wound.

The gash looked angry, the edges inflamed but clean. No signs of serious infection yet, though that would change quickly without proper treatment. I reached for the small first-aid kit someone at the church had handed me when I asked if they had one.

"This will hurt," I warned as I uncapped the small bottle of hydrogen peroxide.

Matt's jaw tightened. "Just do it."

As I cleaned the wound, my eyes never stopped moving, scanning the room in methodical sweeps. The volunteer at the food table—young woman, early twenties, no visible threat. The security guard by the main entrance—retired police, based on his stance and the way he assessed newcomers. The elderly man distributing blankets—harmless. The middle-aged woman leading prayers in the far corner—potential ally if we needed one, her kind eyes suggesting someone who would help without question.

Matt's hand closed around mine as I pressed a clean gauze pad to his side. His fingers were cold, still not fully warmed from our time in the water. "Any sign of pursuit?" he asked, his voice barely audible.

"None yet." I secured the bandage with medical tape; my movements were practiced and efficient. "But Sarah's not the type to give up easily."

The boathouse attack played through my mind in vivid detail—the precision of the assault, the cold calculation in Sarah's eyes as she'd scanned the water for our bodies. She'd been willing to kill us both to protect her elaborate fiction, to maintain the frame she'd constructed around me. And she'd nearly succeeded.

"I know." I cut him off gently. "For now, we need food and rest."

As if on cue, a volunteer announced that the evening meal was being served. People began queuing up near the long tables where steam rose from industrial-sized trays of what smelled like beef stew. My stomach clenched at the thought of food, reminding me that we hadn't eaten since before the boathouse attack nearly twelve hours ago.

"I'll go," I said, patting Matt's arm. "You stay put."

He nodded, conserving energy. We both knew his wound, while not life-threatening, had taken more out of him than he wanted to admit. The pain lines around his mouth had deepened in the past hour, and his normally alert eyes had developed a glassy quality that concerned me.

I joined the food line, keeping my head down and my posture stooped to maintain our cover. The volunteers worked efficiently, ladling stew into plastic bowls and handing out slices of bread with practiced movements. One of them—a teenage girl with braces—smiled at me as she passed me a bowl. I mumbled thanks without meeting her eyes, playing my role while continuing to scan the room.

That's when I saw him.

A small figure moved among the volunteers, carrying a tray of bread slices with careful concentration. Dark hair fell across his forehead in a way that struck me as instantly familiar—the same cowlick that Sarah had absentmindedly brushed back when she'd been playing the role of concerned friend. The boy turned slightly, revealing a profile that made my heart stutter in my chest.

Tommy Winters.

Sarah's nine-year-old son was here, in this shelter, helping serve food to the homeless. The same child I'd seen in Sarah's immaculate home, playing with toy cars on a perfect lawn. The same child who had watched his mother with wary eyes, flinching slightly when she'd corrected him too sharply.

I froze, my bowl of stew halfway to my chest, as Tommy moved along the serving line. His movements were careful and deliberate—a child trying very hard to do everything correctly. I recognized the behavior of someone accustomed to harsh consequences for small mistakes. It was the same hyperawareness I'd observed in other children from controlling homes, the constant self-monitoring that became second nature when living with unpredictable authority.

My mind raced through possibilities. Was this simply community service, a mother involving her child in charitable work? Or was Sarah here too, somewhere in this crowded room, watching and waiting? Had she somehow tracked us to this shelter, using her son as innocent camouflage for her hunt?

Tommy handed a slice of bread to an elderly woman, his smile shy but genuine. There was nothing calculated in that expression, nothing that suggested he was part of any trap. Just a child doing what his mother had instructed, unaware of his role in a larger, darker game.

I moved back toward Matt, food in hand but appetite gone, my eyes never leaving Tommy's small form as he continued his volunteer work. The coincidence was too great. Sarah Winters was here, or close by—of that I was certain. And that meant we were no longer as safe as I'd thought.

Chapter 38

I RETURNED to Matt with two bowls of stew and information far more valuable than food. "Tommy Winters is here," I whispered, settling beside him against the wall. "Sarah's son."

Matt's eyes widened slightly. I placed my hand over his, steadying him. "This isn't a coincidence. Sarah must be here too." We both understood the implications: our temporary sanctuary had just become another trap in Sarah's elaborate game.

"You sure it's him?" Matt asked, his voice low as he took the bowl from me.

"Positive."

I picked up my spoon but didn't eat, my attention fixed on Tommy as he moved between the food tables. "He's helping serve, which means Sarah must be volunteering too. I need to see if I can talk to him."

Matt's expression tightened with concern. "That's risky, Eva."

"So is walking into another of Sarah's traps blind." I set my untouched bowl aside. "Children notice things adults don't think they reveal. If Sarah's been planning all this for years, Tommy might have seen something useful."

For fifteen minutes, I watched Tommy work while scanning the room for Sarah. Eventually, I spotted her supervising a group of volunteers organizing donated clothing at the far end of the room. Her back was to us, her hair pulled into a casual ponytail—the picture of selfless community service. My stomach turned at the performance, knowing what lurked beneath the carefully constructed façade.

When Sarah finally headed toward the kitchen area, disappearing through swinging doors, I saw my opportunity. I squeezed Matt's shoulder and stood, moving casually through the crowded room toward the corner where Tommy now stood folding napkins. I approached from an angle that wouldn't be immediately visible from the kitchen, adopting the slightly stooped posture of our homeless disguise.

"Need some help with those?" I asked, keeping my voice gentle as I stopped beside him.

Tommy looked up, his eyes widening slightly as recognition flickered across his face. "You're the lady from TV," he said, his voice hushed but not frightened. "The one they said hurt people."

I crouched down to his eye level, maintaining a non-threatening distance. "My name is Eva Rae," I said, deliberately omitting my last name. "I came and visited you at your house, remember? And no, I didn't hurt anyone. Sometimes grown-ups make mistakes about things like that."

Tommy studied my face with the unfiltered intensity only children can manage. "Mom says you're dangerous," he said, then added with surprising candor, "but you don't look dangerous. You look tired."

A smile tugged at my lips despite the gravity of our situation. "I am tired," I admitted. "It's hard when people think you did something you didn't do."

He nodded with unexpected understanding. "That happens to me sometimes. Mom gets mad about things I didn't do."

The opening was perfect—a natural segue that any trained interviewer would recognize. During my years with the FBI, I'd interviewed dozens of children, learning to follow their lead rather than directing them too forcefully. Now I employed those same techniques, keeping my body language open and my voice conversational.

"That must be hard," I said, picking up a napkin and beginning to fold it, mirroring his activity to establish a connection. "What kinds of things does your mom get mad about?"

Tommy shrugged, his small fingers working deftly at folding. "When I go places I'm not supposed to. Or when I talk to people she doesn't like." He glanced toward the kitchen doors, then added in a lower voice, "Or when I ask about the special room."

I kept my expression neutral despite the alarm bells ringing internally. "Special room?"

He nodded, continuing to fold napkins as we spoke. "In our basement. Mom has a lock on it. I'm not allowed to go in there, ever." His eyes darted toward the kitchen again. "She gets really mad if I even ask about it."

"Have you ever seen inside this room?" I asked, careful to maintain my casual tone while my heart raced.

Tommy shook his head. "Once I peeked when she left the door open a little. I saw lots of pictures on the wall and a desk with a computer on it. Mom was really angry when she caught me." His voice dropped further. "She didn't let me have dinner that night and made me stay in my room all weekend."

The punishment revealed more about Sarah's controlling nature—the disproportionate response to a child's natural curiosity. I handed him another folded napkin, our fingers briefly touching in a gesture meant to reassure.

"Does your mom have friends who visit?" I asked, thinking of Collins and his connection to Sarah.

Tommy's face brightened slightly. "Mr. Collins used to come over. He was nice. He brought me books about space and answered my questions. Mom acted different when he was there—more smiley." His expression fell. "But he stopped coming. Mom said he did something bad and couldn't visit anymore."

"When did he stop visiting?"

"A while ago. Before..." He hesitated, clearly choosing his words carefully. "Before Mom started acting weird."

"Weird how?" I prompted gently.

Tommy looked down at the napkins, his fingers stilling. "She talks to herself a lot now. When she thinks I'm asleep, I can hear her in her room, having whole conversations with nobody there." He fidgeted with the hem of his shirt. "And sometimes she gets really happy for no reason, like something good happened but she won't tell me what. Then other times she gets super mad and breaks things."

The clinical part of my brain cataloged these behaviors—mood swings, possible delusions or hallucinations, episodes of rage—classic signs of deteriorating mental stability. But the part of me that was a mother recognized something else in Tommy's description: fear. This child was afraid in his own home.

He glanced nervously toward the kitchen doors again. "She's been watching the news a lot. She has a special notebook where she writes things down when they talk about you on TV."

I felt a chill that had nothing to do with my still-damp clothes. Sarah was documenting the manhunt, tracking the progression of her frame in real-time. The level of obsession suggested she was becoming more unstable, more unpredictable.

"Tommy," I said carefully, "that special room in your basement—do you know if your mom keeps other things there? Maybe things that belonged to Mr. Collins?"

His eyes widened slightly. "I don't know, but..." He leaned closer, his voice barely audible. "Last week I saw her carrying a box down there. It had a gun inside. I wasn't supposed to see, but I was getting water, and she didn't know I was in the kitchen."

My blood ran cold—a gun—possibly the murder weapon used on Collins and the woman they found downtown. Before I could ask another question, Tommy's gaze darted past my shoulder, fear flashing across his face.

"She's coming back," he whispered urgently. "You should go. She gets really mad when—"

I nodded, straightening up and moving away with casual deliberation, as if I'd simply been passing by. The information Tommy had provided confirmed my worst suspicions about Sarah while adding new, disturbing dimensions to the picture. Whatever was in that basement room might be the key to unraveling her entire frame-up—and potentially saving both our lives.

Chapter 39

I TURNED AWAY from Tommy just as the kitchen doors swung open. Sarah emerged carrying a fresh tray of bread, her volunteer's smile firmly in place. I kept my head down, moving laterally through the crowd rather than directly back toward Matt. But something—perhaps the movement itself, or some sixth sense born from her obsession—caught Sarah's attention. Her eyes swept the room in a practiced scan that betrayed her casual demeanor, settling on me with laser focus. For a fraction of a second, her smile faltered, the mask slipping to reveal the predator beneath before snapping back into place so quickly that anyone else would have missed it. But I'd seen it. And worse, she'd seen me.

Our eyes locked across the crowded room—hers blue and calculating, mine steady despite the danger. It was a moment of mutual recognition, a silent acknowledgment that the game had entered a new phase. The pleasant mask she wore for the benefit of those around her remained intact, but her eyes told a different story. They held the cold precision I'd witnessed on the dock after the boathouse attack—the unfiltered gaze of a hunter assessing prey.

I maintained my casual pace as I wove through the tables, keeping other shelter occupants between us as much as possible.

Sarah placed her tray on the serving table with deliberate care, her movements unhurried but purposeful. She was too smart to create a scene here, surrounded by witnesses. But the calculated glance she directed toward the exit told me everything—she was already planning her next move.

When I reached Matt, I slid down beside him without looking back at Sarah. "We've been made," I murmured, picking up my abandoned bowl of stew and pretending to eat. "Sarah spotted me."

Matt's posture shifted subtly, his body angling toward the nearest exit while maintaining our cover of two homeless people sharing a meal. "How bad?"

"Full recognition." I took a spoonful of the now-cold stew, forcing myself to swallow despite my churning stomach. "But she won't do anything here. Too many witnesses."

I told him everything Tommy had revealed—the locked basement room, Sarah's erratic behavior, the gun she'd hidden, Collins' visits that had mysteriously stopped. With each detail, Matt's expression grew grimmer.

"That basement is our best lead," he said, keeping his voice low. "Whatever evidence connects her to the murders is probably there."

"Along with whatever she's planning next," I agreed. "Tommy mentioned she keeps a notebook tracking the news coverage about me. She's documenting her own frame-up."

"Narcissists often keep trophies," Matt observed, the detective in him analyzing despite our desperate situation. "She'd want to preserve her 'accomplishment.'"

Across the room, Sarah had moved to Tommy's side, placing a hand on his shoulder in a gesture that appeared affectionate to casual observers. But I noted the tension in her fingers, the slight curl of possession in the way she held him. Tommy's body language shifted immediately—shoulders stiffening, expression becoming more controlled. The natural animation I'd seen during our conversation disappeared, replaced by the careful neutrality of a child walking on eggshells.

"Look at how she's holding him," I whispered to Matt. "That's not protection, it's possession."

Matt nodded, his eyes tracking the pair as Sarah leaned down to whisper something in Tommy's ear. The boy nodded mechanically, his earlier warmth extinguished. "She's using him," Matt said, his voice hardening. "Bringing him here wasn't a coincidence."

"No," I agreed, the realization crystallizing with sickening clarity. "She knew we'd need shelter after the boathouse. This church outreach center is the only one within walking distance of the bay that offers overnight accommodation without ID checks." I watched as Sarah guided Tommy toward the donated clothing area, her arm wrapped possessively around his shoulders. "She predicted our movements, then positioned herself and Tommy here as bait."

"But why Tommy? Why expose her son to this?"

"Because she knows I won't risk harming a child," I said, remembering Rule Seven of The Profiler's Code: Truth before badge. The principle that had guided my FBI career—that finding justice should supersede institutional loyalty or personal safety—extended naturally to the protection of innocents. Sarah had studied me thoroughly enough to know that I would hesitate to take any action that might endanger Tommy. "She's using him as a shield."

Sarah was now helping Tommy into his jacket, her movements efficient but controlling—adjusting his collar, tugging the zipper higher than necessary, her hands constantly touching, directing. She glanced our way again and this time made no effort to hide her recognition. A small, knowing smile curved her lips before she returned her attention to Tommy.

"She's leaving," Matt observed. "Taking Tommy with her."

"And expecting us to follow," I finished. The trap was elegantly simple—Sarah knew we needed to access that basement room, and she was using Tommy's safety to control how and when we'd make the attempt.

Matt shifted, wincing as the movement pulled at his bandaged side. "So, what's our play? We can't let her dictate the terms of engagement, but we need what's in that basement."

I watched Sarah guide Tommy toward the exit, her posture relaxed but her eyes constantly scanning—a predator aware that her prey was watching.

"She'll be watching for us," I said.

We gathered our meager belongings as Sarah and Tommy disappeared through the shelter's main doors. The cold calculation in her parting glance had contained something else—a trace of anticipation, almost excitement. This wasn't just a strategy for her anymore. The game had become personal, feeding whatever twisted obsession drove her.

As we prepared to leave through a side exit, I thought of Tommy—the careful way he'd spoken about his mother, the fear that had flashed across his face when she'd returned. He was both pawn and prize in Sarah's elaborate game, and that made him the most vulnerable player on the board.

"We need to be careful," I said quietly, adjusting my ragged coat around my shoulders. "It's not just our lives at stake anymore."

Matt nodded, his expression grim as he followed my gaze toward the door where Tommy and Sarah had exited. "No matter what evidence we find, we need to make sure he's protected when this all comes crashing down."

The weight of that responsibility settled across my shoulders as we slipped out into the gathering darkness. Sarah Winters had framed me for murder, destroyed my reputation, and threatened everything I held dear. But her most unforgivable crime might be what she was doing to her own son—using him as both weapon and hostage in a war of her own creation.

As we disappeared into the shadows between streetlights, I made a silent promise to Tommy that I would end this—not just for my sake, but for his. Truth before badge. Some principles transcended personal survival.

Chapter 40

THEN:

Ann's fingertips brushed against her phone in her pocket as she pushed through Granger's side entrance, scanning the parking lot one final time before letting the heavy door swing shut behind her. Her shoulders dropped imperceptibly when she found Tom waiting by the time clock, his usual morning greeting replaced by a grim nod toward his office door. Her stomach twisted—nothing good ever came from private conversations in that cramped back room with its perpetually flickering fluorescent light and walls too thin for genuine privacy.

"Before you clock in," Tom said, his voice low enough that the kitchen staff couldn't hear. "Need to talk to you."

Ann followed him into the office, her feet suddenly heavy, as if her body instinctively resisted whatever conversation awaited. Tom's office hadn't changed in the years she'd worked at Granger's—the same metal desk drowning under stacks of invoices and employee records, the same small window overlooking the kitchen's prep area, the same framed photo of Tom with his wife at the restaurant's grand opening fifteen years earlier. The familiarity that once felt comforting now seemed insufficient protection against the storm she sensed brewing.

Tom gestured toward the single chair facing his desk, then closed the door behind them. The soft click of the latch engaging sounded unnaturally final in the confined space.

"I got a call yesterday," Tom began, settling into his creaking desk chair, not quite meeting Ann's eyes. "From Officer Hale."

Ann's throat constricted, her body's reaction immediate and visceral at the mere mention of Marcus's name. She gripped the edge of her chair, fingers pressing into the worn padding as if seeking an anchor in suddenly turbulent waters.

"He says you've been making accusations," Tom continued, his discomfort evident in the way he rearranged papers on his desk that didn't need rearranging. "Telling people he's stalking you. That he planted some device on your car." He finally looked up, his expression caught between concern for a long-time employee and worry about potential liability. "He's threatening legal action, Ann. Defamation. Says you're damaging his reputation."

A bitter laugh escaped her before she could contain it—short, sharp, and edged with hysteria. "His reputation," she repeated, the words tasting like copper in her mouth. "He breaks into my apartment, follows me home, plants tracking devices on my car, and he's worried about his reputation?"

Tom's brow furrowed, his hands stilling on the papers. "These are serious allegations against a respected officer, Ann. The community trusts Marcus. He's been on the force for nearly a decade without complaints."

"Because victims are too scared to report," Ann countered, her voice suddenly steadier as anger temporarily displaced fear. "Or when they do report, no one believes them."

Something in Tom's expression shifted—not quite belief yet, but no longer the dismissal she'd grown accustomed to seeing whenever she mentioned Marcus's surveillance.

"Look, I can see you're genuinely distressed," he said, his tone softening. "And that's why I wanted to talk privately—before this escalates further."

Ann's hands trembled as she pulled her phone from her pocket, unlocking it with fingers that felt stiff and clumsy. "I have proof," she said, navigating to her photo gallery with practiced efficiency. "Not just my word."

She placed the phone on Tom's desk, turning the screen so he could see the first image—Marcus's patrol car, number 37, at 2:17 a.m. three nights earlier.

"This is a half-mile from his patrol route," she explained, swiping to show similar photos taken on different nights, each meticulously timestamped. "And this one—same car, different angle, 3:45 a.m. He sits there for hours, Tom. Watching my windows."

Tom leaned forward, squinting at the small screen, his professional skepticism battling with the evidence before him. "Could be a coincidence," he suggested, though his tone lacked conviction. "Maybe there were calls in your area."

"Every night? For weeks?"

Tom's expression darkened as he studied the photo. "But still—"

"There's more." Ann set her phone aside, reaching into her purse with unsteady hands. She withdrew a small plastic bag containing the black electronic device she'd carefully removed from beneath her car. She placed it on the desk between them, the object's sinister purpose unmistakable despite its innocuous appearance.

"This was under my car," she said. "Installed without my knowledge or consent. After I found it, I had a mechanic friend check it out." She swallowed hard, fighting to keep her voice steady. "It's a tracking device, Tom."

Tom reached for the bag hesitantly, as if the device might somehow activate through the plastic. He held it up to the flickering fluorescent light, examining the smooth black casing.

"Jesus," he muttered, the word barely audible. "So, it's true?"

Tom set the device down carefully. He rubbed his hand across his face, the gesture stripping away years of professional distance, revealing genuine concern beneath.

"Why didn't you bring this to me sooner?" he asked, though his tone suggested he already knew the answer.

"I tried," Ann replied, the words emerging more exhausted than accusatory. "You told me I was overreacting. That I should be flattered by his attention."

Tom winced, recognizing his own dismissive words reflected back at him. "I thought—" He paused, reconsidering. "I'm sorry, Ann. I should have listened."

The simple acknowledgment—so long awaited—hit Ann with unexpected force. Her eyes burned with sudden tears that she refused to let fall, blinking rapidly to dispel them. This wasn't a time for emotional release; it was a moment to press her advantage, to cement the ally she'd finally found.

"What do I do now?" she asked, her voice steadying. "He has the entire police department behind him. Who would even take my report seriously?"

Tom was silent for a long moment, his gaze fixed on the tracking device still sitting between them. When he spoke again, his voice carried a new resolve.

"My brother-in-law," he said finally. "Works for the state police. Internal investigations division." He looked up, meeting Ann's eyes directly. "This isn't just a personal issue anymore. If an officer is abusing his position, planting surveillance devices—that's corruption. That's something the state-level guys take very seriously."

A fragile hope unfurled in Ann's chest—not quite relief, not yet, but the first breath of possibility that her nightmare might have witnesses beyond her own frightened documentation.

"Will he help?" she asked, hardly daring to believe after so many closed doors, so many dismissals.

"I'll call him today," Tom promised, sliding the device back across the desk toward her. "Keep this safe. Document everything, like you've been doing." He hesitated, then added with grim certainty, "And Ann? Don't be alone if you can help it. Not until we get this sorted."

Ann nodded, reclaiming the device with careful fingers. She recognized the shift in Tom's demeanor—the transition from skepticism to belief, from dismissal to concern. It should have felt like victory. Instead, it highlighted how serious her situation had become. If even Tom, who'd known Marcus for years, now saw the danger, then her instincts had been right all along.

She was being hunted by a man with a badge, and the hunt was accelerating toward its endgame.

The last customer shuffled out of Granger's at 10:17, leaving behind a coffee cup with lipstick on the rim and a tip too small for the time they'd occupied the table. Ann wiped down the surface with mechanical efficiency, her movements precise despite the exhaustion that pulled at her limbs as if gravity had doubled. She hadn't slept properly in days—perhaps weeks—and the constant vigilance required to monitor the dining room while avoiding Marcus and his colleagues had drained what little energy remained after her restless nights. All she wanted was the temporary sanctuary of her apartment with its new locks and security camera, the small fortress she'd created against the watching eyes that followed her movements through the world.

"I'll walk you out," Tom said, appearing beside her as she collected her purse from the break room locker. His keys jangled in his hand, the restaurant's alarm remote already poised between his fingers.

The simple acknowledgment—that her fear was valid, her danger real—created a complicated knot of emotion in Ann's chest. Relief that someone finally believed her. Gratitude for the small protection Tom offered. Terror that even this knowledgeable ally might not be enough against what awaited her beyond the restaurant's walls.

They moved through the closing routine with practiced efficiency—lights dimmed, alarm system primed, back door secured. Tom held the employee exit open, gesturing for Ann to precede him into the parking lot. The spring night air carried a hint of chill, raising goosebumps on Ann's forearms as she stepped outside.

The employee parking area was dimly lit, shadows stretching between the few remaining vehicles. Lena's car was gone, as was Chef Cho's—only Tom's aging pickup and Ann's Honda remained, separated by three empty spaces. Ann's eyes performed their habitual scan—left to right, right to left, checking each potential hiding spot, each darkened corner where a figure might lurk unseen.

"All clear," Tom said, misinterpreting her hesitation as a request for him to check the surroundings. He moved ahead of her, keys jingling with each step, the sound unnaturally loud in the quiet lot.

Ann followed, her own keys already positioned between her knuckles in the defensive formation she'd adopted weeks ago. She kept close to Tom's back, using his larger form as both shield and guide through the darkness. The security light above her parking space flickered erratically, creating strobing shadows that transformed ordinary objects into potential threats.

Tom reached her car first, his stride faltering as he approached the passenger side. "Ah, hell," he muttered, the words emerging as a sigh of resignation rather than surprise.

Ann moved beside him, following his gaze to her front passenger-side tire. Even in the unreliable light, the damage was unmistakable—the rubber completely deflated, the tire sitting flat against the asphalt. Her throat tightened as Tom crouched beside it, pulling out his phone to illuminate the damage.

"That's no nail," he said, voice hardening as his flashlight beam revealed a clean, precise slice across the sidewall. "Someone did this deliberately."

Ann's keys slipped from her suddenly trembling fingers, clattering against the asphalt with a sound that made her flinch. "He's escalating," she whispered, the words emerging with such certainty that Tom didn't bother questioning who "he" might be. They both knew.

Tom straightened, retrieving her fallen keys and pressing them gently back into her palm. "I'll call roadside assistance," he said, already pulling out his phone. "You can leave the car here overnight. I'll drive you home."

Ann nodded mechanically, her eyes still fixed on the damaged tire. The cut was surgical in its precision—not a jagged tear or puncture, but a clean slice that would ensure complete deflation without the dramatic noise of a blowout. Calculated. Controlled. A message rather than mere vandalism.

"They'll be here in twenty minutes," Tom said after completing the call. He leaned against the hood of her car, arms crossed over his chest as they prepared to wait. "My brother-in-law's coming into town tomorrow. Said he'd meet us here, take your statement officially."

Ann felt a flicker of hope, quickly extinguished by practical reality. "Will it matter?" she asked, voice hollow. "It's my word against his. A waitress versus a respected officer."

"It's not just your word anymore," Tom reminded her, gesturing toward the slashed tire. "It's physical evidence. It's the tracking devices. It's the documented pattern." He hesitated, then added more quietly, "And it's my word too now, as a witness. I've known Marcus for years. People will listen when I say something's not right."

Chapter 41

THE STREETLIGHTS CAST long shadows across Sarah's perfect suburban lawn as we sat in our newly "borrowed" pick-up truck a block away. Tommy's words about the locked room in the basement echoed in my mind as I studied the house through binoculars, watching parents stream toward the elementary school three doors down for what appeared to be an evening function. The timing couldn't have been better if we'd planned it.

"Science fair night," Matt murmured beside me, checking his watch. "Should give us at least ninety minutes." He winced as he shifted in the driver's seat, his hand instinctively moving to the bandage beneath his shirt.

"Let me see it," I said, lowering the binoculars.

"It's fine," he insisted, but the tightness around his eyes told a different story. The gash along his ribs from our escape through the bay had stopped bleeding, but the crude first aid we'd managed in the church shelter wouldn't prevent infection much longer. We were both running on borrowed time—physically and tactically.

I scanned the street once more, confirming that there were no suspicious vehicles or lurking figures. Sarah's house sat like a perfect dollhouse in a row of similar structures, its yellow paint and white shutters maintaining the façade of normalcy that she wore as skillfully as her smile. Lights were off except for a single lamp visible through the living room window—the carefully staged appearance of an empty home.

"If Tommy was telling the truth."

"He was." I tucked the binoculars into our bag of supplies—flashlights, gloves, the burner phone with its precious camera. "I've interviewed enough children to know when they're hiding something. Tommy wasn't hiding—he was asking for help the only way he knew how."

Matt nodded, his trust in my judgment unwavering despite our increasingly desperate circumstances. We'd been partners long enough that he knew when to question me and when to follow my lead. This was the latter.

"Let's move," I said, checking the time. "Side approach through the neighbor's yard." The property next door offered the best cover—mature oak trees and a neglected hedge that had grown wild enough to shield our approach.

We slipped from the car, staying low as we crossed the quiet street. My body protested, but I pushed the discomfort aside, focusing instead on the tactical challenge before us. The side yard between the houses was narrow but navigable, shadows providing cover as we moved silently toward the back of Sarah's property.

"There," Matt whispered, pointing to a half-window set into the foundation, partially obscured by ornamental grasses. A cellar window—our access point to whatever secrets Sarah had hidden beneath her perfect home.

I crouched beside it, running my fingers along the frame to check for security measures. No wires, no obvious alarm triggers. Just a simple latch that had rusted partially open from neglect.

"Cover's just screwed in," I murmured, pulling a multi-tool from my pocket. "Four points, corroded from moisture." I worked methodically, as I loosened each screw. The metal was soft with age, yielding easily to pressure.

Matt kept watch, his breathing controlled but audible in the quiet night. The distant sounds of the science fair—children's excited voices, occasional applause—provided acoustic cover for our work. The final screw gave way, and the window cover came loose in my hands. I set it carefully aside, revealing a black opening just large enough for an adult to squeeze through.

"I'll go first," I said, pulling on gloves. "Keep watch for another minute, then follow."

Matt nodded, his face half-illuminated by the ambient glow of streetlights filtering through the trees. In that moment, with shadows playing across the familiar planes of his face, I allowed myself a brief acknowledgment of what we were risking. Not just our freedom or my reputation, but potentially our lives. Sarah had already demonstrated her willingness to kill.

I lowered myself through the window feet-first, holding the frame to control my descent. The drop was about six feet. I landed silently, knees bending to absorb the impact.

The basement air hit me immediately—damp and musty with underlying chemical notes that didn't belong in a residential home. Bleach, ammonia, and something else I couldn't immediately identify. A single bare bulb near the stairs cast sickly yellow light across the concrete floor, leaving corners in deep shadow. I moved aside from the window, scanning the space as my eyes adjusted.

Matt's legs appeared at the opening, followed by his torso as he eased himself through the tight space. I saw him bite back a groan as the movement pulled at his injured side. He dropped the final few feet, landing with less grace than I had but managing to stay quiet.

"You okay?" I whispered, steadying him with a hand on his arm.

He nodded, straightening with effort. "Let's find that room."

The basement was larger than I'd expected, extending beneath the entire footprint of the house. Metal shelving units lined one wall, holding neatly labeled plastic bins—"Christmas," "Summer Clothes," "Tommy's toys"—the ordinary storage of family life. The washer and dryer sat against another wall beside a utility sink stained with rust. But it was the opposite wall that drew my attention—blank concrete without shelving or storage, a single door set into its center.

We moved toward it with practiced silence, communication

reduced to hand signals and exchanged glances developed during our days as fugitives. I pointed to unusual marks on the concrete floor—something heavy had been dragged from that door to the stairs. Matt indicated water stains along the baseboards, suggesting recent cleaning with an excessive amount of liquid.

The door itself was solid wood, painted white like everything in Sarah's world, but showing signs of frequent use—the paint around the handle was worn away, revealing darker layers beneath. Taped to its center was a hand-lettered sign in childish pencil script: "Welcome Home."

My skin crawled at the implication. This wasn't just a storage room or workspace. This was a shrine awaiting its subject.

Matt's hand found mine in the dim light, squeezing once. I met his eyes, seeing my own determination reflected there. Whatever lay beyond that door represented the culmination of Sarah's obsession—and potentially our only chance to clear my name.

The lock hung open, the hasp unbolted. An invitation. Or a trap.

I reached for the handle, feeling cold metal beneath my gloved fingers. With one steadying breath, I pushed the door open.

Chapter 42

LIGHT SPILLED from the room in a sickly yellow glow, revealing a space that stopped my breath in my chest. What had once been a standard basement room had been transformed into a meticulous museum of obsession. Three walls were covered floor to ceiling with photographs, clippings, and handwritten notes arranged in concentric patterns that spiraled outward from central images. The fourth wall held a desk with multiple monitors, keyboards, and stacks of journals. My training had prepared me for many things, but the sight before me—the physical manifestation of a mind fractured by delusion—sent ice through my veins. This wasn't just evidence of Sarah's involvement. It was proof of a fixation so profound, so consuming, that murder had become merely a tool in service to her fantasy.

"My God," Matt whispered beside me, his voice barely audible as we stepped into Sarah's inner sanctum.

I moved toward the leftmost wall, where Richard Collins' life had been dissected and displayed with clinical precision. At the center hung a professional headshot—Collins in a suit, smiling confidently at the camera. Around it, photographs spiraled outward in chronological order, the dates meticulously noted in red ink beside each image. Collins leaving his office building. Collins at a coffee shop, stirring his drink. Collins jogging in a park. Each shot progressively closer, more intimate, as if the photographer had grown bolder with time.

The outer rings of the spiral showed a disturbing progression—shots through the windows of Collins in his home, in his bedroom, sleeping. Some appeared to have been taken with a telephoto lens; others so close they could only have been captured by someone inside his apartment. Intermingled with the photos were handwritten notes on pink stationery:

You looked at her today. The woman from accounting. Why can't you see she's not right for you?

I watched you sleep for an hour last night. You looked so peaceful. One day, I'll be beside you when you wake up.

You ignored my email AGAIN. This is your last chance.

The final image showed Collins' body, positioned on plastic sheeting in what appeared to be this very basement, two bullet wounds visible.

I turned away, my stomach churning, only to find myself facing the second wall—my wall. My own face stared back at me from hundreds of images spanning years of my life. Photos from official FBI press conferences. Surveillance shots from outside my home. Images captured through my kitchen window while I cooked dinner. Me picking up my granddaughter from daycare. Matt and I walking along the beach three years ago, our hands almost but not quite touching.

"Matt," I managed, my voice strangled. "Some of these are from like five years ago." I stepped closer, examining dates written with the same meticulous precision. The earliest photos dated back nearly six years—long before I'd ever set foot in Bookmark Haven or heard the name Sarah Winters.

"She's been stalking you for years," Matt said, his face pale in the yellow light. "This isn't opportunistic framing. This was always her endgame."

The revelation hit me like physical pain. Sarah hadn't simply seized an opportunity to frame me when circumstances aligned. She had engineered those circumstances, positioning herself in my orbit, waiting for the perfect moment to spring her trap.

I forced myself to study the wall methodically, as I would any evidence board. The photos of me showed a progression, too—from distant surveillance to closer observation. But unlike Collins' wall, where admiration had twisted into possessiveness and finally rage, my images were overlaid with something else. Red X marks were drawn across my face. Notes scrawled beside them in increasingly frantic handwriting:

She doesn't deserve him. She never did.

She'll be gone soon. Then everything will be as it should be.

THREE WAYS TO KILL HER:

1. Make it look like suicide (too suspicious for an FBI agent)

2. Random attack (too many variables)

3. Frame her for murder (PERFECT—use her own methods against her)

Matt had moved to the third wall—his wall—and stood frozen before it. Unlike the others, his images showed no progression from distant to close. Every photograph was intimate from the start—Matt leaving our home, Matt at physical therapy working with his prosthetic leg, Matt sleeping. Hundreds of images spanning years, many clearly taken with a telephoto lens from strategic vantage points.

Around his central image—a candid shot of him laughing that I recognized from a barbecue three summers ago—Sarah had arranged dried flowers, locks of hair I prayed weren't actually his, and handwritten poems that made my skin crawl with their delusional intimacy.

"She thinks she's in love with you," I said, the horror of Sarah's fractured reality becoming clear. "She's claiming what she believes is hers."

"And Tommy," Matt added, his voice hollow. "Creating her perfect family."

I turned to the fourth wall, where a massive corkboard dominated the space above the computer desk. Newspaper clippings of my FBI cases formed the foundation, with red strings connecting them to a handwritten analysis of my investigation methods. She had studied my techniques, my thought processes, my tendencies—learning how I built cases so she could frame me more effectively.

Matt moved to a large sheet of butcher paper pinned beside the corkboard—a timeline showing my movements over the past month.

"She documents everything," Matt said, tracing his finger along the timeline. "Like she's creating a record of her accomplishment."

I moved to the desk, pulling open drawers. The top drawer contained nothing but pink stationery—identical to the note found on the woman's body who was found downtown. The second drawer held a gun in a plastic bag, a .38 caliber revolver that matched the murder weapon and my service weapon. The third contained prescription bottles—multiple antipsychotic medications with Sarah's name on them. None had been refilled in months.

"Matt," I said, lifting a file from beneath the keyboard. Inside were newspaper clippings about the woman, Alice Mercer, alongside very recent surveillance photos of her at work, at home, shopping. "This was the second victim, but there's another file here."

Matt took the second folder, opening it to reveal similar documentation of a woman I didn't recognize. The label read "Target Three—Margaret Wells." The most recent photo showed her entering a building I recognized as the *Tampa Bay Times* headquarters—she was a reporter.

"She's planning another murder," I said, the timeline suddenly making terrible sense. "Each killing advances her narrative about me being an unstable FBI agent having gone on a killing spree."

My hands shook slightly as I pulled out the burner phone, beginning to photograph everything—the walls, the timeline, the gun, the medications, the files on each victim. The flash illuminated the room in harsh bursts, revealing new details with each image: a calendar with important dates circled in red; a shelf containing items stolen from my home; a drawer filled with the unmistakable red hairs from my brush labeled with dates.

"She knew we'd come here," Matt said suddenly, pointing to an entry on the timeline for today's date: *Eva Rae and Matt discover my special room. Now they understand.*

The implication chilled me. Sarah hadn't just tracked our movements or predicted our actions. She had orchestrated them. The school function tonight wasn't coincidental—it was deliberate, a calculated absence to allow us to find this room.

"This isn't just evidence," I realized aloud, continuing to photograph everything. "It's the next stage of her game. She wanted us to see all of this."

The sound came without warning—tires crunching on gravel above, the distinctive purr of an engine I recognized immediately. My eyes met Matt's across the room, alarm mirrored in both our faces.

"That's her car," he whispered unnecessarily. "She's home."

"The school function—it should have lasted at least another hour." My mind raced through possibilities. "Unless she never went at all. Unless this was—"

"The plan all along," Matt finished, already moving toward the door. "We need to get out through the cellar window."

I pocketed the burner phone with its precious evidence and scanned the room one last time for anything essential we might have missed. The car door slammed above us, followed by the sound of footsteps on the front porch. No child's voice accompanied them—no sign of Tommy. Sarah had come alone.

We slipped back into the main basement area, easing the shrine door closed behind us. The cellar window we'd entered through suddenly seemed impossibly distant—at least twenty feet of open space to cross, with no cover and a floor that creaked with every step. The front door opened above, followed by the thud of something heavy being set down.

Matt and I froze, communicating with eyes and subtle gestures honed through years of partnership and days on the run. I pointed toward a stack of storage bins that might provide temporary cover.

He nodded, and we moved in silent synchronization, keeping low to the ground.

Keys jangled above, then dropped into what I imagined was the ceramic bowl Sarah kept on the entryway table. Footsteps moved across the floor—not toward the basement stairs, but into what would be the kitchen. The refrigerator door opened and closed. A cabinet squeaked on its hinges.

We reached the storage bins, crouching behind them as the floorboards above us groaned with Sarah's movement. She was alone, moving with purpose rather than the casual patterns of someone simply arriving home. The footsteps paused, then changed direction. My breath caught as I recognized the new trajectory—she was heading toward the basement door.

The overhead light switched on, illuminating the stairwell and sending yellow light spilling across the concrete floor. From our hidden position, I could see the stairs but not the doorway at their top. Another moment passed—silence except for the pounding of my heart and Matt's controlled breathing beside me.

Then came the sound of a foot on the top stair, followed by another. Sarah was coming down, her descent measured and unhurried, as if she had all the time in the world. As if she knew exactly what—or who—waited for her below.

Chapter 43

THEN:

Ann gripped the steering wheel as if it were the only solid thing left in her dissolving world, her knuckles whitening with each mile that separated her from Granger's. The evening shift had ended twenty minutes ago, but tension still coiled at the base of her neck, sending tendrils of pain up into her skull. She checked the rearview mirror for the fourteenth time since pulling out of the restaurant parking lot—no patrol car, no sign of Marcus. Not yet. The momentary relief this observation provided evaporated almost instantly, replaced by the certainty that absence of evidence wasn't evidence of absence. He was out there somewhere, watching, waiting, planning his next move in their invisible chess match.

The road stretched before her, mostly empty at this hour, streetlights creating rhythmic patterns of illumination and shadow across the asphalt. Ann had deliberately chosen this route—a winding path through residential areas rather than her usual direct drive home.

Ann turned left where she would normally have turned right, deliberately adding ten minutes to her commute. Her eyes darted to the side mirror, then to the rearview, then to the dark spaces between houses where a vehicle might be hiding. The dashboard clock read 11:17 p.m.

She was so focused on the mirrors, on the shadows, on the imagined threat lurking just beyond her perception, that the sudden flash of blue and red lights behind her hit with the force of physical impact. Ann's foot jerked reflexively toward the brake pedal, her heart launching into a frantic rhythm that seemed to shake her entire body. The police cruiser had appeared as if materialized from her fears—no headlights visible in her mirrors a moment before, now suddenly, terrifyingly present.

"No, no, no," she whispered, easing her car toward the curb with trembling hands. This was it—whatever endgame Marcus had been working toward. She hadn't even made it home.

The car settled against the curb, engine still running, as Ann's mind raced through limited options. Run? Fight? Beg? Each possibility dissolved against the reality of her situation—alone on a dark street. Her breath fogged the driver's side window as she watched the cruiser door open, a uniformed figure emerging into the cone of streetlight.

Not Marcus.

The realization brought no relief, only confusion. Officer Ramirez approached with measured steps, flashlight beam swinging across the interior of Ann's car before settling on her face. A second officer—male, unfamiliar—emerged from the passenger side, hanging back slightly as Ramirez reached the window.

Ann's trembling finger found the button to lower the glass, the mechanical whir seeming unnaturally loud in the silent street. "Where is he?" she demanded before Ramirez could speak, her voice tight with fear. "Where's Marcus?"

If Ramirez was surprised by the question, her professional demeanor revealed nothing. "Good evening, Ms. Porter. License and registration, please."

"No," Ann said, the word emerging sharper than intended. "I want to know where Officer Hale is. Is he in another car? Watching from somewhere?" Her eyes darted past Ramirez's shoulder, scanning the darkened street for signs of Marcus's presence.

"Officer Hale has been deliberately removed from any interaction with you, Ms. Porter," Ramirez stated, her tone maintaining that perfect, infuriating neutrality that all the officers seemed to have mastered. "Your license and registration, please."

The unexpected statement momentarily stunned Ann into compliance. She fumbled in her purse for her wallet, extracted her license with unsteady fingers, then reached across to the glove compartment for the vehicle registration. As she handed both items to Ramirez, her mind struggled to process this new information. Deliberately removed? What did that mean?

"Am I… being arrested?" Ann asked, her voice smaller now, uncertainty creeping in where righteous indignation had been moments before.

"No, Ms. Porter. This isn't a traffic stop, though you were exceeding the speed limit by seven miles per hour." Ramirez examined the documents briefly before returning them. "I need you to step out of the vehicle, please."

Ann's hand froze halfway to receiving her license. "Why?"

"Please step out of the vehicle," Ramirez repeated, her tone remaining even but carrying a new edge of authority that brooked no argument.

With reluctance born of deep suspicion, Ann unbuckled her seatbelt and opened the door, her legs feeling strange and disconnected as she stood beside her car. The night air felt cool against her heated skin, the distant sound of highway traffic providing a surreal background to whatever was unfolding.

The second officer approached now, his face half-shadowed beneath the brim of his hat. He carried something in his hands—a thick manila envelope, its official appearance sending a fresh jolt of anxiety through Ann's system.

"Ms. Porter," Ramirez said, standing at a precise, professional distance, "I've been tasked with serving you with these documents." She gestured toward the envelope the other officer was now extending toward Ann.

Ann made no move to take it. "What is this?" she demanded, fear transforming rapidly into anger. "More lies? More fabricated evidence? I know what Marcus is doing. I have proof—"

"This is a restraining order, Ms. Porter," Ramirez interrupted, her voice cutting through Ann's rising panic with clinical precision. "Filed by Officer Marcus Hale against you. You are being legally ordered to maintain a distance of at least five hundred feet from Officer Hale at all times. The complete terms are detailed in the documentation."

The words hit Ann with physical force, her body swaying slightly as if pushed backward by their impact. A restraining order. Against her. Filed by Marcus. The inversion of reality was so complete, so perfectly backward that for several seconds she could only stare at the envelope still extended toward her.

"That's not..." she began, then stopped, her voice failing as the enormity of the situation began to penetrate her consciousness. "That's not right. He's the one stalking me. He's the one who put a tracking device on my car, who—"

"All the evidence is documented within," the second officer said, pushing the envelope closer to Ann. "You need to accept service of these papers, Ms. Porter."

With numb fingers, Ann finally took the envelope, its weight seeming disproportionate to its size. She stared at the official seal on the front, at Marcus's name printed beneath the word "Petitioner," at her own name under "Respondent." The world tilted slightly around her, streetlights blurring as tears of confusion and rage filled her eyes.

"This isn't right," she whispered, clutching the envelope against her chest as if it contained something dangerous. "This is what he's been planning all along. To make me look like the stalker when he's the one who's been following me."

Neither officer responded to her statement, their expressions remaining professionally impassive in the harsh interplay of streetlight and shadow.

Ann tore open the manila envelope with trembling fingers, her body still pressed against the side of her car for support. The first page bore the county courthouse seal, official and damning in its formality. "TEMPORARY RESTRAINING ORDER AND NOTICE OF HEARING" proclaimed the bold text at the top, followed by Marcus's full name—Marcus James Hale—and her own, the legal terminology transforming them into petitioner and respondent in some twisted inversion of her reality. She flipped to the next page, breath catching in her throat as she began to read the detailed allegations against her.

"Respondent has engaged in a pattern of stalking behavior against Petitioner for approximately three months, including but not limited to: surveillance of Petitioner's residence, workplace, and daily movements; documentation of Petitioner's activities; repeated unwanted contact; and creating false allegations against Petitioner."

The document continued with clinical precision, listing twenty-seven specific instances with dates, times, and locations. Ann's eyes darted frantically across the pages, each entry landing like a physical blow.

"March 12, 7:35 p.m.: Respondent observed parked outside Petitioner's residence for 47 minutes."

"March 17, 6:22 a.m.: Respondent followed Petitioner's patrol vehicle through five consecutive turns off his designated route."

"March 29, 11:40 p.m.: Respondent documented approaching Petitioner's apartment door, attempting to determine if he was home."

"No," Ann whispered, her voice thin and reedy in the night air. "I never—I wasn't...."

But her denials died as she turned to the next page and found herself staring at a series of grainy security camera images.

There she was, unmistakably, standing outside what appeared to be Marcus's apartment door. The timestamp read 11:42 p.m. on March 29, her face captured in profile as she leaned toward the door, one hand raised as if listening or preparing to knock. Ann's mind reeled, struggling to place the memory.

She flipped to the next page with mounting desperation, only to find dashboard camera footage showing her Honda following a patrol car at a consistent distance through residential streets. Four separate images, four different dates, her vehicle clearly identifiable by the license plate in front.

"This isn't possible," Ann said louder, looking up at Officer Ramirez, who stood watching her with that same impassive expression. "These are fabricated. I never followed him. I've been trying to avoid him!"

Ramirez made no response, her silence somehow more devastating than any accusation could have been.

Ann returned to the documents, her hands now shaking so violently that the papers rattled. The next section contained sworn statements from witnesses. Her neighbor, Rosa Alvarez's name leaped from the page, the betrayal striking Ann with such force that her knees nearly buckled.

"I observed Ms. Porter's behavior becoming increasingly fixated on Officer Hale over a period of approximately eight weeks," Rosa's statement read. "She began documenting his movements, photographing his vehicle, and expressing paranoid beliefs that he was stalking her despite no evidence to support these claims. When I suggested she might be misinterpreting ordinary encounters, she became defensive and increasingly secretive about her surveillance activities."

Daniel Reed's statement followed, equally damning: "As a regular customer at Granger's Restaurant, I witnessed Ms. Porter's gradual obsession with Officer Hale develop over several months. She would constantly watch him when he dined at the establishment, sometimes neglecting other customers to hover near his table. On multiple occasions, I observed her taking photographs of him without his knowledge or consent."

Ann's breathing grew shallow, spots dancing at the edges of her vision as she turned to the next section of the file. Here were printouts of online purchase records—a GPS tracking device identical to the one she'd found beneath her car, ordered from a specialty surveillance website, the transaction linked to her own credit card.

The shipping confirmation showed delivery three days before she'd "discovered" it beneath her vehicle.

"No," she breathed, the denial feeling increasingly hollow against the mounting evidence. "I didn't buy this. Someone used my card, someone—" But even to her own ears, the explanation sounded desperate, fabricated.

The final pages delivered the killing blow to her already crumbling reality. Email records showed messages sent from her account to various fake addresses she had supposedly created, then forwarded back to herself—messages containing the exact threats and warnings she had believed came from Marcus. Technical data showed that all the emails originated from her laptop's IP address and were sent between 2:00 a.m. and 4:00 a.m. on multiple nights when she'd been alone in her apartment, allegedly documenting her "stalker's" activities.

Ann's legs finally gave out. She slid down against her car until she was crouching on the pavement, the papers clutched to her chest, her mind fracturing under the weight of contradictory realities. Everything she had documented, everything she had believed, everything she had feared—all of it inverted, transformed into evidence of her own obsession rather than Marcus's pursuit.

"This is insane," she whispered, looking up at Officer Ramirez with pleading eyes. "He's been following me. He planted the tracking device. He broke into my apartment. He cut my tire. He's been watching me for weeks." Her voice cracked on the final word, desperation leaking through each syllable.

Ramirez's expression softened almost imperceptibly—not with belief, Ann realized with horror, but with pity. The kind of pity reserved for someone who had lost touch with reality, who couldn't recognize the truth when presented with overwhelming evidence.

"The tracking device," Ann tried again, her voice strengthening with desperate certainty. "I found it under my car. I didn't put it there. I couldn't have—"

Ann's mind raced, trying to remember whether she had ever verified that the tracking device she'd shown Lena was actually functional, whether she had ever tested whether it was actively transmitting to somewhere, to someone. She had no proof. The thought was so disturbing she physically recoiled from it, the papers slipping from her grasp and scattering across the damp pavement.

"This can't be right," she whispered, more to herself than to the officers standing witness to her unraveling. "I'm not making this up. I'm not crazy. He did this. He did all of this."

Officer Ramirez gathered the scattered papers from the pavement with methodical care, her movements unhurried and precise as she straightened the edges against her thigh. The action—so normal, so mundane—stood in stark contrast to the way Ann's world was splintering around her. When Ramirez spoke, her voice carried the practiced neutrality of someone who had delivered devastating news many times before.

"Officer Hale began documenting your behavior approximately six weeks ago, Ms. Porter, after you were observed photographing him during routine visits to Granger's Restaurant and later following him to his home, and taking pictures of his patrol car in the middle of the night as it was parked outside." Ramirez handed the reorganized papers back to Ann, who accepted them with numb fingers. "At first, he believed it was a misunderstanding, perhaps a curious civilian interest in law enforcement. When your behavior escalated to following his patrol routes and appearing often near his residence, he opened an official investigation."

Ann shook her head, the motion becoming more frantic with each word Ramirez spoke. "No. No, that's backward. He started coming to the restaurant constantly and always sat in my section. Always watching me. I documented it because no one believed me."

Ann pressed her hands against her temples, as if she could physically hold her fracturing reality together. "But the tracking device," she whispered, clinging to the one piece of concrete evidence she had held in her own hands. "I found it under my car. I showed it to people. It was real."

Ramirez nodded, and the acknowledgment sent a surge of

desperate hope through Ann's chest—until the officer continued speaking. "The tracking device was real, yes. As the documentation shows, you purchased it online three weeks ago." She gestured toward the papers Ann still clutched. "What you showed to your coworkers was indeed a real tracking device—one that you had placed under your own vehicle."

"That's impossible," Ann breathed, though the certainty in her voice had begun to waver. "I would never—I couldn't have—why would I do that?"

"The investigation suggests you were creating evidence to support your belief that Officer Hale was stalking you," Ramirez explained, her clinical tone somehow more devastating than an accusation would have been.

Ann's breathing became shallow and rapid, her chest constricting as if bound by invisible wires. The world around her—the quiet street, the police cruiser with its lights still flashing, the two officers standing before her—began to blur at the edges. She pressed her back more firmly against her car, needing its solid presence to remain upright.

"But I remember," she insisted, her voice cracking. "I remember discovering the tracking device. I remember his patrol car driving past the restaurant during my shifts. I remember seeing it parked outside of my apartment complex at 2:00 a.m."

The second officer shifted his weight, his hand moving to rest casually near his holster as Ann's voice rose in pitch and volume. The subtle movement—not quite reaching for his weapon but preparing for the possibility—registered in Ann's peripheral awareness, adding another layer of surreal horror to the moment. They thought she was dangerous. Unstable.

"Memory is complex, Ms. Porter," Ramirez said, maintaining her distance as she spoke. "Especially when influenced by strong beliefs and emotions. The evidence suggests you've been experiencing a type of delusional disorder that has altered your perception of reality."

"No," Ann whispered, the single syllable containing all her

desperate denial. "No, I know what happened. I know what I saw. My tire… it was slashed."

"We suspect you might have done that yourself, Ms. Porter." Ramirez's expression shifted slightly, something like genuine concern breaking through her professional facade. "The investigation found evidence suggesting you may have been experiencing dissociative episodes—periods where you were taking actions you later didn't remember or attributed to someone else. Like when you told your colleague your place had been broken into. In reality, you probably left the door open yourself, or maybe forgot to close it."

The suggestion that she couldn't trust her own mind, her own memories, sent waves of nauseating panic through Ann's body. She looked down at the papers in her hands—the photographs showing her outside Marcus's apartment, the records of her vehicle following his patrol route, the purchase receipts for surveillance equipment—and for one terrible moment, she couldn't be certain whether they represented an elaborate frame-up or evidence of actions she had no memory of taking.

"The terms of the restraining order require you to maintain a minimum distance of five hundred feet from Officer Hale at all times," Ramirez continued, her tone shifting back to professional detachment. "You are prohibited from contacting him through any means—electronic, written, or through third parties. You are barred from visiting the police station without prior legal authorization. Violation of these terms is a criminal offense that could result in your arrest."

Ann barely heard the recitation of terms, her mind caught in a loop of contradicting realities. Had she really stood outside Marcus's apartment at nearly midnight? Had she followed his patrol car through residential streets? Had she purchased a tracking device and planted it on her own vehicle? Slashed her own tire? The possibility that she had done these things without remembering them—or worse, while believing she was the victim rather than the perpetrator—was too horrifying to comprehend.

"The court has also recommended a psychological evaluation," Ramirez added, her voice seeming to come from very far away. She handed her a business card for a facility. Ann took it but threw it on the passenger seat without even looking at it. "We can provide resources and referrals if you—"

"No," Ann interrupted, sudden clarity cutting through her confusion. She couldn't stay here, couldn't continue this conversation, couldn't bear the weight of what was being suggested. She needed to escape, to think, to sort through the collapsing architecture of her reality somewhere safe. "I understand the terms."

In one fluid motion, she pushed herself away from the car, gathered the scattered papers into the envelope, and reached for her door handle. The second officer tensed visibly but made no move to stop her as she slipped back into the driver's seat.

"Ms. Porter," Ramirez began, stepping forward, "I strongly recommend—"

But Ann had already slammed the door shut, turned the key in the ignition, and thrown the car into drive. The tires squealed against the pavement as she accelerated away from the officers, from their judgmental eyes that suggested she had been living in a reality entirely of her own creation.

As streetlights flashed past her window in rhythmic succession, Ann's gaze caught on her own reflection in the rearview mirror—eyes wide and desperate, face pale with shock. For one terrible moment, she didn't recognize the person staring back at her. The realization settled over her with suffocating weight: if the evidence was true, if the documentation wasn't fabricated... then she had been the stalker all along—the hunter rather than the hunted—the threat rather than the victim.

The road blurred before her as tears filled her eyes, the restraining order lying on the passenger seat beside her—physical proof of a reality she couldn't bear to accept but could no longer deny.

Chapter 44

SARAH'S FOOTSTEPS on the basement stairs echoed like a death knell. Each measured step brought her closer to our hiding place, the rhythm steady and unhurried—a predator confident in cornering her prey. Matt's eyes met mine in the dim light, a silent question passing between us. We had seconds, not minutes, to make a decision. The storage bins would conceal us for moments at most, and Sarah knew exactly what she was looking for, what she was hunting.

I pointed toward the far corner of the basement, where the water heater created a shadow deep enough to potentially shield our escape. Matt nodded, understanding instantly. When Sarah reached the midpoint of the stairs, we moved in perfect synchronization, sliding from behind the storage bins toward the deeper darkness as she descended. My heart hammered against my ribs, each beat feeling loud enough to give us away.

Sarah paused on the third-to-last step, a gun clutched in her hand. "I know you're down here," she called, her voice carrying that same pleasant lilt I'd heard when she'd offered us cookies in her perfect kitchen. "There's no need to hide. We're all friends here, aren't we?"

The water heater stood against the wall adjacent to the cellar window we'd entered through. If we timed it perfectly, we might reach the window while Sarah was distracted, checking her shrine. Matt gripped my arm, drawing my attention to the hammer hanging on a pegboard nearby. I gave a slight nod as he reached for it—we needed any advantage we could get.

Sarah reached the bottom of the stairs, her shadow stretching across the concrete floor. "Eva? Matt? Don't you want to see what else I've prepared for you?" She moved toward the shrine door, her back momentarily to us.

That was our chance.

We sprinted for the window, abandoning stealth for speed. Behind us, Sarah turned at the sound of our footsteps, her pleasant mask falling away. "No!" she shrieked, her voice transforming into something feral and raw. "You can't leave yet!"

Matt reached the window first, boosting me toward the opening without hesitation. I scrambled through, feeling the rough edge of the frame tear my shirt as I emerged into the night air. I turned immediately, reaching back to help Matt, who was already struggling to hoist himself up with one arm, the hammer still clutched in his other hand.

Sarah's fingers closed around his ankle just as I grabbed his wrists. For a moment, we were locked in a grotesque tug-of-war, Matt suspended between us, his face contorted with pain as the pull aggravated his wound. Then he kicked backward with his prosthetic leg, the solid impact breaking Sarah's grip. I hauled him upward with strength born of desperation, both of us tumbling onto the damp grass outside.

"Run," I gasped, pulling him to his feet. We sprinted across the darkened yard, not toward the street where we might be visible, but toward the neighboring property.

By dawn, we'd managed to "borrow" an unlocked car from a restaurant parking lot, leaving behind our burner phone number and a promise to return it—a crime of necessity that Matt's police ethics and my FBI training both rebelled against. We drove to the seediest part of Tampa, where questions weren't asked, and cash was the only currency that mattered.

The motel clerk barely glanced at us when I slid sixty dollars across the counter, his bloodshot eyes more interested in the small television behind the desk than in the identities of his customers. The room smelled of cigarettes and industrial cleaner, the carpet worn to threads in high-traffic areas. But it had a lock, a bathroom, and most importantly, a television.

Sleep came in fitful bursts, both of us too wired from adrenaline and too aware of our vulnerability to fully surrender to exhaustion. When morning finally broke, harsh sunlight filtering through the thin curtains, I sat on the edge of the sagging mattress and turned on the television.

The breaking news banner flashed across the bottom of the screen before the sound even kicked in. My body went rigid as I recognized the hotel in the background—the upscale Bayshore Plaza where I had stayed during my trip here, in the days before the book signing event. Crime scene tape cordoned off the entrance, uniformed officers moving efficiently around the perimeter while plainclothes detectives consulted near a parked ambulance.

"—third victim found early this morning by housekeeping staff," the reporter was saying, her expression professionally somber. "Sources close to the investigation confirm that, like the previous victims, this body was also found with a note of admission of guilt, written by former FBI agent Eva Rae Thomas, who remains at large."

The camera panned to show a gurney being wheeled out, a sheet-covered form strapped to its surface. Forensic technicians in blue gloves moved methodically through the scene, placing numbered markers beside evidence.

"Tampa Police is once again warning that Thomas should be considered armed and extremely dangerous. The FBI has joined the manhunt, with agents from the Behavioral Analysis Unit arriving to assist local authorities."

My own face appeared on screen again—my official FBI photo side by side with a grainy surveillance image from a gas station we'd stopped at days ago. Beneath the photos, the words "ARMED AND DANGEROUS" pulsed in red.

Matt's hand came to rest on my shoulder, his touch warm and steady despite everything we'd been through. "She's accelerating her timeline," he said quietly, his gaze fixed on the screen. "I didn't think she'd strike again this fast. I should have warned the reporter—what was her name again? Margaret Wells, yes. I could have...."

"You couldn't have done anything. Chances are she wouldn't have listened to you," Matt said. "You're the most wanted woman in this city right now. Why would she believe you?"

"She's panicking," I continued, forcing myself to analyze the situation professionally despite the sick feeling in my gut. "We weren't supposed to escape the basement. We weren't supposed to find the evidence. Now, she's improvising."

The reporter continued her grim narrative, each word confirming my worst fears: "Police have not released the victim's identity, but witnesses report seeing a woman matching Thomas's description near the hotel yesterday evening."

The footage showed a redheaded woman on a surveillance camera, but I knew it wasn't me. It was Sarah wearing a wig. Sarah wasn't just framing me anymore. She was becoming me—inserting herself into the narrative as my doppelgänger, ensuring witnesses would place "me" at the crime scene. The precision of her planning made my blood run cold. She had studied me, stalked me, and now she was systematically destroying everything I had built, all in service to her delusional fantasy of claiming Matt and creating her perfect family.

And she was winning.

Chapter 45

AFTER A RESTLESS SLEEP, I got up the next morning and couldn't remain still. The motel walls seemed to close in with each passing hour, the worn carpet beneath my feet developing a visible path from my repetitive pacing. The television's morning news programs continued to broadcast updates about Margaret Wells's murder, each report adding details that linked the crime more firmly to me. They were analyzing my career now, forensic psychologists and former colleagues dissecting my methods and my cases, searching for the moment when I had supposedly snapped. It was surreal watching strangers dismantle the life I'd built, using Sarah's carefully planted evidence to construct a monster wearing my face.

"She doesn't just want to frame me," I said suddenly, stopping mid-stride as the full picture crystallized in my mind. Matt looked up from his position by the window, where he'd been keeping watch through a narrow gap in the curtains. "This is complete identity absorption." I resumed pacing, my thoughts racing ahead of my words. "In Sarah's mind, she's not just removing me—she's replacing me. Each murder isn't just evidence against me; it's her audition for my role." I gestured toward the muted television. "She's demonstrating that she understands my methodology better than I do, that she's more worthy of being Eva Rae Thomas than I am."

"And claim everything that was yours," Matt added quietly.

"This isn't just an obsession—it's a complete psychological transference. She wants to erase me and become me in the same gesture."

Matt watched me carefully, his expression reflecting both professional assessment and personal concern. "You're talking about a whole other level of delusion."

"Because it's been festering for years," I explained. "Each rejection she has gotten, even from Collins, reinforced her belief that she deserves better, that happiness is being kept from her by others. She's not just stalking or obsessing—she's constructing an entirely new reality where she gets everything she believes she's entitled to."

"Each kill becomes more public, more dramatic than the last," Matt said. "She wants attention now—needs it to complete the frame."

"We need to ensure Tommy's safety throughout this," I said, thinking of Sarah's son with his careful movements and watchful eyes. "Whatever we do, he can't be collateral damage in his mother's delusion."

Matt's expression softened. "You're right. We should contact social services anonymously, make sure he's removed from the situation before we confront Sarah."

"She'll have contingencies for that," I warned. "She's too controlling to leave Tommy's whereabouts to chance, especially now that she knows we've seen her shrine."

"Then we build that into our plan," Matt decided. "Approach when Tommy is at school or with a relative—"

The burner phone chimed with a text message notification, interrupting our planning. We both stared at it for a moment. I reached for it slowly, a sense of dread building in my chest even before I unlocked the screen.

The image loaded gradually in the poor reception of our motel room—first a pair of frightened eyes, then the rest of a young face I recognized immediately. Tommy Winters stared into the camera, his expression a mixture of confusion and terror. A bruise darkened his left cheek, fresh enough that it hadn't fully developed. Below the photo, a message in stark black text:

Only you can save him now.

My hand trembled slightly as I showed the phone to Matt, watching his face harden as he processed what we were seeing. "She's using him as bait," I said, my voice tight with a fury I rarely allowed myself to feel. "And she knows I can't ignore it."

I paused in my preparations, the full weight of what we were facing settling over me. "She's going beyond what we anticipated. Using her own son as leverage shows how far out she is—the maternal protection instinct is usually the last to break down, even in severe psychosis."

Matt studied the photo again, his jaw tightening. "There's no timestamp or location data attached."

"She doesn't need to provide it," I said. "She knows exactly where I'll go."

"Back to her house," Matt concluded, his expression grim. "Into what's almost certainly a trap."

"She's counting on my training, my instinct to protect an innocent child. She knows I'll come, regardless of the risk."

"Then we don't give her what she's expecting," Matt said. "There has to be another approach, one she won't anticipate."

As we sat down to plan our counter-strategy, I kept seeing Tommy's frightened eyes in my mind. Despite everything—the manhunt, the framing, my destroyed reputation—it was the terror in that child's face that crystallized my resolve. Sarah had studied my cases extensively, learned my methods, and analyzed my techniques. But she had miscalculated on one critical point: I had spent my entire career hunting predators who exploited the vulnerable.

And I had never failed to find them.

"She thinks she knows me," I said, checking the burner phone one last time before powering it off. "Let's show her how wrong she is."

Chapter 46

THEN:

Ann stared at the wall in the walk-in closet, which she always kept closed with a lock, and at the dozens of photographs of Marcus Hale. Her fingers traced the red strings that connected his patrol routes to her apartment, to the restaurant, to the places she had convinced herself he followed her. The strings vibrated slightly under her touch, as if still alive with the energy of her delusion. She had built this monument to her obsession meticulously, piece by piece, photograph by photograph. Now she would dismantle it with the same precision.

The first photograph came down with a soft pop as she removed the thumbtack. Marcus was exiting the police station, unaware of her presence across the street. She remembered taking this one—the satisfaction she'd felt capturing what she'd believed was evidence, the rush of vindication. Now the memory twisted in her stomach, acid and shame rising in equal measure. Ann placed the photo face down on her coffee table and reached for the next.

Marcus at the coffee shop. Marcus walking his German Shepherd. Marcus pumping gas. Each image represented hours of surveillance, of watching, of waiting. Each was a testament not to his obsession with her, but hers with him. The wall began to empty, leaving behind a constellation of tiny holes in the plaster that mapped the geography of her delusion.

Her fingers trembled as she untied the red strings, rolling them into a neat ball out of habit before forcing herself to throw it into the growing pile of evidence. The maps came down next—his patrol routes highlighted in yellow, his apartment building floor plan marked with his unit number, the streets between her apartment and his tracked with time notations for optimal surveillance.

"It wasn't real," she whispered to the empty room, her voice sounding foreign to her ears. "None of it was real."

But it had felt real. That was the terrifying part. Every connection she'd made, every pattern she'd identified, every moment of fear and hypervigilance—all of it had been as solid and undeniable as the floor beneath her feet. It was a reality constructed entirely inside her mind, yet experienced with the full force of truth.

Ann gathered the photos and papers into a stack, feeling their weight—the physical manifestation of months of obsession. She carried them to the kitchen, opened a drawer, and removed a pair of scissors. The blades caught the dim light as she positioned them over the first photograph. For a moment, her hand refused to close, to make the first cut across Marcus's face.

"Do it," she commanded herself, and the scissors snipped, slicing through his left eye and down across his cheek. The violence of the action shocked her, but she continued, cutting each photo into smaller and smaller pieces until Marcus was reduced to confetti. Her movements became faster, more frantic, the scissors working mechanically as she destroyed the physical evidence of her fixation.

Maps followed, then notes, then printed emails she had convinced herself he had sent. The kitchen counter disappeared beneath drifts of shredded paper, each piece a fragment of the elaborate fiction she had constructed around herself. When the scissors began to cramp her hand, Ann moved to tearing the papers directly, her nails catching and tearing on the glossy photo paper, leaving tiny wounds that stung with sweat.

Three hours into her destruction, she turned to her laptop. Digital evidence would be harder to truly eradicate, but she had to try. Ann opened folder after folder of surveillance notes, timestamp records, and patrol schedules downloaded from public records requests. She highlighted them all and dragged them to the trash icon, watching as the deletion progress bar slowly filled.

But when she reached the photo folder—4,327 images of Marcus captured over three months—her finger hesitated over the delete button. These were different somehow. Personal. They represented not just her delusion but the strange intimacy she had constructed with a man who barely knew she existed. In these images, she had captured moments no one else had seen: Marcus laughing on his phone in his car, Marcus absently scratching his dog behind the ears, Marcus with his guard down in ways he rarely allowed in public.

Ann's heart raced as she quickly created a new folder buried deep in her financial records, labeled innocuously as "backup receipts." With quick, furtive movements—as if someone might be watching even now—she transferred selected images to the hidden location. Not all of them. Just the ones where his smile reached his eyes. Just the ones where he looked peaceful. Just the ones that had made her feel connected to him.

The clock on her laptop showed 3:47 a.m. She had been at this for hours, and dawn approached with its threat of revealing light. Ann rubbed her eyes, gritty from strain and dried tears. The trash bin icon showed thousands of deleted files, but the secret folder held forty-three carefully selected photographs—a kernel of her obsession preserved like a tumor she couldn't quite excise.

In the bathroom, Ann washed her face, avoiding her reflection in the mirror. She couldn't bear to see whatever might look back at her—the woman who had convinced herself she was a victim while systematically stalking a police officer, who had manipulated her friends into supporting a delusion, who had destroyed her career and reputation over an elaborate fiction.

Back in the living room, she surveyed her progress. The wall was bare except for the faint shadow where papers had protected the paint from fading. The physical evidence was destroyed, shredded beyond recognition, and stuffed into three black garbage bags by the door. Her apartment looked almost normal now—almost like the home of someone whose mind wasn't fractured, who didn't construct elaborate persecution narratives, who didn't obsessively document the movements of strangers.

Yet as the first gray light of dawn seeped through her blinds, Ann found herself opening the hidden folder on her laptop once more. Forty-three images of Marcus Hale looked back at her, his existence distilled into moments she had stolen from him without his knowledge or consent. Her finger hovered over the delete button again, her breathing shallow and quick.

"Tomorrow," she whispered, closing the laptop without deleting the folder. "I'll delete them tomorrow."

The lie settled between her and the screen, transparent but necessary. Ann knew she wouldn't delete them tomorrow, or the next day, or perhaps ever. Some part of her obsession remained, buried but intact, like a seed that would sprout again given the right conditions.

She tied the garbage bags closed with trembling hands. The physical evidence was gone, but the map of her delusion remained imprinted on her mind, as indelible as the tiny holes dotting her closet wall. As Ann slumped onto her couch, exhaustion finally overtaking her, the hidden folder of photographs pulsed in her awareness like a second heartbeat—the last piece of Marcus she couldn't bring herself to destroy.

Early morning light sliced through the gaps in Ann's blinds, casting thin stripes across her sleeping form on the couch. She jerked awake, disoriented, her neck stiff from the awkward angle. For one merciful moment, her mind was blank—then yesterday's revelations crashed back into her consciousness. The restraining order. The evidence. The wall of photographs, now torn down and stuffed into garbage bags by her door. Ann pushed herself upright, wincing at the protest of muscles held tight with tension all night. She had to leave. Now.

Before they came for her.

She yanked the largest suitcase from her closet, its wheels catching on the carpet as she dragged it to her bedroom. Clothes came off hangers in bunches, hangers clattering to the floor as she stuffed garments haphazardly into the open bag. No time to fold. No time to sort. Just grab, pack, and run.

"They have evidence," she whispered to herself, the sound of her own voice startling in the quiet apartment. "They'll be coming to take me away."

Her hands shook so violently that she dropped a stack of T-shirts twice before managing to stuff them into a duffel bag. Sweat beaded along her hairline despite the cool morning air. Her heart hammered against her ribs with such force that she pressed her palm against her chest, as if she could physically restrain its frantic rhythm.

Ann paused at her dresser, catching sight of herself in the mirror—hair wild, eyes ringed with exhaustion, skin pale and clammy. She barely recognized the woman staring back at her. Was this what madness looked like? The thought flitted across her consciousness before she pushed it away, returning to her frenzied packing.

No, it wasn't, she told herself. They were the ones who were crazy. Not her. This was what gaslighting looked like. They had changed the narrative of her reality, making her doubt herself.

She wasn't going to let them.

Ann's hands gripped the steering wheel so tightly her knuckles bleached white against the black plastic. The morning streets unfolded before her, familiar yet suddenly foreign, as if she were seeing them through someone else's eyes. Every traffic light, every pedestrian, every passing car registered in her hypervigilant mind as a potential threat or witness. She had stuffed her Honda to capacity—clothes and personal items crammed into every available space, the trash bags of shredded evidence secured in her trunk like bodies she was disposing of.

Her breath came in shallow pulls that never quite filled her lungs, leaving her lightheaded as she navigated the town she had called home for years. A town she now had to flee. A town where everyone—her boss, her coworkers, even her neighbor Rosa with her seemingly genuine concern—had turned against her, convinced by Marcus's elaborate manipulation that Ann was the unstable one, the stalker rather than the stalked.

The digital clock on her dashboard read 7:32 a.m. Early enough that the streets remained relatively empty, most residents still at breakfast tables or morning showers. Ann had chosen this hour deliberately—less chance of being seen, less traffic to navigate, less likelihood of running into anyone who might try to stop her.

She took the long way out of town, avoiding Granger's Restaurant and the apartment building where Lena lived. The last thing she needed was another confrontation, another person telling her that she needed "help," that her perception of reality was distorted. Ann knew what she had experienced. Despite the evidence they'd shown her—evidence that had momentarily shaken her certainty—she clung to her version of events. They were the ones who didn't understand. They were the ones who had been fooled.

The route she had chosen took her past the police station—a mistake she realized too late as the brick building came into view. Ann's foot instinctively eased off the gas pedal, her car slowing as she approached. She should have planned better, should have checked a map, should have—

Movement on the station steps caught her eye. Two figures emerged into the morning light—Marcus Hale and Officer Ramirez, deep in conversation as they descended toward the parking lot. Ann's breath stopped entirely, her body freezing except for her eyes, which locked onto Marcus's tall form with the precision of a predator tracking prey.

He looked tired. Even from this distance, she could see the slight droop in his shoulders, the way he rubbed at the back of his neck as he listened to whatever Ramirez was saying. A surge of something that wasn't quite concern and wasn't quite satisfaction rushed through Ann's system. Had he been up all night because of her? Was he stressed about the restraining order? Did he miss her?

Her hand moved toward the turn signal—an automatic response born of weeks spent following his movements, documenting his routine. The familiar urge to track him, to know where he was going and what he was doing, flooded her system like a physical craving—just one more time. Just to see where he went after leaving the station. Just to—

"No." The word emerged sharp and loud in her quiet car, startling even herself. Ann jerked her hand away from the turn signal, gripping the steering wheel again with both hands. She forced her foot down on the accelerator, her gaze fixed deliberately on the road ahead as she passed the station.

"Don't look back," she whispered to herself. "Just keep driving. Steady pace."

But her eyes betrayed her, darting to the rearview mirror where Marcus's figure was still visible, growing smaller with each second but burning into her consciousness nonetheless. It took every ounce of willpower to keep the car moving forward, away from him, away from the pull he exerted on her fractured psyche.

The town gradually thinned into suburbs, then into scattered rural properties, then into the empty highway that would carry her away from everything familiar. Only when the "Now Leaving" sign disappeared behind her did Ann allow herself to exhale fully, her shoulders dropping from their position near her ears, her death grip on the steering wheel easing slightly.

Days along with hundreds of miles passed beneath her tires, the landscape changing from forest to farmland to swamps. Ann drove mechanically, her mind cycling through memories, justifications, explanations—constructing and reconstructing narratives that allowed her to remain the victim rather than the perpetrator in her own story.

They could say what they wanted. She knew the real truth.

On the third day, a gas station appeared on the horizon, its sign flickering even in the morning light—some electrical issue causing the fluorescent bulbs to pulse arrhythmically. Ann's fuel gauge hovered just above empty, forcing her to pull into the cracked concrete lot. The place looked deserted except for a single attendant visible through the convenience store's streaked glass.

Ann filled her tank methodically, the smell of gasoline sharp in her nostrils as she watched the numbers climb on the pump display. Her phone vibrated in her pocket—had been vibrating periodically throughout her drive, though she'd ignored it until now. With the pump running, she had no excuse to continue her avoidance.

Six new messages. Lena, Miriam, Chef Cho, Tom Granger. Their names lined up on her screen like an indictment.

Lena: "Ann, please call me. I'm worried about you. We can figure this out."

Ann's thumb moved automatically, deleting the message without fully letting the words sink in. She didn't need Lena's false concern. Didn't need the pity of someone who had abandoned her when she needed support most.

Miriam: "I'm so sorry about everything. The restaurant isn't the same without you. Please call when you're ready to talk."

Delete.

Chef Cho: "Porter. Heard what happened. Know a good lawyer if you need one. Text me."

Ann paused, momentarily surprised by the offer. Then suspicion bloomed—was this another trap? Another attempt to locate her, to bring her back, to force her into "treatment" she didn't need? Her thumb moved again. Delete.

The final message was from Tom Granger, sent less than an hour ago: "It's not too late to get help. Everyone makes mistakes. What matters is how we handle them afterward. The offer still stands—Granger's will cover the first month at the facility. Please consider it, Ann. For your own sake."

Her finger hovered over the delete button, but something stopped her. A tiny crack appeared in the fortress of her conviction—a moment of clarity that whispered: What if they're right? What if I really did imagine all of it?

The gas pump clicked off, jarring her from the uncomfortable thought. Ann returned the nozzle to its holder and screwed her gas cap back into place. As she slid back into the driver's seat, her gaze fell on a business card, which had fallen from the passenger seat onto the floor.

New Horizons Psychiatric Treatment Center.

The place Officer Ramirez had suggested. Ann picked up the card, turning it over in her fingers, feeling its weight and solidity.

For one brief, terrifying moment, the possibility opened before her—that everything she believed might be wrong, that her mind had constructed an elaborate fiction, that she needed the kind of help this card represented.

Then the moment passed, the crack in her conviction sealing shut as quickly as it had appeared.

"They're all just gaslighting me," Ann muttered, tossing her phone onto the passenger seat beside the business card. "I'm the only one who knows the truth."

She started the engine and pulled back onto the empty highway, accelerating quickly as if she could outrun the doubts that had momentarily surfaced. The road stretched before her, empty and promising—a clean slate, a new start, a place where no one knew her name or her history.

Ann refused to acknowledge the small voice whispering that no matter how far she drove, the real problem remained seated right beside her, inescapable as her own shadow.

As she stopped at a roadside diner to eat, the neon lights flickered as she slid into a vinyl booth. She'd barely glanced at the menu when movement on the mounted TV caught her eye—a redheaded woman with a confident posture speaking into a forest of microphones.

"Who's that?" she asked, nodding toward the screen as the waitress refilled ketchup bottles nearby.

The waitress followed her gaze and smiled. "Eva Rae Thomas. FBI hotshot. Just cracked that serial case nobody could solve down in Tampa." She nodded toward the screen. "Got a book out now about how she gets inside killers' heads. Half the women in Florida want to be her, the other half want to meet her."

"Eva Rae Thomas," she whispered, rolling each syllable across her tongue like a hard candy. Her lips curved into a smile that didn't reach her eyes. "I think I want to be you, too."

The broadcast switched to a studio anchor, her name appearing in bold white letters across the bottom of the screen.

"Sarah Winters," she murmured, fingertip tracing the name in the condensation of her water glass. "That's perfect."

Chapter 47

THE MOTEL ROOM walls seemed to pulse with each heartbeat, closing in tighter with every passing minute. I couldn't stop staring at Tommy's frightened face on the burner phone screen, the bruise on his cheek a violent splash against his pale skin. Sarah had crossed a line I hadn't anticipated—using her own child as bait. The calculated cruelty of it churned my stomach, even as the analytical part of my brain admired the tactical precision. She knew exactly which button to push to force my hand.

"We need a different approach," I said, resuming my pacing across the worn carpet. Five steps one way, turn, five steps back—the limited geography of our temporary prison.

Matt sat on the edge of the bed, wincing as he adjusted his position to accommodate his injured ribs. The makeshift bandage we'd applied was holding, but the strain showed in the tightness around his eyes.

"Eva Rae, you know this is a trap," he said, his voice gentle but firm. "She's manipulating you with the one thing she knows you can't ignore." He gestured toward the television, muted but still broadcasting my face next to the word "MANHUNT" in angry red letters. "Your face is plastered across every screen in Florida. You step outside, someone will recognize you."

I stopped pacing long enough to give him a hard look. "Rule Seven of The Profiler's Code, Matt. 'Truth before badge.' The ultimate loyalty is to finding the truth, even when it conflicts with official positions." I tapped the phone screen where Tommy's frightened eyes stared back at me. "And the truth is there's an innocent child caught in the middle of this."

"That's not how that rule was meant to be applied," Matt countered, shifting again with a barely suppressed groan. "It's about not letting departmental politics interfere with investigations, not charging headfirst into an obvious trap."

"Then how about the unwritten rule? The one that says we protect innocents, regardless of personal cost." I resumed pacing, the thin carpet offering minimal cushion against the concrete subfloor. "Tommy didn't ask for any of this. He's a victim of his mother's delusion as much as we are."

Matt pushed himself to his feet, moving to block my path. His face was pale with pain but determined. "And how exactly do you plan to protect him if you're dead or in custody? Sarah has orchestrated three murders, framed you perfectly for each one, and nearly killed us at the boathouse. She's not suddenly going to make a convenient mistake.

"She already has," I insisted, sidestepping him to continue my circuit of the room. "Using Tommy this way shows she's desperate. Her plan is unraveling."

"Or it's exactly what she planned all along—forcing you into the open by exploiting your protective instincts." Matt followed me with his eyes as I moved. "That's what makes it such an effective trap. She studied you enough to know you'd never ignore a child in danger, even at the cost of your own safety."

I stopped at the grimy window, peering through a crack in the curtains at the parking lot beyond. Afternoon sun glinted off windshields, creating miniature beacons in the asphalt expanse. Somewhere out there, a nine-year-old boy was living in terror of his own mother, witnessing her descent into murderous obsession.

"What would you have me do?" I asked, turning back to Matt. "Ignore him? Let her do God knows what while we hide in this room?"

"I want you to think like the FBI profiler you are, not like—" He cut himself off, but I heard the unspoken words anyway.

"Not like a mother?" I finished, my voice sharper than intended. "Is that what you were going to say?"

Matt's expression softened. "Not like someone personally invested. You taught me that emotional distance is crucial to clear thinking in cases like this."

"Rule Three," I acknowledged. "'Maintain emotional distance.' A profiler who becomes emotionally invested loses objectivity and risks missing crucial details."

"Exactly."

"But I've already broken that rule, Matt. The moment Sarah made this about us—about you and me—objectivity went out the window." I gestured at the bandage visible beneath his shirt. "We're both bleeding from this case. Literally."

The burner phone rang before he could respond, its harsh electronic tone shattering our standoff. Juan Ramirez's number flashed on the screen. Matt and I exchanged a look—Juan was our only remaining lifeline to the outside world.

I answered, putting the call on speaker. "Go ahead, Juan."

"She's got company." Juan's voice came through with uncharacteristic urgency, background noise suggesting he was calling from inside a vehicle. "I've been watching the house since dawn. The place is now packed with police. I think they're waiting for you, expecting you to come there. She probably told them you would."

My eyes met Matt's across the room. "What about Tommy?"

"I don't know. He could be in there with her."

Matt moved closer to the phone. "She could be hurting him right in front of the police?"

"Stay on her," I instructed. "But maintain distance. She's proven more resourceful than we anticipated."

"Copy that." Juan's voice dropped lower. "Be careful, Eva Rae.

Whatever's happening with her, it's accelerating." The line went dead.

I looked at Matt. "What do we do? We have to get inside that house and save Tommy before it's too late."

"I agree, but how? The entire Tampa Bay police department and the FBI are waiting outside, ready to grab you as soon as you get there. Me too, for that matter, for helping a fugitive. We'll never make it past them. All their focus is on you."

"Then we change their focus," I said. "I have an idea."

Part V

Chapter 48

I ENTERED Tampa Mall through the east entrance, moving with the measured confidence of a woman who belonged there. My right hand rested casually inside my jacket pocket, fingers brushing against the cold metal of the gun I'd secured from Juan's emergency supplies. Every face I passed was a potential witness, every security camera a deliberate part of my plan. The weight of what I was about to do settled across my shoulders like a familiar burden—not unlike the weight I'd carried during my most dangerous FBI operations. Only this time, I wasn't operating with the authority of a badge. I was creating chaos by design.

The plan had come together in the predawn hours, after Juan had met with us in the park.

"We need to draw the police away," I'd told Matt and Juan. "Create a situation that forces them to leave the house."

Matt had understood immediately. "A distraction. Something that would pull police resources away from her neighborhood."

"Something that plays into her narrative about me," I'd added, the idea crystallizing with terrible clarity.

With a gun in my pocket that Juan had provided for me, I scanned my surroundings with the automatic threat assessment I'd developed through years of field work. Two security guards near the central corridor, speaking into shoulder-mounted radios. Four visible security cameras covering the main walkways. Emergency exits at forty-foot intervals, each marked with illuminated signs. The morning crowd was modest but growing—mostly elderly mall-walkers getting exercise before the stores opened, young mothers with strollers, and retail employees arriving for their shifts.

Perfect. Enough witnesses to spread the word, not enough to create unmanageable chaos.

I made my way toward the center where the fountain was, passing storefronts still dark and shuttered. A cleaning crew mopped the gleaming floor, their yellow caution signs creating islands in the walkway that I navigated around. An elderly couple nodded as they passed, the woman's smile flickering briefly in my direction. I wondered if she recognized me from the news or simply saw another middle-aged woman on a shopping spree.

The fountain opened before me—a circular space in the center of it all. I glanced toward the food court. Workers arranged chairs around tables, filled napkin dispensers, and wiped counters with practiced movements. The ceiling stretched high above, skylights allowing morning sun to illuminate the area better than the mall's fluorescent lighting. I noted the positions of each security camera, the service corridors marked "Staff Only," and the wide entrance to the main shopping concourse.

I selected my position carefully—central enough to be visible from multiple angles, close enough to the service corridor for a quick exit, far enough from innocent bystanders to minimize risk. I had taken the magazine out for now, so there would be no bullet, and no one would be hurt, except for the scare. The chaos would be controlled, contained. No one would be hurt if everything went according to plan.

My heart maintained its steady rhythm as I settled by the fountain, removing my sunglasses and tucking them into my pocket. I wanted the cameras to capture my face clearly.

Two security guards passed nearby, their conversation about weekend plans carrying across the quiet space. Neither gave me a second glance—just another woman waiting, meeting someone, or maybe waiting for the coffee shop to open. I let them pass, counting seconds in my head.

The burner phone in my pocket vibrated once—Juan's signal that they were in position outside Sarah's house. I gave myself thirty more seconds, using the time to scan the food court once more. A young family had settled two tables away, their toddler banging a plastic toy against the table surface. The mother looked exhausted, with dark circles beneath her eyes, suggesting sleepless nights with her child. I waited until she bent to retrieve something from a diaper bag, ensuring her attention was diverted.

I stood smoothly, withdrawing the gun from my pocket in a single fluid movement that my body remembered from thousands of practice drills. The weapon felt impossibly heavy in my hand, its presence instantly transforming me from an anonymous shopper into a public threat. Before doubt could intrude, I raised my arm and fired three bullet-less shots into the concrete ceiling above.

The sound cracked through the open space like thunder, echoing off hard surfaces and silencing all other noise for one suspended moment.

Then came the screams.

The frozen tableau shattered into frantic movement. Parents grabbed children, elderly couples clutched each other, and food service workers ducked behind counters. Security guards spun toward the sound, hands moving to their weapons as they shouted commands that were lost in the growing panic.

"Gun! She has a gun!"

"Everyone down!"

"This way—emergency exit!"

I moved with the surging crowd, allowing the human current to carry me toward the main corridor. The gun, now hidden again in my pocket, had served its purpose. My face had been captured on every security camera in the food court. Within minutes, those images would be transmitted to law enforcement across Tampa Bay.

"That's her!" a woman's voice cut through the chaos behind me. "That's the FBI killer from the news!"

I didn't turn, didn't acknowledge the recognition. Instead, I peeled away from the main flow of fleeing shoppers, slipping through a service door marked "Staff Only".

I jogged down the hallway. In the distance, I could hear alarm systems activating, the piercing electronic wail adding to the confusion.

By now, Matt and Juan would be entering Sarah's house, using the window I'd created with my desperate diversion. All available police would be coming here in a matter of seconds.

I pushed through a final door and emerged into morning sunlight at the rear of the mall. A service area stretched before me—dumpsters, delivery trucks, the ordinary infrastructure of retail commerce. No people visible yet, though I could hear sirens approaching from multiple directions.

The burner phone vibrated in my pocket again—two short pulses, our code for "mission proceeding." Matt and Juan were inside Sarah's house. The distraction had worked.

I slipped between two delivery trucks and made my way toward the drainage ditch that would lead me to our predetermined rendezvous point.

The true cost of what I'd just done would come later—a new charge added to the growing list of alleged crimes, another nail in the coffin of my reputation. But if it gave Matt and Juan the time they needed to save Tommy, it would be worth it.

As I disappeared into the trees beyond the mall's property line, leaving the wail of sirens and shouts of confusion behind, I allowed myself one moment of grim satisfaction. For the first time since this nightmare began, Sarah Winters wasn't dictating the terms of engagement.

We were.

Chapter 49

I REACHED OUR RENDEZVOUS POINT–AN abandoned gas station—ten minutes after leaving the mall, my lungs burning. The small building's boarded windows and graffiti-covered walls made it invisible to casual observers, perfect for our needs. Juan had left the rusty back door unlocked as planned. I slipped inside, checking my burner phone every few seconds for updates from Matt and Juan.

The abandoned store smelled of mildew and old gasoline, its shelves long stripped bare by scavengers. I positioned myself by a narrow gap in the plywood covering the windows, watching the road for any sign of pursuit while keeping the phone clutched in my hand. Every minute felt stretched to the breaking point, each passing car making my heart stutter until it proved to be just another commuter on their morning drive.

The burner phone vibrated at last. A text from Matt: "In. But no one here. No Tommy."

Damn it!

The phone vibrated again: "No Sarah either. She must have taken him somewhere. We will gather evidence and take folders with us."

My stomach tightened. The shrine we'd discovered in her basement would be good evidence. "Take everything you can."

Twelve minutes since they'd entered the house. I checked my watch compulsively, calculating how much longer their window would remain open. The phone remained silent for what felt like an eternity, but was actually only three minutes.

When it finally vibrated, the message chilled me to the bone: "Found something new in her calendar."

Before I could respond, a call came through—Matt breaking protocol, which meant whatever they'd discovered couldn't wait. I answered immediately.

"Eva Rae." His voice was tight with urgency. "Sarah's planning to kill Tommy and herself. "

The world seemed to tilt beneath me. "What?"

"She's written it all in the calendar. She's taking him to a cabin in the Ocala Forest."

I pressed my back against the wall, needing its solidity as my mind processed this horror. "When?"

"Today." There was a pause, the sound of pages turning. "She's been preparing the cabin for days. Setting the stage."

A distant siren wailed through the phone connection. Matt's voice dropped lower. "We've got to get out of here. Juan's downloading everything we can from her computer. I'm taking the files, the calendar, and the photos. The maps to the cabin, her detailed plans, everything."

"Where exactly is the cabin?" I asked, already moving toward the back door, calculating routes and travel times.

"Ocala National Forest, eastern edge, near Alexander Springs. There's a service road marked on her map that leads to an isolated cabin. She's labeled it 'Final Scene.'"

I knew the area—remote, heavily wooded, with scattered vacation properties that stood empty most of the year. Perfect for what Sarah had planned. "How long ago did she leave?"

"Who knows? She could have left last night."

The thought of Tommy's confused face as his adoptive mother

prepared to make him the final victim in her elaborate performance made my chest constrict with rage and fear.

"I'm sending everything to media contacts now," Matt said, the sound of rapid typing audible in the background. "The calendar pages, photos of her shrine, everything we've found. If we can't stop her, at least the truth will come out."

Another siren wailed, closer this time. "They're coming," Juan's voice came through faintly. "Time's up."

"Go," I urged. "Get out now."

"What about you?" Matt asked, concern evident despite the urgency of their situation.

"I'm heading to the cabin. Sarah doesn't know we've discovered her plan. I might be able to reach them before—" I couldn't finish the sentence, the words sticking in my throat.

"Eva Rae, wait for us. She's dangerous, more unstable than we realized. The calendar entries from the last few days show complete dissociation from reality. She's writing as if she's already become you."

"That's exactly why I can't wait," I replied, already moving toward the rear exit. "Tommy doesn't have hours left—he might not even have minutes."

The sound of a door closing came through the phone, followed by muffled footsteps. Matt and Juan were leaving the house, hopefully seconds before the police returned.

"We're out," Matt confirmed breathlessly. "Heading to the car now. We'll meet you by the cabin. Don't go in alone, Eva. Please."

"I'll try to wait," I said, both of us knowing it was likely a lie. "Be careful."

I ended the call, tucking the phone into my pocket as I slipped out the back door of the abandoned gas station.

I had spent my career stopping killers before they claimed their next victims. Now I was racing to prevent a twisted mirror version of myself from committing her ultimate crime—a performance designed specifically for my eyes, using Tommy's life as her final, devastating prop.

As I stood outside the building waiting for Matt and Juan, I saw a truck parked in the back of the parking lot. I didn't even think about it for a minute. I had watched Matt hot-wire enough cars to know exactly how it was done.

There was no time to waste.

Chapter 50

I ABANDONED my stolen vehicle about half a mile from the cabins and continued on foot through the dense forest of longleaf pine trees. I couldn't risk Sarah seeing my truck as I approached the area. Sarah's cabin appeared through the trees like something from a twisted fairy tale—weathered wood siding and moss-covered roof. I spotted her car immediately and knew that's where they were. I crouched behind a fallen oak, its rotting trunk providing cover as I studied the clearing. Sarah's blue Honda sat parked at an angle near the front steps, driver's door still ajar as if she'd been in a hurry, or wanted it to look that way.

Time was a luxury I didn't have. Matt and Juan would be at least twenty minutes behind me—assuming they'd evaded police after leaving Sarah's house. Twenty minutes might as well be twenty hours for Tommy. I'd seen enough crime scenes to know how quickly situations involving unstable perpetrators could deteriorate, especially when children were involved.

I circled the cabin's perimeter, staying within the treeline, my footfalls silent on the carpet of pine needles despite the persistent ache radiating through my body. Each movement required calculation—balancing stealth against speed, caution against urgency. My

FBI tactical training took precedence over my less stable emotions, providing a framework of practiced protocols that kept panic at bay. Assess. Plan. Execute.

The cabin sat isolated at the end of the service road, backing against a steep hill that would make approach from that direction impossible. Two small windows faced the front clearing, curtains drawn but light visible through thin gaps. A larger window on the west side offered better visibility. I moved toward it in a low crouch.

I pressed my back against the rough wooden siding beneath the window, listening. A child's muffled sob came from inside, followed by a woman's voice—too low to make out words, but carrying that distinctive lilt I'd come to recognize as Sarah's "sweet" persona. The false warmth in her tone now chilled me more than outright threats ever could.

Slowly, I raised myself just enough to peer through a gap where the curtains didn't quite meet. The cabin's interior came into focus—a single main room with a small kitchenette to the left and doors leading to what I assumed were bedrooms to the right. A stone fireplace dominated the far wall.

Tommy sat tied to a wooden chair in the center of the room, a rope securing his small wrists to the armrests. His face was streaked with tears, eyes wide with terror as he tracked Sarah's movements around the room. No visible injuries, at least not yet. That was something.

Sarah paced in a pattern that seemed almost choreographed—three steps toward Tommy, pause, gesture with the gun, four steps to the fireplace, pause, mutter something to herself, then repeat. She was wearing an outfit disturbingly similar to ones I often wore—dark slacks, a simple button-down shirt, and practical shoes. Her blonde hair had been replaced with a red wig. The transformation wasn't just psychological anymore; she was physically becoming "me" for her final act.

The gun in her right hand was a .38 revolver—the same caliber used to kill Collins. The same we had found in her basement, I assumed. She held it with uncomfortable familiarity, her index finger resting alongside the trigger guard rather than on the trigger itself.

I studied her body language, the indicators of mental state that I'd been trained to recognize. Her movements carried a jittery energy—steps too precise, turns too sharp. Her free hand twitched at her side, fingers spreading and contracting in an unconscious rhythm. Micro-expressions flashed across her face between longer periods of eerie calm—flickers of rage, satisfaction, even something like tenderness when she looked at Tommy. Classic signs of a fractured psyche struggling to maintain control.

Sarah stopped suddenly, cocking her head as if listening to something. Her lips moved in what appeared to be a response to an unheard voice. Tommy's eyes widened further, his body shrinking back against the chair as much as his restraints would allow.

I needed to get inside. Now.

The front door wasn't an option—too exposed, too noisy. I eased away from the window, continuing my circuit of the cabin. At the rear, I found what I was looking for—a back entrance, likely leading to a storage area, based on the cabin's typical layout. The wooden door showed signs of water damage, the frame slightly warped from seasonal swelling and contraction.

I entered a small storage room cluttered with fishing gear and dusty camping equipment. Light spilled through a doorway ahead, connecting to what appeared to be a narrow hallway running alongside the main room. Moving silently despite the debris underfoot, I positioned myself just inside this hallway, where shadows provided cover while offering a partial view of Sarah and Tommy.

From this vantage point, I could hear Sarah's voice clearly for the first time—the gentle, singsong quality that had once seemed so genuine now overlaid with something brittle and false.

"It won't hurt, sweetheart," she was saying to Tommy as she made another circuit of the room. "It will be quick, just like falling asleep."

Tommy's frightened whimper cut through me like physical pain. I pressed myself against the wall, calculating angles and distances, noting the positions of each piece of furniture that might provide cover or obstruct my view. Sarah was approximately fifteen feet from my position, Tommy another six feet beyond her. The gun remained in her right hand, occasionally rising to emphasize points in her one-sided conversation.

I slowed my breathing, forcing my heart rate down through practiced control. The hallway's shadows concealed me for now, but any movement toward the main room would expose me immediately. I needed to understand exactly what Sarah was planning before I revealed myself—I needed to know the script she was following in order to disrupt it effectively.

I settled deeper into my hiding place, becoming part of the cabin's shadows as Sarah continued her delusional monologue to Tommy, unaware that her carefully orchestrated final scene had gained an unscripted audience.

Chapter 51

"THE POLICE WILL FIND us tomorrow morning," Sarah told Tommy, her voice carrying the practiced warmth of a mother reading a bedtime story. She knelt in the center of the room, uncapping a piece of chalk with deliberate care. "They'll find you first, right here." She drew a child-sized outline on the wooden floor, her movements precise and almost tender. "Poor Tommy, killed by the deranged FBI agent who'd been stalking his mother for months. Such a tragedy." Her tone conveyed none of the horror her words described, as if discussing a minor inconvenience rather than the murder of a child—her child.

From my hidden position in the hallway, I watched Sarah rise smoothly from her kneeling position, the gun held casually at her side as if it were nothing more threatening than a TV remote. Tommy's eyes followed her movement, his small chest rising and falling in rapid, shallow breaths.

"After they find you," Sarah continued, moving to another spot near the fireplace, "they'll find me." She began drawing a second outline, larger this time. "Right here, executed by the same woman who killed poor Richard Collins, Alice Mercer, and that nasty Wells woman." She glanced up at Tommy with a smile that belonged on a

PTA volunteer, not a woman mapping out a double murder. "And do you know what the best part is, sweetie?"

Tommy shook his head, his lower lip trembling.

"The best part is that evil Eva Rae will be found right there." She gestured toward the cabin's front door, marking a third chalk outline. "She'll have my—I mean her gun in her hand, having turned it on herself when she realized what she'd done. It's the perfect ending to our story."

My fingers tightened involuntarily against the wall as Sarah's plan unfolded before me. The precision of her staging—the positions, the narrative she was creating—revealed a mind that had studied crime scene analysis extensively—my crime scene analysis. She'd read my books and my case files, and learned how I interpreted physical evidence. Now she was using that knowledge to create the perfect frame, right down to the spatial relationships between bodies that would suggest a specific sequence of events to investigators.

"See these marks?" Sarah set down the chalk and picked up a small spray bottle. "This is for the blood spatter. It has to be just right." She spritzed liquid in an arc that caught the firelight—water now, but intended to show where real blood would land. "I studied Eva Rae's Lakeside Killer case very carefully. She testified about blood spatter patterns for three days during that trial."

She returned to Tommy, crouching before him with the gun dangling between her knees. "The medical examiner will determine that you were killed instantly—a single shot to the temple." She raised the gun, pressing the cold metal barrel against Tommy's head. "You won't feel a thing, I promise."

Tommy jerked away from the touch, a broken sob escaping his lips. "Please, Mom. Please, don't do this."

"Shhh." Sarah stroked his hair with her free hand. "I'm not your mom anymore, remember? Today I'm Eva Rae Thomas, troubled FBI agent, unable to distinguish between her cases and reality." She lowered her voice to a conspiratorial whisper. "It's method acting, Tommy. I have to become her completely."

I shifted my weight, calculating distances and angles. Sarah stood approximately twelve feet from my position, the gun alternating between casual gestures and deliberate threats to Tommy. The main room offered little cover—a coffee table, an armchair, and the wooden chair to which Tommy was secured. If I rushed her, she'd have time to swing the gun toward me or, worse, toward Tommy. If I announced myself from a distance, I'd give her time to take Tommy hostage. She was expecting me, yes, but not so soon. She thought there was still time. Tommy had to go first, then me as I came through the door, and then she'd kill herself if she ever followed through with the last part. I had a feeling she was going to hurt herself instead to make it look like I shot her and Tommy. But I wasn't going to wait around to see if I was right. I had a small advantage now, a very small one.

But there were no perfect options—just varying degrees of risk.

Tommy's eyes darted around the room, searching for escape or help. For a moment, I thought he might have sensed my presence, but his gaze moved past the hallway entrance without pausing.

"Did you know she has four children and a granddaughter?" Sarah's tone shifted again, envy threading through the forced pleasantness. "A perfect little family. And a partner who looks at her like she's the center of the universe." She picked up a framed photograph—one I recognized with a jolt as having been stolen from my home. My family. "She didn't deserve any of it. I tried to be her friend. Tried writing to her, email after email, message after message on Facebook, but she never answered. I even tried calling her, but she rejected me. Can you believe that? Me?"

I swallowed hard. I received thousands of emails and messages every month and didn't have time to answer them all. People from all over wanted to know about profiling stuff, and I couldn't reply to all of them. I tried to do as many as I could, but it was simply too much. I didn't remember the call, but I might have thought it was spam if I didn't know the number.

I now realized this was why she was so mad at me. Once again, she had felt rejected by someone who was her obsession.

The gun waved carelessly as Sarah paced, her movements becoming less controlled, more erratic. "But I fixed that. I took it all away from her, piece by piece. Her reputation. Her freedom. And now, her future." She smiled at Tommy with genuine warmth that somehow chilled me more than her anger. "And you helped me, sweetheart. My perfect little helper."

Tommy strained against his restraints, the rope cutting into his wrists as he struggled. "I want to go home," he whimpered. "Please, Mommy. Let me go home."

"This is our home now," Sarah replied firmly. "Our final home." She checked her watch—an expensive men's model that looked out of place on her slender wrist. Matt's watch, I realized with a surge of anger. He hadn't been able to find it for months. Another trophy stolen from my life.

I shifted position for a better view. The wound had reopened at some point during my approach to the cabin, blood seeping through my makeshift bandage to stain my shirt. The pain created a red haze at the edges of my vision that I pushed aside through practiced compartmentalization. Pain was information, not an obstacle. Not when Tommy's life hung in the balance.

Sarah returned to Tommy's side, the gun trailing along his cheek in a grotesque caress. "Just a little longer now. I need to finish setting the stage." Her voice dropped to a whisper. "I need it to be perfect. She deserves a perfect ending."

I weighed my options one final time, recognizing that each passing moment increased the risk to Tommy. Sarah's behavior was becoming more unpredictable, and the transitions between her methodical planning and emotional outbursts were coming more rapidly. The window for relatively safe intervention was closing.

I could wait for Matt and Juan, but their arrival might trigger Sarah's endgame immediately. I could attempt to create a distraction, but in the confined space of the cabin, that carried its own risks. Every option carried the possibility of catastrophic failure.

But doing nothing guaranteed it.

Decision made, I eased away from the wall. I needed her focused on me, not Tommy. I needed her obsession to override her murder plan, even briefly.

I took a steadying breath and stepped from the shadowed

hallway into the main room, keeping my hands visible at my sides. Sarah's back was to me as she adjusted Tommy's position in the chair, murmuring something about sight lines and body positioning.

"That's not how this story ends, Sarah," I said, my voice steady and clear in the cabin's close air.

Sarah froze, her spine stiffening at the sound of my voice. Tommy's eyes widened, hope and terror warring in his expression as he looked past his captor to where I stood.

The game had changed. Sarah's carefully orchestrated murder scene had just acquired an unplanned element—the real Eva Rae Thomas, not the fiction she'd created in her fractured mind, had made her entrance too early.

And I had no intention of following her script.

Chapter 52

THE TRANSFORMATION WAS INSTANTANEOUS. Sarah's body language shifted—shoulders dropping, face softening, eyes widening with a perfect blend of surprise and relief. Her grip on the gun loosened slightly as she stepped behind Tommy's chair, one hand coming to rest on his small shoulder in a gesture that would have looked protective to anyone who hadn't just witnessed her plotting his murder.

"Eva! Thank God you're here," she exclaimed, her voice rising to a breathless pitch that contained precisely calibrated notes of distress. "This woman kidnapped my son! I managed to track them here." The performance was ridiculous—the concerned mother protecting her child from a threat—and was made even more so by the chalk outlines on the floor that told a very different story.

I remained perfectly still, my eyes never leaving the gun in her right hand. It hung loosely at her side now, but I had witnessed enough standoffs to know how quickly that could change. One wrong word, one threatening movement, and Sarah's finger would find the trigger with practiced ease.

"We both know that's not true," I replied, my voice deliberately calm and measured. I kept my hands visible at my sides, maintaining an open posture despite every instinct screaming to attack and try to wrestle the gun from her. "Those chalk outlines tell the real story, don't they, Sarah?"

Tommy's eyes darted between us, his breathing rapid and shallow. The rope binding his wrists had left angry red marks where he'd struggled against it. Sarah's fingers tightened on his shoulder, the gesture appearing comforting but functionally restraining.

"I don't know what you're talking about," Sarah insisted, her voice still pitched in that carefully crafted register of confusion and distress. "This woman—she broke into my house and took Tommy. She's been stalking us for weeks." She shifted slightly, adjusting her grip on the gun without raising it. "I'm so glad you found us. We need to call the police right away. Oh, wait, we can't. They'll just arrest you, now won't they?"

I took one measured step forward, then another, moving in a subtle arc that would eventually position me between Sarah and the door. Sarah countered by taking a small step to her right, maintaining the distance between us. We were circling each other now in the cabin's confined space, engaged in a physical chess match where every movement carried potential consequences.

"The police are already on their way," I said, which wasn't a lie. Matt and Juan would have contacted them by now. "They have everything, Sarah. Your calendar, where you wrote everything, every detail of your plans. The photographs. The shrine in your basement."

A flicker of something—uncertainty? anger?—passed across Sarah's face before the mask of concerned motherhood reasserted itself. "I don't know what kind of game you're playing, but we need to get Tommy to safety." She leaned down slightly, her lips close to Tommy's ear. "It's okay, baby. Agent Thomas is here to help us."

Tommy's eyes met mine, fear and desperate hope mingling in his gaze. He knew the truth, had lived with Sarah's deteriorating mental state for months, years even. I gave him the slightest nod, a silent promise that I wouldn't leave him.

"In your basement shrine, you have surveillance photos of me dating back years, even taken in my own home," I said, watching as this fact landed like a physical blow against her constructed reality. "Photos taken outside my home, through my kitchen window, of my children. You studied my cases, collected newspaper clippings, and created detailed analyses of my investigation methods."

Sarah's smile remained fixed, but something shifted in her eyes—a hardening, a retreat into some internal space where her fractured psyche could maintain its delusions despite the assault of reality. "That's not true," she insisted, though her denial lacked the conviction of moments before.

"The calendar," I continued, taking another step in our slow dance of position. I was now angled to cut off direct access to the front door, though Sarah still had a clear path to the hallway leading to the back entrance. "You wrote about watching Matt at physical therapy. You wrote that Tommy would 'adapt quickly once Matt moves in.' That 'by Christmas, it will be as if we were always a family.'"

Tommy flinched at these words, his small body trembling beneath Sarah's hand. He'd heard this before, I realized—had been living with Sarah's delusions long enough to recognize them when spoken aloud.

"Stop it," Sarah whispered, her grip on the gun tightening almost imperceptibly. "You're confusing things. Twisting everything."

"May 2nd entry," I continued, each revelation another strategic blow to her psychological defenses. "'Everything proceeds according to plan. The teacher's murder has accelerated the manhunt, just as I intended.'"

"STOP IT!" Sarah's voice cracked, the carefully modulated tones giving way to something raw and jagged. The gun lifted slightly, though not yet pointing directly at me. "You're lying. You broke into my house. Planted things. Trying to make me look crazy."

Sarah's breathing had become irregular, her chest rising and falling in an uneven rhythm. The hand holding the gun trembled slightly, matching the increasing instability of her psychological state. "No, no, no," she muttered, almost to herself. "That's not what happened. You stalked me for years, and you planted those things in my house to make me look bad. I know that's what happened. The news said that you had gone rogue, that you were armed and dangerous, and had potentially lost your mind. Don't twist reality. Don't gaslight me. The police will believe me. They've been hunting you for a long time."

Tommy watched the exchange with wide, frightened eyes, his small body curled as far away from Sarah as his restraints would allow. A tear tracked down his cheek, but he remained silent, somehow understanding that any intervention from him might shatter the fragile standoff.

"We were supposed to be a family. I did everything right. I learned everything about you. Became you." She looked down at her clothing—the outfit chosen to mimic my style—with a mixture of pride and revulsion. "I'm better at being Eva Rae Thomas than you ever were."

The gun rose another inch, her grip steadying as the fractured parts of her personality seemed to align around a single purpose. The chalk outlines on the floor, the carefully staged murder scene, the planned narrative—all of it was unraveling. And Sarah Winters, who had spent years constructing her elaborate fantasy, was watching it collapse around her.

In her eyes, I could see the terrifying calculation taking place—the realization that her original plan was no longer viable, but that she still held a gun, still controlled the immediate situation. The frozen smile remained fixed on her face, a grotesque contrast to the hatred blazing in her eyes as she made her decision.

And in that moment, I knew with absolute certainty that whatever script Sarah had so carefully prepared had been abandoned. We were now in uncharted territory, with a woman whose grip on reality had finally, completely shattered.

Chapter 53

I WATCHED HER EYES—THOSE windows to the fractured mind behind them—tracking the micro-expressions that betrayed her internal chaos. The slight twitch at the corner of her left eye, the irregular rhythm of her breathing, the constant shifting of her weight from foot to foot. All textbook indicators of a psyche in critical collapse.

"How long, Sarah?" I asked, keeping my voice deliberately calm, neutral. "How long have you been planning this?"

A smile crawled across her face—not the practiced warmth of "Sweet Sarah," but something feral and uncontrolled. "Since the first time I saw you. On television. The Westwood Strangler case." She tilted her head, studying me with an intensity that made my skin crawl. "You were explaining how you created a psychological profile that led to the killer's capture. So confident. So... perfect."

My mind flashed back to that case—six years ago, a series of strangulations in a quiet suburb outside of Tampa.

"You understood him," Sarah continued, her voice taking on a dreamy quality. "The killer. You understood what drove him when no one else could." Her free hand moved in small, agitated circles as she spoke. "I knew then. I knew you'd understand me too. That we were connected."

I shifted my weight slightly, calculating distances and angles. Six feet to Tommy. Ten feet to Sarah.

"What happened with Richard Collins, Sarah?" I asked, deliberately using his full name to humanize him.

Her face hardened at the mention, the pleasant mask dropping completely for a moment. "He rejected me. After everything I did for him." The words came out in short, harsh bursts. "I brought him coffee every morning. Made myself... available. Had him over for dinner often. " Her expression twisted with remembered rage. "Then he had the nerve to tell me he wasn't interested. That I was 'too intense.' That I made him 'uncomfortable.'"

Tommy whimpered softly behind me, the sound barely audible but enough to remind Sarah of his presence. Her eyes flicked to him briefly, then back to me.

"So, you killed him," I prompted, needing to keep her talking, to buy time.

"He deserved it," she said matter-of-factly. "But it wasn't a waste. I realized he could serve a greater purpose." Her smile returned, this time carrying a ghastly pride. "The first piece in my masterpiece. I studied the forensics from your Lakeside Killer case—the angle of entry, the powder residue patterns. Did it exactly the same way." She leaned forward slightly, her voice dropping conspiratorially. "I even used the same caliber weapon that you use."

"And then you planted his body in my car," I finished, the pieces finally locking into place.

Sarah nodded, pleased, as if I'd passed some twisted test. "I knew you'd appreciate the details. The precision." She gestured with the gun toward the chalk outlines. "Just like this. The perfect frame."

I took another small step toward Tommy, maintaining eye contact with Sarah. "We're not the same, Sarah," I said quietly. "I catch killers. I don't become them."

Her face contorted, the dueling aspects of her personality warring visibly for control. "You're wrong! We're exactly the same! Two sides of the same coin." Her voice rose, cracking with emotion.

"I became you—studied your cases, learned your methods. I can anticipate your every move because I know how you think!"

Tommy's frightened gaze met mine as I edged closer to him, my body now completely between him and Sarah. I could feel the heat radiating from his small form, hear the shallow rhythm of his terrified breathing.

"You don't know me, Sarah," I said, allowing a hint of steel to enter my voice. "If you did, you'd know I never give up. I never stop hunting those who hurt the innocent." I gestured toward Tommy with a slight nod. "I never allow children to become collateral damage."

Something shifted in Sarah s demeanor—a subtle hardening, a calculation taking place behind her eyes. "He was supposed to be part of our new family. Mine and Matt's." The gun lifted slightly, her grip steadying. "But he's been… difficult. Uncooperative." The clinical detachment in her tone when discussing the child she'd adopted just two years ago, sent ice through my veins. "Children are so adaptable. I could have found another who would appreciate what I offered."

A whisper of sound from outside—too faint for Sarah to notice in her agitated state, but clear to my trained ear. The soft crunch of careful footsteps on pine needles—a hushed voice. Matt and Juan had arrived, positioning themselves around the cabin's perimeter. Help was mere yards away, yet the moment had never been more dangerous.

Sarah's head tilted slightly, her senses finally registering the intrusion. "What was that?" The gun came up fully now, no longer casually held but gripped with deadly intent. "Who's out there?" Her voice had risen an octave, the sweet facade completely gone, replaced by raw panic.

"It's over, Sarah," I said quietly, holding her gaze. "The evidence has already been found. Your written descriptions of your plan in your calendar, your shrines, the surveillance photos—all of it. Matt and Juan were at your house this morning while you were focused on me."

Her eyes widened, darting between me and the cabin windows.

"You're lying," she hissed, though uncertainty crept into her voice. "No one will believe you. I've made sure of that."

"The media already has copies of everything," I continued, watching as each word landed like a physical blow. "Your detailed accounts of killing Collins, the teacher, the reporter. Your plans for today. It's all public now."

Sarah's hand trembled, the gun wavering between pointing at me and dropping to her side. The sound of footsteps grew closer, multiple sets approaching from different directions. Her eyes darted wildly around the cabin, the cornered animal inside her recognizing the closing trap.

"No," she whispered, more to herself than to me. "No, that's not how it's supposed to go. That's not the ending I wrote." Her knuckles whitened around the gun's grip as fresh determination hardened her features. "I still have this," she said, raising the weapon decisively. "I can still write the ending my way."

Chapter 54

"NO ONE WILL BELIEVE YOU," Sarah repeated, but her voice had lost its earlier confidence, replaced by something brittle and desperate. Her eyes darted between me and the cabin door, tracking the sounds of approaching footsteps outside. I watched her finger twitch against the trigger guard of the revolver—a subtle, rhythmic movement that my FBI training instantly recognized as the prelude to action. Tommy's frightened breathing behind me punctuated the cabin's heavy silence, each shallow gasp a reminder of exactly what was at stake.

"You don't understand what you've done," Sarah hissed, all traces of her "Sweet Sarah" persona now obliterated. Her face contorted with a rage so pure it transformed her features into something barely recognizable. "Years of planning. Years of watching, waiting, and preparing. And you think you can just walk in and ruin everything?"

"It's over, Sarah," I said, keeping my voice level despite the adrenaline surging through my system. "Even if you kill us both right now, the evidence is already out there—all of it."

Her face paled, then flushed with splotchy anger. "Shut up!" The gun lifted higher, steadying as her indecision crystallized into purpose. "You have no idea what I'm capable of. No idea what I've already survived."

I cataloged the warning signs—dilated pupils, perspiration beading along her hairline, the slight tremor in her voice that belied her attempt at control. Sarah Winters had crossed the threshold from dangerous obsession to acute psychotic break.

"The police know everything," I continued, deliberately pushing the very buttons that would most destabilize her. "The whole world will know what you did."

I took a careful step closer to Tommy, my eyes never leaving Sarah's. "They'll know how you stalked Matt and me for years. How you tried to frame me for your crimes."

"STOP IT!" she screamed, spittle flying from her lips. The gun jerked upward with the force of her emotion.

I saw the decision in her eyes a split second before her finger moved to the trigger—that final neural connection that transforms thought into irrevocable action. Time seemed to compress, my senses heightening as they always did in moments of extreme danger. I started to move, to go for the weapon, but I was a fraction too slow.

I felt the impact before I heard the sound—a hot poker driving into my shoulder, spinning me backward with its force. My back slammed against the cabin wall, legs buckling as fire spread through my chest and arm. Warm wetness bloomed across my shirt front, the copper tang of blood filling my nostrils.

"That's better," Sarah said, her voice unnaturally calm after her previous outburst. She stepped forward, studying me with detached interest as I slumped against the wall, pressing my hand to the wound in a futile attempt to stem the bleeding. "Now you can watch the ending I wrote. The one where you lose everything."

She pivoted smoothly, redirecting the gun toward Tommy. The boy shrank back against the chair, his small face white with terror, tears streaming silently down his cheeks.

"You ruined everything," she told him, her voice conversational despite the madness burning in her eyes.

"Sarah," I gasped, struggling to push myself upright against the wall, my hand slipping in my own blood. "He's just a child. Your child."

She laughed—a hollow, broken sound devoid of humor. "He was never my child. He was a prop. A necessary element for the perfect family I was creating." She stroked Tommy's hair with her free hand, the gesture perversely gentle while the gun remained pointed at his chest. "But props can be replaced."

Tommy's eyes found mine over Sarah's shoulder, wide with terror but also something else—a desperate trust that I wouldn't abandon him. The same look I'd seen countless times in my career, from victims who believed I could save them when no one else could. I had never failed them. I would not fail him.

I gathered every ounce of strength remaining in my battered body, ignoring the screaming pain from my wounds, the lightheadedness from blood loss, the trembling weakness in my limbs. With a final, desperate surge, I launched myself from the wall, driving my good shoulder into Sarah's back.

She staggered forward with a surprised cry, the gun jerking upward as she fought to maintain her balance. I clamped my hand around her wrist, forcing the weapon away from Tommy, driving her backward into the rickety coffee table. It collapsed beneath our combined weight, sending us sprawling across the worn floorboards in a tangle of limbs and desperation.

Sarah fought with the strength of madness, her nails raking across my face as she struggled to bring the gun to bear. I locked my fingers around her wrist, applying pressure to the nerve points that might force her to release the weapon. Blood from my shoulder wound slicked our grip, making it nearly impossible to maintain control.

We rolled across the cabin floor, crashing into the base of Tommy's chair, sending it skidding several inches across the wooden boards. Sarah's knee drove into my wounded shoulder, sending a wave of agony so intense that my vision momentarily whited out. In that second of weakness, she wrenched her arm free.

The gun discharged with a deafening crack.

Tommy cried out—a sound that cut through me more painfully

than any bullet could. The cabin fell into sudden, shocked silence, the echo of the gunshot fading against the wooden walls.

I scrambled to my knees, ignoring my own injuries as I lurched toward Tommy. The bullet had hit him in the abdomen. Blood was gushing out, and he looked at me, terrified.

"It's okay," I whispered, working frantically at the ropes binding his wrists with blood-slippery fingers. "I've got you. You're going to be okay." The words came automatically, professionally, even as my heart hammered with terror at the sight of his blood.

Sarah had recoiled to the far wall, the gun hanging limply from her fingers as she stared at Tommy's wound with an expression of horrified fascination. For the first time since I'd known her, her face showed a single, unified emotion rather than the fractured masking of her multiple personas. She looked utterly lost, as if the script she'd been following had finally, irrevocably shattered.

I freed Tommy's hands and gathered him carefully against me, my blood mingling with his as I pressed my palm against his wound. His small body trembled against mine, his tears hot against my neck as he clung to me with desperate strength.

"I didn't mean—" Sarah began, her voice small and uncertain. Then her expression shifted, calculations resuming behind her eyes as she tightened her grip on the gun once more. The moment of genuine horror had passed, replaced by the cold pragmatism of a survivor assessing her remaining options.

Outside, the footsteps had reached the cabin door. Sarah's eyes fixed on the entrance, then returned to me and Tommy, the gun rising once more in her blood-streaked hand.

Chapter 55

I RAN toward her with one sole purpose: to knock her back against the wall and get the gun from her hand. As I leaped, Tommy made his move. I caught glimpses of his movements through the chaos—as Sarah was forced up against the wall, and then fought back, pushing me away. As we ended up in a battle on the floor, the gun flew away. While Sarah and I grappled across the cabin floor, Tommy's fingers had found my burner phone that had fallen out of my pocket. The dial clicked as he turned it—three deliberate numbers that seemed to echo in the cabin despite our violent struggle.

"Nine-one-one, what's your emergency?" The operator's voice carried across the room, tinny but distinct through the speaker.

Tommy's voice quavered, barely audible over the sounds of Sarah and me fighting. "My mom shot me." The words came out small and frightened, yet determined. Then he ran to the bathroom and shut the door.

I saw the flash of confusion in Sarah's eyes when she heard him speak—not just at the realization that he'd reached the phone, but at his words.

Sarah realized what he was doing. Her focus had been so

completely on me, on our violent struggle, that Tommy's actions had registered only peripherally until that moment. I watched her expression transform from rage to something worse—a cold, calculating hatred that chilled me more than her previous frenzy.

"You ungrateful little—" she snarled, shoving herself away from me with unexpected force. She ran after him, kicking open the bathroom door. I heard her speak to Tommy, and then I set off after her. Inside the bathroom, I lunged for her, fingers grasping at her shirt, her hair, anything to keep her from reaching Tommy. My hand closed around her ankle, and she stumbled, but not before swinging the gun toward me with deliberate aim.

The second shot exploded through the cabin with deafening finality. White-hot pain blossomed in my chest as the bullet tore through me, sending me crashing back against the wall. Blood spread across my shirt in a warm, wet rush as my legs gave out beneath me.

Through the haze of pain and encroaching shock, I heard the operator's voice become more urgent.

"Hello?" The voice on the phone cracked. "Are you there?"

Sarah turned toward Tommy, her movements suddenly fluid and purposeful. The gun hung at her side as she crossed the bathroom in three long strides.

Sarah grabbed the phone and hung up.

I tried to push myself upright, to call out a warning, but my voice emerged as little more than a wet gurgle as blood filled my throat. My vision narrowed to a tunnel that framed the scene before me with terrible clarity. I heard the front door getting kicked in and Matt's voice calling my name.

The silence that followed seemed to press against my eardrums with physical weight. Tommy's quiet sobbing provided the only soundtrack to Sarah's heavy breathing as she stood over him, the gun now trained on his small, trembling form.

"No one interrupts my ending," she said, her voice oddly calm after the violence that had preceded it. "No one ruins what I've written."

I forced my eyes to remain open despite the darkness creeping in from the edges of my vision. Tommy's gaze found mine across the blood-smeared floor, his expression a heartbreaking mixture of terror and apology—as if he'd failed somehow by not completing the call, by not saving us both.

I tried to communicate with my eyes what my failing body could not express in words: You did everything right. You were so brave. Don't give up.

Outside, the faint wail of distant sirens carried through the cabin's thin walls—so far away, but growing closer. Tommy had succeeded after all. Help was coming. Matt was in the cabin with Juan, and I had managed to scream for his help.

The question was whether any of us would still be alive when it arrived.

Chapter 56

CONSCIOUSNESS CAME IN WAVES, each one carrying me briefly to the surface before pulling me back into darkness. Fragments of reality washed over me—harsh fluorescent lights blurring above, the antiseptic smell of hospital disinfectant, the rhythmic beeping of machines monitoring my tenuous hold on life. Voices floated around me, urgent but distant, as if filtering through water. "Blood pressure dropping." "Push another unit." "We're losing her." I tried to speak, to tell them I was still here, still fighting, but my body remained disconnected from my will, a broken vessel that could no longer contain the commands of my mind.

Time lost meaning. Each surfacing felt like breaking through ice into painful awareness, each submersion a relief from the brutal reality of what my body had endured. Two gunshot wounds. Blood loss so severe that twice I heard someone whisper, "I don't know how she's still with us."

During one brief period of clarity, I became aware of pressure around my hand—warm, strong fingers intertwined with mine. Matt's voice cut through the medical jargon surrounding me, his tone brooking no argument.

"I'm not leaving her."

"Sir, you need treatment yourself—"

"Treat me here or don't treat me at all." The pressure on my hand increased slightly. "I'm not leaving this room."

I tried to squeeze back, to let him know I felt his presence, but my body remained stubbornly unresponsive. The darkness pulled me under again, this time dragging me deeper than before.

When I next surfaced, the urgent activity had subsided. The lights seemed dimmer, the voices quieter. Night had fallen, or perhaps they had simply moved me to a different room. Matt's presence remained constant, his hand still wrapped around mine, his breathing slow and measured beside me. Beyond the door to my room, another voice filtered through—Juan's, his tone steady and professional as he spoke with someone in the hallway.

"The journal contains explicit confessions to all three murders," he was saying. "Detailed accounts of how she killed three people. The planning, the execution, the evidence planting—everything."

"And the frame-up of Agent Thomas?" A voice I didn't recognize, probably a detective.

"Meticulously documented. Sarah Winters studied Eva Rae for years. Created an elaborate shrine in her home with surveillance photos dating back five years. The forensic team found Eva Rae's DNA throughout the house—hair samples, fingerprints—all collected and stored for later planting at crime scenes."

"We found the body of Victor Reeves," the detective said. "In the boat house. You said earlier in a statement that was her as well?"

"Yes, he worked for her as far as I have been told. Then he decided to help them instead, and he saved both their lives but lost his own."

The conversation drifted beyond my hearing as another wave of darkness approached. This time, I didn't fight it, allowing myself to sink beneath its surface with the comforting knowledge that evidence of my innocence had survived.

The next emergence brought television sounds—a news anchor's professionally modulated voice penetrating my semiconscious state.

"...raising serious questions about whether former FBI agent

Eva Rae Thomas was wrongfully accused. Sources close to the investigation reveal that Sarah Winters, the local bookstore owner now in custody, may have orchestrated an elaborate frame-up targeting Thomas. Police have recovered evidence suggesting Winters committed the murders herself while methodically building a case against Thomas...."

Matt's voice cut through the broadcast. "Turn it off. She needs quiet."

The sound disappeared, replaced by the steady beep of my heart monitor and the soft hiss of oxygen flowing through a tube beneath my nose. I drifted again, this time surfacing to catch fragments of a gentle conversation from somewhere nearby.

Matt's face swam into focus above me, haggard with exhaustion, his eyes ringed with dark circles. Butterfly bandages held together a gash on his forehead. When he saw my eyes open, his expression transformed—relief washing away the worry, if only for a moment.

"Hey," he whispered, leaning closer. "There you are."

I tried to speak, but my throat felt scraped raw from the breathing tube they must have removed at some point. Matt reached for a cup with a straw, gently holding it to my lips. The water felt miraculous against my parched tissues, each painful swallow worth the relief it brought.

"Tommy?" I managed finally, the word barely audible.

"He's safe," Matt assured me, his hand returning to mine. "No serious physical injuries. He got lucky that the bullet didn't hit any vital organs. They're keeping him for observation and psychological assessment, but he's going to be okay." His voice caught slightly. "Thanks to you."

I closed my eyes briefly, allowing that knowledge to sink in. When I opened them again, Matt was still watching me, his expression a complex mixture of relief, exhaustion, and something deeper that I wasn't ready to name.

"Sarah?" The question scratched its way out of my damaged throat.

"In custody. Maximum security at the psychiatric wing." His jaw tightened. "They found the shrine in her house, just like you said.

Everything. Juan made sure all the evidence got into the right hands." A grim smile touched his lips. "The FBI director himself called to apologize for how they handled the case."

I absorbed this information slowly, my mind still struggling through the fog of pain medication and trauma. Vindication should have felt triumphant, but in that moment, all I felt was bone-deep weariness.

"It's over," Matt continued, his thumb tracing gentle circles on the back of my hand. "The nightmare is finally over, Eva. You were right all along, and now everyone knows it."

I managed a weak nod, not trusting my voice for more words. The simple act of consciousness had already drained what little strength I had regained. But before I surrendered again to the waiting darkness, I needed to know one more thing.

"Tommy," I whispered. "What happens to him now?"

Matt's expression softened. "Let's worry about that after you heal. Right now, the only thing that matters is getting you well." He leaned closer, his lips brushing my forehead in a touch so gentle it might have been imagined. "Rest. I'll be here when you wake up."

Chapter 57

THE SOUND of rapid footsteps in the hallway pulled me from the edge of sleep. After two weeks in this room, I'd learned to distinguish between the measured pace of nurses doing their rounds and the hurried stride of someone with purpose. These footsteps were different—eager, almost frantic, accompanied by a younger voice being gently shushed. My heart quickened before my mind fully registered why. Then Christine burst through the doorway, her red hair—so like mine before the silver took over—flying behind her like a banner. Angel followed more cautiously, her young eyes visibly relieved as she saw me propped up against the pillows, awake and alive despite the monitors and tubes that marked the seriousness of my condition.

"Mom!" Christine's voice broke on that single syllable as she rushed to my bedside. At nineteen, my second-oldest had always been the emotional one, wearing her heart like an external organ for all to see. Now she hovered over me, clearly desperate to embrace me but terrified of causing pain. Her eyes cataloged the visible bandages, the IV lines, the monitors with their steady readouts.

"It's okay," I whispered, opening my arms despite the protest from my wounds. "Just be gentle."

Christine carefully leaned down, wrapping her arms around me with the delicacy of someone handling spun glass. I felt her tears against my neck as she pressed her face close. "We thought—" she began, but couldn't finish.

"They said you killed people," Christine whispered against my hair, her voice so low I almost missed it. "On the news. Every day. They said you were dangerous."

I closed my eyes briefly, imagining my daughters watching news reports declaring their mother a murderer, a fugitive. The thought caused a pain deeper than any bullet could inflict. "I know," I said. "But it wasn't true. None of it was true."

Christine straightened, wiping tears from her cheeks with quick, impatient gestures. "Grandma said that from the beginning. She told everyone who would listen that it was all lies."

Angel sat at the foot of my bed, while my teenage son, Alex, remained in the corner, looking shy yet concerned.

Matt, who had remained quietly in the corner since the kids' arrival, cleared his throat softly. "I'm going to grab some coffee," he said, moving toward the door. "Give you all some time."

Our eyes met as he passed the bed, his gaze conveying volumes—tenderness, understanding, the promise of return. I nodded slightly, acknowledging both his tact in giving us privacy and the unspoken connection that had deepened through our shared ordeal.

"Thank you," Christine said to him, the words carrying a weight of gratitude beyond this small courtesy.

When the door closed behind him, Christine finally released the tight control she'd been maintaining. "They wouldn't let us see you," she said, anger and hurt threading through her voice. "For almost two weeks. Even after they said you were innocent, they still wouldn't let us come."

"The doctors wanted to make sure I was strong enough," I explained, gesturing for both girls and Alex to sit in the chairs beside the bed. "And there were still some legal complications to sort out."

"When can you come home?" Angel asked, leaning forward with the focused intensity she'd inherited from me. "Grandma is taking care of Ellie. She has everything ready—she's moved into the guest room so she can help with your recovery."

The question struck me with unexpected force. Home. The concept seemed both achingly familiar and strangely distant after weeks of running, hiding, fighting for my life. "Soon," I promised. "The doctors want me to start physical therapy first, make sure I can manage basic movements. Then I will be coming home."

I met her eyes, then Christine's, seeing in both the desperate need for reassurance that some things in their upended world were still certain. Alex came closer and held my hand. I rubbed it gently.

"I promise," I said, pouring every ounce of conviction I could muster into those two words. "We're going to be okay."

For the first time since they'd entered the room, I saw their shoulders relax slightly, the weight they'd been carrying visibly lightening. It wasn't everything—recovery, for all of us, would be a long road with many challenges ahead. But it was a beginning, a step back toward the light after weeks of darkness. And for now, that was enough.

Epilogue

THREE MONTHS LATER

Chapter 1

THE WITNESS BOX felt like a cage despite its open sides, the polished oak rail pressing against my palms as I leaned forward to speak into the microphone. My shoulder throbbed beneath the blazer I'd chosen specifically for this testimony—navy blue, structured, professional enough to remind the jury of my FBI credentials without appearing intimidating. Three months after Sarah's bullets tore through my body, the wounds had closed but not truly healed, much like the psychological damage she'd inflicted. I shifted slightly on the hard wooden seat, trying to find a position that didn't aggravate the scar tissue as the prosecutor approached with measured steps.

"Agent Thomas," he began, though we both knew the title was a courtesy rather than a current fact. "Please describe for the court what you discovered in the defendant's home."

I drew a careful breath, aware of the packed gallery behind me. The scratch of pens against notepads created a constant whisper of sound, like insects in tall grass. Matt sat in the front row, his face a mask of supportive neutrality that couldn't quite hide the tension in his jaw. Behind him, the sea of unfamiliar faces leaned forward, hungry for details of the case that had dominated headlines for months.

"I found a hidden room in Sarah Winters' basement," I began, my voice steadier than I expected. " Inside was what I can only describe as a shrine dedicated to me."

The prosecutor nodded encouragingly. "Please elaborate on the contents of this shrine."

"The walls were covered with surveillance photographs spanning approximately six years," I continued, the clinical language of testimony helping me maintain distance from the visceral horror of that discovery. "Images of me at my home, shopping, with my family, at work. There were items stolen from my residence—family photographs, personal effects, even strands of hair collected from my hairbrush. She had written everything down in files that detailed her daily observations of my movements, preferences, and habits."

The courtroom had fallen so silent that I could hear the ancient heating system clicking beneath the floorboards. I didn't need to turn to know that every eye was fixed on me, including hers. I could feel Sarah's gaze like a physical touch, probing for weakness.

"And what did these files reveal about the defendant's intentions?" the prosecutor asked.

"They documented an elaborate plan to frame me for the murders of Richard Collins, Alice Mercer, and Margaret Wells." My fingers tightened imperceptibly on the rail. "Sarah detailed how she collected my DNA to plant at crime scenes and studied my investigative methods to anticipate my responses. She even knew I would follow her to the cabin."

The prosecutor approached with evidence bags containing photocopies of Sarah's files.

"Could you describe for the court what happened at the cabin?" The prosecutor's voice gentled slightly, acknowledging we had reached the most difficult part of my testimony.

I swallowed against the sudden dryness in my throat. The courtroom seemed to recede slightly around me as memories surged forward—the cabin's musty air, the chalk outlines on the floor, Tommy's terrified eyes.

"Sarah Winters had taken nine-year-old Tommy, her adopted son, to a remote cabin in Ocala National Forest." My voice remained level through years of professional training, though something inside me trembled. "She had drawn chalk outlines on the floor, indicating where bodies would be positioned. When I arrived with Matthew Miller and Juan Ramirez to rescue Tommy, she shot me twice—once in the shoulder and once in the chest. She also shot Tommy in the abdomen."

A murmur rippled through the courtroom. The judge tapped her gavel once, restoring silence.

"I understand this is difficult," the prosecutor said. "But could you explain how you determined Ms. Winters was responsible for the previous murders?"

"In the cabin, Sarah directly confessed to killing Richard Collins, Alice Mercer, and Margaret Wells while she held us at gunpoint."

Throughout my testimony, Sarah had maintained her carefully constructed persona—head slightly bowed, shoulders curved inward to appear smaller, dabbing occasionally at her eyes with a tissue that remained suspiciously dry. The blue dress she wore, with its modest neckline and knee-length hem, had been chosen to project innocence and vulnerability. Her blonde hair, pulled back in a simple bun, emphasized a face that had once appeared warm and trustworthy to me.

"Agent Thomas," the prosecutor said, "can you identify the person who shot you and Tommy Winters in the cabin that day?"

"Yes," I replied, my gaze finally moving directly to Sarah. "Sarah Winters. The defendant. We later learned that her real name is Ann Porter. She changed her name to hide that she had done this before. She had stalked a police officer in Minneapolis years before she turned her obsession toward me. It's all in the police records that we have obtained from up there, including a restraining order that the same officer had to get against her."

Our eyes locked across the courtroom. For a fraction of a second, the mask slipped. The wounded innocence disappeared, replaced by something cold and venomous that I recognized from the cabin—pure, undiluted hatred burning in eyes that suddenly seemed darker, deeper. Her lips tightened imperceptibly, the corners pulling downward in a suppressed snarl. Then, just as quickly, the mask slid back into place, her eyes downcast, shoulders slumped in apparent defeat.

The exchange lasted less than a heartbeat, but I knew others had seen it too. A juror in the front row straightened, blinking rapidly. The prosecutor's stance shifted subtly, more confident.

"No further questions, Your Honor," he said, returning to his table.

Sarah's defense attorney rose for cross-examination, but the damage had been done. Her performance had cracked at the crucial moment, revealing the truth beneath the carefully constructed fiction. My testimony concluded thirty minutes later, and I returned to my seat beside Matt, who squeezed my hand beneath the table. It didn't take the jury long to reach a verdict. They found her guilty of every count.

Judge Marina Hemphill adjusted her silver-rimmed glasses, her expression grave as she reviewed the papers before her. A woman in her sixties with iron-gray hair and the composed demeanor of someone who had presided over hundreds of cases, she commanded absolute silence with a single raised finger when whispers threatened to disrupt the proceedings.

"Ann Porter," she began, her voice carrying to every corner of the hushed courtroom, "having been found guilty of three counts of first-degree murder, two counts of attempted murder, one count of kidnapping a minor, and numerous lesser charges, this court sentences you to life imprisonment without the possibility of parole."

The official words washed over me like a physical wave, dissolving a tension I'd carried for months. My shoulders relaxed incrementally, breath coming easier than it had since entering the courtroom.

Sarah remained motionless as the sentence was delivered, her expression unchanged. Only I noticed the slight tremor in her hands, the tightening around her eyes. Her carefully constructed world had finally, irrevocably collapsed. As officers approached to lead her away, she turned one last time, her gaze finding mine across the crowded room.

This time, she didn't bother with the mask. The hatred blazed openly, a promise that even concrete walls and iron bars wouldn't extinguish her obsession. I met her eyes steadily, refusing to look away until the courtroom doors closed behind her.

It was over, not in the way any of us had expected when the nightmare began, but over nonetheless. I exhaled slowly, feeling the weight of the past months begin to lift, even as I recognized that some scars—visible and invisible—would remain with me forever.

Chapter 2

THE COURTHOUSE DOORS felt impossibly heavy as I pushed through them with Matt at my side, the transition from climate-controlled dimness to Florida sunshine momentarily blinding. I squinted against the sudden brightness, my body tensing instinctively at the wall of noise that greeted us—shouted questions from reporters, the mechanical whir and click of cameras, the general buzz of a crowd hungry for a statement from the exonerated FBI profiler whose case had dominated national headlines for months. The stone steps stretched before us like an exposed gauntlet we would have to run, no shelter from the attention I'd never sought nor welcomed.

"Agent Thomas! How does it feel to see justice served?"

"Will you be returning to the FBI?"

"What's your response to the Bureau's handling of your case?"

The questions overlapped into unintelligible noise as Matt placed a protective hand against my lower back, gently guiding me forward. The gesture wasn't possessive but supportive, understanding that my body was still a map of healing wounds and that the press of bodies around us threatened more than just my privacy.

"No comments today," Matt repeated firmly as cameras thrust toward us, lenses glinting like predatory eyes in the midday sun.

I kept my face composed, years of media training kicking in despite my determination to leave that life behind. The FBI had taught me well—how to reveal nothing, how to maintain professional distance, how to keep my expression neutral even when surrounded by chaos. Ironic that these skills served me now, after the Bureau had so quickly assumed my guilt.

Halfway down the steps, the crowd parted like a reluctant sea.

The café two blocks from the courthouse offered sanctuary from the press and curious onlookers. I sank into the chair Matt pulled out for me, grateful for the relative anonymity of the seating. My body still ached from the tension of testimony and the lingering effects of my injuries, but here, with the courthouse no longer visible and Matt's steady presence across from me, I could feel my shoulders beginning to loosen, my breath coming easier. A waitress approached with professional disinterest—perhaps not recognizing us, or more likely, offering the courtesy of treating us like normal customers rather than subjects of the morning's headline news.

"You okay?" Matt asked after she'd left with our orders. His eyes studied my face with the careful attention he'd developed during my recovery, searching for signs of fatigue or pain.

"I'm fine," I assured him. "Better than fine, actually. It feels like…" I paused, searching for the right words. "Like I can finally exhale."

Matt nodded, his fingers drumming lightly against the metal tabletop—a habit I'd come to recognize as his mind working through complex problems. "I've been thinking," he began, the rhythm of his fingers increasing slightly. "About what comes next."

"And?" I prompted when he hesitated.

His expression shifted, enthusiasm replacing contemplation as he leaned forward. "I want to start a private investigation firm. Specializing in wrongful accusations." The words tumbled out with an energy I hadn't seen from him in a very long time. "Using my cyber expertise to find evidence that the authorities miss or misinterpret. Helping people who've been framed, like—"

"Like me," I finished quietly.

"Exactly." His hands stilled, palms flat against the table as he looked directly into my eyes. "I want you to join me, Eva. Your profiling skills, my tech background—we'd make one hell of a team."

The waitress returned with our coffees, interrupting briefly as she set down cups and a small plate of biscotti neither of us had ordered. "On the house," she murmured with a quick, sympathetic smile before retreating again.

I wrapped my fingers around the warm ceramic, considering Matt's proposition. The idea resonated in unexpected ways—using my skills without the bureaucracy that had failed me, helping others navigate the nightmare I'd barely survived, working alongside the man who had remained steadfast when everyone else believed the worst of me.

"Yes," I said simply, my lips curving into what felt like the first genuine smile in months.

Matt's eyebrows lifted slightly, as if he'd expected more resistance. "Just like that?"

"Just like that." I sipped my coffee, relishing both its rich bitterness and the rightness of this decision. "I can't go back to the Bureau, not after everything. But I'm not ready to stop using what I know, either. This feels…" I searched for the word. "Fitting."

Matt reached across the table, his fingers finding mine in a gesture that had become familiar during my hospital recovery. "Partners, then."

The word carried multiple meanings, professional and personal boundaries blurring in ways we hadn't fully articulated yet. I squeezed his hand in acknowledgment of all those layered meanings.

"Have you heard anything new about Tommy?" I asked, shifting the conversation to the other topic that had occupied our thoughts since leaving the hospital.

Matt's expression softened at the boy's name. "His case worker called yesterday. He's doing okay in the temporary placement, but she says he still asks about you."

"And about you," I added, remembering my last visit with Tommy, how he had carefully shown me a drawing of three stick figures—a woman with red hair, a man with a "special leg" as he called Matt's prosthetic, and a smaller figure between them.

"I've been thinking about that too," Matt said, his voice quieter now. "The case worker mentioned Tommy will need a permanent placement soon. Preferably with someone who understands his trauma, who can help him process what happened with Sarah."

The implication hung between us, neither quite ready to speak it aloud until Matt continued, "I've jumped ahead and started the foster parent application process. I thought that we could..."

My heart stuttered at the suggestion—not from reluctance but from the sudden expansion of possibility it represented. "You mean, us becoming Tommy's foster parents?"

Matt nodded, watching my reaction carefully. "I know it's fast, and there's still so much we're figuring out, I mean, we already have a house full of kids, but—"

"Yes," I interrupted, the certainty in my voice surprising even me. "He needs stability and understanding. He needs people who were there, who know what he survived."

"It won't be easy," Matt cautioned, though I could see relief and something like joy lighting his eyes. "He'll have nightmares, trust issues. The psychologists say Sarah's manipulation affected him profoundly."

"None of it will be easy," I agreed, thinking of my own ongoing therapy sessions, the nightmares that still woke me gasping for breath. "But since when have we taken the easy way out? And we understand trauma, both of us. He deserves a chance at healing, at family."

Matt's smile widened, the lines of worry that had become etched around his eyes during my hospital stay momentarily smoothing away. "I'll call the case worker this afternoon."

As if on cue, my phone vibrated in my pocket, Christine's familiar ringtone cutting through the café's ambient noise. I answered quickly, my maternal instincts immediately alert to the strain in her voice.

"Mom?" The single word carried a weight of barely controlled panic.

"I'm here," I assured her. "What's wrong?"

"Please, come home soon," Christine said, her voice tight with stress. "It's… it's bad."

Matt was already signaling the waitress for our check, responding to the change in my expression.

"What's going on?" I asked, standing and gathering my purse, my body already preparing for action despite the protest from healing muscles.

"It's Chris," Christine replied. "Ellie's father. He's back in town, and he just served me. He wants custody of Ellie. Says I'm unfit as a mother."

My expression hardened, protective instinct overriding any lingering discomfort or fatigue. "I'm coming home now," I said firmly, making eye contact with Matt, who nodded in immediate understanding.

We left payment on the table and moved quickly toward Matt's car. My daughter needed me, and after months of fighting to survive, to clear my name, to rebuild my life, I found comfort in the simplicity of this truth: I was still a mother first, and my family needed me.

As Matt navigated through downtown traffic with practiced efficiency, I found myself mentally shifting from the courtroom battle behind us to the personal one ahead. Chris had never been in Ellie's life. He had left town when he found out Christine was pregnant, unwilling to be a part of it. Why was he back now? Why had he chosen now to file for custody—when our family had just begun to heal from the trauma of the past months—it seemed calculated for maximum damage.

But he would find, as Sarah had, that threatening my family was the quickest way to discover exactly how resilient, how determined, how unstoppable I could be when those I loved were at risk.

THE END

Afterword

Dear Reader,

Thank you for purchasing and reading *A Cry for Help (Eva Rae Thomas #21)*. The idea for this story came to me when I read an article about a waitress who had a stalker. He came in every day where she worked and sat in her section, and when she refused to date him, he killed her. Of course, this book is not much like the real story, as I have changed everything up completely. In this case, it turns out that the woman is actually the stalker, but that's the fun of writing fiction.

You can read about the woman here if you want to know more:

https://www.telegram.com/story/news/crime/2017/01/13/stalkers-murder-conviction-upheld-in-pipe-bomb-killing/22688170007/

As always, I am so grateful for your support, and I encourage you to leave a review if possible.

Take care,

Willow

About the Author

Willow Rose is a multi-million-copy best-selling Author and an Amazon ALL-star Author of more than 100 novels.

Several of her books have reached the top 10 of ALL books in the Amazon store in the US, UK, and Canada.

She has sold more than six million books that are translated into many languages.

Willow's books are fast-paced, nail-biting pageturners with twists you won't see coming.

That's why her fans call her The Queen of Plot Twists.

Willow lives on Florida's Space Coast. When she is not writing or reading, you will find her surfing and watching the dolphins play in the waves of the Atlantic Ocean.

Published by BUOY MEDIA LLC

Cover design by Juan Villar Padron,
https://www.juanjpadron.com

Special thanks to my editor Janell Parque
http://janellparque.blogspot.com/